LETHAL

SANDRA BROWN

LETHAL

GRAND CENTRAL
PUBLISHING

New York   Boston

Grand Central Publishing
Hachette Book Group
237 Park Avenue
New York, NY 10017
www.HachetteBookGroup.com

Printed in the United States of America

First Edition: September 2011

10 9 8 7 6 5 4 3 2 1

Grand Central Publishing is a division of Hachette Book Group, Inc.
The Grand Central Publishing name and logo is a trademark of Hachette Book Group, Inc.

Library of Congress Cataloging-in-Publication Data
  Brown, Sandra
    Lethal / Sandra Brown. — 1st ed.
       p. cm.
    ISBN 978-1-4555-0147-2 (regular ed.) — ISBN 978-1-4555-0413-8 (large print ed.)
    I. Title.
  PS3552.R718L48 2011
  813'.54—dc22   2011010210

LETHAL

Chapter 1

—⇒•⇐—

"Mommy?"

"Hmm?"

"Mommy?"

"Hmm?"

"There's a man in the yard."

"What's that?"

The four-year-old came to stand at the corner of the kitchen table and gazed yearningly at the frosting her mother was applying to the top of the cupcake. "Can I have some, Mommy?"

"*May* I have some. When I'm done, you can lick the bowl."

"You made chocolate."

"Because chocolate is your favorite, and you're my favorite girl," she said, giving the child a wink. "And," she added, drawing out the word, "I've got sprinkles to add as soon as I'm finished with the icing."

Emily beamed, then her face puckered with concern. "He's sick."

"Who's sick?"

"The man."

"What man?"

"In the yard."

Emily's statements finally penetrated that innate mom-screen that filtered out unimportant chatter. "There's really a man outside?" Honor placed the iced cupcake on the platter, returned the spatula to the bowl of frosting, and absently wiped her hands on a dishtowel as she stepped around the child.

"He's lying down because he's sick."

Emily trailed her mother as she made her way from kitchen to living room. Honor looked through the front window, turning her head from one side to the other, but all she saw was the lawn of St. Augustine grass sloping gradually down to the dock.

Beyond the dock's weathered wood planks the waters of the bayou moved indolently, a dragonfly skimming the surface and causing an occasional ripple. The stray cat, who refused to take Honor seriously when she told him that this was *not* his home, was stalking unseen prey in her bed of brightly colored zinnias.

"Em, there's not—"

"By the bush with the white flowers," Emily said stubbornly. "I saw him through the window in my room."

Honor went to the door, unlocked it, slid the bolt, stepped out onto the porch, and looked in the direction of the rose of Sharon shrub.

And there he was, lying facedown, partially on his left side, his face turned away from her, his left arm outstretched above his head. He lay motionless. Honor didn't even detect movement of his rib cage to indicate that he was breathing.

Quickly she turned and gently pushed Emily back through the door. "Sweetie, go into Mommy's bedroom. My phone is on the nightstand. Bring it to me, please." Not wanting to frighten her daughter, she kept her voice as calm as possible, but hurriedly took the steps down off the porch and ran across the dewy grass toward the prone figure.

When she got closer, she saw that his clothing was filthy, torn in places, and bloodstained. There were smears of blood on the exposed skin of his outstretched arm and hand. A clot of it had matted a whorl of dark hair on the crown of his head.

Honor knelt down and touched his shoulder. When he moaned, she exhaled with relief. "Sir? Can you hear me? You're hurt. I'll call for help."

He sprang up so quickly she didn't even have time to recoil, much less to defend herself. He struck with lightning speed and precision. His left hand shot out and closed around the back of her neck, while with his right hand he jammed the short, blunt barrel of a handgun into the slight depression where her ribs met. He aimed it upward and to the left, directly in line with her heart, which had ballooned with fright.

"Who else is here?"

Her vocal cords were frozen with fear; she couldn't speak.

He squeezed the back of her neck and repeated with sinister emphasis, *"Who else is here?"*

It took several tries before she was able to stammer, "My...my dau—"

"Anybody besides the kid?"

She shook her head. Or tried. He had a death grip on

the back of her neck. She could feel the pressure of each individual finger.

His blue eyes cut like lasers. "If you're lying to me..."

He didn't even have to complete the threat to coax a whimper from her. "I'm not lying. I swear. We're alone. Don't hurt us. My daughter...she's only four years old. Don't hurt her. I'll do whatever you say, just don't—"

"Mommy?"

Honor's heart clenched, and she made a feeble squeaking sound, like that of a helplessly trapped animal. Because she still couldn't turn her head, she shifted only her eyes toward Emily. She was several yards away, standing in her endearingly duck-kneed stance, blonde curls wreathing her sweet face, chubby toes peeking out from beneath the pink silk flower petals that decorated her sandals. She was clutching the cell phone, her expression apprehensive.

Honor was engulfed with love. She wondered if this would be the last time she would see Emily healthy and whole and untouched. The thought was so horrible, it brought tears to her eyes, which, for her child's sake, she rapidly blinked away.

She didn't realize her teeth were chattering until she tried to speak. She managed to say, "It's okay, sweetheart." Her eyes shifted back to the face of the man who was only a trigger pull away from blowing her heart to smithereens. Emily would be left alone, and terrified, and at his mercy.

Please. Honor's eyes silently implored him. Then she whispered, "I beg you."

Those hard, cold eyes magnetized hers as he gradually eased the pistol away from her. He lowered it to the ground, placing it behind his thigh where Emily couldn't see it. But the implicit threat remained.

He removed his hand from around Honor's neck and turned his head toward Emily. "Hi."

He didn't smile when he said it. Faint lines formed parentheses on either side of his mouth, but Honor didn't think they had been grooved there by smiling.

Emily regarded him shyly and dug the toe of her sandal into the thick grass. "Hello."

He extended his hand. "Give me the phone."

She didn't move, and when he snapped the fingers of his outstretched hand, she mumbled, "You didn't say please."

Please appeared to be a foreign concept to him. But after a moment, he said, "Please."

Emily took a step toward him, then drew up short and looked at Honor, seeking permission. Although Honor's lips were trembling almost uncontrollably, she managed to form a semblance of a smile. "It's okay, sweetie. Give him the phone."

Emily bashfully closed the distance between them. When she was within touching distance, she leaned far forward and dropped the phone into his palm.

His blood-smeared hand closed around it. "Thanks."

"You're welcome. Are you gonna call Grandpa?"

His eyes shifted to Honor. "Grandpa?"

"He's coming for supper tonight," Emily announced happily.

Holding Honor's stare, the man drawled, "Is that right?"

"Do you like pizza?"

"Pizza?" He looked back at Emily. "Yeah. Sure."

"Mommy said I can have pizza for supper because it's a party."

"Huh." He slid Honor's cell phone into the front pocket of his dirty jeans, then encircled her biceps with his free hand and pulled her up as he stood. "Looks like I got here just in time, then. Let's go inside. You can tell me all about tonight's party." Keeping a grip on Honor's arm, he propelled her toward the house. Her legs were so shaky they barely supported her as she took those first few stumbling steps. Emily got distracted by the cat. She chased after him, calling, "Here, kitty," as he slunk into a hedge on the far side of the yard.

As soon as Emily was out of earshot, Honor said, "I've got some money. Not much, a couple hundred dollars maybe. A few pieces of jewelry. You can take anything I own. Just please don't hurt my daughter."

And all the time she was babbling, she was scanning the yard in frantic search of something she could use as a weapon. The water hose wound up on its spool at the edge of the deck? The pot of geraniums on the bottom step? One of the bricks embedded in the ground, lining the flower bed?

She would never get to one of them in time, even if she could wrench herself from his grasp, which she knew from the strength of it would be difficult if not impossible. And in the process of a struggle, he would simply shoot her. Then he'd be left to do with Emily what he would. Thoughts of that brought bile to her throat.

"Where's your boat?"

She turned her head and looked at him blankly.

Impatiently, he hitched his chin toward the empty dock. "Who's got the boat out?"

"I don't have a boat."

"Don't bullshit me."

"I sold the boat when...A couple of years ago."

He seemed to weigh her honesty, then asked, "Where's your car?"

"Parked in front."

"Keys in it?"

She hesitated, but when he increased the pressure of his grip, she shook her head. "Inside. On a wall hook by the kitchen door."

He started up the steps of the porch, pushing her along in front of him. She felt the pistol bumping against her spine. She turned her head, about to call out to Emily, but he said, "Leave her for now."

"What are you going to do?"

"Well, first…" he said, opening the door and pushing her inside ahead of him. "I'm going to make sure you aren't lying to me about anyone else being here. And then… we'll see."

She could feel the tension in him as he propelled her from the empty living room then down the short hallway toward the bedrooms. "There's no one here except Emily and me."

He gave the door of Emily's bedroom a push with the barrel of the pistol. The door swung open to a panorama of pink. No one was lying in wait. Still mistrustful, he crossed the room in two wide strides and yanked open the closet door. Satisfied that no one was hiding inside it, he gave Honor a shove back into the hall and toward the second bedroom.

As they approached, he growled close to her ear, "If there's someone in here, I shoot you first. Got it?" He hesitated as though giving her a chance to change her claim that she was alone, but when she remained silent, he kicked the door open with the toe of his boot, sending it crashing against the adjacent wall.

Her bedroom looked ironically, almost mockingly, serene. Sunlight coming through the shutters painted stripes on the hardwood floor, the white quilted comforter, the pale gray walls. The ceiling fan caused dust motes to dance in the slanted beams of light.

He shoved her toward the closet and ordered her to open the door. He relaxed only marginally when he glanced into the connecting bathroom and discovered it also empty.

He faced her squarely. "Where's your gun?"

"Gun?"

"You have one somewhere."

"No I don't."

His eyes narrowed.

"I swear," she said.

"Which side of the bed do you sleep on?"

"What? Why?"

He didn't repeat the question, just continued to stare at her until she pointed. "The right."

Backing away from her, he moved to the nightstand on the right side of the bed and checked the drawer. Inside were a flashlight and a paperback novel but no lethal weapon. Then to her shock, he shoved the mattress, linens and all, off the bed far enough for him to search beneath it, finding nothing except the box spring.

He motioned with his chin for her to lead him from the room. They returned to the living room and went from there into the kitchen, where his eyes darted from point to point, taking it all in. His gaze lit on the wall hook with her car keys hanging from it.

When she saw his notice, she said, "Take the car. Just go."

Ignoring that, he asked, "What's in there?"

"Laundry room."

He went to that door and opened it. Washing machine and clothes dryer. Ironing board folded into a recession in the wall. A rack on which she dried her delicates, some of which were hanging there now. An array of lace in pastels. One black bra.

When he came back around, those Nordic eyes moved over her in a way that made her face turn hot even as her torso became cold and clammy with dread.

He took a step toward her; she took a corresponding step back, a normal response to mortal danger, which is what he posed to her. She didn't delude herself into believing otherwise.

His entire aspect was menacing, starting with his chilling eyes and the pronounced bone structure of his face. He was tall and lean, but the skin on his arms was stretched over muscles that looked as taut as whipcord. The backs of his hands were bumpy with strong veins. His clothes and hair had snagged natural debris—twigs, sprigs of moss, small leaves. He seemed indifferent to all that, just as he did to the mud caked on his boots and the legs of his jeans. He smelled of the swamp, of sweat, of danger.

In the silence, she could hear his breathing. She could hear her own heartbeat. She was his sole focus, and that terrified her.

Overpowering him would be impossible, especially since one jerk of his index finger would fire a bullet straight into her. He stood between her and the drawer where butcher knives were stored. On the counter was the coffee pot, still half filled with this morning's brew, still hot enough to scald him. But in order to reach either it or the knives, she would have to get past him, and that didn't seem likely. She doubted she could outrun him, but even if she could make it beyond the door and escape, she wouldn't leave Emily behind.

Reason or persuasion seemed the only options open to her.

"I've answered all your questions truthfully, haven't I?" she said, her voice low and tremulous. "I've offered to give you my money and whatever valuables—"

"I don't want your money."

She motioned toward the bleeding scratches on his arms. "You're hurt. Your head has been bleeding. I'll...I'll help you."

"First aid?" He made a scoffing sound. "I don't think so."

"Then what...what do you want?"

"Your cooperation."

"With what?"

"Put your hands behind your back."

"Why?"

He took a couple of measured steps toward her.

She backed away. "Listen." She licked her lips. "You don't want to do this."

"Put your hands behind your back," he repeated, softly but with emphasis on each word.

"Please." The word was spoken on a sob. "My little girl—"

"I'm not going to ask you again." He took another step closer.

She backed away and came up against the wall behind her.

One last step brought him to within inches of her. "Do it."

Her instinct was to fight him, to scratch and claw and kick in an effort to prevent, or at least to delay, what seemed to be the inevitable. But because she feared Emily's fate if she didn't comply with him, she did as ordered and clasped her hands together at the small of her back, sandwiching them between her and the wall.

He leaned in close. She turned her head aside, but

he placed his hand beneath her chin and brought it back around.

Speaking in a whisper, he said, "You see how easy it would be for me to hurt you?"

She looked into his eyes and nodded numbly.

"Well, I *won't* hurt you. I promise not to hurt you or your kid. But you gotta do everything I say. Okay? Have we got a deal?"

She might have derived some level of comfort from the promise, even if she didn't believe it. But she suddenly realized who he was, and that sent a bolt of terror through her.

Breathlessly, she rasped, "You're…You're the man who shot all those people last night."

Chapter 2

C oburn. C-o-b-u-r-n. First name Lee, no known middle
initial."

Sergeant Fred Hawkins of the Tambour Police Department removed his hat and wiped sweat off his forehead. It
had already gone greasy in the heat, and it wasn't even nine
o'clock yet. Mentally he cursed the heat index of coastal
Louisiana. He'd lived here all his life, but one never got
used to the sultry heat, and the older he got the more he
minded it.

He was in a cell phone conversation with the sheriff of
neighboring Terrebonne Parish, giving him the lowdown
of last night's mass murder. "Chances are that's an alias, but
it's the name on his employee records and all that we have
to go on at present. We lifted prints off his car...Yeah, that's
the damnedest thing. You'd think he would've sped away
from the scene, but his car is still parked in the employee
lot. Maybe he thought it would be spotted too easily. Or, I
guess if you go and kill seven people in cold blood, you're

not thinking logically. Best we can tell, he fled the scene on foot."

Fred paused to take a breath. "I've already put his prints into the national pipeline. I'm betting something will turn up. A guy like this has gotta have priors. Whatever we get on him will be passed along, but I'm not waiting on further info, so you shouldn't either. Start looking for him A.S.A.P. You got my fax?...Good. Make copies and pass them out to your deputies for distribution."

While the sheriff was assuring Fred of his department's capacity for finding men at large, Fred nodded a greeting to his twin brother, Doral, who joined him where he was standing outside his patrol car.

It was parked on the shoulder of the two-lane state highway in a sliver of shade cast by a billboard sign advertising a gentleman's club that was located near the New Orleans airport. Sixty-five miles to the exit. The coldest drinks. The hottest women. Totally nude.

All sounded good to Fred, but he forecast that it would be a while before he could seek entertainment. Not until Lee Coburn was accounted for.

"You heard right, Sheriff. Bloodiest crime scene I've ever had the misfortune of investigating. Full-scale execution. Sam Marset was shot in the back of the head at close range."

The sheriff expressed his disgust over the viciousness of the crime, then signed off with his pledge to be in touch if the murderous psycho was spotted in his parish.

"Windbag could talk the horns off a billy goat," Fred complained to his brother as he disconnected.

Doral extended him a Styrofoam cup. "You look like you could use a coffee."

"No time."

"Take time."

Impatiently Fred removed the lid from the cup and took a sip. His head jerked back in surprise.

Doral laughed. "Thought you could use a little pick-me-up, too."

"We ain't twins for nothing. Thanks."

As Fred drank the liberally spiked coffee, he surveyed the line of patrol cars parked along the edge of the road. Dozens of uniformed officers from various agencies were milling around nearby, some talking on cell phones, others studying maps, most looking befuddled and intimidated by the job at hand.

"What a mess," Doral said under his breath.

"Tell me something I don't know."

"As city manager, I came out to offer any help that I or the City of Tambour can provide."

"As lead investigator on the case, I appreciate the city's support," Fred said drolly. "Now that the official bullshit is out of the way, tell me where you think he ran to."

"You're the cop, not me."

"But you're the best tracker for miles around."

"Since Eddie was killed, maybe."

"Well, Eddie ain't here, so you're it. You're part bloodhound, too. You could find a flea on a pissant."

"Yeah, but fleas ain't as slippery as this guy."

Doral had arrived dressed not as a city official, but as a hunter, fully expecting that his twin would recruit him to join the manhunt. He took off his dozer cap and fanned his face with it as he gazed toward the edge of the woods where those involved in the search were gathering.

"That slipperiness of his has got me worried." Fred would admit that only to his brother. "We gotta catch this son of a bitch, Doral."

"Like right effing now."

Fred chugged the rest of his bourbon-laced coffee and tossed the empty cup onto the driver's seat of his car. "You ready?"

"If you're waiting on me, you're backing up."

The two joined the rest of the search party. As its appointed organizer, Fred gave the command. Officers fanned out and began picking their way through the tall grass toward the tree line that demarcated the dense forest. Trainers unleashed their search dogs.

They were commencing the search here because a motorist who'd been changing a flat on the side of the road late last night had seen a man running into the woods. He hadn't thought anything about it until the mass slaying at the Royale Trucking Company warehouse was reported on the local news this morning. The estimated time of the shooting had roughly corresponded with the time he'd seen an individual—whom he couldn't describe because he'd been too far away—disappearing into the woods on foot and in a hurry. He'd called the Tambour Police Department.

It wasn't much for Fred and the others to go on, but since they didn't have any other leads, here they were, trying to pick up a trail that would lead them to the alleged mass murderer, one Lee Coburn.

Doral kept his head down, studying the ground. "Is Coburn familiar with this territory?"

"Don't know. Could know it as good as he knows the back of his hand, or could be he's never even seen a swamp."

"Let's hope."

"His employee application said his residence before Tambour was Orange, Texas. But I checked the address and it's bogus."

"So nobody knows for sure where he came from."

"Nobody to ask," Fred said dryly. "His coworkers on the loading dock are dead."

"But he's been in Tambour for thirteen months. He had to know somebody."

"Nobody's come forward."

"Nobody would, though, would they?"

"Guess not. After last night, who'd want to claim him as a friend?"

"Bartender? Waitress? Somebody he traded with?"

"Officers are canvassing. A checker at Rouse's who'd rung up his groceries a few times said he was pleasant enough, but definitely not a friendly sort. Said he always paid in cash. We ran his Social Security number through. No credit cards came up, no debts. No account in any town bank. He cashed his paychecks at one of those places that do that for a percentage."

"The man didn't want to leave a paper trail."

"And he didn't."

Doral asked if Coburn's neighbors had been interviewed.

"By me personally," Fred replied. "Everybody in the apartment complex knew him by sight. Women thought he was attractive in that certain kind of way."

"What certain kind of way?"

"Wished they could fuck him, but considered him bad news."

"That's a '*way*'?"

"Of course that's a '*way*.'"

"Who told you that?"

"It's just something I know." He nudged his twin in the ribs. "'Course I understand women better than you do."

"Piss up my other leg."

They shared a chuckle, then Fred turned serious again. "Men I talked to said they knew better than to mess with Coburn, which wasn't a problem, because he came and went without even a nod for anybody."

"Girlfriends?"

"None that anybody knew of."

"Boyfriends?"

"None that anybody knew of."

"You search his apartment?"

"Thoroughly. It's a one-room efficiency on the east side of town, and not a damn thing in it to give us a clue. Work clothes in the closet. Chicken pot pies in the freezer. The man lived like a monk. One thumbed copy of *Sports Illustrated* on the coffee table. A TV, but no cable hookup. Nothing personal in the whole damn place. No notepad, calendar, address book. Zilch."

"Computer?"

"No."

"What about his phone?"

Fred had found a cell phone at the murder scene and had determined that it didn't belong to any of the bullet-riddled bodies. "Recent calls, one to that lousy Chinese food place that delivers in town, and one came in to him from a telemarketer."

"That's it? Two calls?"

"In thirty-six hours."

"Well, damn." Doral swatted at a biting fly.

"We're checking out the other calls in his log. See who the numbers belong to. But right now, we know nothing about Lee Coburn except that he's out here somewhere, and that we're gonna catch shit if we don't find him." Lowering his voice, Fred added, "And I'd just as soon return

him in a body bag as in handcuffs. Best thing for us? We'd
find his lifeless body floating in a bayou."

"Townsfolk wouldn't complain. Marset was highly
thought of. Practically the freaking prince of Tambour."

Sam Marset had been the owner of the Royale Trucking Company, president of the Rotary Club, an elder at St.
Boniface Catholic Church, an Eagle Scout, a Mason. He
had chaired various boards and was usually grand marshal
of the town's Mardi Gras parade. He had been a pillar of
the community whom folks had admired and liked.

He was now a corpse with a bullet hole in his head, and,
as if that one hadn't been enough to kill him, another had
been fired into his chest for extra measure. The other six
shooting victims probably wouldn't be missed much, but
Marset's murder had warranted a televised press conference earlier that morning. It had been covered by numerous community newspapers from the coastal region of the
state, and all of the major New Orleans television stations
were represented.

Fred had presided, flanked at the microphone by city
officials, including his twin. The New Orleans P.D. had
loaned Tambour police a sketch artist, who'd rendered a
drawing of Coburn based on descriptions provided by
neighbors: Caucasian male around six feet three inches
tall, average weight, athletic build, black hair, blue eyes,
thirty-four years of age according to his employee records.

Fred had concluded the press conference by filling television screens with the drawing and warning locals that
Coburn was believed still to be in the area and should be
considered armed and dangerous.

"You laid it on pretty thick," Doral said now, referring
to Fred's closing remarks. "No matter how slippery Lee

Coburn is, everybody's going to be after his hide. I don't think he has a prayer of escaping the area."

Fred looked at his brother and raised one eyebrow. "You mean that honestly, or is that wishful thinking?"

Before Doral could reply, Fred's cell phone rang. He glanced at the caller ID and smiled across at his brother. "Tom VanAllen. FBI to the rescue."

Chapter 3

———⊰◦⊱———

Coburn gradually backed away from the woman, but even then, her fear of him was palpable. Good. He needed her to be afraid. Fear would inspire cooperation. "They're searching for you," she said.

"Behind every tree."

"Police, state troopers, volunteers. Dogs."

"I heard them yelping early this morning."

"They'll catch you."

"They haven't yet."

"You should keep running."

"You'd like that, wouldn't you, Mrs. Gillette?"

Her expression became even more stark with fear, so the significance of his knowing her name hadn't escaped her. He hadn't randomly selected her house in which to take refuge. It—she—had been a destination.

"Mommy, the kitty went into the bushes and won't come out."

Coburn's back was to the door, but he'd heard the little

girl come in from outside, had heard the soles of her sandals slapping against the hardwood floor as she approached the kitchen. But he didn't turn toward her. His gaze remained fixed on the kid's mother.

Her face had turned as white as chalk. Her lips looked practically bloodless as her eyes sawed back and forth between him and the kid. But Coburn gave her credit for keeping her voice light and cheerful. "That's what kitties do, Em. They hide."

"How come?"

"The kitty doesn't know you, so maybe he's afraid."

"That's silly."

"Yes, it is. Very silly." She shifted her gaze back to Coburn and added meaningfully, "He should know you won't do anything."

Okay, he wasn't dense. He got the message. "If you do," he said softly, "he'll scratch, and it will hurt." Holding her frightened stare, he slid the pistol into the waistband of his jeans and tugged the hem of his T-shirt over it, then turned around. The kid was staring up at him with blatant curiosity.

"Does your boo-boo hurt?"

"My what?"

She pointed to his head. He reached up and touched congealed blood. "No, it doesn't hurt."

He stepped around her as he crossed to the table. Ever since coming into the kitchen, his mouth had been watering from the aroma of freshly baked cake. He stripped away the paper cup of a cupcake and bit off half of it, then ravenously crammed the rest of it into his mouth and reached for another. He hadn't eaten since noon yesterday, and he'd been slogging through the swamp all night. He was starving.

"You didn't wash," the kid said.

He swallowed the cupcake practically whole. "What?"

"You're supposed to wash your hands before you eat."

"Oh yeah?" He peeled the paper off the second cup-cake and took a huge bite.

The kid nodded solemnly. "It's the rule."

He shot a look at the woman, who had moved up behind her daughter and placed protective hands on her shoulders. "I don't always go by the rules," he said. Keeping an eye on them, he went to the fridge, opened it, and took out a plastic bottle of milk. He thumbed off the cap and tilted the bottle toward his mouth, drinking from it in gulps.

"Mommy, he's drinking from—"

"I know, darling. But it's okay just this once. He's very thirsty."

The kid watched in fascination as he drank at least a third of the milk before stopping to take a breath. He wiped his mouth with the back of his hand and replaced the bottle in the fridge.

The kid wrinkled her nose. "Your clothes are dirty and stinky."

"I fell in the creek."

Her eyes widened. "On accident?"

"Sorta."

"Did you have wings on?"

"Wings?"

"Can you do a face float?"

Clueless, he looked at the mother. She said, "She learned to do a face float in swim class."

"I still have to wear my wings," the little girl said, "but I got a gold star on my fertisicate."

Nervously, the mother turned her around and ushered her toward the doorway into the living room. "I think it's time for Dora. Why don't you go watch while I talk to…to our company."

The child dug her heels in. "You said I could lick the bowl."

The mother hesitated, then took a rubber spatula from the bowl of frosting and handed it down to her. She took it happily and said to him, "Don't eat any more cupcakes. There s'pposed to be for the birthday party." Then she skipped out of the room.

The woman turned to him, but said nothing until they heard the voice track of the TV show come on. Then, "How do you know my name?"

"You're Eddie Gillette's widow, right?" She merely stared at him. "It's not that tough a question. Yes or no?"

"Yes."

"So, unless you've remarried…"

She shook her head.

"Then it stands to reason your name is Mrs. Gillette. What's your first name?"

"Honor."

Honor? He'd never known anybody by that name. But then this was Louisiana. People had strange names, first and last. "Well, Honor, I don't have to introduce myself, do I?"

"They said your name is Lee Collier."

"Coburn. Pleased to meet you. Sit down." He indicated a chair at the kitchen table.

She hesitated, then pulled the chair from beneath the table and slowly lowered herself into it.

He worked a cell phone out of the front pocket of his jeans and punched in a number, then hooked a chair leg with the toe of his boot and sat down across the table from her. He stared at her as he listened to the telephone on the other end ring.

She fidgeted in her seat. She clasped her hands together in her lap and looked away from him, then, almost defiantly, brought her gaze back to his and held it. She was scared half to death but trying not to show it. The lady had backbone, which was okay by him. He would much rather deal with a little moxie than bawling and begging.

When his call was answered by an automated voice mail recording, he swore beneath his breath, then waited for the ding and said, "You know who this is. All hell's broke loose."

As soon as he clicked off, she said, "You have an accomplice?"

"You could say."

"Was he there during the . . . the shooting?"

He merely looked at her.

She wet her lips, pulled the lower one between her teeth. "They said on the news that seven people were killed."

"That's how many I counted."

She crossed her arms over her middle and hugged her elbows. "Why did you kill them?"

"What are they saying on TV?"

"That you were a disgruntled employee."

He shrugged. "You could call me disgruntled."

"You didn't like the trucking company?"

"No. Especially the boss."

"Sam Marset. But the others were just shift workers, like you. Was it necessary to shoot them, too?"

"Yes."

"Why?"

"They were witnesses."

His candor seemed to astonish and repel her. He watched a shudder pass through her. For a time, she remained quiet, simply staring at the tabletop.

Then slowly she raised her head and looked up at him. "How did you know my husband?"

"Actually I never had the pleasure. But I've heard about him."

"From whom?"

"Around Royale Trucking, his name pops up a lot."

"He was born and raised in Tambour. Everybody knew Eddie and loved him."

"You sure about that?"

Taken aback, she said, "Yes, I'm sure."

"Among other things, he was a cop, right?"

"What do you mean by 'among other things'?"

"Your husband, the late, great Eddie the cop, was in possession of something extremely valuable. I came here to get it."

Before she could respond, the cell phone still in his pocket, hers, rang, startling them both. Coburn pulled it from his pocket. "Who's Stanley?"

"My father-in-law."

"Grandpa," he said, thinking back to what the kid had said out in the yard.

"If I don't answer—"

"Forget it." He waited until the ringing stopped, then nodded toward the cupcakes. "Whose birthday is it?"

"Stan's. He's coming for dinner to celebrate."

"What time? And I don't advise you to lie to me."

"Five-thirty."

He glanced at the wall clock. That was almost eight hours from now. He hoped to have what he was after and be miles away from here by then. A lot depended on Eddie

Gillette's widow and how much she knew about her late husband's extracurricular activities.

He could tell her fear of him was genuine. But her fear could be based on any number of reasons, one of them being that she wanted to protect what she had and was afraid of him taking it away from her.

Or she could be entirely innocent and afraid only of the danger he posed to her and her kid.

Apparently they lived alone out here in the boondocks. There hadn't been a trace of a man in the house. So when a bloodstained stranger showed up and threatened the isolated widow with a pistol, she would naturally be afraid.

Although living singly didn't necessarily equate to virtue, Coburn thought, reminding himself that he lived alone.

Looks could be deceiving, too. She looked innocent enough, especially in the getup she was wearing. The white T-shirt, blue jean shorts, and retro white Keds were as wholesome as home-baked cupcakes. Her blonde hair was in a loose ponytail. Her eyes were hazel, veering toward solid green. She had the scrubbed appearance of the classic all-American girl next door, except that Coburn had never lived next door to anybody who looked as good as she did.

Seeing the skimpy undies on the drying rack in the laundry room had made him realize how long it had been since he'd lain down with a woman. Looking at the soft mounds underneath Honor Gillette's white T-shirt and her long, smooth legs made him aware of just how much he'd like to end that spell of abstinence.

She must have sensed the track of his thoughts, because when he lifted his gaze from her chest to her eyes, they were regarding him fearfully. Quickly she said, "You're in a lot of trouble, and you're only wasting time here. I can't help you. Eddie didn't own anything extremely valuable." She raised her hands at her sides. "You can see for yourself how simply we live. When Eddie died, I had to sell his fishing boat just to make ends meet until I could return to teaching."

"Teaching."

"Public school. Second grade. The only thing Eddie left me was a modest life insurance policy that barely covered the cost of his funeral. He'd been with the police department only eight years, so the pension I receive each month isn't much. It goes directly into Emily's college fund. I support us on my salary, and there's little left for extras."

She paused to take a breath. "You've been misinformed, Mr. Coburn. Or you jumped to the wrong conclusion based on rumor. Eddie had nothing valuable and neither do I. If I did, I would gladly hand it over to you in order to protect Emily. I value her life more than anything I could ever own."

He looked at her thoughtfully for several moments. "Nicely put, but I'm not convinced." He stood up and reached for her, encircling her biceps again and hauling her up out of her chair. "Let's start in the bedroom."

Chapter 4

His street name was Diego.

That's all he'd ever been called, and, as far as he knew, that was the only name he had. His earliest memory was of a skinny black woman asking him to fetch her cigarettes, or her syringe, and then hurling abuse at him if he was too slow about it.

He didn't know if she was his mother or not. She didn't claim to be, but didn't deny it the one time he'd asked her. He wasn't black, not entirely. His name was Hispanic, but that didn't necessarily signify his heritage. In a city of Creoles where mixed bloodlines were historical and commonplace, he was a mongrel.

The woman of his memory had operated a hair-braiding salon. The business was open only when she felt like it, which was seldom. If she needed quick cash, she gave blowjobs in the back room. When Diego was old enough, she sent him out to solicit clients off the streets. He lured in women with the promise of getting the tightest braids in New Orleans. To men, he hinted of other pleasures to be found beyond the glass bead curtain that separated the establishment from the gritty sidewalk.

One day he came in after scrounging for something to eat and found the woman dead on the floor of the filthy bathroom. He stayed until the stink of her got to be too much even for him, then he abandoned the place, leaving her bloated corpse to become somebody else's problem. From that day on, he had fended for himself. His turf was an area of New Orleans where even angels feared to tread.

He was seventeen years old and wise beyond his years.

His eyes showed it as he looked at the readout on his vibrating cell phone. *Private caller.* Which translated to The Bookkeeper. He answered with a surly, "Yeah?"

"You sound upset, Diego."

Pissed, more like it. "You should have used me to take care of Marset. But you didn't. Now look at the mess you've got."

"So you've heard about the warehouse and Lee Coburn?"

"I got a TV. Flat-screen."

"Thanks to me."

Diego let that pass without comment. The Bookkeeper didn't need to know that their working relationship wasn't exclusive. He did occasional jobs for other clients.

"Guns," he said scornfully. "They're noisy. Why shoot up the place? I would have taken out Marset silently, and you wouldn't have a circus going on down there in Tambour."

"I needed to send a message."

Don't fuck with me, or else. That was the message. Diego supposed that anyone who'd crossed The Bookkeeper, and had heard about the mass murder, was looking over his shoulder this morning. Despite the amateurish handling of Marset's execution, no doubt it had been an effective wake-up call.

"They haven't found Lee Coburn yet," Diego said, almost as a gibe.

"No. I'm closely monitoring the search. I hope they find him dead, but if not, he'll have to be taken out. And so will anyone he's had contact with since leaving that warehouse."

"That's why you're calling me."

"It will be tricky to get close to someone in police custody."

"I specialize in tricky. I can get close. I always do."

"Which is why you're the man for this job, should it become necessary. Your skills would have been wasted on Marset. I needed to make noise and leave a lot of blood. But now that it's done, I want no loose ends."

No loose ends. No mercy. The Bookkeeper's mantra. Anybody who shied away from the wet work usually became the next victim.

A few weeks earlier, a Mexican kid had escaped the overloaded truck that was smuggling him into the States. He and a dozen others were destined for slavery of one type or another. The kid must've known what the future held for him. During a refueling stop, while the truck driver was paying for his gasoline, the kid got away.

Fortunately, a state trooper who was on The Bookkeeper's payroll had found him hitchhiking on the westbound lane of the interstate. The trooper had hidden him and had been ordered to dispose of the problem. But he'd turned squeamish.

The Bookkeeper had contracted Diego to go in and do his dirty work for him. Then, a week after Diego killed the boy, The Bookkeeper hired him to take care of the driver whose carelessness had allowed the kid to escape, along with the trooper who had shown himself to be greedy but gutless.

No loose ends. No mercy. The Bookkeeper's uncompromising policy instilled fear and inspired obedience.

But Diego wasn't scared of anybody. So when The Bookkeeper asked him now, "Did you find the girl who got away from the massage parlor?" he replied in a flippant manner, "Last night."

"She's no longer a problem?"

"Only to the angels. Or the devil."

"The body?"

"I'm not an idiot."

"Diego, the only thing more annoying than an idiot is a smart-ass."

Diego raised his middle finger at the phone.

"Someone else is calling in, so I must go. Be ready."

Diego slid his hand into his pants pocket and fondled the straight razor for which he was famous. Although The Bookkeeper had already disconnected, Diego said, "I stay ready."

Chapter 5

Engrossed in her program, Emily gave Honor and Coburn no notice as they passed through the living room.

When they reached Honor's bedroom, she jerked her arm free from his grip and rubbed her bruised biceps. "I don't want to get shot, and I certainly wouldn't risk Emily's life or run away and leave her behind. The manhandling is unnecessary."

"That's for me to decide." He nodded toward the computer on the writing desk. "Was that your husband's computer?"

"We both used it."

"Boot it up."

"There's nothing on it except my personal emails, school records of my students, and lesson plans for each month."

He just stood there, looking dark and dangerous, until she went to the desk and sat down. It seemed to take an eternity for the computer to boot. She stared into the monitor, looking at the blurred reflection of herself, but all the while aware of him, standing close, emanating odors of the swamp, his body heat, and a distinct threat of violence.

From the corner of her eye, she looked at his hand. It was relaxed, resting against his thigh. Even so, she knew it could squeeze the life from her body if he put it around her throat. The thought of it wrapped around Emily's sweet, soft neck made her ill.

"Thank you, Mr. Coburn," she whispered.

Several seconds elapsed before he asked, "For what?"

"For not harming Emily."

He didn't say anything.

"And for keeping the pistol out of her sight. I appreciate that."

Another few seconds ticked past. "Nothing to be gained by scaring the kid." The computer asked for a password. Honor quickly typed hers in. It showed up as black dots in the box.

"Wait," he said before she could hit Enter. "Backspace and type it again. Slowly this time."

She pecked out the letters again.

"What does the *r* stand for?"

"Rosemary."

"H, r, Gillette. Not a very original password. Easy to guess."

"I've got nothing to hide."

"Let's see."

He reached over her shoulder and began maneuvering the mouse. He navigated through her emails, even those that had been deleted, and all her documents, which contained nothing that would interest him unless he was in second grade.

At one point, she asked politely, "Would you like to sit down?"

"I'm fine."

He might be, but she wasn't. He was leaning over her, occasionally making contact with her back and shoulder, his arm brushing hers as he scooted the mouse around.

Finally he was satisfied that the files he'd opened were useless to him. "Did Eddie have a password?"

"We used the same one, as well as the same email address."

"I didn't see any emails to or from him."

"They've all been deleted."

"Why?"

"They were taking up space on the computer."

He didn't say anything, but she felt a tug on her ponytail and realized that he was winding it around his fist. When he had a tight grip, he turned her head toward him. She closed her eyes, but she could feel the pressure of his gaze on the top of her head.

"Open your eyes."

Given her recent thoughts on the strength of his hands, she did as he ordered because she was afraid not to. She was on eye level with his waist. The proximity of her face to his body, and the intimacy it suggested, was disconcerting, as she supposed he intended. He wanted there to be no doubt as to who was in charge.

But perhaps she could turn this to her advantage. Her nose was inches from the outline of the pistol beneath his T-shirt. Her hands were free. Could she—

No. Even before she had finished formulating the thought, she cast it aside. Eddie had taught her how to shoot a handgun, but she'd never been comfortable handling any firearm. She couldn't secure the pistol and fire it before Coburn knocked it aside or yanked it from her. Any attempt to do so would only anger him. And then what? She didn't hazard to guess.

Using her fisted ponytail as leverage, he tilted her head back until she was looking up into his face. "Why did you delete your husband's emails?"

"He's been gone for two years. Why would I keep them?"

"They could have had important information in them."

"They didn't."

"She says, sounding real sure about it."

"I am," she snapped. "Eddie wouldn't have been so careless as to put important information in an email."

He held her stare as though gauging the strength of her argument. "Do you do your banking on this computer?"

"No."

"Pay any accounts?"

She shook her head as much as his hold on her hair would allow. "Neither of us used it for personal business."

"What about his work computer?"

"It belonged to the police department."

"It wasn't given to you?"

"No. I suppose another officer has use of it now."

He studied her face for another long moment, and must have determined that she was telling the truth. He released her hair and backed away. Relieved, she stood up and moved away from him and toward the door. "I'm just going to check on Emily."

"Stay where you are."

His eyes made a sweep of the room and did a double take when something on top of the dresser grabbed his attention. He crossed quickly to the bureau and picked up the picture frame, then thrust it into her hands. "Who are these guys?"

"The oldest one is Stan."

"Eddie's father? He's in awfully good shape for a man his age."

"He works at it. That's Eddie standing next to him."

"The other two? Twins?"

"Fred and Doral Hawkins. Eddie's best friends." Smiling over the fond memory, she ran her fingers across the glass sealing the photograph. "They'd gone on an overnight fishing trip into the Gulf. When they put in the following afternoon, they posed on the pier with their catch and asked me to take this picture."

"Is that the boat you sold?"

"No, that was Doral's charter boat. Katrina took it. Now he's our city manager. Fred is a policeman."

He looked at her sharply, then tapped the glass inside the frame. "This guy's a cop?"

"He and Eddie enrolled in the police academy together and graduated in the same class of new officers. He—" She broke off and looked away from him, but he caught her chin and jerked her head back to him.

"What?" he demanded.

She saw no point in hedging. "Fred is spearheading the manhunt for you."

"How do you know?"

"He conducted a press conference this morning. He pledged your swift capture and justice for the seven men you killed. Allegedly."

He absorbed that, then released her chin and took the frame from her. To her consternation, he turned it over and began folding back the metal tabs so he could remove the easel back.

"What are you doing?"

"What does it look like?"

He took it apart and, inside, found only what she knew he would: the photograph, a piece of stiff backing, and the glass. He stared hard at the photograph and checked the date printed on the back of it. "They seem like a real chummy quartet."

"The three boys became friends in grade school. Stan practically raised the Hawkins twins along with Eddie. They've been a great help to us since he died. They've been especially attentive to Emily and me."

"Yeah?" He gave her a slow once-over. "I'll bet they have."

She wanted to lash out at him for what his smirk insinuated. But she held her tongue, believing it was beneath her dignity to defend her morals to a man who was smeared with his victims' blood. She did, however, take the photograph from him and return it and the pieces of the frame back to the top of her bureau.

"How'd he die?" he asked. "Eddie. What killed him?"

"Car accident."

"What happened?"

"It's believed he swerved to miss hitting an animal, something. He lost control and went headlong into a tree."

"He was by himself?"

"Yes." Again she looked wistfully at the photograph that had so perfectly captured her husband's smiling face. "He was on his way home from work."

"Where's his stuff?"

The question yanked her from the poignant reverie. "What?"

"His stuff. You're bound to have kept his personal belongings."

In light of their conversation, his wanting to go through Eddie's effects was the height of insensitivity, and it offended her almost more than having been threatened with a pistol. She met his cold, unfeeling eyes head-on. "You're a cruel son of a bitch."

His eyes turned even more implacable. He took a step toward her. "I need to see his stuff. Either you hand it over to me, or I'll tear your house apart looking for it."

"Be my guest. But I'll be damned before I'll help you."

"Oh, I doubt that."

Catching his malevolent implication, her gaze swung beyond his shoulder toward the living room where Emily was still enjoying one of her favorite shows.

"Your kid is all right, Mrs. Gillette. She'll stay all right so long as you don't play games with me."

"I'm not playing games."

"So we understand each other, neither am I."

He spoke softly, malevolently, and his point was made. Furious with him, and with herself for having to capitulate without putting up more of a fight, she said coolly, "It would be helpful if you told me what you're looking for."

"It would be helpful if you quit jerking me around."

"I'm not!"

"Aren't you?"

"No! I have no idea what you want or even what you're talking about. Gold bars? Stock certificates? Precious stones? If I had something like that, don't you think I would have liquidated it by now?"

"Cash?"

"Do I look like I have a lot of cash at my disposal?"

"No. You don't. But you wouldn't make it obvious, because that would be stupid."

"Stupid in what way?"

"If you were suddenly flush with cash, people would be on to you."

"People? What people? On to me? I don't understand."

"I think you do."

During this heated exchange, he'd been coming ever

closer until now they were toe to toe. His sheer physicality made her feel trapped. It was hard not to move away from him, but she refused to dance that dance again. Besides, she wouldn't give him the satisfaction of knowing how effective his intimidation tactics were.

"Now, for the last time," he said, "where's Eddie's stuff?"

She defied him with her glare, her upright posture, her sheer force of will. Telling him to go straight to hell was on the tip of her tongue.

But Emily giggled.

In her sweet, piping voice she addressed something to the characters on the program, then squealed in delight and clapped her hands.

Honor's bravado evaporated. She lowered her defiant chin, and rather than telling him to go to hell, she said, "There's a storage box under the bed."

Chapter 6

It wasn't a long commute between Tom VanAllen's home and the FBI's field office in Lafayette. Often, he considered it not long enough. It was the only time of his day in which he could switch off and think of nothing more complicated than to stay in his lane and drive within the speed limit.

He wheeled into his driveway and acknowledged that his house looked a little tired and sad compared to others in the neighborhood. But when would he have time to do repairs or repaint when something as necessary as mowing the lawn was only done sporadically?

By the time he entered through the front door, those self-castigating thoughts had already been pushed aside by the urgency of the situation in Tambour.

Janice, having heard him come in, hurried into the entryway, cell phone in hand. "I was just about to call you to ask when you'd be home for lunch."

"I didn't come home to eat." He took off his suit jacket

and hung it on the hall tree. "That multiple murder in Tambour—"

"It's all over the news. The guy hasn't been caught yet?"

He shook his head. "I've got to go down there myself."

"Why must you? You dispatched agents early this morning."

Royale Trucking Company conducted interstate trade. When the carnage was discovered inside the warehouse, Tom, as agent in charge of the field office, had been notified. "It's politic for me to review the situation in person. How's Lanny today?"

"Like he is any other day."

Tom pretended not to hear the bitterness underlying his wife's voice as he headed down the central hallway toward the room at the back of the house where their thirteen-year-old son was confined.

In fact, where he and Janice were also confined. Sadly, this room was at the epicenter of their lives, their marriage, their future.

An aberrant accident in the birth canal had cut off their son's oxygen and left him with severe brain damage. He didn't speak, or walk, or even sit alone. His responses to any stimuli were limited to blinking his eyes, but only on occasion, and to making a guttural sound, the meaning of which neither Tom nor Janice would ever be able to interpret. They had no way of knowing if he even recognized them by sight, or sound, or touch.

"He's soiled himself," Tom said upon entering the room and being hit with the odor.

"I checked him five minutes ago," Janice said defensively. "I changed the sheets on his bed this morning and—"

"That's a two-person job. You should have waited for me to help you."

"Well, that could have been a wait, couldn't it?"

Quietly Tom said, "I had to leave earlier than usual this morning, Janice. I had no choice."

She blew out a gust of air. "I know. I'm sorry. But after changing his bed, I had to do laundry. It's not even lunchtime, and I'm exhausted."

He stayed her as she moved toward the bed. "I'll take care of this."

"You're in a hurry to get away."

"Five minutes won't matter. Will you fix me a sandwich, please? I'll eat it on the way down to Tambour."

After seeing to Lanny, he went into their bedroom and changed out of his suit and into outdoor clothes. Before day's end, he would probably be called upon to join the manhunt. He had little or nothing to contribute to such an undertaking, but he would make the gesture of pitching in.

He dressed in jeans and a short-sleeved white shirt, and slipped on an old pair of sneakers, reminding himself to check the trunk of his car for the rubber boots he used to wear whenever he went fishing.

He used to do a lot of things he no longer did.

When he walked into the kitchen, Janice's back was to him. She was preoccupied with making his sandwich so he studied her for several seconds without her being aware of it.

She hadn't retained the prettiness that she'd had when they first met. The thirteen years since Lanny's birth had taken a visible toll. Her movements were no longer graceful and fluid, but efficient and brisk, as though if she didn't hurry up and accomplish the task at hand, she would lose the wherewithal to do it.

The slender young body she'd boasted had been whittled away and now she could be described as gaunt. Work and worry had etched lines around her eyes, and the lips that had always been on the verge of smiling were perpetually drawn with disappointment.

Tom didn't blame her for these changes in her appearance. The changes in him were just as disagreeable. Unhappiness and hopelessness were stamped indelibly onto their faces. Worse, the changes weren't only physical. Their love for each other had been drastically altered by the ongoing tragedy that their life together had become. The love he felt for Janice now was based more on pity than passion.

When first married, they'd shared an interest in jazz, movies, and Tuscan cooking. They'd planned to spend a summer in Italy attending cooking classes and drinking the regional vintages during sun-drenched afternoons.

That was just one of their dreams that had been shattered.

Every single day Tom asked himself how long they could go on in their present state. Something must change. Tom knew it. He figured Janice did, too. But neither wanted to be the first to wave a white flag on their commitment to their helpless son. Neither wanted to be the first to say, "I can't do this any longer," and suggest doing what they had pledged never to do, which was to place him in a special care facility.

The good ones were private and therefore costly. But the exorbitant expense was only one obstacle. Tom wasn't certain what Janice's reaction would be if he suggested they amend their original policy regarding Lanny's care. He was afraid she would talk him out of it. And equally afraid that she wouldn't.

Sensing his presence, she glanced over her shoulder. "Ham and cheese with brown mustard?"

"Fine."

She folded plastic wrap around the sandwich. "Do you plan to stay away overnight?"

"I can't leave you alone with Lanny for that long."

"I would manage."

Tom shook his head. "I'll come back. Fred Hawkins will share with me all his case notes."

"You mean the oracle of the Tambour Police Department?"

Her sarcasm made him smile. She'd known the Hawkins twins from her last year of high school, when her father had decided to move "to the country" and had taken Janice out of the parochial academy in New Orleans and transferred her to the public school in Tambour. While the distance wasn't that far, the two environments had been worlds apart.

Janice had experienced a reeling culture shock and had never quite forgiven her parents for uprooting her during that all-important senior year and transplanting her in "Bubbaville." She considered everyone in Tambour a hick, starting with, and in particular, Fred Hawkins and his twin, Doral. It amazed her that one had become an officer of the law, the other a city official. Even by Tambour's standards, the twins had exceeded her expectations of them.

"Everybody in Tambour wants the head of Sam Marset's killer on a pike, and they're breathing down Fred's collar to get it," Tom told her. "The coroner estimates time of death for all seven victims at around midnight, so Fred is"—he glanced at the clock on the microwave oven—"almost twelve hours into the investigation, and he doesn't have any substantial leads."

Janice winced. "The scene was described as a blood-bath."

"The photos my men sent back weren't pretty."

"What was the owner of the company doing in the warehouse at that time of night?"

"That struck Fred as odd, too. Mrs. Marset was of no help because she was out of town. Fred's thinking is that maybe this Coburn created some kind of problem, got into a fight with a coworker, something serious enough for the foreman to call Marset. They'll check phone records, but a reason for Marset's being there at that unusual hour hasn't been established yet."

"Is Lee Coburn a habitual troublemaker?"

"His employment record didn't indicate that. But no one claims to know him well."

"I gathered that by Fred's press conference. Beyond a description and a police artist sketch, they don't seem to have much."

"He put false information on his job application."

"They didn't check it out before they hired him?"

"An oversight I'm sure the human resources staff is regretting."

"Why did he lie on his application, I wonder. To hide a police record?"

"That was the general consensus. But so far his fingerprints haven't turned up any prior arrests."

Janice frowned. "He's probably one of those wackos who slips through the cracks of society until he does something like this. Then everybody takes notice. What I don't get is why these nutcases go after innocent people. If he bore a grudge against the company, why didn't he just wreck one of the trucks? Why go on a killing spree?"

When Tom had first met Janice, she'd been a feeling, compassionate human being who often championed the underdog. Over the years her tolerance level had steeply declined.

"Apparently Coburn doesn't have the outward markings of a wacko," he said.

"Wackos rarely do."

Tom conceded her point with a tip of his head. "Coburn had recently been placed in charge of shipping manifests. Maybe he cracked under the pressure of new responsibility."

"That's plausible." Her expression indicated that she knew something about cracking under pressure.

Tom took a canned drink from the fridge. "I'd better be off. Fred's waiting on me. If you need me, call. I've always got my cell phone."

"We'll be fine."

"I turned Lanny when I cleaned him, so you don't have to do that for a while."

"Don't worry about us, Tom. Go. Do your job. I'll handle things till you get home, whenever it is."

He hesitated, wishing he could think of something to say that would brighten her day, wishing there *was* something to say. But he knew there wasn't, so he trudged from his house with the overgrown lawn, feeling the burden of their lives weighing heavily on his shoulders because he didn't know how to make it better.

He felt no more confident about improving the situation in Tambour.

Chapter 7

—➤◦◄—

Honor retrieved the sealed rubber box from under her bed.

Coburn replaced the mattress, then, without ceremony, dumped the contents of the storage box onto her snowy white comforter and began pawing through Eddie's personal effects.

First to attract his attention were Eddie's diplomas from high school, LSU, and the police academy. He removed the first from its leather folder and searched the folder itself. But when he ripped away the moire lining, Honor protested, "There's no need to do that!"

"I think there is."

"I'm saving those documents for Emily."

"I'm not doing anything to the documents."

"Nothing's hidden behind the lining."

"Not in this one." He tossed the first aside and reached for another, subjecting it to the same vandalism. When he was done with them, he examined Eddie's wristwatch.

"Pretty tricked-out watch."

"I gave it to him for Christmas."

"Where'd you buy it?"

"What difference does it make?"

"A local store?"

"I ordered it online. It's a knockoff of a fancy one."

"How much did it cost?"

"Around three hundred dollars."

"Not thousands?"

"Do you want to see the receipt?"

"No, but you've contradicted yourself. You said you didn't use the computer for personal business."

Wearily she sighed. "I've ordered things."

"Did Eddie?"

"I never knew him to."

He held her stare, then let it go and moved on to Eddie's death certificate. "Broken neck?"

"He died instantly. Or so I was told."

She hoped he'd died immediately and hadn't suffered. The medical examiner had told Stan and her that even if he had survived the neck injury, he probably would have died of his extensive internal injuries before reaching the hospital.

After perusing the death certificate, Coburn thumbed through the guest book for the funeral service.

"Whatever you're looking for isn't in there." It was breaking her heart to see items that were precious only to her handled by a man with blood on his hands, literally and figuratively.

She was especially incensed when he picked up Eddie's wedding ring. It had been on Eddie's finger from the day they'd stood at the altar and exchanged their vows until she'd been called to the morgue to identify his body.

Holding the ring close, Coburn read the inscription inside. "Ah. What's this?"

"Our wedding date and initials."

He read the engraving again, then bounced the ring in his palm as he regarded it thoughtfully. Finally he looked up at her and, after a moment, extended his hand. She held out hers. He dropped the ring into her palm and her fingers closed around it.

"Thank you."

"I don't need it anymore. I memorized the engraving."

He went through Eddie's wallet several times, then actually turned the leather inside out. It produced nothing except expired credit cards, Eddie's driver's license—he examined the laminate to make sure it was sealed all the way around—and Social Security card. There were pictures of her and Emily that had been trimmed to fit the clear plastic sleeves.

He picked up the empty key ring and dangled it in front of her face. "A key ring without keys?"

"I took off the house key and hid it outside in case I ever lock us out. The keys to the squad car and Eddie's locker were returned to the police department."

"Do you have a safe deposit box?"

"No."

"Would you tell me if you did?"

"If it guaranteed Emily's safety, I'd drive you to the bank. But I don't have a safe deposit box."

He continued to examine and question her about each article arrayed on her comforter, which he'd soiled with his muddy clothes. But it was an exercise in futility as she'd known it would be. "You're wasting your time, Mr. Coburn. Whatever you're looking for isn't here."

"It's here. I just haven't found it yet. And you can drop the 'mister.' Just plain Coburn will do."

He came off the bed, planted his hands on his hips, and made a tight circle as he looked around the room. She had hoped he would quickly find whatever it was he was after, then leave without harming either Emily or her. But the fruitlessness of his search was beginning to frustrate him, and that didn't bode well. She feared that she and Emily would become the scapegoats for his mounting frustration.

"Bank statements, tax records. Where's all that?"

Afraid not to cooperate, she pointed overhead. "Storage boxes in the attic."

"Where's the access?"

"In the hall."

He dragged her along behind him as he left the bedroom. Reaching high above his head for the slender rope, he pulled down the trapdoor, then unfolded the sectioned ladder and motioned to her. "Up you go."

"Me?"

"I'm not leaving you down here alone with your daughter."

"I'm not going to run away."

"That's right. I'm going to see that you don't."

To protest his logic would be futile, so she started up the ladder, acutely aware of her exposed legs and the view he was getting of her backside. She climbed as quickly as possible and was actually glad to be stepping up into the attic, when it had always been a place she would rather avoid. She associated attics with cobwebs and rodents. And attics were sad places, dark depositories where the cast-off articles of one's life were sent to molder.

She yanked the string on the bare bulb in the ceiling. The file storage boxes were right where she knew they would be. She picked up the first one by the open slots in its sides. Coburn waited in the narrow opening to take it from her and carry it down. They repeated the procedure until all had been removed from the attic.

"This is pointless," she said as she dusted her hands and reached for the string to turn off the light.

"Wait a minute. What about those?" He'd poked his head up through the opening and had taken a look around, spying the boxes that Honor had hoped would escape his notice. They were standard packing boxes sealed with tape. "What's in those?"

"Christmas decorations."

"Ho-ho-ho."

"There's nothing in them that you've asked to see."

"Hand them down."

She didn't immediately obey. Looking down at him, she wondered if she could jam her foot into his face hard enough to break his nose. Possibly. But if she missed, he might trap her up here in the attic, leaving him alone with Emily. As galling as it was to take the coward's way, Emily's safety demanded it.

One by one, she handed the other three boxes down to him.

By the time she had descended the ladder and raised the trapdoor back flush with the ceiling, he was stripping the sealing tape off one of the boxes. When he pulled back the flaps, it wasn't tinsel that blossomed out, but a man's shirt.

He looked up at her, the obvious question in his eyes.

She remained stubbornly silent.

Finally he said, "He's been dead how long?"

His implication smarted because she'd asked herself many times how long she was going to keep perfectly good clothing boxed in her attic when needy people could use it.

"I gave away most of his clothes," she said defensively.

"Stan asked if he could have Eddie's police uniforms, and I let him keep those. Some things I just couldn't..."

She left the statement unfinished, refusing to explain to a criminal that some articles of Eddie's clothing brought back distinctively happy memories. Giving away those items would be tantamount to letting go of the memories themselves. As it was, they were inexorably dimming without any help from her.

Time marched on, and recollections, no matter how dear, faded with its passage. She could now spend an entire day, or even several, without thinking about Eddie within the context of a specific memory.

His death had left a hole in her life that had seemed bottomless. Gradually that void had been filled with the busyness of rearing a child, with the busyness of life itself, until, over time, she had learned how to enjoy life without him.

But the enjoyment of living came with a large dose of guilt. She couldn't escape feeling that even the smallest grain of happiness was a monumental betrayal. How dare she relish anything ever again, when Eddie was dead and buried?

So she had saved articles of his clothing that held special memories for her, and by keeping them, kept her survivor's guilt at bay.

But she wasn't about to discuss any of this psychology with Coburn. She was spared from having to say anything when Emily appeared.

"Dora's over and so's Barney, and I'm hungry. Can we have lunch?"

The kid's question reminded Coburn that he hadn't eaten anything in twenty-four hours except the two rich cupcakes. A search through the boxes from the attic would take time. He would eat before tackling them. He motioned the widow into the kitchen.

After clearing the cupcakes and bowl of frosting off the table, she fixed the kid a peanut butter and jelly sandwich. He asked for one for himself and watched as she made it, afraid she might slip something into his. Ground-up sleeping pills, rat poison. He was short on trust.

"You gotta wash your hands this time." The kid placed a step stool with her name painted on it in front of the kitchen sink. She climbed onto it. Even standing on tip-toe, she was barely able to reach the taps, but somehow she managed to turn them on. "You can use my Elmo soap."

She picked up a plastic bottle with a bug-eyed red character grinning from the label. She squirted some liquid soap into her palm, then handed the bottle to him. He glanced at Honor and saw that she was watching them with apprehension. He figured that as long as she was nervous about his being close to the kid, she wasn't going to try anything stupid.

He and the kid washed their hands, then held them beneath the faucet to rinse.

She tilted her head back and looked up at him. "Do you have an Elmo?"

He shook the water off his hands and took the towel she passed him. "No, I don't have a...an Elmo."

"Who do you sleep with?"

Involuntarily, his gaze darted to Honor and made a connection that was almost audible, like the clack of two magnets. "Nobody."

"You don't sleep with a friend?"

"Not lately."

"How come?"

"Just don't."

"Where's your bed? Does your mommy read you stories before you go to sleep?"

He dragged his attention off Honor and back to the kid. "Stories? No, my mom, she's...gone."

"So's my daddy. He lives in heaven." Her eyes lit up. "Maybe he knows your mommy in heaven!"

Coburn snorted a laugh. "I doubt it."

"Are you scared of the dark?"

"Emily," Honor interrupted. "Stop asking so many questions. It's rude. Come sit down and have your lunch."

They gathered around the table. The widow looked ready to jump out of her skin if he so much as said *boo*. She didn't eat. Truth be told, he was as discomfited by this domestic scene as she was. Since being a kid, he'd never talked to one. It was weird, carrying on a conversation with such a little person.

He scarfed the sandwich, then took an apple from the basket of fruit on the table. The kid dawdled over her food.

"Emily, you said you were hungry," her mother admonished. "Eat your lunch."

But he was a distraction. The kid never took her eyes off him. She studied everything he did. When he took the first crunching bite of the apple, she said, "I don't like the peel."

He shrugged and said through a mouthful, "I don't mind it."

"I don't like green apples, either. Only red."

"Green's okay."

"Guess what?"

"What?"

"My grandpa can peel an apple from the top to the bottom without it breaking. He says he likes to make a long curl of the peel, just like my hair. And guess what else."

"What?"

"Mommy can't do it because she's a girl, and Grandpa says boys do it best. And Mommy doesn't have a special magic knife like Grandpa's."

"You don't say." He glanced across at Honor, who'd rolled her lips inward. "What kind of special magic knife does your grandpa have?"

"Big. He carries it in a belt around his ankle, but I can't ever touch it 'cause it's sharp and I could get hurt."

"Huh."

Honor scraped back her chair and shot to her feet. "Time for your nap, Em."

Her face puckered into a frown of rebellion. "I'm not sleepy."

"It's rest time. Come on."

Honor's voice brooked no argument. The child's expression was still mutinous, but she climbed down from her chair and headed out of the kitchen. Coburn left the remainder of the apple on his plate and followed them.

In the frilly pink bedroom, the kid got up onto the bed and extended her feet over the edge of it. Her mother removed her sandals and set them on the floor, then said, "Down you go. Sleepy time."

The little girl laid her head on the pillow and reached for a cotton quilt so faded and frayed that it looked out of place in the room. She tucked it beneath her chin. "Would you hand me my Elmo, please?" She addressed this request to Coburn.

He followed the direction of her gaze and saw a red stuffed toy lying on the floor near his mud-caked boot. He recognized the grinning face from the bottle of hand soap. He bent down and picked it up. The thing began to sing, startling him. He quickly handed it to the kid.

"Thank you." She cradled it against her chest and sighed happily.

It occurred to Coburn that he didn't recall a time in his life when he'd experienced that kind of contentment. He wondered what it was like to fall asleep without having to worry over whether or not you'd wake up.

Honor bent down and kissed her child's forehead. The kid's eyes were already closed. He noticed that her eyelids looked almost transparent. They had tiny purple veins criss-crossing them. He'd never noticed anyone's eyelids before, unless it was seconds before they drew a gun on him. Then that person usually had died with that telltale squint intact.

As they left the bedroom, the toy was still singing a silly little song about friends. Honor pulled the door shut behind them. He glanced at the boxes lined up along the wall, then took her cell phone from his jeans pocket and handed it to her. She looked at him curiously.

"Call your father-in-law. You know, the one who works at staying fit. The one with the big magic knife strapped to his ankle. Tell him the party's off."

Chapter 8

The Royale Trucking Company's warehouse was cordoned off with crime scene tape. The vicinity just outside
that barrier was jammed with official vehicles and those of
onlookers who'd converged to gawk. They were collected
in groups, exchanging the latest rumors surrounding the
mass murder and the man who had committed it.

Allegedly committed it, Stan Gillette reminded himself as
he parked his car and got out.

Before leaving his house, he'd assessed his image in the
full-length bathroom mirror with a critical eye. He'd patted his flat stomach, run his hand over his closely cropped
hair, adjusted his starched collar, checked the crease in his
pants legs, the shine on his shoes, and had determined that
the discipline he'd acquired during his military career had
served him well in civilian life.

He'd never resented the U.S. Marine Corps' near-
impossible standards. In truth, he wished they'd been

stricter. If being a Marine was easy, everybody would be one, right? He'd been born one of the few, the proud.

He was conscious of the authoritative figure he cut as he made his way through the crowd. People parted for him to pass. An air of command came naturally to him. Which is why he had decided to visit the scene of last night's crime, and why no one challenged him as he made his way up to the yellow tape.

Inside it and several yards away, Fred Hawkins was engrossed in conversation with a handful of other men, Doral among them. Stan caught Doral's eye, and, looking grateful for the interruption, he jogged over.

"Hell of a mess we've got here, Doral," Stan said.

"A regular cluster-you-know-what." Doral took a cigarette from the pack in his shirt pocket and held a lighter to it. Noticing Stan's frown of disapproval, he said, "Hell, I know, but this situation...And I was two weeks into being a nonsmoker."

"I'm sixty-five today, and I ran five miles before dawn," Stan boasted.

"Big deal. You run five miles before dawn every day."

"Unless there's a hurricane blowing."

Doral rolled his eyes. "And then you only run two and a half."

It was an old joke between them.

Doral angled his exhale away from Stan, looking at him askance. "I figured wild horses couldn't keep you away for long."

"Well, I appreciate your returning my calls and keeping me updated, but there's nothing like being in the thick of it." He was watching Fred, who was gesturing broadly as he talked to the men around him.

Following the direction of Stan's gaze, Doral nodded at the tall, skinny man who was giving Fred his undivided attention. "Tom VanAllen just got here. Fred's filling him in."

"What's your take on him?"

"He's the best kind of feeb. Not too bright. Not too ambitious."

Stan chuckled. "So if this investigation goes south—"

"He catches the flak. Most of it anyway. If the feds can't get to the bottom of this, how the hell can the local P.D. be expected to?"

"It makes good copy."

"That's the idea. Shift the heat off Fred and onto the feds. 'Course we'll be keeping close watch over everything they do."

"Give me the behind-the-scenes details."

Doral talked for several minutes, but didn't tell Stan much that he didn't already know or hadn't surmised. When Doral wrapped up, Stan asked, "No eyewitnesses?"

"Nope."

"Then how's it being laid on this Coburn?"

"Only seven employees clocked in last night. Count Sam coming in, and that means eight people were here at midnight when the shooting started. Coburn's the only one unaccounted for. At the very least he's a person of interest."

"What motive would he have had?"

"He locked horns with the boss."

"Fact or conjecture?"

Doral shrugged. "Fact. Until somebody says otherwise."

"What do you know about the man?"

"Well, we know he ain't caught yet," Doral said with exasperation. "Men and dogs have been all over that area where it's believed he ran into the woods, but nothing's turned up. Lady who lives around there says her rowboat's missing, but she suspects the neighbor's kids took it and didn't bring it back. Officers are checking out that lead. We'll see."

"Why aren't you out there searching? If anybody can find him—"

"Fred wanted to escort VanAllen out there, make sure he got seen on TV, establish that the feds are on the case. As city manager I personally welcomed VanAllen into the fray."

Stan processed all that, then asked, "What about the murder weapon?"

"Coroner says a large-caliber handgun killed Sam. The rest were shot with an automatic rifle."

"And?"

Doral turned to his mentor. "Nary a firearm found at the scene."

"Leading us to assume that Coburn is heavily armed."

"And has nothing to lose, which makes him dangerous. Public enemy number one." Doral noticed his brother waving at them. "That's my cue to come rescue him." He threw down his cigarette and ground it out.

Stan said, "Tell Fred I'll join the volunteers later this evening."

"Why not now?"

"Honor's cooking me a birthday dinner."

"Out at her place? Long way out there. When are you going to persuade her to move into town?"

"I'm making headway," Stan lied, knowing that Doral was ribbing him about his running argument with his daughter-in-law.

Stan wanted her to move into town. She demurred. He understood her wanting to stay in the house that she and Eddie had moved into as newlyweds. They'd put a lot of themselves into making it a home, spending most week-ends applying elbow grease until they'd got it the way they wanted it. Naturally she would feel a strong bond to the place.

But it would be easier for him to keep an eye on her and Emily if they lived closer to him, and he didn't plan to give up the argument until Honor came around to his way of thinking.

"I'll catch up with you after the party," he told Doral. "But it won't be late."

"Hopefully we'll have Coburn by then. If not, ask around if you don't see me or Fred right away. We'll need you."

"Challenging?"

"Not to Fred and me."

Coburn figured Honor Gillette would jump at the chance to speak to her father-in-law, but she put up an argument. "He's not due here until five-thirty. You'll be gone by then."

He hoped so, too. But he didn't want the old man showing up early. He nodded at the phone in her hand. "Make up something. Convince him not to come."

She used speed dial to place the call.

"Don't try anything cute," Coburn warned. "Put it on speaker."

She did as he asked, so he heard the crispness in the man's voice when he answered. "Honor? I tried to call you earlier."

"I'm sorry. I couldn't get to the phone."

Immediately he asked, "Is something wrong?"

"I'm afraid the party has to be postponed. Em and I both came down with a bug. A stomach virus. I'd heard that one was going around. Two of the kids in Vacation Bible School—"

"I'm on my way."

Coburn gave his head a hard shake.

"No, Stan," she said quickly. "We'd expose you, and there's no sense in your getting it, too."

"I never catch these things."

"Well, I'd feel awful if you did. Besides, we're fine."

"I could bring you Gatorade, soda crackers."

"I've got all that. And the worst is past us. Em's been able to keep down some Sprite. She's napping. We're feeling a little wrung out, but I'm sure this is one of those things that runs its course within twenty-four hours. We'll have your party tomorrow evening."

"I hate to postpone it for Emily's sake. She's going to love her present."

She smiled wanly. "It's *your* birthday."

"Which entitles me to spoil my granddaughter if I've a mind to."

Background noise, which had been loud during their conversation, turned into a racket.

"What's all the noise? Where are you?" Honor asked.

"Just leaving Royale's warehouse. If you've been sick you might not have heard about what happened here last night." He encapsulated it. "Fred's in charge of the posse. Doral briefed me."

Her eyes on Coburn's, she said, "This man sounds dangerous."

"He should be scared silly. Regardless of the holiday, every badge in five parishes is on the lookout. They'll run this murderer to ground soon enough, and when they do he'll be lucky if they don't string him up in the nearest tree. Everybody's jumpy and wants to avenge Sam Marset."

"Any fresh leads?"

"A woman's boat was stolen overnight. They're checking that out now. And the FBI is on board."

Honor gave an appropriate murmur that could have been interpreted any number of ways. Stan Gillette must have taken it to mean that she was weary.

"Rest while you can. I'll call later to check on the two of you, but in the meantime, if you need anything—"

"I'll call, I promise."

They exchanged goodbyes and Stan Gillette clicked off. Coburn extended his hand and, with reluctance, Honor dropped her cell phone into it. Meanwhile he was using his own phone to redial the number he'd called earlier. He got the same recorded message. "What holiday is it?"

"Yesterday was the Fourth. Since it fell on Sunday—"

"Today's the national holiday. Shit. I didn't think of that."

He pocketed both phones, then stood there considering the boxes he intended to pillage. "How long will the kid sleep?"

"An hour. Sometimes a little longer."

"Okay, into the bedroom."

He nudged her elbow, but she balked. "Why? I thought you wanted to go through the files."

"I will. After."

Her expression went slack with fear. "After?"

"After."

Chapter 9

———◆———

He nudged her toward the bedroom. Her heart was hammering, and as she entered the room, she frantically looked about for a possible weapon.

"Sit on the bed."

There was nothing she could reach and utilize before he shot her, but the least she could do was to make a stand. She turned to face him and defiantly asked, "Why?"

He'd removed the pistol from the waistband of his jeans. He wasn't pointing it at her, but even holding it down at his side and lightly tapping his thigh with the barrel was threat enough. "Sit down on the end of the bed."

She did as told but with attitude.

He backed up through the doorway and into the hall. Keeping his eyes on her, he used his foot to push the opened box of clothing from the hallway into the bedroom, moving it along the hardwood floor until it was within her reach.

"Pick out some clothes I can wear. It makes no difference to me what it is, but it might to you. I don't want to defile some sacred garment."

It took her a moment to comprehend that she wasn't about to be raped, and that all he wanted from her was a change of clothing. But not mere clothing. Clothes that Eddie had worn.

She started to tell him that he could rot in his bloodstained clothes for all she cared. But he would only take something from the box himself, so what would be the point?

She knelt beside the box and rifled through the garments, choosing a worn pair of jeans and an LSU Tigers T-shirt. She held them up for his inspection.

"Underwear? Socks?"

"I didn't keep any."

"Okay, bring the clothes with you into the bathroom."

"Into the bathroom? What for?"

"A shower. I'm sick of my own stink."

She looked through the connecting door into the bathroom, then came back to him. "Leave the door open. You can see me from here."

"Not an option." He flicked the barrel of the pistol toward the bathroom.

Slowly she stood up and walked toward it. He motioned for her to sit on the lowered commode lid, which she did, watching with dread as he closed the door and flipped the lock.

He opened the shower stall door and turned on the water, then, after setting the pistol on a decorative shelf well out of her reach, he tugged off his cowboy boots one at a time. Socks came next. He whipped off his T-shirt and tossed it to the floor.

She stared at intersecting lines of grout on the tile floor, but within her peripheral vision she could see a lean torso with a fan of hair over the pectorals. A barbed-wire tattoo banded the left biceps.

She had hoped he would forget the cell phones in his jeans pockets, but she saw him take them out and set them on the shelf beside the pistol. He also took from his pockets a wad of currency and a piece of paper that had been folded into a tight rectangle about the size of a playing card. These, too, went onto the shelf.

Then his hands moved to the fly of his jeans and deftly worked the metal rivets from their well-worn holes. Without the least compunction, he pushed the jeans down his legs and stepped out of them, kicking them aside. Last came a pair of undershorts.

Honor's heart was thudding so hard she felt each pulse against her eardrums. She'd forgotten, or rather hadn't allowed herself to remember, the particular essence of a naked man, the shape of the male body, the intriguing textures.

Perhaps because she feared Coburn, because he posed a physical threat, she was acutely aware of his nakedness as he stood only inches from her emanating a very real, dominant, primitive masculinity.

Beneath Eddie's clothes that were lying in her lap, her hands curled into fists. Despite her determination not to be cowed, she'd kept her eyes open. But now they seemed to shut tightly of their own volition.

After what seemed like an eternity, she sensed him moving away from her and stepping into the shower stall. He didn't close the door. When the spray of hot water hit him, he actually sighed with pleasure.

That was the instant she'd been waiting for. She shot to her feet, dumping the garments to the floor, and, hands outstretched, lunged for the shelf.

Only to find it empty.

"I figured you would try."

Angrily, she spun toward the stall. He was casually working the bar of soap into a lather between his hands, water sluicing over him. With a smug smile, he tipped his head toward the narrow window high in the shower wall. On the tile ledge, safe and dry, were the pistol, the cell phones, the money, and the folded piece of paper.

With a strangled cry of despair, she launched herself toward the door and turned the lock. She even managed to yank the door open before a soapy hand shot over her shoulder and slammed it shut, then remained flat against it. He placed his other hand at her hip, the heel of it pressing against the bone, his palm and fingers tightly fitting themselves to the curve of her belly.

The wet imprint of his hand was as distinct and searing as a brand as he crowded up behind her, mashing her between him and the door. From the corner of her eye she had a close-up view of the barbed-wire tattoo, which looked as unyielding as the hard muscle it encircled.

She froze with fear. He didn't move either, except for the rapid rise and fall of his chest against her back. Her clothing acted as a sponge to his wet skin. Water dripped off him and trickled down the backs of her bare legs. Soap bubbles dissolved into liquid on his hand that was still flattened against the door.

His breath was rapid and hot against her neck. He bent his head downward toward her shoulder even as his hips angled up. It was an oh-so-subtle adjustment of two body parts, perfectly synchronized and corresponding. But it was enough to cause Honor's breath to catch in her throat.

"Jesus." The word was spoken in a barely audible groan

that came from deep within his chest and wasn't in the least religiously inspired.

Honor didn't dare shift her position, didn't dare even breathe, afraid of what the slightest motion might provoke.

Half a minute ticked by. Gradually, the tension in his body ebbed, and he relaxed his hold, but only marginally. In a gravelly voice, he said, "We had a deal. You cooperate, you don't get hurt."

"I didn't trust you to keep to the agreement."

"Then we're even, lady. You just lost all trust privileges." He released her and backed away. "Sit down and stay there, or so help me God..."

He made his point so emphatically that he didn't even bother locking the bathroom door again. Her knees gave way just as she reached the commode. She sat down on it heavily, grateful for the support.

He got back into the shower stall, and although she didn't look in that direction, she sensed him picking up the bar of soap from off the floor, then washing and rinsing in cycles in order to get the filth off himself.

She smelled her shampoo when he uncapped the plastic bottle. Knowing he would have to duck his head beneath the spray in order to rinse it, she wondered if she dared try again to get through the door. But she didn't trust her legs to support her, and she didn't trust what he would do if she tried and failed again.

The room had become cloudy and warm with steam by the time he turned off the faucets. She sensed him reaching through the open shower door and whipping a towel off the rack. A few moments later, he picked up Eddie's old jeans and pulled them on, then the faded purple T-shirt.

"My head is bleeding again."

When she looked up, he was still working the T-shirt over his damp torso with one hand, and with the other was trying to stanch the bleeding from his scalp. Bright red blood was leaking through his fingers.

"Hold the towel against it. Press it hard." She stood up and opened the medicine cabinet above the sink. "You'd better douse it with peroxide."

She passed the bottle to him. He uncapped it and did as she suggested, liberally pouring the peroxide directly over the wound. She winced. "Is it deep? You may need stitches."

"This'll do for now."

"How did it happen?"

"I was running with my head down, trying to see the ground. Ran into a low tree branch." He tossed the bloody towel to the floor. "What do you care?"

She said nothing to that, but she didn't believe he actually expected her to reply. He retrieved the items from the window ledge in the shower stall. He slid the pistol into the waistband of Eddie's jeans. They were a bit short, Honor noted, and the waistband was a tad too large. The cell phones, money, and odd piece of paper went into the front pockets. Then, gathering up his socks and boots, he said, "You can open the door now."

As they left the bathroom, Honor said, "While we were locked up in there, someone could have come along searching for you. You would have been trapped."

"That had occurred to me, but I wasn't too worried about it. Thanks to your father-in-law I know where they're concentrating the search."

"Where you stole the boat?"

"It's miles from here. It'll take them a while to pick up my scent again."

*   *   *

"Are you *shore?*" Mrs. Arleeta Thibadoux squinted doubtfully. "'Cause they're crazy, mean kids, always into trouble of one kind or another. I 'spect they do drugs."

Tom VanAllen had yielded the floor to Fred Hawkins, letting the police officer interview the owner of the small boat that had gone missing in the approximate area where Lee Coburn had last been seen. Or was thought to have last been seen. That he was the man the motorist with the flat tire had spotted as he ran into the woods couldn't be confirmed either, but it was all they had, so they were following it up as though it was a strong lead.

The trio of boys of questionable repute, who lived a quarter mile from Mrs. Thibadoux, had been interrogated and dismissed as the suspected boat thieves. Last night, they'd been in New Orleans with several friends prowling the French Quarter. They'd slept over—passed out, more accurately—in the van belonging to one of those friends and had just straggled home, hungover and bleary-eyed, just as Tambour police had arrived to question them.

This had been explained to Mrs. Thibadoux, who wasn't quite ready to rule them out as the culprits. "I had to holler at them just a few days ago. Saw them down there at the dock messing around with my boat."

"Their friends can vouch for their whereabouts since eight o'clock last night," Fred told her.

"Hm. Well." She sniffed. "That boat weren't worth much, anyhow. I hadn't took it out since my husband died. Thought many times about selling it but never got around to it." She grinned, revealing a space where a critical tooth should have been. "It'll be worth more money now if that killer got away in it. If you find it, don't let nobody do nothing to it."

"No, ma'am, we won't."

Fred tipped his hat to her and made his way past the bird dogs sprawled on her porch. As he came down the steps, he opened a stick of gum, offering the pack to Tom.

"No thanks." Tom swiped a trickle of sweat off his forehead and waved at the swarm of gnats that had taken a liking to him. "You think Coburn took her boat?"

"Could've just got loose from her dock and drifted with the current," Fred said. "But she swears it was secure. In any case, we gotta assume it was Coburn and try to locate it."

Frustration made Fred's reply sound terse, even obligatory. Tom could tell that the police officer's patience was wearing thin. The longer Coburn was at large, the better his odds for escaping. Fred was beginning to feel the pressure. He was giving the chewing gum a workout.

"My office called while you were talking to Mrs. Thibadoux," Tom said. "The search of the trucks hasn't yielded anything."

The first thing he'd done last night, after being alerted to the multiple murder, was to order that all the trucks in the Royale fleet be stopped along their routes and thoroughly searched.

"I didn't expect it to," Fred said. "If Coburn had an accomplice who whisked him away in a company truck, or a buddy who provided him a getaway, he could have been dropped anywhere."

"I'm aware of that," Tom said testily. "But the drivers are being held and questioned all the same. And using the company manifests, we're checking out anyone who was in that warehouse within the past month. Coburn could have forged an alliance with someone who worked for any of the companies Royale does business with. Maybe more than one."

"Nothing's missing from the warehouse."

"That we know of," Tom stressed. "Coburn could have been stealing for a while, a little at a time, and it just hadn't caught up with him yet. Maybe his embezzlement wasn't exposed until yesterday, and when Sam challenged him, he went haywire. Anyhow, I've got agents working that angle."

Fred shrugged as though to say it was the federal government's time and manpower that were being wasted. Sardonically he said, "You can question Coburn about that when we catch him."

"If it's us."

"It'll be us," Fred growled with resolve. "He's still in the area or I'm not three-quarters Coonass."

"What makes you so sure?"

"I can feel him like hairs on the back of my neck standing on end."

Tom didn't argue. Some law enforcement officers had innate crime-solving skills that had inspired their career choice. Tom wasn't one of them. He'd always wanted to be an FBI agent, to work in that environment, but he'd never deluded himself into believing that he possessed extraordinary powers of detection or deduction. He relied strictly on training and procedure.

He knew he didn't call to mind the sexy, glamorous image of an FBI agent that Hollywood portrayed—steely-eyed, iron-jawed men defying machine-gun bullets as they chased gangsters in fast cars.

The perils Tom faced were of another kind altogether.

He cleared his throat to shake off that disturbing thought. "So you think Coburn is out there somewhere." He shaded his eyes against the sun, which hadn't yet slipped below the tree line. He could hear the search helicopter hovering not too far away but couldn't see it in the glare. "Chopper might spot the boat."

"Might. But probably won't."

"No?"

Fred relocated his gum to the other side of his mouth. "It's been up there going on two hours. I'm thinking Coburn's too smart to let himself be sighted that easily. It's not like that chopper can sneak up on him. Meanwhile we've got police boats trolling miles—"

A sharp whistle drew their attention to the ramshackle boat dock fifty yards from Mrs. Thibadoux's dwelling. Doral Hawkins was waving his arms high above his head. VanAllen and Fred jogged down the grassy slope that was littered with junk, relics from salvage yards and garage sales that had been purchased, then left to the mercy of salt air.

They joined Doral and several uniformed officers who were grouped around an area on the bank of the bayou. "What have you got, brother?" Fred asked.

"Partial footprint. Even better, blood." Doral proudly pointed out what was obviously spatters of blood near a distinct depression in the cool mud.

"Hot damn!" Fred went down on his haunches to better examine the first real clue they'd found.

"Don't get too excited," Doral said. "Looks like the heel of a cowboy boot. Could belong to one of those idiot teenagers the old lady was ranting about."

"She said they were down here at her dock only a few days ago," Tom remarked.

"We'll check out their footwear," Fred said. "But one of the ladies who works in the Royale offices sounded like she had the hots for Coburn. Described him in detail. Right down to his boots." He grinned up at the other two men. "She said she never saw him in anything except cowboy boots."

"What do you make of the blood?" Tom asked.

"It's a few drips, not a puddle, so he couldn't be hurt too bad." Fred slapped his thighs as he stood up and called back to one of the other officers, "Get the lab boys from the sheriff's office down here."

He put another pair of officers in charge of cordoning off the area. "Twenty feet wide. From the house down to the water. And tell Mrs. Thibadoux to keep her damn dogs away from here."

"They might pick up his scent," Tom said hopefully.

Fred scoffed. "Not that sorry pack. Where were they when Coburn was stealing her boat?"

Good question. Strangers were milling all over the property and none of the dogs had even growled.

Doral, who'd been staring out over the sluggish water of the bayou, used his thumb to push his dozer cap farther back on his head. "I hate to throw a wet blanket over this, but if Coburn put into the bayou here—"

"We're screwed," Fred said, catching his twin's meaning.

"What I was thinking," Doral said unhappily.

Tom hated to show his ignorance, but he had to ask. "What were you thinking?"

"Well," Doral said, "from here, Coburn could've gone in any one of five directions." He pointed out the tributaries that converged into the widest section of the bayou behind the Thibadoux property.

"All five of those channels branch off into others, and those into others. It's a network. Leaving us with miles of waterways and swamp to cover." Fred's elation had rapidly dissipated. Looking out over the watery view, he placed his hands on his hips. "Shit. We should have had this son of a bitch in custody by now."

"Won't argue with you there," Doral said.

"He worked on the loading dock, for crissake," Fred grumbled. "How smart can he be?"

Tom refrained from pointing out the obvious, but he did say, "It's like he chose this point on purpose, isn't it? Like he knew that these creeks came together at this spot."

"How could he know that if he's not from around here?" Doral asked.

Fred took the wad of chewing gum from his mouth and pitched it overhand into the dark, murky waters of the bayou. "It means he had an escape route all planned out."

Tom's cell phone vibrated. He took it from his pocket. "My wife," he told the two men.

"You'd better take it," Fred said.

Tom didn't talk to anyone about his circumstances at home, but he was certain people talked about them behind his back. Lanny was never mentioned, but everybody acquainted with the VanAllens, even by name, knew about their son. Someone as disabled as Lanny aroused pity and curiosity, which is why Tom and Janice had never taken him out in public. They wanted to spare not only themselves but their helpless son the humiliation of having people gawk.

Even their friends—former friends—had revealed a morbid curiosity that got so uncomfortable that he and Janice had severed all connections. They no longer socialized with anyone. Besides, their friends had borne normal, healthy children. It was painful to listen to their talk about school plays, birthday parties, and soccer games.

He turned his back and answered the call. "Is everything okay?"

"Fine," she replied. "I'm just calling to check on you. How's it going?"

"We just got a breakthrough, actually." He shared with

her the recent discovery. "Good news, it's likely that we've picked up his trail. Bad news, it leads into the bayou. That's a hell of a lot of swampy territory to cover."

"How long will you be?"

"I was about to head back. Don't hold supper on me, though. I've got to stop at the office before coming home. How's Lanny?"

"You always ask that."

"I always want to know."

She sighed. "He's fine."

Tom was about to thank her for the update when he bit back the words. It was offensive to him, this feeling that he should thank her for answering a question about their son's well-being. "I'll see you in a while," he said and immediately disconnected.

Finding the footprint and blood had galvanized the flagging officers involved in the manhunt. Fresh search dogs had been sent for. Mrs. Thibadoux was yelling from her back porch that somebody would have to pay for any damages done to her yard or dock. Fred and Doral ignored her as they reorganized and divided responsibilities among the various agencies.

Tom figured this would be a good time for him to slip away. His departure would go unnoticed, and he wouldn't be missed.

Chapter 10

———⇒»·◦·«⇐———

Darkness would impede the search for Coburn.

Which made The Bookkeeper unhappy to see that the sun was going down.

Sam Marset's execution had required an entire week of thought and planning, and The Bookkeeper had braced for its repercussions. A backlash was to be expected, even hoped for, because the louder the communal gasp over such a bloody deed, the stronger the impact was on those who had to be taught a lesson.

Case in point, the state trooper. His funeral procession had stretched for miles. Uniformed officers from numerous states had turned out for it, little knowing, or perhaps not caring, that he was an amoral bastard who took graft for looking the other way whenever trucks bearing drugs, or weapons, or even human beings traveled along the stretch of Interstate 10 that he patrolled.

It had also been reported to The Bookkeeper that on occasion the trooper would avail himself of one of the girls before returning her to the hellish cargo hold of whatever vehicle was transporting her. It was said that he preferred virgins and that he didn't return her in the condition in which he'd found her.

When his body was discovered behind the left rear wheel of his patrol car, his head nearly severed, newspaper editorialists and television pundits had decried the violence and demanded that the decorated trooper's killer be captured and made to pay the ultimate penalty for the brutal slaying. But within days the public outrage had been shifted to the breaking news of a Hollywood starlet's premature release from rehab.

Such was modern society's moral decay. If one couldn't beat it, one might just as well wallow in it. Having reached that conclusion several years ago, The Bookkeeper had set out to build an empire. Not one of industry or art, nor of finance or real estate, but of corruption. That was The Bookkeeper's stock-in-trade. Dealing solely in that commodity, the business had flourished.

In order to succeed in any endeavor, one had to be ruthless. One acted boldly and decisively, left no loose ends, and extended no mercy to competitors or traitors. The last person to have learned The Bookkeeper's policy the hard way was Sam Marset. But Marset had been the township of Tambour's favorite son.

So as the sun slid below the horizon and darkness encroached, The Bookkeeper acknowledged that the ripples of killing him had taken on the proportion of a tidal wave.

All because of Lee Coburn.

Who *must* be found. Silenced. Exterminated.

The Bookkeeper was confident of that happening. No matter how clever the man believed himself to be, he

couldn't escape The Bookkeeper's widespread and inescap-
able net. It was likely that he would be killed by his eager
but clumsy pursuers. If not, if he was brought into custody,
then Diego would be called upon to eliminate the problem. Diego was excellent at stealth. He would find a way to
get to Coburn in an unguarded moment. He would apply
his razor deftly and feel the hot gush of Coburn's blood on
his hands.

The Bookkeeper envied him that.

By sundown, Honor's house looked like storm damage.

Emily had awakened from her nap on schedule. A juice
box, a package of Teddy Grahams, and unlimited TV view-
ing had kept her pacified. But even her favorite Disney
DVDs didn't altogether distract her from their visitor.

She tried to maintain a running dialogue with Coburn,
pestering him with questions until Honor shushed her with
uncharacteristic harshness. "Leave him alone, Emily." She
was afraid her daughter's chatter, to say nothing of Elmo's
singing, would irritate him to the point of taking drastic
measures to stop it.

While he was tearing through every book in the living
room shelves, Honor told Emily that he was on a treasure
hunt, and that he didn't want to be bothered. Emily looked
doubtful of the explanation, but returned to her animated
movie without argument.

The afternoon wore on. It was the longest of Honor's
life, longer even than the days immediately following
Eddie's death, which had taken on the aspects of a dread-
ful dream from which she couldn't awaken. Time ceased
to be relevant. One hour bled into the next. While she'd
been in a benumbed state, days had passed with hardly any
notice from her.

But today, time was extremely relevant. Each second mattered. Because eventually they would run out.

And then he would kill them.

Throughout the day, she had refused to accept that as an outcome, afraid that acknowledging it would make it a certainty. But as the day drew to a close, she could no longer delude herself. Time was running out for her and Emily.

As Coburn upended pieces of furniture to search the undersides, she clung to a single ray of hope: He hadn't killed them immediately, which would have been more expedient than his having to cope with them. She supposed they'd been spared a sudden death only because he thought she could be useful to his search. But if he became convinced that she knew nothing and her usefulness ran out, what then?

Dusk claimed the last of the sunlight, and Honor's hope went with it.

Coburn switched on a table lamp and surveyed the havoc he'd wreaked on her orderly house. When his eyes landed on her, she saw that his were bloodshot, making the blue irises look almost feral as they glowered at her from deeply shadowed sockets. He was a man on the run, a man with a mission that he'd failed to accomplish, a man whose frustration had reached a breaking point.

"Come here."

Honor's heart began beating painfully hard and fast. Should she throw herself over Emily in an attempt to protect her, or attack him, or plead for mercy?

"Come here."

Keeping her expression impassive, she approached him.

"Next I'll start tearing into the walls and ceilings, pulling up floors. Is that what you want?"

She almost collapsed with relief. He wasn't finished

yet. She and Emily still had time. There was still hope for rescue.

Denying that her house concealed a treasure hadn't made a dent in his resolve, so she took another tack. "That would take a lot of time. Now that it's dark, you should leave."

"Not till I get what I came for."

"Is it that important?"

"I wouldn't have gone to all this trouble if it wasn't."

"Whatever it is, you've spent precious hours looking for it in the wrong place."

"I don't think so."

"I *know* so. It's not here. So why don't you leave now while you still have a chance of getting away?"

"Worried about my welfare?"

"Aren't you?"

"What's the worst that could happen?"

"You could die."

He raised one shoulder. "Then I'd be dead, and none of this would matter to me. But right now, I'm alive, and it does matter."

Honor wondered if he truly was that indifferent to his own mortality, but before she could address it, Emily piped up. "Mommy, when is Grandpa coming?"

The DVD had ended, and all that remained on the TV screen were exploding fireworks. Emily was standing beside her, Elmo held in the crook of her elbow. Honor knelt down and rubbed her hand along Emily's back.

"Grandpa's not coming tonight after all, sweetheart. We're going to have the party tomorrow. Which will be even better," she said quickly in order to prevent the protest she saw forming on Emily's lips. "Because, silly me, I forgot to get party hats. We can't have Grandpa's party without hats. I saw one that looks like a tiara."

"Like Belle's?" she asked, referring to the character in the DVD.

"Just like Belle's. With sparkles on it." Lowering her voice to an excited whisper, she said, "And Grandpa told me that he has a surprise present for you."

"What is it?"

"I don't know. If he'd told me, it wouldn't be a surprise, would it?"

Emily's eyes were now shining. "Can I still have pizza for supper?"

"Sure. Plus a cupcake."

"Yea!" Emily raced toward the kitchen.

Honor stood up and faced Coburn. "Her dinner is past due."

He pulled his lower lip through his teeth, glanced toward the kitchen, then hitched his chin in that direction. "Make it quick."

Which wouldn't be a problem, because by the time they entered the kitchen, Emily had already taken her pizza from the freezer. "I want pep'roni."

Honor cooked the small pizza in the microwave. As she set it in front of Emily, Coburn asked, "You got any more of those?"

She heated him a pizza, and when she served it, he ate as greedily as he had at lunch.

"What are you eating, Mommy?"

"I'm not hungry."

Coburn looked at her and arched an eyebrow. "Stomach virus?"

"Spoiled appetite."

He shrugged indifferently, went to the freezer, and helped himself to another pizza.

When it came time for Emily's cupcake, she insisted that Honor also have one. "So that it's a real party," she chirped.

Honor placed cupcakes on Dora the Explorer paper plates and, to please Emily, served them ceremoniously.

"Don't forget the sprinkles."

Honor brought the jar from the counter and passed it to Emily. Coburn was about to take a bite of his cupcake when Emily tapped his hand where it rested on the table. He jerked it back as though he'd been struck by a cobra.

"Company first. You need sprinkles."

He looked down at the extended jar of sprinkles as though it was a moon rock, then said a gruff thanks, took it from Emily, and shook the candies onto his cupcake before passing the jar back to her.

He was jumpy, his nerves rubbed raw by exhaustion, the signs of which had become more apparent. The ceiling light above the dining table cast shadows on his prominent cheekbones, making the lower half of his face appear all the more lean and taut. The set of his shoulders and the heavy quality of his breathing were evidence of his weariness. Honor caught him several times blinking rapidly as though trying to stave off sleepiness.

Reasoning that fatigue would slow his reactions and dull his senses, Honor determined to watch and wait for an opportunity to make her move. She needed only one nanosecond of weakness, one blink when his guard was down.

The problem was, she was exhausted too. Emotions ranging from terror to rage had been supercharged all day, leaving her totally depleted of energy. Emily's bedtime came as a relief. Honor changed her into pajamas.

While she was using the bathroom, Honor said to Coburn, "She can sleep in my bed."

"She can sleep in her bed."

"But if she's with me, you can watch both of us at the same time."

He gave one firm negative shake of his head. Arguing would be futile. She wouldn't leave the house without Emily, and he knew that. Separating them ensured that she wouldn't try to escape.

While Honor read the compulsory bedtime story, Coburn searched Emily's closet, pushing aside the hangers and tapping the back wall. He removed her shoes from the floor and knocked on the planks with the heel of his cowboy boot, listening for a hollow spot.

He squeezed every stuffed toy in Emily's menagerie, which caused Emily to giggle. "Don't forget to hug Elmo," she said, and trustingly handed the toy up to him.

He turned it over and ripped open the Velcro on the back seam.

"No!" Honor cried.

He shot her a look filled with suspicion.

"That's just access to the battery," Honor said, knowing that Emily would be traumatized to see Elmo disemboweled. "Please."

He examined the inside of the toy, even removed the batteries and checked beneath them, but, eventually, satisfied that the toy wasn't concealing anything, he closed it up and returned it to Emily.

Honor continued reading. The bedtime story reached its happ'ly-ever-after conclusion. Honor listened to Emily's bedtime prayer, kissed both her cheeks, and then hugged her extra close, prolonging the embrace because she feared that this might be the last time she would tuck her daughter in for the night.

She tried to preserve the moment, seal it inside her

heart and mind, memorize the smell and feel of Emily's sweet little body, which felt incredibly small, fragile, and vulnerable. Maternal love pierced her heart.

But eventually she had to let go. She eased Emily back onto her pillow and forced herself to leave the room. Coburn was lurking in the hallway just outside the door. As she pulled it shut, she looked up into the unfeeling mask of his face.

"If you...do something to me, please don't let her see. She's no threat to you. No purpose would be served by harming her. She—"

A cell phone rang.

Determining that it was hers, he took it from his pocket, glanced at the readout, and passed it to her. "Same as before. Put it on speaker. Find out what you can about the hunt for me, but don't make it obvious."

She answered with, "Hi, Stan."

"How are you feeling? Emily okay?"

"You know how kids are. They bounce back from these things quicker than adults do."

"The party still on for tomorrow night, then?"

"Of course." Looking into Coburn's bloodshot eyes, she asked, "Any news about the fugitive?"

"He's still on the loose, but it's only a matter of time. He's been out there going on twenty-four hours. He's either already dead or weakened to the point of being easy prey."

He told her about the stolen boat and the place at which Coburn had launched it. "Dozens of boats are searching the waterways and will be through the night. The whole area is crawling with lawmen."

"But if he has a boat—"

"Not a very reliable one from what I understand. Nobody thinks it will get him far."

"It might have sunk already," Honor ventured.

"Then unless he sunk with it, they'll pick up his trail. They've got excellent trackers and dogs going over solid ground."

He urged her to rest well, then they said good night and signed off. As Coburn took the phone from her, she felt disheartened. Stan's news didn't bode well for her and Emily. As Coburn's chances of escape dwindled, so did theirs.

But rather than reveal the desperation she felt, she played up the hopelessness of his situation. "Instead of tearing into the walls of my house, why don't you get out of the area while you can? Take my car. Between now and daylight, you could cover—"

Her words came to an abrupt halt when she heard the throaty growl of a small motor, getting closer, growing louder. She spun away from Coburn and bolted toward the living room.

But if Coburn's reflexes had been slowed by exhaustion, they were boosted by the sound of the motorboat. He was on her before she got halfway across the room. One arm closed around her waist like a pincer and hauled her up against him as his other hand clamped down hard over her mouth.

"Don't go stupid on me now, Honor," he whispered in her ear. "Get out there before they reach the porch. Talk loud enough for me to hear. If I sense that you're trying to send them a signal, I won't hesitate to act. Remember that I'm 'prey' to them, so I've got nothing to lose. Before you get cute, think about me standing over your daughter's bed."

The boat's motor was now idling. She saw lights dancing through the trees, heard masculine voices.

"You got it?" he repeated, shaking her slightly.

She nodded.

Gradually he released her and withdrew his hand from her mouth. She turned around to face him. She gasped, "I beg you, don't hurt her."

"It's up to you."

He spun her around and prodded her lower spine with the barrel of the pistol. "Go."

Her legs were shaking. She gripped the doorknob and took several deep breaths, then pulled the door open and stepped out onto the porch.

Two men were coming up the path from the dock, sweeping her property with their flashlights, the bright beams penetrating the shrubbery. They wore badges on their uniform shirts. Gun belts were strapped to their hips. One of them raised his hand in greeting.

"You Mrs. Gillette?"

"Yes."

"Don't be alarmed, ma'am. We're sheriff's deputies."

Remembering Coburn's instructions, she took the porch steps down to ground level. She knew he'd be watching from the window in Emily's bedroom. His warning echoed inside her head, making her stomach pitch.

Trying to disguise her fear as curiosity, she asked, "Is something wrong? What can I do for you?"

They introduced themselves by name and produced their identification. "We're searching for the suspect in last night's mass murder in Tambour."

"I heard about that. It was awful."

"Yes, ma'am. We have reason to think that the suspect is still in the region."

"Oh."

The deputy gave the space between them a reassuring pat. "He could be miles from here, but we're canvassing all the houses along this bayou, hoping someone can provide us with useful information." He rattled off a basic physical description of the man hiding inside her house. Honor envisioned him standing over Emily with a pistol in his hand.

So when the second deputy asked, "Have you seen anyone fitting that description, ma'am?" she replied immediately. "No."

"Anyone passing by here today in a small craft?"

She shook her head. "But I wasn't paying particular attention. My daughter and I have been down with a stomach virus."

"Sorry to hear that."

Honor acknowledged that with a bob of her head.

"Are you out here alone, ma'am?"

"Just my daughter and me."

"Well, please be on the lookout, Mrs. Gillette, and if you see anything unusual, call 911 immediately."

"Of course."

"Best keep all your doors and windows locked, too."

"I always do."

One of the deputies was already tipping his hat. The other took a step back.

They were about to leave! What could she do? She had to do something! A hand signal?

I'm "prey" to them, so I've got nothing to lose.

"We won't disturb you any longer. Have a good evening."

They turned and started walking away.

She couldn't let them go! *For godsake, do something, Honor!* But what could she do without putting Emily's life in danger?

It's up to you.

Yes, it was up to her. Up to her to save her daughter's life. But how. *How?*

Suddenly one of the deputies did an about-face. "Oh, Mrs. Gillette?"

She held her breath.

"I knew your husband," he said. "He was a fine officer."

Her heart sank and along with it her hope of alerting them to the imminent danger she was in. She mumbled, "Thank you."

Then he touched his hat brim again, turned, and continued down the slope toward the dock.

She turned, went up the steps, and reentered the house. Coburn was standing in the opening between the living room and the hallway, between her and Emily.

"Turn on the porch light. Stand where they can see you and give them a wave."

She followed his instructions, doubting that the deputies were looking back toward her, but even if they were, it was unlikely they could see the tears sliding down her cheeks.

The deputies got aboard their boat, revved the engine, and made a slow U-turn in the bayou. In seconds they were out of sight. The drone of the motor diminished to nothingness.

Honor closed the door. She leaned into it and pressed her forehead against the smooth wood. She sensed Coburn moving up behind her.

"Good girl. Emily is safe and sound and sleeping like a baby."

His smug inflection was the final straw. The emotions that had been building inside her all day reached a boiling point. Without even thinking about it, or pausing to consider the consequences, she spun around and glared at him.

"I'm sick of you and your threats. I don't know why you came here or what you want, but I won't go along with it anymore. If you're going to kill me anyway, I had just as soon you do it now. If not..." Reaching behind her, she twisted the doorknob and pulled open the door. "If not, shut up and get out of my house!"

He reached out to close the door. Seizing the opportunity, Honor jerked the pistol from the waistband of his jeans. But she fumbled with its unexpected weight. He gave her wristbone a hard chop. She cried out in pain as the pistol fell from her hand onto the floor and slid across the polished hardwood.

Both of them went for it at once. Honor dropped to the floor at the same time he kicked the pistol out of her reach. She scrambled across the floor after it. All she needed to do was get hold of it long enough to pull the trigger once. The deputies would hear the gunshot.

Her knees and elbows banged painfully against the wood floor as she belly-crawled toward the handgun. She touched the cool metal, but instead of getting a grip, her fingers nudged the pistol farther away by a mere inch.

Coburn had straddled her back and was crawling over her, reaching beyond her, trying to get hold of the gun before she did.

Straining every muscle, she extended her whole body. Her hand closed around the pistol barrel.

But before she could retract her arm and take full possession of it, he pinned her wrist to the floor with fingers that seemed made of steel. "Let it go."

"Go to hell."

Trying to throw him off, she squirmed under his weight.

He only pressed down tighter, squeezing the breath from her. "Let it go."

Instead, she yanked on her hand hard, wrenching it free of his grip.

He cursed profusely as she drew the pistol under her body, clutching it tightly to her chest.

Then they wrestled.

Honor lay as flat as possible, but he worked his hands between her and the floor and tried to pry the weapon from her hand. It became a life-or-death struggle for ownership, and he outlasted her. She was gasping for air by the time he secured the pistol grip and worked it out of her weakening fingers.

He yanked it out from under her. Honor, moaning in defeat, went limp and began weeping.

He flipped her over onto her back. He was on his knees, still straddling her. His hands, one of them in possession of the pistol, were planted on his thighs. He was breathing hard, and his face was contorted with fury.

And she thought, *This is it. This is the moment I die.*

But to her astonishment, he tossed the pistol aside, then placed both hands on her shoulders and leaned down on her heavily. "Why the *fuck* did you...? It could have discharged and blown a hole right through you. Stupid, idiotic thing to do, lady. Don't you know what..." Seemingly at a loss for words, he gave her shoulders a hard shake. "Why'd you do that?"

Her reason for doing it should have been obvious: She'd been fighting for her life. Why was he asking such a dumb question?

Her breath coming in pants, she said, "Just tell me— and please make it the truth—are you going to kill us?"

"No." His eyes bored into hers, and, in a rougher voice, he repeated, "*No.*"

She wanted desperately to believe him, which is perhaps why she was close to doing so. "Then why should I pay any attention to your threats? Why do anything you say?"

"Because you have a vested interest."

"Me? I don't even know what you're looking for! Whatever it is, this *thing* you're after—"

"Is the *thing* that got your husband killed."

Chapter 11

It was well past the dinner hour when Tom returned home. He found Janice in Lanny's room giving him his sponge bath, which they performed each evening before changing him into pajamas. In the morning, they dressed him in a track suit. Of course it made no difference what he wore, but changing his clothes was a much-needed nod toward normalcy.

Tom set his briefcase on the floor and began rolling up his shirtsleeves. "Honey, why didn't you wait on me?"

"I didn't know when you'd be home, and I wanted to get him settled for the night so I could put my feet up."

"I'm sorry. I wanted to get some paperwork done on Tambour before tomorrow, because tomorrow will be crazy. It always is after a holiday. And now with this crisis, it'll be doubly nuts."

When he reached the bed, he elbowed her aside. "Sit down. I'll finish." Before dipping the sponge into the tub of warm water, Tom bent over his son and kissed his forehead. "Hi, Lanny."

Lanny's eyes remained fixed. The lack of response filled Tom with a familiar despair. He dipped the sponge in the water and, after squeezing out the excess, applied it to Lanny's arm.

"How's that going?" Janice asked.

"What?"

"The crisis in Tambour?"

Lanny's arm was dead weight when Tom lifted it to wash his armpit. "The suspect is still at large. I think he'd be a fool to hang around here. It seems to me that he'd hitch a ride with a truck-driving pal and get as far away from southern Louisiana as possible."

"Is there such a person as a truck-driving pal?" She had settled herself into the La-Z-Boy recliner and tucked her feet beneath her. The large chair served as a bed for one of them if Lanny was having a rough night.

"None identified as yet, but we're checking with companies that do business with Royale. Fred Hawkins thinks it's a waste of time. He thinks Coburn is still in the area." He smiled across at her. "He feels him like standing hairs on the back of his neck."

"Good Lord," she scoffed. "What's next? Reading chicken innards? I hope he's not relying on a sixth sense to find a mass murderer."

"It'll take some smarts."

"Is Fred Hawkins up to the task?"

Tom began washing Lanny's legs and feet. "He's certainly motivated. Mrs. Marset made a personal call to the superintendent of police and put the squeeze on him, which he passed along through the rank and file. Marset's church is conducting a candlelight prayer vigil tonight.

Heat is coming from God and government, and Fred is beginning to feel it."

"He sounded pretty confident a while ago."

She motioned toward the TV sitting on a dresser opposite the bed, which remained on around the clock in the hope that some programming might stimulate a reaction from Lanny. The picture was on now, but the audio had been muted.

"Fred fielded questions from reporters live on the evening news," Janice said. "He seemed convinced that the footprint and blood spatters you found this afternoon were a major boon."

It pleased Tom that she seemed suitably impressed by his contribution, which he had exaggerated slightly.

Taking advantage of her attention, he expanded the story. "Did I tell you about Mrs. Arleeta Thibadoux?" His anecdote about the colorful and semi-toothless woman actually coaxed a laugh from Janice. He detected a trace of the woman he'd fallen in love with and proposed marriage to.

He remembered that day as one of the happiest of his life, rivaling even their wedding day in his memory. After he'd slipped the solitaire diamond ring on her finger, they'd made love on the sagging bed in his stuffy, cramped apartment. It had been ardent, sweaty, and athletic, and afterward they'd celebrated their engagement by sharing a bottle of beer.

He wished he could turn back the clock to that afternoon and once again see Janice's cheeks flushed, her lips soft and smiling, her eyes lambent with satiation and happiness.

But if he turned back the clock to that day, they wouldn't have Lanny.

The next thought that flashed through his mind was involuntary but treacherous, and he was instantly shamed by it.

He dropped the sponge into the plastic tub and looked over at Janice. Judging from her expression, her thoughts were moving along a similar track, or one close enough to make her feel equally guilty.

She came out of the chair as though trying to outrun her own thoughts. "I'll go fix dinner while you're finishing up here. Omelets okay?" Without waiting for him to reply, she left the room as though the devil was after her.

Ten minutes later they sat down to their omelets and ate in virtual silence, exchanging only brief snippets of forced conversation. Tom remembered times when they couldn't say enough, when they would talk over each other relating the events of the day.

When he finished his meal, he carried his plate to the sink and ran water over it, then mentally braced himself and turned to his wife.

"Janice, let's talk."

She set her fork on the rim of her plate and placed her hands in her lap. "About what?"

"Lanny."

"Specifically?"

"It may be time to readjust our thinking about his care."

There, he'd said it.

Lightning didn't strike him, nor did the statement spark a reaction from his wife. She just stared up at him with an expression as closed as a storm shutter.

He pressed on. "I think we should revisit the possibility— just the possibility—of placing him in a facility."

She looked away from him and rolled her lips inward. Giving her a moment, he cleared the remainder of the dishes and utensils from the table and carried them to the sink.

Finally she broke the tense silence. "We made promises to him, and to each other, Tom."

"We did," he said somberly. "But when we pledged to keep him with us always, I think we nursed a kernel of hope that he would develop to some extent, acquire some capabilities. True?"

She neither denied nor admitted having held out such a feeble hope.

"I don't think that's ever going to happen." That was something both of them knew, but had never acknowledged out loud. Saying it had caused Tom's voice to crack with emotion.

Tight-lipped, Janice said, "All the more reason why he needs the best of care."

"That's just it. I'm not sure we're providing it." She took immediate offense, but he spoke before she could. "That's not a criticism of you. Your patience and endurance amaze me. Truly. But caring for him is killing you."

"You're exaggerating."

"Am I? It's shredding you, body and soul. I see evidence of it daily."

"You can look into my soul?"

Her sarcasm was more effective than a flat-out rebuke would have been. He rubbed his eyes, the activities of the day catching up with him, and then some. "Please don't make this subject even more difficult than it already is. It hurts me even to suggest moving him to a facility. Don't you know that?"

"Then why bring it up?"

"Because one of us had to. We're eroding as human beings, Janice. And I'm not just thinking about us. I'm thinking about Lanny. How do we know that we're doing what's best for him?"

"We're his parents."

"Loving parents, yes, but untrained in how to care for him. There are specialists for patients like Lanny."

She stood up and wandered the kitchen as though looking for a means of escape. "This is a pointless conversation. Even if we agreed that it would be best, we can't afford the private facilities. As for some modern-day Bedlam operated by the state, forget it. I would never put him in a place like that."

The implied suggestion that he would bothered him, but he didn't let himself be drawn into an argument. He stuck to the core of the matter. "We owe it to ourselves, and to him, to visit some of the better places and see what they're like." He hesitated, then asked, "Would you be open to doing that if finances weren't a consideration?"

"But they are."

"If they weren't," he said insistently.

"Are you planning on winning the lottery?"

Again, he felt the sting of her sarcasm, but he let it pass. He'd said enough for one night. He'd given her food for thought. He'd known that broaching this subject would automatically make him out to be the bad guy, but one of them had to be, and it wasn't going to be Janice.

She'd been valedictorian of her high school class, an honor graduate from Vanderbilt, a rising star in an investments firm. Then fate cruelly interrupted not only her promising career path but the sum total of her life.

She'd had to sacrifice everything for Lanny, which made admitting defeat untenable to her. In her mind, placing Lanny in a facility was full-scale surrender, as good as an admission that—yet again—she had been denied the opportunity to finish something she'd started.

He sighed. "I'd better get to bed and sleep while I can. I won't be surprised if I get a call in the middle of the night."

"What for?"

"The agents I left in Tambour know to call me with any developments." He paused at the door. "You look done in, too. Coming?"

"Not yet. I'm tired but not sleepy. I think I'll stay up for a while."

"Playing your word game with your cell phone friend in Japan?"

"Singapore."

He smiled. Playing the games were her one form of recreation, and it had become almost an addiction. "I hope you win."

"I'm leading by forty-three points, but I've got a *j* that's challenging me."

"You'll come up with a word for it," he said with confidence. "But don't stay up too late."

Two hours later, Tom was still alone in their bed. He got up and padded barefoot down the hall. After looking in on Lanny, he found Janice in the den, staring raptly into the screen of her cell phone, totally engrossed in a pastime that apparently was much more enjoyable to her than sleeping with him.

Without her ever knowing that he'd been watching her, he turned away and retraced his steps to their bedroom.

Chapter 12

⟫◦⟪

Coburn gradually withdrew his hands from Honor's shoulders. He got off her and retrieved the pistol, tucking it back into his waistband. She continued to lie there staring up at him.

"That was a damn stupid thing to do," he said. "If you'd accidentally pulled the trigger, one of us could be dead, and if it turned out to be you, I'd be stuck with your kid."

It was a harsh thing to say, which is why he'd said it. Her daughter was the button to push when he wanted something from her, and right now he wanted her to stop gaping like a beached perch.

He knew she heard him, because she blinked. But she remained perfectly still, and for one panicked moment he wondered if she'd been seriously injured during their struggle.

He wondered why he cared.

"Are you all right?"

She nodded.

Relieved of that worry, he turned away and looked at the mess he'd made of her house. When he'd arrived this morning, everything had been in its place. Lived in, but tidy and neat. Homey. Smelling of fresh cake.

Now the place was in shambles, and he had nothing to show for his ransacking.

Dead end.

Which more or less summarized the life and times of Lee Coburn, who would leave the world with seven brutal murders as his only legacy. Seven victims who hadn't been given a chance, who'd died before they knew what had hit them.

Swearing beneath his breath, he rubbed his temples. He was tired. No, more than tired. Weary. Weary of loading and unloading those goddamn trucks. Weary of the sad, one-room apartment that he'd been living in for the past thirteen months. Weary of life in general, and of *his* life in particular. As he'd told Gillette's widow, if he died, which he probably would soon, he'd be dead, and none of it would matter.

But hell if it didn't matter *now*. As he lowered his hands from his forehead, he realized he wasn't quite ready to let the devil take him.

"Get up."

She stirred, rolled to her side, and pushed herself into a sitting position. He reached down. She studied his hand for several seconds, then clasped it and let him pull her up.

"What did you mean?"

Her voice was breathless and shaky, but he knew what she was referring to. Instead of addressing the question, he propelled her toward the hallway and then into her bedroom, where he released her hand. Going to the bed, he whipped back the comforter, which had been spotless, but was now stained and grimy because of him.

"I gotta lie down, which means you gotta lie down."

She stood where she was, looking at him as though she didn't understand the language.

"Lie down," he repeated.

She moved to the bed, but stood on the opposite side of it, staring across at him like he was an exotic animal she'd never seen before. She wasn't acting right. All day long, he'd been studying her reactions to things he said and did, so that he would know what her weaknesses were and what fears he could tap into in order to manipulate her.

He'd seen her terrified, supplicant, desperate, and even pissed off. But this was a new expression, and he didn't know what to make of it. Maybe she'd banged her head on the floor when she was fighting for control of the pistol.

"What you said about Eddie..." She paused to swallow. "What did you mean?"

"What did I say? I don't remember."

"You said that the thing you're after had got him killed."

"I never said that."

"That's exactly what you said."

"You must've heard me wrong."

"I didn't hear you wrong!"

Well, good. She was acting normal again, not like a zombie had taken over her body. Her compact, shapely body that had felt real good against his.

"Eddie's death was an accident," she declared.

"If you say so." He turned away and started rifling through the heap of clothes he'd removed from her bureau drawers earlier as he'd searched them.

He sensed her approach only a heartbeat before she

grabbed him by the arm and brought him around to face
her. He allowed it. She wasn't going to stop with this until
she got an explanation. Not unless he gagged her, and he
really didn't want to do that unless she forced him to.

"What did you come here to find?"

"I don't know."

"Tell me."

"I don't know."

"Tell me, damn you!

"*I don't know!*"

He pulled his arm free and bent down to pick up a pair
of stockings. Sheer, black stockings. When he turned back
to her, she searched his eyes.

"You honestly don't know?" she asked.

"What part of 'I don't know' don't you understand?"

He reached for her hand and began wrapping the
stocking around her wrist. She didn't resist. In fact, she
seemed oblivious to what he was doing.

"If there's anything about Eddie or how he died that
you can tell me...Please," she said. "Surely you can understand why I want to know."

"Actually I don't. He'll stay dead. So what difference
does it make?"

"It makes a huge difference. If his death wasn't an accident, as you imply, I'd like to know why he died and who
was responsible." She placed her hand over his. He stopped
winding the stocking around her wrist. "Please."

Her eyes were various shades of green that were constantly changing. He'd noticed that the first thing, when
they'd been out in the yard and he'd thrust the barrel of
the pistol into her belly. Then her eyes had gone wide with
fear. He'd seen them spark with anger. Now they glistened
with unshed tears. And, always, those shifting hues.

He looked down at their joined hands. She lifted hers off his, but didn't break eye contact. "You don't think Eddie's car crash was an accident?"

He hesitated, then shook his head.

She breathed through her lips. "You think someone caused the crash and made it look like an accident?"

He didn't say anything.

Her tongue swept across her lips. "He was killed because of something he had?"

He nodded. "That someone else wanted."

"Something valuable?"

"The people who wanted it thought so."

He watched the play of emotions in her face as she digested that. Then her gaze refocused on him. "Valuable to you?"

He gave a brusque nod.

"Like cash?"

"Possibly. But I don't think so. More like the combination to a lock. Account number in a Cayman Islands bank. Something like that."

She shook her head with perplexity. "Eddie wouldn't have had anything like that. Unless he was holding it for evidence."

"Or…"

His insinuation finally sank in and she recoiled from it. "Eddie wasn't party to any criminal activity. Surely that's not what you're suggesting."

He snuffled a laugh. "No, of course not."

"Eddie was as honest as the day is long."

"Maybe. Maybe not. But he got crosswise with the wrong person."

"Who?"

"The Bookkeeper."

"Who?"

"Did Eddie know Sam Marset?"

"Yes, of course."

"Why 'of course'?"

"Before we got married, Eddie moonlighted by working as a security guard for Mr. Marset."

"At the warehouse?"

"The whole compound."

"For how long?"

"Several months. They'd had a few break-ins, minor vandalism, so Mr. Marset hired Eddie to patrol at night. The break-ins stopped. Nevertheless, Mr. Marset liked the peace of mind that having a guard provided. But Eddie declined his offer of a permanent position." She smiled faintly. "He wanted to be a cop."

"How well did you know him?"

"Sam Marset? Only casually. He was an elder at our church. He and I served one term together on the Historical Preservation Society."

"Church elder, historical society, my ass," he snorted. "He was a greedy, unscrupulous son of a bitch."

"Who deserved to be shot in the head."

He raised one shoulder. "Quick and painless."

The statement and his matter-of-fact tone seemed to repel her. She tried to back away from him, only then realizing that her wrist was bound.

Honor's head began to swim as she clawed at the stocking around her wrist. "Take this off me. Take it *off*!"

He grabbed the hand frantically trying to unwind the stocking and began wrapping the other stocking around that wrist. "No. No!" She batted at his hands, then at his face with her free hand.

He dodged her flailing hand. Swearing, he pushed her back onto the bed and was on her in a heartbeat. His knee held down her left arm while he quickly tied her right hand to the iron headboard.

Only the fear of awakening Emily kept her from screaming bloody murder. "Let me go!"

He didn't. He hauled her left hand up and wrapped the end of the stocking around one of the curved iron rails, ruthlessly knotting it. Frantically she tugged on the bindings. Panic had her gasping. "Please. I'm claustrophobic."

"I don't give a shit." He came off the bed and stood looking down at her, breathing hard from exertion.

"Untie me!"

He not only ignored the demand, he left the room.

She bit down hard on her lower lip to keep from screaming. He'd left about six inches of give on each hand, permitting the backs of her hands to lie against the pillow beside her head, but the slack didn't lessen her feeling of entrapment. Overwhelmed by panic, she renewed her effort to get free.

But soon it became apparent that her attempts were futile and that she was only wasting her strength. She forced herself to stop struggling and to take deep, calming breaths. But reason had never succeeded in ridding her of claustrophobia, and it didn't now. It only ameliorated it enough for her to slow down her heart rate and respiration to levels that weren't life-threatening.

She could hear Coburn moving through the house. She supposed he was checking the locks on doors and windows. The irony of that caused a bubble of hysterical laughter to escape her before she could catch it.

The hallway light went out. Coburn reentered the bedroom.

She made herself lie still and to speak as evenly as possible. "I'll go crazy. Really. I will. I can't stand it."

"You don't have a choice. Besides, you've got no one to blame but yourself."

"Just untie me and I promise—"

"No. I've got to sleep. You've got to lie here beside me."

"I will."

He shot her a skeptical look.

"I swear."

"We had a deal. You welshed on it. Twice. And almost shot one of us in the process."

"I'll lie here and not move. I promise I won't do anything. Okay?"

Their recent tussle had reopened his scalp wound. A thin trickle of blood slid down his temple. He swiped at it, then looked at the red streaks on his fingers before wiping them on the leg of his jeans. Eddie's jeans.

"Did you hear me?"

"I'm not deaf."

"I won't try to get away. I swear. Just untie my hands."

"Sorry, lady. You blew what trust I had in you, and I didn't have any to start with. Now lie still and be quiet or I'll stuff something into your mouth and then you really will feel claustrophobic."

He set the pistol on the nightstand, then switched off the lamp.

"We have to keep a light on," she said, keeping her voice low. The thought of a gag terrified her. "Emily is afraid of the dark. If she wakes up and the light isn't on, she'll get scared and start crying. She'll come looking for me. Please. I don't want her to see me like this."

He hesitated, then turned away. Her eyes followed his dark form as he went into the hallway and switched on the overhead light. His silhouette showed up large and menacing as he came back into the bedroom.

He seemed even more menacing when he lay down on his back inches from her. She hadn't been in bed with anyone since Eddie. Emily, of course. But Emily's forty pounds hardly made an impression in the mattress. She didn't rock the bed when she climbed onto it or create a decline, which caused Honor to focus on keeping to her side rather than rolling against him.

The motions and sounds of his settling down beside her harkened back to the familiar, yet it felt strange. This man lying close to her wasn't Eddie. His breathing was different. His sheer presence felt different from Eddie's.

And somehow *not* touching seemed more intimate than if they were.

Once he was settled comfortably, he didn't stir. From the corner of her eye, she looked over to see that he'd closed his eyes. His fingers were loosely clasped and resting on his abdomen.

She lay as straight, still, and stiff as a plank, trying to talk herself out of having a full-blown panic attack. She was bound and unable to get free, true. But, she told herself sternly, she wasn't in mortal danger. She counted her heartbeats in order to keep the rate of them under control. She made each breath long and deep.

But these exercises worked no better than reason.

Her anxiety continued to mount until she began pulling against the bindings, straining against them with as much effort as she could muster.

"You're only making them tighter," he said.

"Undo them."

"Go to sleep."

A sob burbled out of her and she started jerking at the

bindings until the headboard banged rhythmically against the wall.

"Stop that!"

"I can't. I told you I couldn't stand it, and I *can't*."

She began to pull so viciously against the stockings that the recoil caused the backs of her hands to rap painfully against the iron rails of the headboard. The pain caused her panic to rise until she was bucking like someone demented. Her legs bicycled as though trying to outrun the feeling of suffocation. Her heels pushed hard against the mattress. Her head thrashed from side to side on the pillow.

"Shh, shh. Calm down. You're okay. Shh."

Realization came to her gradually. Coburn was leaning over her. He was holding one of her hands in each of his, his thumbs planted solidly in her palms. His voice was a soothing whisper.

"Shh." His thumbs began massaging small circles into her palms. "Take deep breaths. You'll be fine."

But she didn't breathe deeply. Following one stuttering exhale, she didn't breathe at all. And when he angled his head back to look down into her face, he stopped breathing too.

His face was close to hers, close enough that she could see his eyes as they looked down at her mouth, then at her chest, making her achingly aware of her breasts. Not even the semi-darkness could dim the blue intensity of his eyes when they reconnected with hers.

In order to stop her convulsing, he'd placed his leg across her thighs. His lap was pressed against her hip. His arousal was unmistakable. And Honor knew that her perfect stillness was a giveaway that she felt it.

It seemed like an eternity that they lay there, frozen in

that position, but it was probably only a few seconds. Then he swore viciously as he released her hands and rolled off her. He lay as before on his back, close but not touching. Only now he placed one forearm across his eyes.

"Don't pull another stunt like that."

It hadn't been a stunt, but she didn't refute him. He hadn't specified what her punishment would be if she freaked out again. But the gruffness in his voice warned her against testing him.

Chapter 13

One hour shy of daylight the boat belonging to Arleeta Thibadoux was discovered. It appeared to have been dragged into a grove of cypress trees for concealment.

Two deputy sheriffs had been poling their way through the swamp when one of them spotted it with his high-powered light. He and his partner used their cell phones to spread the word, and within half an hour of the discovery, two dozen exhausted but exhilarated law enforcement officers had converged on the site.

Fred Hawkins, who'd been at the police station in downtown Tambour when he got word, was able to get fairly close to the site in the helicopter on loan from N.O.P.D. As soon as the chopper set down, he was picked up in a small motorboat by fellow officers, who conveyed him the rest of the way. Doral was already at the scene when he arrived.

"It took on water," Doral told him, getting straight to the point. He aimed his flashlight into the partially submerged hull. "At least we have a new starting point."

"We don't know for certain it's Coburn."

"It's either him or a bizarre coincidence." Doral used the beam of the flashlight to spot the blood smears on the oar. "Still bleeding from somewhere. The hell of it is..."

He didn't finish, but used the flashlight to cut a swath across the surrounding landscape. It was a monotonous, gray, desolate wilderness with nothing to distinguish one square yard of it from another except for whatever form of deadly wildlife might be lurking within its deceptive placidity.

"Yeah." Fred sighed, catching his brother's drift. "But as you said, it gives us a fresh start."

"You'd better call it in."

"Right." Fred made the call.

Over the next half hour, more officers arrived, were briefed, and then dispatched to cover new territory. The FBI agents from Tom VanAllen's office were alerted. "Get word to Tom," Fred told them. "He needs to know about this immediately. I may need to call on the feds for reinforcement. They've got better toys than we do."

As he lit a cigarette, Doral pulled Fred aside. "What about Stan? Should I call him, get him to round up some of yesterday's volunteers to pitch in?"

Fred consulted the eastern horizon, or what he could see of it through the dense cypress grove. "Let's wait till after daylight. Stan knows more about stalking than you and I have forgot. But some of those other boys would be more harm than help."

Doral exhaled a plume of smoke. "Don't bullshit a bullshitter, brother. You don't want a bunch of volunteers in this posse any more than you want all these extra badges. Or the feds. You don't want anybody to tree Lee Coburn but your own self."

Fred grinned. "You always could read me like a book."

"'Cause we think alike."

They rejoined the others. Maps were consulted. Waterways, which formed intricate loops, were assigned to be explored. "Coburn will be needing drinking water," Fred reminded the group. Since the oil spill, no right-minded individual would drink water from any of these channels. "Anybody know of any fishing cabins, camps, shacks, sheds, anything like that in this general vicinity? Anyplace he could find potable water?"

Several possibilities were mentioned. Men were sent to check them out. "Approach with caution," Fred warned them as they set off in the small boats they'd been trolling in all night. "Cut your engines before you get close."

Doral volunteered to take the road less traveled, and Fred let him. "If anybody can slog through that area without getting lost, you can. Keep your phone handy, and I'll do the same. You see anything, call me first."

"You don't have to ask me twice. Meanwhile, are you going back to the police station?"

"What, and have reporters bugging me?" Fred shook his head. "Look here." Their map had been spread out on a section of relatively dry ground. The twins hunkered down over it and Fred traced his finger along a faint blue line indicating a long, narrow channel. "See where this eventually leads?"

"To Eddie's place."

The twins looked long and hard at each other. Fred spoke first. "Bothers me some."

Doral said, "You read my mind. Stan was supposed to go out there yesterday evening for a birthday dinner, but he told me later that Honor had canceled the get-together because she and Emily were sick with a stomach thing. Wouldn't hurt to check on them."

Fred refolded the map and stuck it in the back pocket of his uniform trousers. "I'll feel better once I have. Besides, somebody has to search that bayou. Might as well be me."

When Honor woke up, what surprised her most wasn't that her hands had been cut free from the headboard, but that she had awakened at all. She hadn't expected to fall asleep and was amazed that she had. The light outside was pinkish with predawn.

She was alone in the bed.

She vaulted off it and raced to Emily's room. The door was ajar, just as she'd left it last night. Emily was sleeping peacefully, a tumble of butter-colored curls on her pillow, her face buried in her "bankie," her plump hand clutching Elmo.

Honor left her and rushed through the living room and into the kitchen beyond. The rooms were empty, dim, and silent. Her keys were missing from the hook beside the back door, and when she looked through the window, she saw that her car wasn't parked out front.

Coburn was gone.

Perhaps the cranking motor of her car was what had awakened her. But the house had a still quality, indicating to her that his departure might have been earlier than that.

"Thank God, thank God," she whispered as she rubbed her hands over her chilled upper arms. They were covered with gooseflesh, but that was evidence that she was alive. She hadn't believed that he would go, leaving her and Emily unscathed. But miraculously they had survived an excruciatingly long day and night spent with a mass murderer.

Relief made her weak.

But only for a moment. She must alert the authorities to what had happened. They could pick up his trail from here. She could call them, give them her car tag number. They—

The surge of thought was rudely interrupted by a new realization. How would she call anyone? Her cell phone was last in Coburn's possession, and she no longer had a landline. Stan had tried to dissuade her from having it disconnected, but she'd argued that it was a monthly expense for something that had become superfluous.

That argument came back to haunt her now.

She quickly went back through the house looking for her phone. But she didn't find it, nor had she expected to. Coburn was too clever to have left it behind. Taking it would delay her from notifying the authorities and give him crucial time in which to get farther away.

Without a phone, car, or boat—

Boat.

That's what had awakened her! Not her car coming to life, but a boat motor idling down. Now that she was fully awake, she recognized the difference, because she'd been around boats all her life.

She ran to her front door, unbolted it, and practically leaped across the porch and clambered down the steps, landing hard on the ground and pitching forward. She broke her fall with her hands, then scrambled down the slope, her sneakers slipping on the dewy grass. She managed to keep on her feet the rest of the way to the dock.

Her footfalls thudded hollowly on the weathered boards, startling a pelican on the opposite bank. With a noisy flapping of wings, he took flight. She shaded her eyes against the rising sun as she looked in both directions of the bayou for signs of a boat.

"Honor!"

Her heart lurched and she spun in the direction of

the shout. Fred Hawkins steered a small fishing boat from beneath the leafy cover of a willow.

"Fred! Thank God!"

He goosed the motor and reached the dock within seconds. Honor was so glad to see him, she almost missed the rope he tossed her. She knelt down and wound it around a metal cleat.

Fred had barely got his footing on the dock when Honor flung herself against him. His arms went around her. "Honor, Christ, what's wrong?"

She gave his large torso a hard squeeze, then let him go and stepped back. There would be time later for gratitude. "He's been here. The man you're after. Coburn."

"Son of a— I got this weird premonition about thirty minutes ago when we found...Are you okay? Emily?"

"We're fine. Fine. He...he didn't hurt us, but he—" She paused to gulp air. "He took my car. My phone. That's why I was running down to the dock. I thought I'd heard a boat. I—"

"You're sure it was Coburn who stole—"

"Yes, yes. He showed up here yesterday."

"He's been here all that time?"

She nodded furiously. "All day yesterday. All night. I woke up just a few minutes ago. He was gone. I don't know what time he left."

Her chest was hurting from breathing so hard. She pressed her fist against it.

Sensing her distress, Fred placed his hand on her shoulder. "All right, slow down. Catch your breath and tell me everything that happened."

She swallowed, took several deep breaths. "Yesterday morning..." In stops and starts, she described Coburn's arrival and the daylong ordeal. "Two sheriff's deputies came by last night." Breathlessly she recounted what had happened. "Maybe I should have tried to communicate to them that he was inside, but so was Emily. I was afraid he would—"

"You did the right thing," he said, giving her shoulder a reassuring squeeze. "Is he injured? We found blood on the trail."

She explained about his head wound. "It was a fairly deep gash, I think. He was scraped and scratched from going through brush, but otherwise he wasn't hurt."

"Armed?"

"He had a pistol. He threatened me with it. At one point last night, we fought over it. I had it, but he got it back."

He dragged his hand down his weary face. "Jesus, you could have been killed."

"I was so afraid, Fred. You have no idea."

"I can guess. But the important thing is that he took shelter and then moved on without hurting you."

"He didn't come here for shelter. He knew who I was. He knew Eddie. At least he knew of Eddie. He came here for a reason."

"What the hell? Was he somebody Eddie had arrested?"

"I don't think so. He said he'd never met him. He said... He...he..." She couldn't control her stuttering, and Fred sensed that.

"Okay. You're all right now." He muttered words of concern that were liberally sprinkled with profanities. He placed his arm around her shoulders and turned her toward the house. "I've got to call this in. Let's go inside."

Honor leaned against him heavily, relying on his support as they made their way up the slope. Now that the crisis was past and she and Emily were no longer in danger, she was trembling. With the arrival of help, the courage it had taken to protect herself and Emily abandoned her.

As her friend had said, she could have been killed. She'd thought for sure she would be.

The full impact of how narrowly she had escaped death struck her and brought her close to tears. She'd heard of this phenomenon, of people acting with incredible valor during a crisis situation, then coming apart completely after surviving it.

"He ransacked the house," she told Fred as they approached the porch. "He was insistent that Eddie died with something valuable in his possession."

Fred snorted with incredulity. "Not the Eddie I knew."

"I tried to tell him he was wrong. He refused to believe me. He ripped up my house for nothing."

"What was he looking for? Money?"

"No. I don't know. *He* didn't know. Or so he said. But he insisted that this—whatever it is—was the reason Eddie had died."

"He died in a car wreck."

Stepping up onto the porch, she looked up at him and shrugged. "That didn't sway Coburn."

Fred drew up short when they entered the living room and he saw the damage Coburn had done. "Criminy. You weren't kidding."

"He stopped just short of tearing down the walls and pulling up the floors. He was dead certain that I had something that Eddie had died protecting."

"Where'd he get that notion?"

She raised her hands to her sides, indicating to him that she was at a loss. "If you can find that out, maybe you'll uncover his motive for killing those seven people."

He took a cell phone off his belt and started punching in numbers. "I gotta let the others know."

"I'm going to check on Emily."

She tiptoed down the hallway and moved to the door of Emily's room. Peering through the crack, she was relieved to see that Emily had flipped over onto her back, but was still sleeping. If she were awake, she would view Fred's visit as a social one and would be confused if he didn't stop everything and play with her.

Besides that, as the widow of a policeman, Honor knew she faced hours of questioning. Soon she should call Stan to come and take Emily for the rest of the day. He could be overprotective and overbearing, but today she would welcome his help.

For now, she pulled her child's bedroom door securely closed, hoping that she would sleep a while longer.

As she reentered the living room, Fred was where she'd left him, holding his cell phone to his ear. "Mrs. Gillette isn't sure what time he slipped out, so we don't know how much of a head start he's got or which direction he's moving in. But he's in her car. Hold on." He covered the mouthpiece. "What's your tag number?"

She recited it to him, and he repeated it into the cell phone, then described the make and model of her car. He raised his eyebrows in silent query: Was he remembering right? She nodded.

"Put out an APB on the car immediately. Inform the superintendent of this and tell him—*request*—that I need every officer available." After clicking off, he smiled at her with regret.

"In a very short time, cops are gonna be swarming this house inside and out. It's gonna get even more torn up, I'm afraid."

"It doesn't matter, so long as you catch him."

He replaced his phone in the holster at his belt. "Oh, we'll catch him. He couldn't be far."

No sooner had he said the words than the front door burst open and Coburn barged in. He was holding the pistol with both hands, and the muzzle was aimed at the back of Fred's skull. "Don't you fucking move!" Coburn yelled.

Then, a bright red starburst exploded out the center of Fred Hawkins's forehead.

Chapter 14

Honor clamped her hands over her mouth to trap her scream and watched in horrified astonishment as Fred's body fell face first onto the floor.

Coburn stepped over it and strode toward her.

On an adrenaline surge, she spun around and bolted down the hallway. He grabbed her arm from behind. As he brought her around, she swung her other fist at his head.

Cursing liberally, he caught her in a bear hug, pinning her arms to her sides, and lifted her off the floor. He backed her into the wall with enough impetus to knock the breath out of her and positioned himself between her legs to make her vicious kicking ineffectual.

"Listen! Listen to me!" he said, his breath striking her face in hot pants.

She fought like a wildcat to get free, but when her limbs proved useless, she tried to bang her forehead against his. He jerked his head back in the nick of time.

"I'm a federal agent!"

She went perfectly still and gaped at him.

"Hawkins—that's his name?"

Her head wobbled.

"He was the shooter at the warehouse. Him and his twin. Got it? He was the bad guy, not me."

Honor stared at him with stark incredulity as she gulped in air. "Fred is a police officer."

"Not anymore."

"He was—"

"A murderer. I watched him shoot Marset in the head."

"I watched you shoot Fred!"

"I had no choice. He already had his gun in his hand to—"

"He didn't even know you were here!"

"—to kill *you*."

She sucked in a breath and, after holding it for several seconds, exhaled it in a gust. Her swallow was dry. "That's impossible."

"I saw him headed this way in a boat. I doubled back. If I hadn't, you'd be dead now, and so would your kid. I'd have been accused of two more murders."

"Why would...why would...?"

"Later. I'll tell you all of it. But for right now, just believe me when I tell you he would have killed you if I hadn't killed him first. Okay?"

She shook her head slowly. "I don't believe you. You can't be a cop."

"Not a cop."

"Federal agent?"

"FBI."

"Even more unlikely."

"J. Edgar rolls over in his grave every day, but that's the way it is."

"Show me your ID."

"Undercover. Deep cover. No ID. You have to take my word for it."

She gazed into his hard, cold eyes for several moments, then stammered tearfully, "You spent the last twenty-four hours terrifying me."

"Part of the shakedown. I had to be convincing."

"Well, I'm convinced. You're a criminal."

"Think about it," he said angrily. "If I was a killer on the run, you'd have been dead this time yesterday. Fred would have found your body this morning. Your little girl's, too. Maybe floating in the creek out there, a fish buffet, if she hadn't been eaten by gators first."

She hiccupped a sob and looked away from him with revulsion. "You're worse than a criminal."

"That's been said. But for the immediate future, I'm your only chance of staying alive."

Tears of confusion and fear blurred her vision. "I don't understand what I have to do with any of this."

"Not you. Your late husband." He let go of her with one hand and dug into the front pocket of his jeans, producing the folded sheet of paper she had noticed the day before.

"What is that?"

"Your husband was somehow linked to that killing in the warehouse."

"Impossible."

"This might help convince you." He shook out the folds of the paper, then turned it around so she could read what was written. "Your husband's name, circled and underlined and with a question mark beside it."

"Where did you get it?"

"Marset's office. I sneaked in there one night. Found this entry in an old day planner."

"That could mean anything."

"Check the date."

"Two days before Eddie died," she murmured. She looked at Coburn with bewilderment, then tried to snatch the paper from him.

"Un-huh." He yanked it out of her reach and stuffed it back into his pocket. "I might need that for evidence. Along with anything you can testify to."

"I don't know anything."

"We'll talk about that later. Right now, we gotta get you the hell out of here."

"But—"

"No buts," he said with a hard shake of his head for emphasis. "You're getting the kid and going with me now before Hawkins number two shows up."

"Doral?"

"Whatever the hell his name is. You can bet he's speeding his way here."

"The police are on their way. Fred notified them that you'd been here. I heard him."

He released her so suddenly, she nearly slid down the wall. In seconds he was back, a cell phone in each hand. "His official phone," he said, holding it up for her to see. "Last call, an hour ago." He tossed that phone to the floor. "This phone. His burner." His thumb busily worked the keypad. "Last number called three minutes ago. Not the police."

He depressed the icon to redial, and she recognized Doral's voice when he answered. "Everything okay?"

Coburn disconnected immediately. "So now he knows everything's not okay." The phone began ringing almost instantly. Coburn turned it off, crammed it into his jeans pocket, and nodded toward Emily's bedroom. "Get the kid."

"I can't just—"

"You wanna die?"

"No."

"You want your little girl to get snuffed? Wouldn't take too long for him to cut off her air with a pillow over her face."

She recoiled from the horrible image. "You would protect us. If what you say is true, why don't you arrest Doral?"

"I can't blow my cover yet. And I can't turn you over to the police because the whole frigging department is dirty. I couldn't protect you."

"I've known the Hawkins twins for years. They were my husband's best friends. Stan practically raised them. They have no reason to kill me."

He placed his hands on his hips. His chest was rapidly rising and falling with agitation. "Did you tell Fred I came here looking for something?"

She hesitated before giving one bob of her head.

"That's why Fred would have killed you. The Bookkeeper would have ordered it."

"You mentioned this bookkeeper last night. Who is it?"

"I wish I knew. But there's no time to explain that now. You just gotta believe that since Fred can no longer kill you, Doral will."

"That can't be true."

"It is."

He stated it as fact, without mitigation. Two words. *It is.* Still she hesitated.

"Look," he said, "you want to stay here and wring your hands over divided loyalties? Fine. But I'm leaving. I've got a job to finish. You'd be helpful to me, but not necessary. All I'm trying to do is save your skin. If you stay, you'll be at Doral's mercy. Good luck with that."

"He wouldn't hurt me."

"The hell he wouldn't. If he thinks you've got information, he'd hurt you plenty, you or your kid. Make no mistake about that. And then, whether you'd told him anything useful or not, he'd kill you. So stay and die, or come with me. You've got to the count of five to make up your mind. One."

"Maybe you're not lying, but you're wrong."

"I'm not wrong. Two."

"I can't just leave with you."

"When Hawkins gets here, I'll be gone, and you can explain—or try to—how his dearly departed twin wound up with a bullet hole in his head. He probably won't be in a very receptive mood. Three."

"Doral wouldn't raise a finger to me. To Emily? Eddie's child? Out of the question. I know him."

"Like you thought you knew his policeman brother."

"You're wrong about Fred, too."

"Four."

"You're telling me you're the good guy, and I'm supposed to believe it simply because you said it?" Her voice had gone raw and ragged with emotion. "I know these men. I trust them. But I don't know *you*!"

He stared at her for several beats, then put his hand around the front of her neck to hold her head still. He moved his face close to hers and whispered, "You know me. You know I'm who I say."

Her pulse beat rapidly against his strong fingers, but it was his piercing gaze that held her pinned to the wall behind her.

"Because if I wasn't, I would have fucked you last night." He held her for several seconds longer, then dropped his hand and backed away. "Five. Are you coming or not?"

*   *   *

Doral Hawkins hurled an armchair against the wall, then, angered because it hadn't busted up like they do in the movies, he whacked it against the wall again and again until the wood splintered. He punted a thick New Orleans Yellow Pages through the living room window. Then, standing amid the shattered windowpane, he clasped a double handful of his thinning hair and pulled hard as though wanting to rip it from his scalp.

He was in a state. Part agonizing anguish, part sheer animal rage.

His twin lay dead on the floor of Honor's house with a bullet hole bored through the center of his head. Doral had seen worse wounds. He'd inflicted worse. Like the time a guy had bled to death, slowly and screaming, after Doral eviscerated him with a hunting knife.

But his brother's lethal wound was the most obscene of Doral's experience because it was like looking at his own death mask. The blood hadn't even had time to congeal.

Honor wouldn't have killed him. It had to have been that son of a bitch Coburn.

During their last phone conversation, Fred, speaking in a hushed and hurried voice so Honor wouldn't overhear, had told him that their quarry, Lee Coburn, had been making cozy with her all the while they'd been chasing their tails through the pest-ridden swamp looking for him.

"He's there now?" Doral had asked excitedly.

"We're not that lucky. He's split."

"How much head start does he have?"

"Minutes, or could be hours. Honor says she woke up, he was gone. Took her car."

"She all right?"

"In a tizzy. Babbling."

"What was Coburn doing there?"

"The whole house is torn up."

"He knew about Eddie?"

"When he put in on this bayou, I got a sick feeling, and, yeah, looks like."

"How?"

"Don't know."

"What did Honor say?"

"Said he was after something that Eddie had died protecting."

"Fuck."

"My thought exactly."

After a short pause, Doral had asked quietly, "What are you gonna do?"

"Go after him."

"I mean about Honor."

Fred's sigh had come loudly through the cell connection. "The Bookkeeper didn't leave me a choice. When I called in that I was going to check out Eddie's place... Well, you know."

Yes, Doral knew. The Bookkeeper took no prisoners, and it wouldn't matter if it was a family friend, or a woman and child. *No loose ends. No mercy.*

Fred had been torn up about it, but he would do what he had to do, because he knew it was necessary. He was also aware of the severe consequences suffered by anyone who failed to carry out an order.

They'd ended their call with the understanding that he would take care of the problem, so that by the time Doral joined him at the Gillette place, they could report to the sheriff's office the horrifying double murder of Honor and Emily.

They'd chalk up the homicides to Coburn, who was sure to have left his fingerprints all over Honor's house.

There were muddy, blood-stained clothes left in the bathroom, which would prove to be his. Law enforcement personnel would be galvanized. Fred knew the buzz words to
use with the media so they'd take the story and run with it.
Soon the whole state would be salivating for a piece of Lee
Coburn, only suspect in the warehouse massacre, woman
and kid killer.

It had been a good plan, now shot to hell.

Doral spent a critical ten minutes in rage and grief. But,
his fit having subsided, he wiped the mucus and tears from
his face and forced himself to put personal feelings aside
until he could indulge in them properly, and instead to
evaluate the present situation. Which sucked. Big-time.

Most troubling was that Fred's body was the only one
in evidence. There was no sign of Honor and Emily, or of
their remains, in or near the house. If his brother had dispatched them, he'd hidden their bodies very well.

Or—and it was a really troublesome *or*—Coburn had
popped Fred before he'd had a chance to dispatch Honor
and her daughter. If that was the case, where were they
now? Hiding until someone came to their rescue? Possibly.
But that meant that as soon as he found them, he'd have to
kill them, and the thought of that made him queasy.

There was also a third possibility, and it was the worst-
case scenario: Coburn and Honor had escaped together.

Doral gnawed on that. It portended all kinds of trouble, but he didn't know what to do about it. He was a hunter,
not a detective, and not a strategist except when it came to
stalking. Besides, it wasn't up to him to determine what the
next course of action should be. He'd let The Bookkeeper
figure it out.

Like the Godfather in the movie, The Bookkeeper
insisted on hearing bad news right away. Doral placed the

call and it was answered on the first ring. "Have you found
Coburn?"

"Fred's been killed."

He waited for a reaction, but didn't really expect one
and didn't get it. Not even a shocked exclamation, certainly not a murmur of sympathy. The Bookkeeper would
be interested only in hearing the facts and hearing them
immediately.

As uncomfortable as it was to be the bearer of bad
news, Doral described the scene at Honor's house and
passed along everything that Fred had told him before he
was shot. "I got one more call from his cell, but as soon
as I answered, it was cut off. I don't know who placed that
call, and when I dial his number now, I get nothing. The
phone's missing. I found his police-issued one in the hall. I
don't know what happened to Honor and Emily. There's no
sign of them. Fred's pistol is also gone. And…and…"

"More bad news? Spit it out, Doral."

"The house is torn up all to hell. Honor told Fred that
Coburn came here looking for something he thought
Eddie had squirreled away."

The silence that followed was deafening. Both were
thinking about the grave implications of Coburn's search
through Honor's house. They certainly couldn't dismiss it
as a bizarre coincidence.

Doral wisely remained quiet and tried to keep his
gaze from wandering back to his brother's corpse. But he
couldn't help himself, and each time he looked at it, he felt
a burning rage. Nobody humiliated a Hawkins like that.
Coburn would pay and pay dearly.

"Did Coburn find what he was looking for?"

This was the question Doral had most dreaded, because
he didn't have an answer for it. "Who's to say?"

"*You're* to say, Doral. Find them. Learn what they know or retrieve what they have, then dispatch them."

"You don't need to tell me."

"Don't I? I told you and your brother not to let anyone leave that warehouse alive."

Doral felt his face burn.

"And let me emphasize," The Bookkeeper continued, "that there's no room for another mistake. Not when we're on the brink of opening up a whole new market for ourselves."

For months The Bookkeeper had been obsessed with sealing a deal with a new cartel out of Mexico that needed an established and reliable network to provide protection as they trafficked their goods across the state of Louisiana. Drugs and girls going one way, guns and heavy weaponry the other. They were big players, willing to pay substantial sums for peace of mind.

The Bookkeeper was determined to get their business. But it wasn't going to happen unless one hundred percent reliability was guaranteed. Killing Sam Marset was supposed to have been a swift and bloody resolution to a problem. "Make a splash," The Bookkeeper had told him and Fred, tongue in cheek.

But although it would never be admitted, the mass murder had opened up a hornet's nest. They were now in damage control mode, and in order to protect his own interests, Doral would go along. He had no choice.

"The next time I call you, Doral, it'll be from another cell phone. If Coburn's got Fred's phone—"

"He'll have your number."

"Unless your brother did as told and cleared the log each time we talked. But in any case, I'll switch to a new phone."

"Understood."

"Get Coburn."

"Also understood."

He and Fred had had a patsy in place to frame for the warehouse murders. But the dock worker who had managed to escape the bloodbath, this Lee Coburn, had made himself an even better "suspect."

They had counted on finding him within an hour of the killings, hunkered down somewhere, shaking in his boots, praying to his Maker to deliver him from evil. Later, they planned to attest that he'd been fatally shot while trying to escape arresting officer Fred Hawkins.

But Coburn had proved himself to be smarter than expected. He'd eluded Fred and him. And even when being tracked by armed men and bloodhounds, he'd run to Honor Gillette's house and had spent a lot of valuable time searching it. You didn't have to be a rocket scientist…

"You know, I've been thinking."

"I don't pay you to think, Doral."

The insult stung, but he pressed on. "This guy Coburn burst onto the scene a year ago and worked his way into Sam Marset's confidence. I'm beginning to think he's no ordinary loading dock worker, somebody who accidentally got wind of the more lucrative aspects of Marset's operation and decided to horn in. He seems—what's the word? *Overqualified*. Not your average trucking company employee."

After another weighty silence, The Bookkeeper said bitingly, "Did you figure that out all by yourself, Doral?"

Chapter 15

Since Honor's house was outside the city limits, the sheriff's office had jurisdiction. The deputy, who was that department's singular homicide investigator, was a man named Crawford. Doral had failed to catch his first name.

Doral was retelling how he'd come to find the body of his brother when Crawford looked beyond his shoulder and muttered, "Dammit, who's that? Who let him in here?"

Doral turned. Stan Gillette must have talked his way past the uniformed officers stringing crime scene tape around the perimeter of the Gillette property. He paused only briefly on the threshold, then, sighting Doral, made a beeline toward him.

"That's Stan Gillette, Honor's father-in-law."

"Great," the detective said. "The last thing we need."

Doral echoed the detective's sentiment but kept his feelings from showing by assuming an appropriately somber expression as the older man approached.

The former Marine didn't even glance at Fred's body,

which had been zipped into a black plastic bag that was
presently being strapped onto a gurney for transport by
ambulance to the morgue. Instead he barked as though
issuing a subordinate an order:

"It's true? Honor and Emily have been kidnapped?"

"Well, they're not here and Coburn was."

"Jesus Christ." Stan ran his hand over his burred head,
around the back of his neck, uttered a string of curses.
Then he fixed a hard stare on Doral. "What are you doing
here? Why aren't you out looking for them?"

"I will be, soon as Deputy Crawford frees me to go." He
gestured toward the deputy and made a cursory introduc-
tion. "He's investigating—"

"With all due respect to your investigation," Stan said,
interrupting Doral and addressing the deputy with none
of the respect he mentioned, "it can wait. Fred died in the
performance of his duty, which is a risk that every police
officer accepts. He's dead and nothing can bring him back.
Meanwhile two innocent people are missing, most likely
kidnapped by a man believed to be a ruthless murderer."

He tilted his head toward Doral. "He's the best hunter
in the area. He should be out looking for Honor and Emily
in the hope of finding them before they are killed, not
standing here talking to you about somebody who's already
dead. And if you had any gumption at all, you'd also be out
tracking the fugitive and his hostages instead of languish-
ing here in the one place that they're noticeably not in."

His voice had risen with each word so that his statement
ended on a full-blown shout that brought all the activity
going on around them to a halt. Everyone turned to stare.
Stan, his color high, his posture rigid with righteous indignation, seemed not to notice.

To his credit, the deputy didn't wither under Stan's

blistering criticism. He was several inches shorter than both Stan and Doral, and was as physically unimposing as a man could possibly be. But he stood his ground. "I'm here in an official capacity, Mr. Gillette. Which makes *one* of us."

Doral could tell that Stan was about to blow a gasket, but Crawford didn't flinch. "I'll have the ass of whoever let you past the crime scene tape, but as long as you're here, you could try to be helpful. Talking down to me and issuing orders won't get you anywhere except escorted off the premises, and if you resist, you'll be arrested and taken to jail."

Doral thought Stan might even be on the verge of taking out the knife for which he was famous and using it to threaten the gullet of the deputy. Before that could happen, Doral intervened. "Cut him some slack, Crawford. He's just received distressing news. Let me have a word with him. Okay?"

The deputy shifted his gaze from one man to the other. "Coupla minutes while I'm talking to the coroner. Then, Mr. Gillette, I'd like you to walk through the house with me, see if you can spot anything that's missing."

Stan glanced around at the disarray. "How could I possibly determine that?"

"I understand, but it wouldn't hurt to look. Maybe you'll notice something that gives us a clue as to why and where Coburn took them."

"That's the best you can do?" Stan asked.

The deputy merely returned his steely look, then said, "Coupla minutes," and moved away. But suddenly he came back around. "Who notified you? How'd you get here so fast?"

Stan rocked forward and back on the balls of his feet as though he didn't intend to answer. Finally he said, "Yesterday Honor told me that she and Emily were sick. Obviously she was coerced into saying that, purposely to keep me away. This morning I was worried about them and decided to drive out and check on them. When I arrived, I found the house surrounded by police cars. One of the officers told me what it's feared has happened."

Crawford sized him up again, said, "Don't touch anything," then turned away to consult the coroner.

Doral nudged Stan's arm. "Back here."

They moved down the hallway. Doral went past Emily's bedroom, but Stan paused at the open door and then went in. He walked over to the bed and stared down at it for several long moments, then slowly surveyed the room with his eagle eyes.

Looking troubled, he rejoined Doral and followed him into Honor's bedroom. In the salty language of the military, he expressed disgust over the damage done to it.

"Listen," Doral said, needing to get this out before Deputy Crawford reappeared. "Promise you won't fly off the handle."

Stan promised nothing, merely stared at him.

Doral said, "Crawford noticed something and commented on it."

"What?"

Doral indicated the bed. "Looks like two people slept there last night. I'm not making anything of it," he added hastily. "I'm just telling you that Crawford remarked on it."

"Suggesting what?" Stan asked through lips that barely moved. "That my daughter-in-law slept with a man wanted for seven murders?"

Doral raised one shoulder, the gesture both noncommittal and sympathetic. "Is there a chance, Stan, the smallest chance, that she, you know, had met this guy before he showed up here yesterday?"

"No."

"You're sure? You know everybody Honor—"

"I'm sure."

"Every woman that Fred interviewed yesterday— neighbors, women who work at the trucking company— pretty much agree this guy's a stud."

"If Honor is with Lee Coburn," Stan said, his voice vibrating with anger, "she was taken against her will."

"I believe you," Doral said, contradicting his insinuation of only seconds earlier. "The good news is that her and Emily's bodies weren't found here along with Fred's."

For the first time Stan acknowledged Doral's loss. "My condolences."

"Thanks."

"Have you told your mother?"

"I called my eldest sister. She's on her way out to Mama's place now to break the news."

"She'll be heartbroken. First your dad and Monroe. Now this."

Doral's father and the second eldest of the Hawkinses' eight children had died in an offshore rig accident several years ago. Mama would take Fred's death hard. Doral could imagine the weeping and wailing. His sister was better equipped to handle that scene than he was. Besides, he had problems of his own to deal with.

"There's something else you should be aware of, Stan," he said, speaking in a low voice.

"I'm listening."

"Before you got here, Crawford was asking a lot of questions about Eddie."

Stan was taken aback and instantly wary. "What kind of questions?"

"Leading questions. He noticed that Eddie's clothes were strewn all over the place. Old files had been rifled through. He said it looked to him like Coburn was after something that had belonged to Eddie. I dismissed it, but Crawford kept coming back to that.

"The photo of the four of us, taken after the fishing trip?" Doral continued in a hushed voice. "Crawford noticed that it had been removed from the frame. He bagged the whole kit and caboodle as evidence. Yeah," he said, noticing Stan's surprise and displeasure.

"Did you challenge him about it?"

"He said they might be able to lift Coburn's prints off it."

"Flimsy excuse. Anything in the house could have Coburn's fingerprints on it."

Doral raised both shoulders. "I'm just telling you. It was a picture of Eddie, and Crawford's stuck on the idea that Coburn was searching for something that related to him."

"But he didn't say what."

Doral shook his head.

Crawford chose that moment to interrupt. Coming into the room, he said, "Mr. Gillette. Have you noticed anything unusual?"

Stan drew himself up. "Is that supposed to be a joke?" Without waiting for a response, he launched a verbal attack. "As a citizen and taxpayer, I'm demanding that you do whatever is necessary, using whatever resources you have, to bring my daughter-in-law and granddaughter home safely."

Crawford's face turned red, but he kept his voice even. "We all want Coburn apprehended and the safe return of your family."

"That sounds like pro forma bullshit," Stan said. "Save

your banal promises for somebody stupid enough to take heart from them. I want action. I don't care what guidelines your handbook says to follow. I want this criminal found, killed if necessary, and my daughter-in-law and grand-daughter returned to me unharmed. We can make nice then, and not until then, Deputy. And if I'm not getting through to you, I can go over your head. I know the sheriff personally."

"I know what my duties are, Mr. Gillette. And I'll per-form them in accordance with the law."

"Fine. Now that we know where each other stands, you do what you've got to do, and I'll do likewise."

"Don't go taking the law into your own hands, Mr. Gillette."

Stan ignored that, gave Doral a pointed look, and, with-out another word, marched out.

Chapter 16

———⇒•◦•⇐———

This isn't my car."

Coburn took his eyes off the rearview mirror to glance over at Honor. "I ditched yours."

"Where?"

"A few miles from your house where I picked up this one."

"It's stolen?"

"No, I knocked on the door and asked if I could borrow it."

She ignored the sarcasm. "The owners will report it."

"I switched the plates with another car."

"You did all this between leaving my house and coming back to head off Fred?"

"I work fast."

She absorbed all that information, then remarked, "You said you saw Fred in a boat."

"The road follows the bayou. I was driving without headlights. I saw the light on his boat, pulled off the road to check it out. Saw him and recognized him instantly. Figured what he would do if you repeated to him anything of what I'd told you. Went back. Lucky for you I did."

She still didn't look convinced of that, and he couldn't say he blamed her for doubting him. Yesterday when he'd barged into her life, she'd been icing cupcakes for a birthday party. Since then he'd threatened her and her kid at gunpoint. He'd manhandled and wrestled with her. He'd wrecked her house and tied her to her bed.

Now he was supposed to be the good guy who'd talked her into fleeing her home because men she'd known and trusted for years were in fact mass murderers with designs on killing her. Naturally, she'd be more than a little skeptical.

She was nervously running her hands up and down her thighs, now clothed in jeans instead of yesterday's denim shorts. Occasionally she would glance over her shoulder at the little girl, who was in the backseat playing with that red thing. It and the ratty quilt that she called her bankie, along with Honor's handbag, were all that he'd allowed them to bring with them. He'd hustled them away literally with nothing except the clothes on their backs.

At least their clothes belonged to them. He was wearing those of a dead man.

Not for the first time.

In a whisper, Honor asked, "Do you think she saw?"

"No."

On their race through the house, Honor had created a game requiring Emily to keep her eyes shut until they were outside. For expediency, Coburn had carried her from her pink bedroom to the car. He'd kept his hand on the back of her head, her face pressed into his neck, just in case she cheated at the game and opened her eyes, in which case she would have seen Fred Hawkins's body on the living room floor.

"Why didn't you tell me yesterday that you were an FBI agent? Why run roughshod over me?"

"I didn't trust you."

She looked at him with a bewilderment that seemed genuine.

"You're Gillette's widow," he explained. "Reason enough for me to harbor some doubts about you. Then when I saw that photo, saw him and his dad being chummy with the two guys I'd seen kill those seven in the warehouse, heard you extol them as dearest friends, what was I supposed to think? In any case, I was and am convinced that whatever Eddie had, you have now."

"But I don't."

"Maybe. Or maybe you do have it and just don't know that you do. Anyway, I no longer think you're holding out on me."

"What changed your mind?"

"Even if you'd been crooked, I think you'd have given me anything I wanted if I didn't hurt your little girl."

"You're right."

"I came to that conclusion just before dawn this morning. I figured I'd leave you in peace. Then I saw Hawkins on his way to your house. Sudden change of plan."

"Am I truly to believe that Fred killed Sam Marset?"

"I witnessed it." He glanced at her; her expression invited him to elaborate. "There was a meeting scheduled for Sunday midnight at the warehouse."

"A meeting between Marset and Fred?"

"Between Marset and The Bookkeeper."

She rubbed her forehead. "What are you talking about?"

He took a breath, collected his thoughts. "Interstate Highway 10 cuts through Louisiana, north of Tambour."

"It goes through Lafayette and New Orleans."

"Right. I-10 is the southernmost coast-to-coast interstate, and its proximity to Mexico and the Gulf make it a pipeline for drug dealers, gun runners, human traffickers. Big markets are the key cities it passes through—Phoenix, El Paso, San Antonio, Houston, New Orleans—all of which also have major north/south routes that intersect it."

"Essentially—"

"Connecting I-10 to every major city in the continental U.S."

Again she nodded. "Okay."

"Any vehicle you pass on it—everything from a semi, to a pickup, to a family van—might be transporting street drugs, pharmaceuticals, weapons, girls and boys destined for forced prostitution." He looked over at her. "You still following me?"

"Sam Marset owned Royale Trucking Company."

"You get a gold star."

"You're actually saying that Sam Marset's drivers were dabbling in this illegal transport?"

"Not his drivers. Sam Marset, your church elder and historical society whatever. And not dabbling. He's big-time. *Was.* Sunday night put an end to his life of crime."

She thought that over, checked to see that the kid was still distracted by her toy, then asked, "Where do you factor in?"

"I was assigned to get inside Marset's operation, find out who he did business with, so the hotshots could set up a series of stings. It took me months just to gain the foreman's trust. Then, only after Marset gave his approval, I was entrusted with the manifests. His company ships a lot of legal goods, but I also saw plenty of contraband."

"Human beings?"

"Everything except that. Which is good, because I'd have had to stop that shipment, and that would have entailed blowing my cover. As it was, I had to let a lot of illegal contraband go through. But my bosses aren't interested in one truck of dry goods concealing one box of automatic handguns. The bureau wants the people sending and receiving them. I didn't have enough proof yet to catch the big fish."

"Like Marset."

"Him and bigger. But the real prize would be The Bookkeeper."

"Who is that?"

"Good question. The bureau didn't even know about him until I got down here and realized that somebody is greasing the skids."

"You just lost me."

"The Bookkeeper is a facilitator. He goes to the people who're supposed to be preventing all this illegal trafficking, then bribes or strong-arms them into looking the other way."

"He bribes policemen?"

"Police, state troopers, agents at the state weigh stations, the man guarding impounded vehicles, anybody who has the potential of impeding the trafficking."

"The Bookkeeper pays off the official..."

"Then takes a hefty commission from the smuggler for guaranteeing him and his cargo safe passage through the state of Louisiana."

She ruminated on that, then said, "But you didn't learn his identity."

"No. I'm missing a key element." He stopped at a cross-roads and turned his head, giving her a hard look.

"Which you came to my house in search of."

"Right." He took his foot off the brake and accelerated through the intersection. "The DOJ isn't—Department of Justice," he said to clarify—"isn't going to make a case until it knows it can't lose in court. We might make a deal with someone to testify against The Bookkeeper in exchange for clemency, but we also need hard evidence. Files, bank records, phone records, canceled checks, deposit slips, names, dates. Documentation. Proof. I think that's what your late husband had."

"You think Eddie was involved in this?" she asked. "Drugs? Guns? Human trafficking? You are so wrong, Mr. Coburn."

"Truth is, I don't know what side of the business your husband was working. But he was blood brothers with the twins, and in my book that makes him damn suspicious. And being a cop would be an asset, just like it was to Fred."

"Eddie was an *honest* cop."

"You'd think that, wouldn't you? You're his widow. But I saw his bosom buddies mow down seven people in cold blood. I would have been victim number eight if I hadn't gotten away."

"How did you manage that?"

"I was expecting something to happen. The meeting was supposed to be peaceful, no weapons. But I was on high alert because The Bookkeeper is reputed to be a ruthless son of a bitch. Do you remember a few weeks ago—it was on the news—about a Latino kid found in a ditch up near Lafayette with his throat cut?"

"There was no identification on him. Do you know who he was?"

"Not his name. I know he was being transported by one of The Bookkeeper's 'clients' to a place in New Orleans that caters to…" He glanced into the rearview mirror. The kid was singing along with Elmo. "Caters to clients with lots of money and a taste for kinky sex. This kid knew what awaited him. He escaped during a refueling stop.

"Most of these kids are too scared to go to the authorities, but one might get brave. Apparently The Bookkeeper feared as much. His people caught up to this kid before he could do any damage." He looked at her and muttered, "He's probably better off dead. Shortly after the kid's body turned up, a state trooper was found with his throat slit. I have an inkling the two murders are connected."

"Do you think this Bookkeeper is a public official?"

"Could be. Maybe not. I was hoping to learn his identity on Sunday night," he said tightly. "Because something big is brewing. I've just caught whiffs of it, but I think The Bookkeeper is courting a new client. Scary people with zero tolerance for screw-ups."

Again she massaged her forehead. "I refuse to believe that Eddie was involved in anything relating to this. I can't believe it of Sam Marset, either."

"Marset was in it strictly for the money. He was a fat cat who profited off vices, but he wasn't violent. If somebody crossed him, he ruined them. Usually financially. Or caught them with their pants down in a hotel room and blackmailed them. Like that. He was of the mind that the flyblown body of a thirteen-year-old boy being found in a ditch was bad for business.

"And that was only one of the grievances Marset was holding against The Bookkeeper. He demanded that they sit down together, hash out their differences, clear the air. The Bookkeeper agreed."

"But pulled a double-cross."

"To put it mildly. Instead of The Bookkeeper, it was the Hawkins twins who showed up. Before Marset could even voice his outrage over the switcheroo, Fred popped him. Doral had an automatic rifle. He opened fire on the others, taking out my foreman first. The instant I saw them at the door, I smelled a rat and slipped behind some crates, but I knew they'd seen me. When the others were down, they came after me."

He approached a railroad crossing, but didn't let it slow him down. The car bounced over it. "I'd taken the precaution of carrying a pistol to work that night, along with my extra cell phone. I left one phone behind on purpose. That'll throw them off. They'll chase their tails tracking down the calls on it.

"Anyway, I made it out of the warehouse alive and got to an abandoned building. One of the twins searched it, but I hid in the crawl space until he left. Then I hightailed it toward the river, bent on eventually getting to you before they caught up to me." He looked over at her. "You more or less know the rest."

"So what now? Where are we going?"

"I have no idea."

She turned her head so quickly, her neck popped. "What?"

"I didn't plan that far ahead. Actually, I didn't count on living through that first night. I figured I'd either be killed by an overanxious officer or by someone on The Bookkeeper's payroll." He glanced over his shoulder into the backseat. "I sure didn't count on having a woman and kid in tow."

"Well, I'm sorry for the inconvenience we've imposed,"

Honor said. "You can drop us at Stan's house and go on about your business."

He gave a short laugh. "Don't you get it? Haven't you been listening? If Doral Hawkins or The Bookkeeper think you know something that could help convict them, your life's not worth spit."

"I *do* understand. Stan will protect us until—"

"Stan, the man in the one-for-all-and-all-for-one photo with your late husband and the Hawkins twins? *That* Stan?"

"Surely, you don't think—"

"Why not?"

"Stan's a former Marine."

"So am I. Look how I turned out."

He'd made his point. She hesitated, then said staunchly, "My father-in-law would protect Emily and me with his dying breath."

"Maybe. I don't know yet. Until I do, you stay with me and contact nobody."

Before she could say more, they heard the wail of sirens. Within seconds, two police cars appeared where the road met the horizon. They were approaching and closing quickly.

"Doral must have found his brother's corpse."

Though his muscles contracted with tension and he gripped the steering wheel of the stolen car tighter, Coburn maintained his speed and kept his eyes straight ahead. The squad cars screamed past at a high rate of speed.

"Police car," the kid chirped. "Mommy, police car."

"I see it, sweetheart." Honor threw a smile back at her, then came around to him again. "Emily will need food. A place to sleep. We can't just keep driving around in a stolen car, dodging the police. What are you going to do with us?"

"I'm about to find out."

He checked the clock in the car's dashboard and saw that it would be past nine on the East Coast. He took the next turn off the main road. The blacktop soon gave way to gravel and gravel to rutted dirt, and the road finally came to a dead end at a stagnant creek covered with duckweed.

He had three phones. Fred's. Beyond that one last call to his brother, the call log had been empty. But since Fred used that phone for illegal purposes, Coburn hadn't expected to find The Bookkeeper's number highlighted. All the same, he would keep the phone. For safe measure, he removed the battery.

They couldn't use Honor's cell because the authorities could locate it using triangulation. He took the battery from it too.

Which left Coburn's burner, the disposable he'd bought months earlier but had never used until yesterday. He turned it on, saw that he was getting a cell signal, and punched in a number with the hope that today his call would be answered.

"Who are you calling?" Honor asked.

"You jump out of your skin every time I move."

"Can you blame me?"

"Not really."

He looked at her elbows and upper arms, which bore bruises. The backs of her hands were also bruised from her banging them against the headboard when he'd tied her to it. He regretted that he'd had to get physical, but he wouldn't apologize for it. She would have been hurt much worse if he hadn't.

"You don't have to worry about me grabbing you anymore," he told her. "Or waving a pistol at you. No more jitters, okay?"

"If I'm jittery it could be because I saw a man shot dead in my home this morning."

He'd already said what he had to say about that, and he wasn't going to justify it again. If you got a chance to take out a violent criminal like Fred Hawkins, you didn't stop to reason why. You pulled the goddamn trigger. Otherwise, you'd be the one no longer breathing.

How many men had he seen die? How many had he seen die violently? Too many to count or even to remember. But he supposed that for a second-grade schoolteacher's clear green eyes, it was a shocking thing to witness, which she would always associate with him. No help for that. However, this call would put an end to her flinching every time he moved.

He was about to disconnect and try again when a woman answered. "Deputy Director Hamilton's office. How can I direct your call?"

"Who're you? Put Hamilton on."

"Whom may I say is calling?"

"Look, cut the bullshit. Give him the phone."

"Whom may I say is calling?"

Damn bureaucrats. "Coburn."

"I'm sorry, who did you say?"

"Coburn," he repeated impatiently. "Lee Coburn."

After a sustained pause, the woman at the other end said, "That's impossible. Agent Coburn is deceased. He died more than a year ago."

Chapter 17

Diego's cell phone vibrated, but just to be ornery, he waited several seconds before answering it. "Who's this?"

"Who were you expecting?" The Bookkeeper asked with matching snideness.

"Found your fugitive yet?"

"He's proving to be more of a problem than originally thought."

"You don't say? Those couple of clowns really fucked up, didn't they? Letting him get away like that." He wanted to add, *That's what you get for not giving me the job*, but decided not to press his luck. He didn't rely solely on The Bookkeeper for income, but their business relationship—if you could even call it that—was lucrative.

For years after leaving the hair-braiding salon, he'd lived on the streets, finding shelter where he could, scavenging for food and clothing. He'd survived by a wily intellect that had come to him through some unknown contributor to his cloudy gene pool, and it hadn't taken him long to figure out that barter, theft, and salvaging only got one so much. The only currency that mattered was money.

Diego had applied himself to earning it. He observed and learned and proved to be a quick study. The marketplace for his particular skills was limitless. His business thrived regardless of the economic climate for any other field of commerce. In fact, he was busiest whenever times got hard and the prevailing dog-eat-dog law of the jungle was more strictly enforced.

By his early teens he'd cultivated a reputation for sudden and explosive violence, so even the toughest of the tough respected his slight build and small stature and, for the most part, gave him a wide berth. He had no friends and few competitors because few were as good.

As far as the state of Louisiana was concerned, he didn't exist. His birth had never been recorded, so he never had attended school. Although basically illiterate, he could read a smattering of English, enough to get by. He spoke fluent Spanish, which he'd picked up on the street. He couldn't point out his hometown on a map, but he knew it like the back of his hand. He'd never even heard of long division or the multiplication tables, yet he could tabulate amounts of money in his head with lightning speed. Already he was calculating what he would charge for doing Coburn.

"So is the guy caught yet, or what?"

"No. He got Fred Hawkins."

Diego was surprised by that, but withheld comment.

"Now everyone is really up in arms. If Coburn survives his *arrest*, I want you to be ready to move."

"I've been ready."

"I also may need you to take care of a woman and child."

"That'll cost you extra."

"I'm prepared for that." After a cool silence, The Book-keeper said, "About that whore…"

"Taken care of. I told you."

"Ah, so you did. My mind has been on other matters. I'll be in touch."

The call ended without another word.

None was necessary. They understood each other. They had from the start. A few years back, someone who knew someone had approached him about contract work. Was he interested? He was.

He called the telephone number given to him, listened to The Bookkeeper's recruitment spiel, and figured it was the kind of alliance he liked—loose. He did that first job, he got paid. He and The Bookkeeper had been doing business together ever since.

He slipped the cell phone back into the holster hooked to his belt, hunched his shoulders, and pushed his hands deep into the pockets of his pants. The fingers of his right hand closed securely around the razor.

Since Katrina, some areas of the city had become gang war zones. Diego was an independent operator who'd tried to steer clear of the clashes, but it was impossible to remain neutral, and consequently he'd become the enemy of all the gangs.

He appeared to be focused on the grimy pavement beneath the rubber soles of his high-tops, but in truth, his eyes were darting and watchful, suspecting that danger lurked in each shadow, constantly anticipating an ambush.

He didn't fear much from cops. They were a joke. Some-times a bad joke, but still laughable and not something he worried about.

In that deceptively stooped posture, he slunk down the

sidewalk, turning left into the first alley he came to, scattering cockroaches and two cats on the prowl. For the next five minutes, he wove his way through abandoned buildings filled with rusting industrial equipment or refuse left by homeless people who'd used the structures as temporary camps.

The labyrinth of alleyways was no maze to Diego. He knew every square inch of it. He took a different and circuitous path through it each time, so he could be certain that no one was following him. Nobody could find him if he didn't want to be found.

After years of living wherever he could take shelter, he now had a permanent residence, although it wasn't on any postman's route. He circled the vacant building twice before approaching a padlocked door to which he held the only key. Once he was in, he bolted the metal door from the inside.

Total darkness enveloped him, but it was no impediment. He easily navigated the hallways, whose walls were black with mold. They were perpetually damp. Rainwater trickled down three stories to collect in rancid puddles on the uneven floors.

Deep within the bowels of this former bean cannery, Diego had made himself a home. He unlocked the door to the inner sanctum, slipped inside, secured the deadbolt.

The chamber's air was cooler and drier due to a makeshift ventilation system that he'd adapted from the building's original, using scrap materials he'd collected over time. On the floor was an expensive oriental rug he'd stolen off a truck parked in the French Quarter. He'd pretended to be one of the deliverymen. No one had challenged him when he slung the carpet over his shoulder and walked away with it. All the room's furnishings had been similarly obtained. Twin lamps shed a welcoming glow.

She was sitting on the edge of the bed, brushing her hair with a brush that Diego had shoplifted yesterday. He'd paid for the goldfish, though. He'd passed a pet store he'd never taken notice of before. He saw the fish in their tank. Next thing he knew, he was carrying home one of them in a plastic bag. Her smile when he'd presented it to her had been worth triple what he'd paid for the fish.

He'd never had a pet before. Now he had two. The goldfish and the girl.

Her name was Isobel. She was a year younger than he, although she looked even younger than that. Her hair was sleek and so black it was iridescent. It hung straight to her shoulders, forming a glossy curtain against her cheeks.

She was slightly built, with a waist his hands could span. Diego figured he could snap her frail limbs in two with virtually no effort. Her breasts were small, barely tenting the T-shirt he'd stolen for her. And although he'd had many women of all ages and sizes, it was the delicate beauty of Isobel's small body that made him feel feverish, short of breath, and weak with desire.

But he hadn't touched her in that way. Nor would he.

Her fragile, youthful features had made her very popular with the massage parlor's clientele. Men loved being stroked by her small hands. Many requested her. She had regulars. Her delicacy was a turn-on because it made those who sweated over her feel more manly, larger, harder, stronger.

Like thousands of others, she and her family had been promised that she would enjoy a better life in the United States. She was guaranteed a job in a fancy hotel or a fine restaurant, where she would make more money in one week than her father earned in a year.

Once she had paid off the debt of getting her into the States and well situated, which would take only a few years, she would start earning money to send back to her family, possibly enough to pay for her younger brother to come to the U.S. also. It had sounded like a fairy tale come true. She had bade her family a tearful but hopeful goodbye and had climbed into the truck headed for the border.

The hellish trip had taken five days. She and eight others had been crammed into the bed of a pickup and covered with a sheet of plywood. During the journey, they were given very little to eat and drink and few opportunities to relieve themselves.

One of the other girls, no older than Isobel, had become sick with a fever. Isobel had tried to hide the girl's illness, but the driver and the heavily armed man who rode with him discovered it during a rare rest stop. The truck departed without the girl. She was left on the side of the road. The others were warned that they would also be abandoned if they interfered or caused trouble. Isobel had wondered many times if the girl had died before someone found her.

And that was only the beginning of Isobel's nightmare.

When the truck finally reached its destination, she was made to dress in provocative clothing, which was charged against her earnings, and put to work in a brothel.

She didn't know anyone. Even those who'd been trucked into the States with her, and with whom she'd forged a quasi-friendship founded on shared fear and despair, had been sent to other places. She didn't know which city or state she was in. She didn't understand the language that the first leering man crooned to her as he robbed her of her virginity.

Although she hadn't understood his words, she'd comprehended completely what that act had signified. She was ruined, spoiled goods. No kind and caring man would ever want to marry her now. She was disgraced. Her family would disown her. Her choices were now limited to continuing to "entertain" the customers, or to kill herself. But suicide was a mortal sin, a ticket to damnation.

In essence, the only choice left to her had been what kind of hell she would suffer.

Which is why her eyes, as black and fluid as ink, had looked so wounded and haunted the first time Diego had seen her. He'd been sent to deliver a warning to the manager of the massage parlor, whom The Bookkeeper claimed was withholding payment for the protection provided to his latest shipment of girls.

Diego had spotted Isobel as she emerged from one of the "treatment" rooms, clutching a tacky satin robe around her slenderness, tears streaming down her cheeks. When she caught him looking at her, she turned away from him in shame.

He returned a few days later, this time as a client. He asked for her. When she entered the room, she recognized him. With noticeable despondency, she began to undress. He hastily assured her that he only wanted to talk.

Over the next hour, she related her story. It wasn't the tale of woe itself but the mesmerizing way in which she told it that compelled Diego to offer to help her run away. She clasped his hand, kissed it, rained tears onto it.

Now, as he approached the bed, she set aside the hairbrush and smiled at him timidly, her eyes no longer filled with wretchedness, but brimming with gratitude.

He sat down beside her, leaving space between them. "*Como está?*"

"*Bien.*"

He returned her tentative smile, and for a moment they simply gazed at one another. The moment lasted so long that when he raised his hand toward her, she flinched.

"Shh." Gently, he laid his palm against her smooth cheek. He stroked her skin with his thumb, marveling at its velvety texture. He looked at her throat, noticed how slender it was, how vulnerable. Around it, she wore a thin silver chain with a crucifix. He watched her pulse beat faintly beneath the small cross that glittered when it caught the lamplight.

The razor in his pocket felt as heavy as lead.

His standard rate was five hundred dollars.

It would be over quickly. One slash and she would be relieved of her misery. She would have nothing more to fear, not even damnation. He would be liberating her, actually. He would be freeing her from pawing men and her crucified god's harsh judgment. And he would be carrying out The Bookkeeper's directive.

By killing her, Diego would stay in favor with The Bookkeeper, and this lovely girl would never again have her small, sweet body defiled.

But instead of applying the razor to her throat, he stroked it with his fingertips, touched the crucifix, and in softly spoken Spanish reassured her that she was safe now. He told her that he would take care of her, that she didn't need to be afraid any longer, that he would protect her. The nightmare that she'd been living for two years was over.

Diego swore this to her on his life.

And by doing so, he was drawing a line in the sand. He'd been ordered not only to kill Isobel, but also to learn who had helped her to escape the massage parlor, and to kill that person as well.

The Bookkeeper had no idea that Diego himself was responsible.

Taking in the beautiful sight and smell and feel that was Isobel, he had a pair of blunt English words for The Book-keeper. "Get fucked."

Chapter 18

⎯⎯⊷∘⊶⎯⎯

"Tori, you might want to, you know, look at this."

Her receptionist knew better than to interrupt her when she was with a client, especially one as overweight and undertoned as Mrs. Perkins. She gave Amber a withering look, then said to her client, "Six more of those, please."

Groaning, the woman went into a deep squat.

Tori turned to her receptionist and, with asperity, said, "Well. What?"

The receptionist pointed to the row of flat-screen TVs attached to the wall in front of the treadmills. One was tuned to a syndicated talk show, another to an infomercial where a soap opera star was hawking a miracle-working face cream. The third was on a New Orleans station broadcasting late-breaking news.

Tori watched for several seconds. "You interrupted me to watch an update on the Royale Trucking Company shootings? Unless the fugitive is presently in the women's sauna without a towel, why is this my problem?" She turned back to Mrs. Perkins, whose face had gone beet red. Tori thought maybe she should have asked for only five more squats.

"It's your friend," Amber the receptionist said. "Honor? They think she's been kidnapped."

Tori looked quickly at Amber, then back at the TV screen. That's when she recognized Honor's house as the one behind the reporter who was doing a report "live from the scene," as the caption across the bottom of the screen informed the audience.

Astonished, she watched for several seconds before realizing that the audio was muted. "Oh my God, what's he saying?"

"What's going on?" Mrs. Perkins puffed.

Tori ignored her and wove her way through the workout equipment toward the wall of televisions. She grabbed a remote and aimed it at the set. After several tries, she got the sound on and adjusted the volume as high as it would go.

"...feared to have been kidnapped by Lee Coburn, the individual sought in connection to the mass murder at the Royale Trucking Company on Sunday night, where, among six other victims, community leader Sam Marset was fatally shot."

"Come on, come on," Tori muttered impatiently. She wasn't yet convinced that her health club's receptionist hadn't gotten confused. She'd hired Amber strictly for the way she looked in workout gear. She had big hair, teeth, and tits going for her, but was short on gray matter.

This time, however, she'd gotten the information right. When the reporter finally got around to explaining again why he was reporting from Honor's house, Tori listened with mounting incredulity and anxiety.

"See?" Amber whispered in her ear. "I told you."

"Be quiet," Tori snapped.

"Police and FBI agents are on the scene, conducting a thorough investigation, but from what the authorities have pieced together, it's believed that Mrs. Gillette and her four-year-old daughter were forcibly taken from their home. I spoke briefly with Stan Gillette, father-in-law of the believed victim, who declined to be interviewed for this broadcast. He did tell me that so far he hasn't received a ransom demand."

The reporter glanced down and consulted notes. "It appears that a struggle took place inside the house, which has been ransacked. Mr. Gillette said it was impossible to determine if anything was missing. As for the body of police officer Fred Hawkins, which was found inside the house—"

"Jesus," Tori gasped, slapping her hand to her chest.

"—no further information has been forthcoming except that it looked like an execution-style killing." The reporter looked up and into the camera. "Police and other state and local agencies have asked citizens to be on the lookout for the suspect and his supposed hostages. Here's a recent photo of Honor Gillette and her daughter."

The photograph that Honor had sent with last year's Christmas card filled the screen. "Anyone seeing them should alert the authorities immediately. That's all the information I have at this time, but I'll be following this breaking news story throughout the day. Stay tuned for developments as they happen."

The station returned to its broadcast of a game show, morons jumping up and down and squealing over a shiny new vacuum cleaner. Tori muted the sound and tossed the remote into Amber's surprised hands.

"Take over for me with Mrs. Perkins. She's got fifteen

more minutes of cardio. Call Pam and tell her to take my one o'clock with Clive Donovan and to cover my spin class at three. Don't call me unless there's an emergency, and for godsake don't forget to set the alarm and lock the door when you close up tonight."

"Where are you going?"

Tori didn't bother answering as she brushed past Amber. She didn't owe her employee or her clients an explanation. Her best friend had been reported kidnapped. *Kidnapped*, for crissake. And Emily, too.

She had to do something, and she would start by going home and getting herself ready for whatever the rest of the day might bring, although she dreaded to think what that might be.

She was in her office for no longer than it took to grab her cell phone and her handbag, then she left by the employee door at the back of the health club and got into her Corvette. She gunned it to life and roared from the parking lot.

The car was as responsive to Tori's high-speed driving as Tori had been to the clumsy sexual forays of the husband who'd bought the car for her. He'd been a type-A in the boardrooms of his various businesses, but confidence deserted him in the bedroom. Tori had set her mind to making the sweet, shy man feel like King Kong between the sheets. She'd succeeded. To the point that he'd suffered a stroke and died before their first wedding anniversary.

That had been the only one of her three marriages to end involuntarily. She'd been sad for weeks following his death because she'd actually been fond of Mr. Shirah. That's why she'd kept his name when she had two others to choose from in addition to her maiden name. Besides, she liked the sound of it. Tori Shirah. It had an exotic ring to it that suited her style and flamboyant personality.

Her other reason for remembering him fondly was that his legacy to her had financed the construction of her sleek and sexy fitness center, the first and only of its kind anywhere near Tambour.

As she drove, she punched in Honor's cell phone number. It went straight to voice mail. Cursing a red light she sped through, she scrolled her contact list to see if she had a number for Stan Gillette. She did. She called it. Same thing. Straight to voice mail.

She whipped around a school bus that was hauling kids to day camp, and a block later reached the driveway of her condo. She brought the Vette to a screeching halt and within seconds was inside her house. She dropped her purse onto the floor of her entryway, stepped over it, and went down the hallway, pulling her workout top over her head as she went.

She flung the top onto her bed as a voice behind her said, "Are they as firm as they used to be?"

"What the—" She spun around. Leering at her from behind her bedroom door was Doral Hawkins. "What the hell? You scared the shit out of me, Doral!"

"That was the plan."

"You always were an asshole." Indifferent to her bare chest, she placed her hands on her hips. "What are you doing here?"

"I called your club. The bimbo who answered the phone told me you'd just left. I was only a coupla blocks away."

"You couldn't have waited for me outside like a normal person?"

"I could have, but the scenery is better in here."

She rolled her eyes. "*Again*...what are you doing here? You know about Fred, right?"

"I found his body."

"Oh. That's awful."

"Tell me."

"Sorry."

"Thanks."

She was becoming so exasperated, she wanted to shake him. "Maybe I'm dense, Doral, but I still don't get why you're here when your brother's just been murdered. Seems to me like you'd have other things to do besides ogling my tits."

"I have some questions to put to Honor."

"Honor?"

"*Honor?*" he repeated, mimicking her. Dropping the amicable pose, he advanced on her, took her face between his hands, and mashed her features together until they were distorted. "Unless you want that Botoxed face of yours squashed like a ripe persimmon, you'd better tell me now where Honor's at."

Tori didn't frighten easily, but she wasn't a fool either.

She was well acquainted with Doral Hawkins's reputation. Since losing his charter fishing boat to Katrina, he had no visible means of support, beyond the small stipend the city paid him. Yet he lived very well. She had nothing on which to base her suspicion that Doral was participating in something illegal, but she wouldn't be at all surprised to learn that he was.

He and Fred had been perpetual troublemakers in grade and middle school, bullying fellow students and faculty alike. By high school they were committing petty crimes: stealing hubcaps, knocking out the stadium lights with their deer rifles, terrorizing kids who didn't kowtow. Had it not been for Stan Gillette reining them in, they'd probably have gone off the deep end. Some said his influence had saved them from certain incarceration.

To their credit, they had been very good to Honor after Eddie was killed. But rumors had circulated that, despite Stan's intervention and influence, the pair hadn't been altogether converted to the straight and narrow, and that Fred's becoming a police officer had only served to legalize their bullying.

Tori hadn't had an occasion to test the gossip about their propensity for meanness because she rarely crossed paths with them. When they were in school, she had gone out with Doral a few times. He had grown mean and nasty when she'd stopped him at second base and wouldn't let him go any further. He'd called her a cunt, and she'd fired back that even cunts had standards. He had disliked her ever since.

Now he looked mean and dangerous, and he was hurting her. She'd had enough experience with men to know that showing fear was as good as inviting more abuse. She'd been down that rocky road with husband number one. She'd be damned if she'd go down it again. Even with a cretinous thug like Doral, the best defense was an offense.

She shoved her knee into his crotch.

He yelped, dropped his hands from her face to cup his genitals, and hopped backward out of harm's way.

"Don't touch me again, Doral." She grabbed the workout top she'd discarded moments before and pulled it on over her head. "You're ugly, and you're stupid, and what makes you think I know where Honor is?"

"I'm not fucking around, Tori." He pulled a handgun from a holster at the small of his back.

"Oh no, a gun!" she said in a high falsetto. "Is this the point where I'm supposed to faint? Plead for mercy? Put that thing away before you hurt somebody, namely me."

"I want to know where Honor is."

"Well join the freakin' club!" she shouted. "Everybody wants to know where she is. It appears she's been taken hostage by a killer." She could coax tears from her eyes whenever it was convenient to do so, but the ones that flowed now were for real. "I heard about it on TV and came straight here from the club."

"What for?"

"To get ready in case—"

"In case of what?"

"In case of anything."

"You expect to hear from her." He made it sound like an accusation.

"No. I hope I do, but from what they say about this Coburn guy, I fear the worst."

"Like he'll do away with her and Emily."

"Jeez, you're a genius."

He didn't address the insult. "Has she talked to you recently about Eddie?"

"Of course. She talks about him all the time."

"Yeah, but I mean, has she told you something about Eddie? Something important. Did she share a secret about him?"

She tilted her head to one side and peered into his eyes. "Are you still smoking dope?"

He lurched toward her threateningly. "Cut the crap, Tori. *Has she*?"

"No!" she exclaimed, giving his chest a shove. "What are you talking about? I don't know anything about a secret. What kind of secret?"

He studied her for a moment, as though trying to spot signs of deception, then muttered, "Never mind."

"No, not never mind. Why'd you come here? What are

you after? The same guy who shot your brother took Honor and Emily. Why aren't you out looking for them?"

"I'm not sure he *took* them."

That stunned her. "What do you mean?"

He bent closer still. "You and Honor are like this." He held his hand within an inch of her nose and crossed his middle finger over his index. "If she knew this guy—"

"You mean Coburn?"

"Yes, Coburn. Lee Coburn. Did she know him?"

"Where would Honor have met a freight dock worker turned mass murderer?"

He stared at her for a moment longer, then spun away and left the room, sliding the pistol back into the holster at the small of his back as he lumbered down the hall.

"Hold on." Tori grabbed his elbow and brought him around to face her. "What are you getting at? That the kidnapping is some kind of hoax?"

"I'm not getting at anything." He yanked his arm free of her grip and wrapped his fingers around her arm instead. "But I'm gonna be on you like white on rice. If you hear from your pal Honor, you'd do well to let me know."

She hiked her chin up in defiance of the implied threat. "Or what?"

"Or I'll hurt you, Tori, and I bullshit you not. You may be rich now, but you got that way by selling your pussy to the highest bidder. One dead tramp would be no great loss to the world."

Chapter 19

S*on of a bitch!*"

Coburn hissed the profanity under his breath out of deference to the kid. As for her mother, who'd already frowned at him for a slipped *bullshit* earlier, she was now staring at him as though a horn had grown from the center of his forehead.

He waggled the cell phone. "I guess you heard that."

"That Agent Lee Coburn has been dead for over a year? Yes, I heard that."

"Obviously she hasn't got her facts straight."

"Or I bought into your lies and now I'm—"

"Look," he said, angrily cutting her off. "I didn't ask for you either, okay? You want to go back to your house, take your chances with Doral Hawkins and anybody else who's in The Bookkeeper's pocket? Fine. Go. I'll hold the door open for you."

It wasn't fine, of course, and he wouldn't let her go even if she chose to. On her own, she wouldn't live long. He'd been described as cold and heartless, and the adjectives fit. But even he would be uncomfortable sending a woman and four-year-old to certain death. Besides, she would be useful, now and later, toward building a case against The Bookkeeper. She probably knew a whole lot more than she was aware of. Until he'd wrung every last ounce of information from her, she stayed with him.

On the other hand, she and the kid were going to be a major pain in the ass.

He hadn't counted on having to take care of anybody but himself until Hamilton could bring him in, and that was going to be dangerous enough, what with every gun-wielding yahoo within a hundred miles believing him to be a killer and kidnapper. He'd more or less resigned himself to not making it out of this intact, if he lived through it at all.

But now he was responsible for Honor and Emily Gillette, and with that responsibility came the commitment to seeing that they survived even if he didn't.

Essentially taking back his offer to let her go, he said, "Whether you know it or not, you hold the key that will bust open The Bookkeeper's crime ring."

"For the umpteenth time—"

"You've got it. We just have to figure out what it is and where to find it."

"Then drive me to the nearest FBI office and escort me in. We'll all look for it together."

"I can't."

"Because?"

"Because I can't blow my cover. Not yet. Right now Hawkins and The Bookkeeper think that I'm just the freight dock worker who was lucky enough to get away. An eyewitness to the mass murder. Which is bad. But not nearly as bad as an eyewitness who's also an undercover federal agent. If they discover that, the target on my back gets bigger."

"But the FBI would protect you."

"Like Officer Fred Hawkins of the Tambour P.D. was going to protect you?"

He didn't have to spell it out. She connected the dots. "The Bookkeeper has local FBI agents on his payroll?"

"I'm not willing to bet my life against it, are you?" He gave her time to answer. She didn't, which was as good as her saying, *No, I'm not.* "You wouldn't be sitting there if you didn't believe at least some of what I've told you."

"I'm sitting here because I believe that if you'd intended to hurt us, you would have done so as soon as you arrived yesterday. Also, if everything you've told me is true, then our lives, mine and Emily's, are in danger."

"You're right so far."

"But the main reason I came with you has to do with Eddie."

"What about him?"

"You've raised two questions that I want answered. One, was his death really an accident?"

"It was made to look like it, but I don't think it was."

"I have to know," she said with feeling. "If he died of an accident, that's one thing. Tragic, but acceptable. Fate. God's will. Whatever. But if someone caused the crash that killed him, I want them punished for it."

"Fair enough. What's the second question?"

"Was Eddie a bad cop or a good cop? I know the answer to that one. I want you convinced of it, too."

"I don't care one way or the other," he said, meaning it. "He's dead. All I care about is identifying The Bookkeeper and putting him out of business. The rest of it, including your dead husband's reputation, makes no difference to me."

"Well, it makes a huge difference to me. And it will to Stan." She gestured to the cell phone still in his hand. "I should call him, tell him we're okay."

He shook his head and pocketed the phone.

"He'll be beside himself when we turn up missing."

"I'm sure he will be."

"He'll fear the worst."

"That you're at the mercy of a killer."

"He won't know otherwise. So, please—"

"No."

"That's cruel."

"So's life. You can't call him. I don't trust him."

"You mistrust on principle."

"Now you're catching on."

"But you trust me."

He looked at her askance. "What gave you that idea?"

"To have dragged me along with you, you must trust me to some extent."

"Not as far as I can throw you. Probably even less than you trust me. But, like it or not, we're dependent on each other."

"How is that?"

"You need my protection to survive. I need you in order to get what I came after."

"I've told you repeatedly—"

"I know what you've told me, but—"

"Mommy?"

The kid's voice interrupted him. Honor dragged her vexed gaze off him and looked back at her daughter. "What, sweetheart?"

"Are you mad?"

Honor reached over the car seat and patted Emily's knee. "No, I'm not mad."

"Is Coburn mad?"

Hearing the kid say his name caused his gut to clench. He'd never heard his name spoken in a child's voice. It sounded different.

Honor pasted on a smile and lied through her teeth. "No, he's not mad either."

"He looks mad."

"He's not. He's just…just…"

He did his earnest best not to look angry. "I'm not mad."

The kid didn't buy it. Not entirely, but she switched subjects. "I have to tinkle."

Honor looked at Coburn, a silent question in her expression. He shrugged. "If she's gotta go, she's gotta go."

"Can we drive to a gas station? I could take her—"

"Un-huh. She can go in the bushes."

Honor debated it for about fifteen seconds, then was prompted with a plaintive "Mom-mee." She opened the car door and got out. As she helped Emily from the backseat, she told her that they were going to have an adventure and led her by the hand to the rear of the car.

Coburn heard nothing more except a few conspiratorial whispers. Emily giggled once. He tried to block out the practical implications of a female having to pee in the great outdoors and instead to concentrate on more pressing problems. Like deciding what to do next. As Honor had said, they couldn't keep driving around in a stolen car.

So where could they go? Not to his place. It was sure to be staked out. He didn't trust Stan Gillette to safeguard them. He was in thick with the Hawkins brothers, so chances were good he was crooked. Honor was certain of his love and loyalty to her and Emily, but Coburn wasn't ready to accept that, not without seeing evidence of it for himself. Gillette could also be a law-abiding former Marine who would feel honor-bound to notify the authorities immediately. In which case he still had to be rejected.

The deed done, Emily opened the passenger-side door and grinned across at him. "I did it!"

"Congratulations."

"Can I ride in front?" she asked.

"No, you cannot." Honor guided her into the backseat.

"But I don't have my car seat."

"No, you don't." Honor shot a condemning glance at Coburn for abandoning the kid seat along with her car. "We'll break the rule just this once," she told Emily as she helped her to buckle up.

When Honor was once again in the passenger seat, Coburn asked, "Do you know of someplace we can go?"

"You mean to hide?"

"That's exactly what I mean. We've gotta stay out of sight until I can get through to Hamilton."

She nodded thoughtfully. "I know where we can go."

Tom VanAllen was awakened early that morning with the startling news that Fred Hawkins was dead and that Honor Gillette and her child were missing from their home. Both the murder and the kidnapping were attributed to Lee Coburn.

When Tom shared this news with Janice, she registered total disbelief, and then remorse. "I feel terrible about the unflattering things I said about Fred yesterday."

"If it's any comfort to you, he would have died instantly. He probably didn't feel a thing." He told her about Doral's finding the body.

"That's horrible. They were so close." After a moment

of silence, she asked, "What were they doing at Honor Gillette's house?"

He told her about the discovery of the boat. "It was a few miles from her house, but near enough to worry them, so Fred went to check on her. According to Doral, when Fred arrived he found that the house had been tossed."

"Tossed?"

He described the condition of the house as it had been described to him by Deputy Sheriff Crawford. "Fred's body was lying just inside the front door. Coburn apparently came up behind him."

"Just like he shot Sam Marset."

"Looks like. Anyway, I need to go, see it for myself."

He hated having to leave the house before helping her with the arduous morning routine of getting Lanny cleaned, dressed, and fed. Because he couldn't chew or swallow, Lanny got his nourishment through a feeding tube. Mealtimes weren't pleasant.

Janice, however, was understanding about duty taking him away. She told him she could handle things at the house and for him not to worry. "This is a crisis situation. You're needed." As she saw him off, she whispered in his ear, "Be careful," and even went up on tiptoe to kiss his cheek.

Most of his work was done sitting behind a desk. He supposed that the exciting elements of this case represented to Janice more of what she'd had in mind when he told her he wanted to become an agent for the FBI. He surprised and pleased her by kissing her back.

He got lost twice on the back roads but finally found the Gillette place, arriving just as Crawford was about to leave. The two introduced themselves and shook hands. Crawford brought him up to speed.

"I've turned it over to our CSU. They've got their hands

full with this one. Your agents have come and gone. They're meeting me back in town, where we'll set up phone lines, organize a task force, divide the labor. Tambour P.D. has offered us space for a command center on their top floor."

"Yes, I talked to my men on my drive down. I emphasized that cooperation is key, and that priority one is to find Mrs. Gillette and the child before they come to harm."

Crawford looked at him with an implied *Duh*, which Tom tried to disregard. "Anything enlightening come from Doral Hawkins?"

"Not much. He says he received an excited call from his brother just as dawn was breaking. Got here as fast as he could. Fred's boat was tied up at the dock. First sign that something was out of joint, the front door of the house was standing open."

"What did he make of the mess inside?" Tom asked.

"You mean in addition to his brother's body? Made the same thing I did of it. Somebody—we gotta presume Coburn—was searching for something."

"Like what?"

"Anybody's guess."

"Was it found?"

"Anybody's guess. Nobody seems to know what Coburn was after. Not Doral, not Mrs. Gillette's father-in-law."

He told Tom about Stan Gillette's untimely arrival at the crime scene and described the former Marine down to his spit-and-polished shoes. "He's a real hard-ass, but in his present situation, I probably wouldn't be a nice guy either," the deputy admitted.

The investigator took his leave, but gave Tom permission to walk through the house. He was conscientious to stay out of the way of the technicians who were painstakingly picking through the mess, trying to gather evidence. He was in and out in a matter of minutes.

His drive back to Lafayette from the Gillette place took over an hour, and when he walked into his office, he did so relieved that the obligatory errand was behind him.

But no sooner had he sat down at his desk than the office line rang. He depressed the blinking intercom button. "Yes?"

"Deputy Director Hamilton is calling from Washington."

Tom's stomach dropped like a plunging elevator. He cleared his throat, swallowed, thanked the receptionist, and depressed the other blinking button. "Agent VanAllen."

"Hi, Tom. How are you?"

"Fine, sir. You?"

Clint Hamilton, with customary brusqueness, cut straight to the reason for the call. "You've got a dung heap of trouble down there."

Tom, wondering how in hell Hamilton had gotten wind of it, hedged. "It's been a busy couple of days."

"Fill me in."

Tom talked for the next five minutes without interruption. Several times, he paused to make sure that they hadn't been accidentally disconnected. During those pauses, Hamilton didn't speak, but Tom could hear him breathing, so he kept talking.

When he finished, Hamilton remained quiet for several moments, long enough for Tom to dab at his damp upper lip with his pocket handkerchief. Hamilton had placed a lot of confidence in him. That faith in his abilities was now being tested, and he didn't want Hamilton to find him lacking.

When Hamilton finally spoke, he stunned Tom with a question. "Was he one of your agents?"

"I beg your pardon?"

"This man Coburn. Was he an agent working undercover for you to investigate Sam Marset's trucking interests?"

"No, sir. I never heard of him until I went to the crime scene at the warehouse and learned from Fred Hawkins the name of the suspect."

"Fred Hawkins who's now dead."

"Correct."

After another noticeable pause, Hamilton said, "Okay, continue."

"I...uh...I forgot—"

"You were telling me that agents from your office are working hand in glove with the Tambour P.D."

"Yes, sir. I didn't want to sweep in there and piss them off. The warehouse murders are their jurisdiction. The sheriff's office has Fred Hawkins's homicide. But once it's determined that Mrs. Gillette has indeed been kidnapped—"

Hamilton rudely interrupted him. "I know about jurisdiction, Tom. Let's go back to Sam Marset. He would have been in a perfect position to engage in illegal interstate trafficking."

Tom cleared his throat. "Yes, sir."

"Has any such connection been drawn?"

"No, nothing so far." He told Hamilton about the search of every truck in the fleet, the questioning of each driver and other employees. "I've assigned agents to track down and interview anyone that we can place in and around that warehouse in the last thirty days, but so far no illegal contraband has been discovered."

"What motive did the suspect have for killing his boss and fellow employees?"

"We're trying to ascertain that, sir. But Coburn's lifestyle is making it difficult."

"In what way?"

"He's been described as a loner. No friends, family, little interaction with coworkers. Nobody knew him well. The people—"

"Give it your best shot, Tom," Hamilton said with palpable impatience. "Take a guess. Why'd he kill them?"

"He was a disgruntled employee."

"A disgruntled employee." Hamilton said it without inflection, certainly without enthusiasm.

Tom thought it smart to keep quiet.

Eventually Hamilton said, "If Coburn's only beef was with his boss, if he wigged out over a slight he suffered on the loading dock, or because he was shortchanged on overtime pay, why'd he go to the house of a dead cop and turn it upside down? If he was fleeing the scene of a mass murder, why'd he hide out with the widow and child for an estimated twenty-four hours? And if he took them, why did he? Why not just dispose of them right then and there? Doesn't that atypical behavior bother you like a popcorn hull stuck in your teeth?"

These weren't rhetorical questions. Tom had worked in the Lafayette field office with Clint Hamilton only briefly, but it had been long enough for him to learn that the man didn't waste his breath on unnecessary words.

When Hamilton was bumped up to Washington, D.C., leapfrogging the district office in New Orleans, he had recommended Tom as his successor, and, even at the time, Tom had been aware that Hamilton's endorsement of him had been met with skepticism by some and vociferous opposition by others. Hamilton had fought for Tom, and he'd won the fight.

Each day when he entered the office where Hamilton had once sat, Tom felt pride in succeeding such an able, revered, even feared agent. He also experienced a cold panic that he wouldn't live up to the other man's standards or expectations. In any capacity.

If he were being baldly honest with himself, he would even go so far as to wonder if Hamilton had tossed him a bone because of Lanny. It made him hot with humiliation and indignation even to consider that his appointment had been extended out of pity, but he feared such was the case.

He also wondered where Hamilton was getting his information. He didn't just know about Marset's murder and what had happened afterward, but he was well informed of the details. Meaning that he had consulted someone in the local office even before calling Tom. That rankled.

However, he didn't want Hamilton to discern his self-doubt, so he affected a confident tone. "I've asked those questions myself, sir. They're unsettling."

"To say the least. They imply that this was no mental malfunction, no ordinary shoot-'em-up by some nutcase with personality issues. Which means, Tom, that you've got your work cut out for you."

"Yes, sir."

"First order of business, find them."

"Yes, sir."

After a pregnant pause the length of an aircraft carrier, Hamilton said a brisk, "I'll be standing by," then clicked off.

Chapter 20

———⟫•⟪———

Following the directions Honor gave him, Coburn drove the stolen car down the narrow dirt lane. It was overgrown with weeds and saplings that knocked against the car's underside. Forty yards from their destination, he rolled to a stop and stared in dismay at the derelict shrimp boat, then turned his head and looked pointedly at Honor.

Defensively she asked, "Do you have a better idea?"

"Yeah. We don't launch it."

He took his foot off the brake and continued on, approaching with caution, although it was virtually impossible that anyone would be lying in wait to ambush them on the hulk. A person would have to be crazy to board the vessel, which seemed about to collapse in on itself at any second.

"Who does it belong to?" he asked.

"To me. I inherited it when my dad died."

Coburn knew virtually nothing about marine craft of any size, but he'd been in coastal Louisiana long enough to recognize an inshore shrimp trawler. "He shrimped in that thing?"

"He lived on it."

The craft looked about as seaworthy as a broken match-stick. It sat half in, half out of a sluggish channel that Honor claimed eventually fed into the Gulf. But from this vantage point, the waterway looked like a stagnant creek.

Coburn guessed that the boat hadn't been afloat for years. Vines had overtaken the hull. The wheelhouse paint, what was left of it, was curled and peeling. Windowpanes that weren't missing altogether were cracked and so coated with grime they barely resembled glass. The metal frame supporting the butterfly net on the port side was bent prac-tically at a forty-five-degree angle, making it look like the broken wing of a great bird.

But for all those reasons, it had been abandoned, prob-ably forgotten, and that worked in their favor.

"Who knows it's here?" he asked.

"No one. Dad brought it here to ride out Katrina, then decided to stay. He lived here till he got sick and went downhill fast. I moved him into a hospice house. He was there less than a week when he died."

"How long ago was this?"

"Only a few months before Eddie's accident. Which made Eddie's dying all the more difficult for me." She smiled ruefully. "But I was glad Dad didn't live to see me widowed. That would have been very upsetting to him."

"Your mother?"

"Died years before that. That's when Dad sold the house, moved onto the boat."

"Does your father-in-law know it's here?"

She shook her head. "Stan didn't exactly approve of my dad's way of life, which was rather...bohemian. Stan discouraged visits with him. He especially didn't like Emily being exposed to him."

"Exposed? Bohemianism is contagious?"

"Stan seemed to think so."

"You know," he said, "the more I hear about this father-in-law of yours, the less I like him."

"He's probably thinking the same of you."

"I won't lose sleep over it."

"I'm sure you won't." She pushed back her hair and, after a moment of staring at the boat, said, "Stan means well."

"Does he?"

That touched a sore spot. She came around to him quickly. "What business is it of yours?"

"Right now, it's my business to know if he'll look for us on this damn heap."

"No."

"Thank you."

He opened his door and got out. A snake slithered past his boot. He swore under his breath. He wasn't especially afraid of snakes, but he'd just as soon avoid them.

He opened the door to the backseat and reached in for Emily, who'd already unbuckled her seat belt and was holding her arms up to him. He lifted her out, then carried her around to the other side and passed her to Honor.

"Don't set her down. I saw a . . ." He stopped himself, then spelled out the word.

Honor's eyes went wide with fear as she inspected the ground. "A water moccasin?"

"I didn't ask."

He slipped the pistol from his waistband, but palmed it quickly when Emily turned to him. "Coburn?"

"What?"

"Are we still on a 'venture?"

"I guess you could call it that."

"Mommy said."

"Then, yeah, we're on an adventure."

"Can we be on it for a long time?" she chirped. "It's fun."

Oh, yeah, this is a blast, he thought as he went ahead of them, cautiously picking his way to the boat. The name of it was barely legible because of the peeling paint, but he could make it out. He gave Honor a significant look from over his shoulder. A look she ignored.

By design, the sides of the hull were shallow. He stepped aboard easily, but his boot settled into a nest of Spanish moss and other natural debris. His trained eyes looked around for signs that someone had been there recently, but cobwebs and forest detritus were evidence that the deck hadn't been disturbed for some time, probably not since the day that Honor's dad had been moved to a hospice house to die.

Satisfied that they were alone, he kicked aside the clump of moss to clear a spot for Emily when Honor passed her up to him. He set her down on the deck. "Don't move."

"Okay, Coburn, I won't."

Once she'd broken the barrier of using his name, it seemed she welcomed every opportunity to do so.

He leaned down, extended his hand to Honor, and helped her up and over. Once aboard, she surveyed the littered deck. Coburn noticed a sadness in her expression before she shook it off and said briskly, "This way."

She took Emily's hand and told her to be careful where she stepped, then led them around the wheelhouse to the door, where she halted and looked back at Coburn. "Maybe you should go first."

He stepped around her and pushed open the door,

which resisted until he put his shoulder to it. The interior of
the wheelhouse was in no better condition than the deck.
The control panel was covered with a littered tarp that had
collected small lakes of scummy rainwater. A tree branch
had broken through one of the windows so long ago that a
good crop of lichen had had time to grow on its bark.

Honor surveyed it with evident despondency. But all
she said was, "Below," and pointed to a narrow passage with
steps leading down.

He descended carefully, and had to duck to keep from
hitting his head when he squeezed through an oval opening into a low-ceilinged cabin. It smelled of mildew and rot,
brine and dead fish, motor oil and marijuana.

Coburn looked behind him at Honor who was poised
on the steps. "He smoked weed?"

She admitted it with a small shrug.

"Do you know where he kept his stash?"

She glared, and he gave her a grin, then turned his
attention back to the compact chamber. It had a two-
burner propane stove that was ghosted over with cobwebs.
The door of the small refrigerator stood open. Empty.

"Electricity?" Coburn asked.

"There's a generator. I don't know if it still works."

Doubtful, Coburn thought. He opened two pantry
doors that revealed mouse droppings but otherwise bare
shelves. There were two bunks separated by an aisle no
more than a foot wide. He pointed to a door at the back of
the cabin. "The head?"

"I don't recommend it. I didn't even when Dad lived
here."

In fact, there was nothing to recommend the boat
except that it seemed watertight. The floor was a mess, but
it was dry.

"Can we stay here?" she asked.

"Hopefully we won't have to for more than a few hours."

"Then what?"

"I'm working on it."

He went to one of the bunks and peeled back the bare mattress, checking beneath it for varmints. Finding none, he turned to Honor and held his hands out for Emily. Honor handed her over. He deposited her on the mattress.

She wrinkled her nose. "It smells bad."

"Tough," Coburn said. "Sit there and don't get down."

"Is this gonna be our house?"

"No, sweetheart," Honor said with forced gaiety as she squeezed into the cabin behind Coburn. "We're just visiting. Remember when Grandpa lived here?"

The child shook her head. "Grandpa lives in a house."

"Not Grandpa Stan. Your other grandpa. He lived on this boat. You used to love coming here to see him."

Emily looked at her blankly.

Coburn could tell that Emily's lost memory of her grandfather caused Honor heartache, but she put up a brave front. "This is part of our adventure."

The kid was perceptive enough to recognize a lie when she heard one, but she was also smart enough to stay quiet when her mother was on the verge of losing it. Seeing through Honor's false enthusiasm, she held her bankie close and turned on Elmo, who broke into cheerful song.

Honor spoke in a whisper. "Coburn, we've got to get some food and water at least."

"By we you mean me."

She had the grace to look chagrined. "I did, yes. I'm sorry." She raised her hands at her sides. "I haven't been here since I buried Dad. I didn't realize..." She ran out of things to say and looked at him with helplessness. "Please let me call Stan."

Rather than go through that tired routine, Coburn opened a narrow closet and found a broom, which he handed to her. "Do your best. I'll be back as soon as I can."

When two hours had passed and he still hadn't returned, Honor began pacing the deck of the trawler, her eyes searching the end of the road that had got them here, willing him to reappear, listening above the call of birds for the welcome sound of an approaching car.

She tried not to convey her concern to Emily, who had become increasingly cantankerous and whiny. She was hot, hungry, thirsty. *Where did Coburn go?* and *When's he coming back?* were questions repeated about every five minutes, until Honor lost what little patience she had remaining and snapped at her. "Stop asking me that."

She didn't know the answers to Emily's nagging questions, but the possible answers terrified her. Her overriding fear was that Coburn had abandoned them.

Her father had chosen to dock his boat here specifically because the surrounding forest was swampy, virtually impenetrable, and would provide some shelter from hurricanes. He'd chosen to "retire" here because he liked the isolation of the place. It was off the beaten path and hard to get to. Moreover, he didn't have to pay rent for a slip at a marina, and here he could avoid other pesky interferences with his freedom, things like rules and regulations, laws and ordinances, fines, and taxes.

He became a virtual hermit, avoiding contact with the outside world as much as possible. To her knowledge, she and Emily were the only other persons ever to come here. Not even Eddie had visited with her.

Coburn had asked her if she knew of a good place to
hide. This was an excellent choice, but now she wished she
had kept it to herself. The qualities that made it a good hiding place were the same ones that might do her in. The
closest connection to civilization was a two-lane state road,
and it was more than five miles from here. She couldn't
walk that, not with Emily in tow, and not without water.

She was stuck here until Coburn returned or...

She didn't allow herself to think of the *or.* When the sun
set and it grew dark, how would she keep Emily from being
afraid? How would she maintain her own courage? She was
completely without resources or means of communication.

Coburn had refused to leave a cell phone with her.

"I swear I won't use it."

"Then why do you want me to leave it?"

"We could have an emergency. A snakebite."

"Stay out of their way, and they won't hurt you."

"I'm sure there are alligators."

"They're not Jaws. They won't jump into the boat."

"You can't just leave us here like this!"

"No, I could tie you up."

That had silenced her. She had wanted to fly at him, but
didn't want to do so in front of Emily. A fight between them
would frighten her, and Honor knew it would be futile anyway,
resulting in nothing except sorer muscles and more bruises.

She absently rubbed at one on her elbow, growing
even more resentful of Coburn's desertion and her own
fear. She wasn't helpless. She'd been a single parent, living
alone, in a remote place, for more than two years. She had
confronted every problem bravely because she'd had no
choice. Sure, Stan, the twins, other friends had been there
to lend support. If she got in a pinch and asked for help,
they came running.

This time was different. She was entirely alone.

But, by God, she wasn't helpless. She—

"Coburn!" Emily cried.

She launched herself from the crate on which she'd been sitting and skipped across the deck, throwing herself against him and wrapping her arms around his knees. "Did you bring me something? Mommy said you were going to bring me some lunch."

Honor's heart was in her throat. He was standing on the deck only yards away from her, but she hadn't heard a sound to signal his approach. He was wearing a baseball cap and sunglasses, which he now removed, hooking one stem on the neck of his T-shirt. Eddie's T-shirt, she reminded herself. His boots and pants legs from midcalf down were wet, dripping water onto the filthy deck.

Seeing that she noticed, he said, "I came around along the creek bank."

Emily was bouncing up and down on her toes. Without taking his eyes off Honor, he fished a Tootsie Pop from the pocket of his jeans and handed it down to her. She didn't even ask Honor's permission before ripping off the purple wrapper.

"What do you say, Emily?"

"Thank you, Coburn. I love grape. Grape's my favorite."

Sourly, Honor thought that any flavor Coburn had brought her would have instantly become her favorite. She didn't even ask permission to have the candy before lunch, but stuck the lollipop into her mouth.

Honor let it pass. "Why did you come by way of the creek? Where's the car?"

"I left it back a piece. Someone could have found you. I didn't want to drive into a trap." He looked at her knowingly. "You thought I'd ditched you here, didn't you?"

Without saying more, he stepped off the boat and began walking toward the road.

Emily pulled the Tootsie Pop from her mouth and wailed, "Where's he going?"

"Good grief, Emily, he'll be right back." Her daughter's blind admiration for him was beginning to grate.

In only a few minutes he returned, driving a pickup truck, whose black paint job had been scoured gray by the salty Gulf air. It was several years old and boasted an LSU Tigers bumper sticker. It looked to Honor like hundreds of other black pickups that had suffered the effects of the corrosive coastal climate, boasting an LSU Tigers bumper sticker. Which she was sure was the very reason he'd stolen it.

He brought it to a stop near the boat, got out, and lifted several bags from the bed. "Give me a hand." He passed the bags up to Honor and went back for more. After handing them up to her, he said, "I'm gonna hide the truck."

"Why?"

"Somebody could shoot out the tires."

She didn't ask how he thought the three of them could make it to the truck on foot in the event of a shootout. Obviously he was more experienced than she in these matters.

By the time he came aboard and clumped down the steps, she'd made three peanut butter and banana sandwiches. She and Emily sat on one bunk, he on the other. Happily Emily asked, "Is this a picnic?"

"Sort of." Honor leaned down to kiss her forehead, feeling apologetic for snapping at her earlier.

The sacks Coburn had carried in contained foods that were ready to eat and didn't require refrigeration. He'd also brought a pack of bottled water, a battery-operated lantern, an aerosol can of insect repellent, wet wipes, and a squeeze bottle of hand sanitizer.

Once she'd been fed, Emily yawned. She protested when Honor suggested that she lie down and rest, but she was soon asleep.

Coburn helped himself to a package of cookies. "You worked wonders on the place."

Honor looked across at him from where she sat fanning Emily with an outdated magazine she'd found in a drawer. "Are you being sarcastic?"

"No."

After he'd left, she'd put the broom to use, sweeping trash from off the floor and cobwebs from every surface. She'd found a couple of sheets folded up in the storage box that formed the platform for one of the bunks. She'd taken them on deck to shake them out, then had spread them over the bunks. The sheets no longer had bugs or larvae in them, although they still smelled of mildew. They were, however, less objectionable than the stained bare mattresses.

"I didn't venture into the head," she admitted.

"Probably wise. I saw a couple of buckets on deck. I'll fill them with creek water. You and Emily can use those."

She was glad that troublesome subject had been addressed, but she moved away from discussing it further. "Now that we've got water, I can wipe down some of the surfaces we're forced to touch."

"Be stingy with the water."

"I will." Then she asked him the questions that had been plaguing her. "Were you able to reach your man? Hamilton?"

"I tried. Same woman answered. I demanded she put him on. She insisted that I was dead."

"What do you make of that?"

He shrugged and bit into a cookie. "Hamilton doesn't want to talk to me yet."

"What do you make of *that*?"

"Nothing."

"You're not worried?"

"I don't panic unless I have to. Wastes energy."

She stored that for later rumination or discussion. "Did you check Fred's cell phone for stored numbers?"

"There were none, which is what I expected. And only one call in his log, that last one to his brother. This phone was a throw-down."

"A burner," she said, remembering the term he'd used before.

"No records. Disposable. Virtually untraceable."

"Like yours."

"Saved for a rainy day. Anyway, my guess is that he used this phone to stay in contact with his brother and The Book-keeper, and that he immediately erased numbers from the call log. If I ever get it into the hands of techies, they can tear into it and see if possibly there's any intel to be had. But for right now, Fred's phone isn't of much help to us. All the same, I'll keep the battery out of it."

"Why?"

"I haven't kept up with the technology, but I think there are experts who can locate a phone even if it's turned off. All they need is the phone number. As long as there's a battery in the phone, it's transmitting a signal."

"Is that true?"

He shrugged. "I've picked up buzz."

"How long would it take? To locate a phone, I mean."

"No idea. That's not my area of expertise, but I'm not going to take any chances."

Forty-eight hours ago, she wouldn't have imagined herself having a conversation about intel and burners and such things. Nor would she have imagined a man like Coburn, who could eat Chips Ahoy at the same time he was discussing a man he'd killed only a few hours earlier.

She didn't know quite what to make of Lee Coburn, and it was disturbing that she wanted to make anything of him at all.

Changing the subject, she asked, "Where'd you get the truck?"

"I got lucky. I spotted a rural mailbox with lots of mail in it, a dead giveaway that the residents are away. House sits way back off the road. The truck keys were hanging on a peg inside the back door. Just like at your house. I helped myself. Hopefully the owners will stay gone for at least a few more days and the truck won't be reported stolen."

"I assume you switched the license plates with another vehicle."

"S.O.P." Reading her blank look, he said, "Standard operating procedure. Remember that if you decide to pursue a life of crime."

"I doubt that will happen."

"So do I."

"I don't think I'm cut out for living on the edge."

He gave her a slow once-over. "You may surprise yourself." When his gaze reconnected with hers, it was hot and intense.

Uncomfortably, she looked away from it. "Did you buy or steal the groceries?"

"Bought."

She remembered the money he'd been carrying in the pocket of the jeans. "You weren't afraid of being identified?"

"The cap and sunglasses were in the console of the truck."

"I recognized you in them."

He chuckled. "They weren't looking at me."

"They?"

"I stopped at a bait shop out in the middle of nowhere. Slow day. No other customers in the place. Only the bottled-water delivery truck in the parking lot."

She cast a glance at the twenty-four bottles encased in plastic. "You stole that off the truck?"

"Piece of cake. When I went into the store, the delivery-man was behind the counter with the cashier. His hand was inside her pants and his mouth was on her nipple. They had eyes only for each other. I grabbed my stuff, paid, and got out quick. They won't remember me at all, only the interruption."

Honor's cheeks burned with embarrassment over the images he'd conjured. She wondered if the story was true, and even if it was, why had he painted such a vivid picture? To fluster her? Well, she was flustered, but if Coburn cared or noticed, he gave no indication of it as he checked his wristwatch.

"I'll try Hamilton again."

Using his own phone, he redialed the number, and this time Honor heard a man answer. "Hamilton."

"You son of a bitch. Why are you fucking me over?"

He replied blandly, "A man in my position can't be too careful, Coburn. If the caller ID is blocked, I don't answer."

"I identified myself."

"After I heard the news, I would have known it was you anyway. You're in a world of hurt. Or should I say a vat of gumbo?"

"Oh, that's real funny."

"Not so much. Mass murder. Kidnapping. You've out-done yourself, Coburn."

"Like I need you to tell me that. If I wasn't in trouble, I wouldn't be calling."

Switching to a more serious tone, the man on the other end said, "Is speculation correct? Do you have the woman?"

"And her kid."

"Are they all right?"

"Yeah, they're fine. We've been picnicking." After a weighty, sustained silence, Coburn said again, "They're *fine.* You want to talk to her yourself?"

Without waiting for an answer, he passed the phone to Honor. Her hands were trembling as she raised it to her ear. "Hello?"

"Mrs. Gillette?"

"Yes."

"My name is Clint Hamilton. I want you to listen carefully. Please, for your child's sake as well as your own, don't underestimate the importance of what I'm about to tell you."

"All right."

"You, Mrs. Gillette, are in the company of a very dangerous man."

Chapter 21

Tori had slammed her front door hard behind Doral, flipped the deadbolt, then for half an hour had railed at herself for not slapping the fire out of Doral Hawkins over his parting remark.

But even long after he'd left her house and she'd had time to calm down somewhat, his threat echoed. It had been unsettling to say the least. She wasn't as afraid for herself, however, as she was for Honor.

Tori was self-sufficient, independent, and accustomed to taking care of herself. But she wasn't above asking for help if she deemed it necessary. She placed a call.

"Tori, sweetheart. I was just thinking about you."

His voice immediately soothed her raw nerves. Matching his sexy tone, she asked, "What were you thinking?"

"I was just sitting here daydreaming, wondering if you're wearing panties."

"Of course not. I'm my horny self. Why do you think I called you?"

That pleased him. He gurgled an ex-smoker's chuckle. He was thirty pounds overweight and had bright capillaries on his nose from imbibing oceans of bourbon over the course of his fifty-eight years. But he could afford to drink the best.

His name was Bonnell Wallace, and he had more money than God, which he kept in the New Orleans bank that had been privately held by his family since the Spanish had governed Louisiana or since the beginning of time, whichever had come first.

His beloved wife of thirty-something years had succumbed to cancer a year ago. Fearing the same fate, Bonnell had tossed the cigarettes, cut back to five or six drinks a day, and joined Tori's health club. Which more or less had sealed his future.

He'd become husband candidate number four, and that was fine by him because he thought the sun rose and set inside the panties she claimed not to be wearing.

"Will you do something for me, Bonnell?"

"You name it, sugar."

"A friend of mine is in danger. The life-or-death kind."

Instantly, he dropped his bantering tone. "Jesus."

"I may need some money on short notice."

"How much?"

Just like that. No questions asked. Her heart swelled with affection.

"Don't agree so fast. I'm talking serious cash. Like a million or more." Tori was thinking in terms of a ransom, and wondered what the going rate was for the safe return of a young widow and her daughter. "I'm good for it. But I may not be able to access my accounts in time."

"Tell me what's going on. How else can I help?"

"Have you heard about the woman and child who were kidnapped this morning?"

He had. Tori filled in the blanks. "I can't even think about what she and Emily might be going through. I don't know what to do, but I can't just sit here and do nothing. With your help, I can at least have cash on standby if her father-in-law gets a call from their abductor. Stan's financially stable, but he won't have that kind of money."

"You just let me know what you need, when you need it, and it's yours." He paused, then said, "I'm only a phone call away, Tori. Good Christ, you must be worried sick. Do you want me to come and stay with you?"

Because of his grown children, and because of her policy that employees of the club were not to date the clientele, they had kept their affair a secret. His willingness to drop everything, leave the bank in the middle of a workday, and rush to her aid signified more than just courtesy and concern.

In a voice choked with emotion, she said, "Have I told you what a sweetheart you are? How important you are to me?"

"You mean it?"

"I do," she said, speaking with an unmitigated honesty that surprised her.

"Well, that's good. Because I feel the same."

When he'd enrolled in her health club, she'd immediately been attracted to his engaging manner. She'd overlooked his portly body and had checked out his portfolio. Realizing his worth, she had set her sights on him.

He, having spent the last five years of his marriage nursing his suffering wife, had been ripe for fun, for sex, for Tori's raunchy teasing, flirting, and flattery. Bonnell

Wallace was a feared and revered businessman, shrewd in all his dealings, but he'd been putty in Tori's talented and well-experienced hands.

However, over time she'd formed an attachment to him that was no longer just about snagging another rich husband. Beneath the flab left by good living, she'd discovered a good heart, a good friend, a good man. She had grown genuinely fond of him, and for her, that was as close as she was ever going to get to true love.

They exchanged air kisses and disconnected reluctantly. As she clutched the phone to her chest, her smile lingered for several minutes. But when her doorbell rang, she dropped her phone, bolted to the door, and flung it open.

On her threshold stood Stan Gillette. If it had been Elvis she wouldn't have been as shocked.

She didn't like Honor's father-in-law, and the dislike was returned. In spades. Neither made a secret of their mutual antipathy. It went beyond being on opposite sides of the conservative/liberal coin.

The only thing they had in common was their love for Honor and Emily, and nothing except that shared love could have brought Stan to her doorstep.

Her heart practically stopped. She gripped the door for support. "Oh, God. They're dead?"

"No. At least I hope not. May I come in?"

Weak with relief, she stood aside. He marched—the only word to describe his tread—across her threshold, which he no doubt equated to the gateway to Gomorrah, then stopped and looked around as though assessing an enemy camp. She supposed that to some extent, he was. Her furnishings were tasteful and expensive, but his lips were set with stern disapproval when he turned to her.

"How did you hear?"

She wondered how the man managed to make a simple question sound like he was about to jam bamboo shoots under her fingernails. But the circumstances called for her to be civil. "I saw it on the news."

"You haven't heard from Honor?"

"Why does everyone keep asking me that?"

His eyes narrowed on her. "Who else asked you that?"

"Doral. He was here when I got home from the club. Like you, he seems to think that Honor's kidnapper would call a time out and let her contact me."

"I don't need your sarcasm."

"And I don't need you implying that if I knew what had happened to Honor and Emily I'd be standing here disliking you with every fiber of my being. I'd be out doing something to bring them safely back. Which begs the question, why aren't *you* out there searching for them instead of stinking up my house with your narrow-minded, judgmental self-righteousness?"

So much for civility.

He bristled. "Can you think for one nanosecond that I care more about insulting you than I do about the welfare of my son's widow and child, the only family I have left?" Tori understood exactly where he was coming from. Her concern for Honor and Emily overrode her hatred of him. Having had her outburst, she backed down. "No, Stan, I don't think that at all. I know you love them." *In your overbearing and possessive fashion,* she was tempted to add, but didn't. "You must be going through hell."

"To put it mildly."

"Why don't you sit down? Can I get you anything? Water? Soft drink? *Stiff* drink?"

He almost smiled before catching himself. "No. Thanks." He didn't sit, but stood in the center of her living room, looking ill at ease.

"I love them, too, you know," she said softly. "How can I help? What do you know that the media doesn't?"

"Nothing. Not really."

He told her about his conversation with Doral and Deputy Crawford. "The house was a wreck. Crawford seemed more interested in knowing what might be missing from it, as if the fact that Honor and Emily were missing were secondary."

"He's a deputy sheriff in a backwater parish. Is he up to the task of getting them back in one piece?"

"I hope so. Of course the FBI is on the case, too. They've also called in assistance from other parishes and the New Orleans P.D." He took a turn around the room, but she could tell he was preoccupied.

"Something is bothering you. What?"

He turned back to her. "It may be nothing." For several seconds, he wrestled with the decision to air his concern, then asked a seemingly unrelated question. "Have you ever tucked Emily in for the night?"

"As recently as two weeks ago. Honor had me out for burgers on the grill. We put Emily down, then kicked back and killed a bottle of wine."

By telling him that, she was hitting below the belt, because he considered her a bad influence on Honor.

From the moment they were introduced, he'd regarded her as a slut, unsuitable friend material for the daughter-in-law of Stanley Gillette. Which, from Tori's standpoint, was just too effing bad. She and Honor's friendship had been forged when they were girls, and it had endured despite the divergent paths their lives had taken.

She admired Honor's way of life, but she didn't envy it. Not for her was the home-and-hearth scene. Marrying your high school sweetheart wasn't her idea of hot romance. Eddie had been an excellent husband and father, and she had liked him for loving Honor and making her happy. His death had been a tragedy.

But Stan kept him alive and present to the point where Honor felt guilty if she as much as contemplated dating. That had been one topic they'd discussed over that excellent bottle of Pinot Noir.

Not for the first time, Tori had urged Honor to start going out, to meet new people, specifically men. "Your period of grieving has been twice the accepted time. You need to kick up your heels, and I mean that in the most literal sense. What's the holdup?"

"It would break Stan's heart if I began dating," Honor had replied wistfully.

Tori had argued that she wasn't married to Stan, and who cared what he thought anyway.

Apparently Honor did. Because she was letting Stan prevent her from having a future. He was keeping her shackled to the past and to a husband who was dead and buried.

But that was an issue for another day. Today, they had to deal with one much more pressing. "What about tucking Emily in?" she asked.

"She always sleeps with two things."

"Her bankie and Elmo."

"They weren't in her bed this morning." While Tori processed that, he continued. "They weren't in Honor's bed either. I didn't see them anywhere."

"A kidnapper who let Em take her bedtime pals along? Hmm." She thought back to Doral's insinuation that the supposed kidnapping might not have been that at all. What was Honor into?

As though reading her mind, Stan said, "I believe in keeping confidences."

She didn't touch that.

"I know how close Honor is to you. I don't understand the friendship. I don't approve of it. But I respect it."

"Okay."

"But these are critical circumstances, Victoria."

His use of her full name underscored how critical the circumstances were. As if she needed him to emphasize that to her.

"If Honor has confided to you—"

"That she's involved with a man named Lee Coburn? Is that what you're waltzing around? Save the dance steps, Stan. The answer is no. Honor doesn't confide in me every thought and feeling she has, but I think I would know if she was seeing someone. Hell, I'd be celebrating it. But if she knew this man at all, I swear to you that I'm unaware of it."

He received her answer with characteristic stoicism. He coughed behind his fist, indicating to her that there was more on his mind. "Crawford asked Doral a lot of questions about Eddie. Crawford seems to be working under the delusion that there's a link to him in all this."

"I guess that explains why Doral asked me about it."

"What did Doral ask you?"

"If Honor had recently revealed a secret about Eddie." She shrugged. "I accused him of being high."

"Then there's no such secret?"

She gaped at him for several seconds, then looked around her familiar living room, almost expecting to see writing on the walls that would explain to her why every-one seemed to have lost their minds. When she came back to him, she said, "Stan, I have no idea what you're talking about."

"I won't tolerate any negative implications about my son."

"The deputy's implications were negative?"

"Not precisely. But it sounds to me as though he's trying to draw a connection between Eddie and what happened at Sam Marset's warehouse on Sunday night. That's preposterous. I don't know why Coburn sought out Honor and turned her house upside down, but both he and Crawford are mistaken if they think Eddie was involved in anything…"

Tori supplied the word he couldn't bring himself to speak. "Illegal." She waited; Stan said nothing. "I agree with you. Eddie was a Boy Scout, a model citizen, an honest cop. So what are you worried about?"

"I'm not."

"Could've fooled me." She folded her arms beneath her breasts and assessed him closely. "A team of wild horses couldn't have dragged you into the home of the scarlet woman of Tambour. But here you are in my den of iniquity asking questions that make no sense to me, but obviously do to you. And to Doral."

He remained stubbornly tight-lipped.

She continued. "Doral's brother was killed this morning. Your daughter-in-law and grandchild are missing. Yet this alleged secret, involving a man who's been dead for over two years, has got the two of you barging in on me when you should be out there overturning every stone in search of my friend and her little girl. What gives, Stan?"

Without a word, he strode to the front door and opened it.

"Wait!" She joined him at the threshold. The look he

gave her would curdle milk. She didn't back down from it, but she moderated her tone. "I don't give a rat's ass what you think of me. In fact, I rather enjoy ruffling your American eagle feathers. But I love Honor. I love Emily. I want them back, whole and sound and safe."

He remained rigid and unmoved, but he didn't storm out.

Still speaking in a quiet, reasonable tone, she continued. "Just so you know, I've made arrangements to have a large sum of cash available if and when you get a ransom demand. Don't be stubborn and proud, Stan. Don't be a priggish idiot. Nobody has to know that the money came from my whoring hands. Let me do this. Not for you. For them."

He remained as taciturn as ever, but he said, "Thank you. I'll let you know."

Chapter 22

Honor's eyes remained fixed on Coburn as the man on the telephone repeated to her how dangerous he was. When she didn't respond, Hamilton prompted her. "Mrs. Gillette?"

"Yes," she said hoarsely, "I...I'm listening."

"Coburn is lethal. He's been trained to be. But the fact that he abducted you instead of killing you—"

"He didn't abduct me, Mr. Hamilton. I came with him voluntarily."

Several seconds ticked by before Hamilton said anything. Then he cleared his throat and politely asked if Coburn was treating Emily and her well.

She thought of his threats, real and implied, and the strong-arming, and the battle royal over possession of the pistol, but she also remembered his snatching up Emily's bankie and Elmo as they fled the house. She thought of his taking a chance on being captured to buy them food and water.

And she thought of his coming back rather than deserting them.

She said to Hamilton, "We're all right."

"I'm glad to hear it. Put Coburn back on."

She passed the phone to him. He said into it, "Talk to me."

"You first."

He talked Hamilton through the mass shooting and everything that had transpired since. He was concise and ended by saying, "I had no choice but to get her and the kid out of there. They'd be dead if I hadn't."

"You're certain that this policeman you killed was Sam Marset's assassin."

"I saw him do it."

"Along with his twin."

"Correct."

Hamilton took a deep breath and expelled it loudly. "Okay. Except for the warehouse killer's identity, and the misconception that Mrs. Gillette was kidnapped, that matches everything Tom VanAllen told me."

"Tom VanAllen. Who's VanAllen?"

"My successor down there."

"When did you talk to him?"

"When it became apparent that you'd kicked up a shit storm."

"You talked to this VanAllen before taking my call?"

"I wanted to get a feel for the situation from his perspective. I wanted it unfiltered. I even asked him if you were an agent from his office working undercover."

"Gee, you're a stitch."

"I needed to know what he knew or suspected."

"I'm kinda interested in that myself."

"As far as local law enforcement is concerned, you're

a friendless dock worker who went postal and shot up the place. That's good. Now that I've talked to you, I'll admit to VanAllen that I tricked him in order to get his unbiased assessment, and then I'll enlist him to help bring you and Mrs. Gillette in. Once you, she, and the child are safe, we'll figure out how to go in and mop up."

Coburn frowned, pulled at his lower lip with his teeth, and looked hard at Honor. Finally, he said, "Negative."

"Excuse me?"

"Negative. I don't want to come in yet."

"Don't worry about your cover. It will remain intact. The official word will be that you died of a self-inflicted gunshot wound during a standoff with federal agents. We'll make arrests based on the intel you've gathered so far, but no one will know where it came from. You'll be reassigned to another part of the country, and no one will be the wiser."

"Sounds swell. Except that I haven't finished the job here."

"You've done well, Coburn," Hamilton argued. "You're getting out alive, which is no small accomplishment. And you've fingered some key people in The Bookkeeper's organization. I've got men from San Antonio to key points east, all the way to the Mississippi/Alabama line, standing by to make arrests, soon as I give them the green light. You took out one of The Bookkeeper's main facilitators this morning."

"But we don't have The Bookkeeper."

"I'm satisfied."

"I'm not. Something big is about to happen. I want to put him out of commission before it does."

"Something big, like what?"

"A new client. A Mexican cartel would be my guess. I think that's why Sam Marset was bumped. He was whining over a couple of his trucks getting stopped and searched. Those two weren't hauling anything except potting soil, but it spooked Marset, because he was guaranteed that none of his trucks would be subject to search. The Bookkeeper wanted to shut him up. He doesn't need a complaint department at any time, but especially not now."

Hamilton considered it, then said, "But the new alliance isn't a sure thing."

"It's pending."

"Can you identify the cartel?"

"No. My time ran out Sunday night."

Again Hamilton took several moments to mull it over. Coburn watched Honor watching him.

Finally Hamilton said, "We'll go with what we've got. With or without this pending arrangement, you've built a case. It's enough."

"That's bullshit, and you know it. No federal prosecutor is going to touch this unless he's got a smoking gun or an eyewitness who'll swear his life away to see justice done, and no one is going to do that even if he's guaranteed a new identity in Outer Mongolia, because everybody's scared shitless of The Bookkeeper.

"It would also be a P.R. nightmare for the bureau. Sam Marset is just a name to you, but in these parts he was looked upon as a saint. Drag his name through the mud without absolute proof of his corruption, make charges that won't stick, and all you'll do is cause resentment among the law-abiding population and put the offenders on red alert.

"Then the DEA will get pissed off and blame us for sending every dealer underground. Same with the ATF, Customs and Border Protection, Homeland Security. Everybody will get skittish and back off stings they had planned, and we'll all slink back to square one with nothing but our dicks in our hands.

"If you bring me in now, that's what will happen. After a week or so, when things have cooled down, the smugglers will return to supplying their customers. They'll go on killing each other, plus a few innocent bystanders now and then whenever a deal goes south, and those casualties will be on your head, and on mine for not finishing my job."

Hamilton waited several beats, then said, "Bravo, Coburn. That was a very impassioned speech, and I hear you." He paused again. "Okay. You stay. But as good as you are, you can't clean this up by yourself, especially now that you're a suspected mass murderer. Badges down there would love to get in their target practice on you. You'll need backup. VanAllen will provide it."

"Nix. The Bookkeeper has informers in every police department, sheriff's office, city hall, and courthouse. Every-freaking-body is on the take."

"You're saying you think VanAllen—"

"I'm saying give me forty-eight hours."

"You can't be serious."

"All right, thirty-six."

"What for?"

Coburn focused more sharply on Honor. "I'm on to something that could blow the top off."

"What is it?"

"I can't say."

"Can't or won't?"

"You pick."

"Shit."

Honor could sense Hamilton's frustration. Through the phone, she heard him blow out another gust of breath.

Finally he said, "This *something* involves Mrs. Gillette, doesn't it?"

Coburn said nothing.

"I'm not a rookie either, Coburn," Hamilton said. "You don't really expect me to believe that you chose her house, out of all the houses in coastal Louisiana, to hide in, and that while you were there, you just up and decided to ransack the place. You can't expect me to believe that without some über-strong motivating factor she came with you of her own free will after watching you fatally shoot a family friend in her living room.

"And you certainly can't expect me to believe that you, of all people, have taken a widow and child under your wing out of the goodness of your heart, when it has come under debate many times whether or not you even possess a heart."

"Aw now, that really hurts my feelings."

"I know Mrs. Gillette's late husband was a police officer. I know that the recently deceased Fred Hawkins was his best friend. Now, call me crazy, but the coincidence of that has got my gut instinct churning, and even on an off day, it's usually pretty damn reliable."

Coburn dropped the sarcasm. "You're not crazy."

"Okay. What's she got?"

"I don't know."

"Does she know who The Bookkeeper is?"

"She says no."

"Do you believe her?"

Coburn stared hard at her. "Yeah."

"Then what's she sitting on?"

"I don't know."

"Stop jerking me around, Coburn."

"I'm not."

Hamilton swore under his breath. "Fine, don't tell me. When you're back in Washington, we'll discuss your insubordination in addition to the long list of offenses that you—"

"You're using scare tactics now? Go ahead, kick me out of your stinking bureau. See if I give a fuck."

Hamilton added even more heat to his voice. "I'll supply VanAllen with whatever it takes to find you and bring you in, by force if necessary, for the safety of the woman and child."

Coburn's jaw turned to iron. "Hamilton, you do that, and they'll likely die. Soon."

"Look, I know VanAllen. I appointed him myself. I grant you, he's no dynamo, but—"

"Then what is he?"

"A bureaucrat."

"That's a given. What's he like?"

"Mild-mannered. Beleaguered, even. His personal life is shit. He's got a special needs son, a tragic case who ought to be in a perpetual care home but isn't."

"How come?"

"Tom doesn't discuss it. If I were guessing, I'd say the expense makes it out of the question."

Again Coburn pulled that thoughtful frown that Honor was beginning to recognize. "Give me forty-eight hours. During that time, you check out VanAllen. If you can convince me that he's honest, I'll come in. With luck, I'll have got the goods on The Bookkeeper by then."

"In the meantime, what are you going to do with Mrs. Gillette and the child?"

"I don't know."

"Let me talk to her again."

Coburn handed the phone to her.

"I'm here, Mr. Hamilton."

"Mrs. Gillette. Have you been following our conversation?"

"Yes."

"I apologize for some of the language."

"Doesn't matter."

"What's your take?"

"On what?"

"On everything that's been discussed."

"Is Lee Coburn his real name?"

He seemed taken aback by the question. It was several seconds before he replied in the affirmative, but she wasn't entirely convinced of his truthfulness.

"Why did the woman in your office say that he was dead?"

"She was under my orders to. For Coburn's protection."

"Explain that, please."

"He's been in a very precarious situation down there. I couldn't risk someone coming to suspect him of being an agent and calling an FBI office and weaseling out verification of it. So I put it through the bureau pipeline that he'd been killed while on assignment. It's even in his service records in case a hacker gets into our system."

"You're the only person who knows he's alive?"

"Me and my assistant who answered the phone."

"And now me."

"That's right."

"So if something happened to Coburn, any information that he'd passed along to me regarding Sam Marset and The Bookkeeper, or anything that I'd picked up inadvertently, would be extremely valuable to the FBI and the Justice Department."

He answered with reluctance. "Yes. And Coburn is

willing to place your life in jeopardy in order to safeguard that information. Tell me the truth. What have you got? What's Coburn after?"

"Even I don't know, Mr. Hamilton."

She figured that he was questioning her veracity during the long silence that followed.

Then he asked, "Are you saying any of this under duress?"

"No."

"Then help me get other agents to you. They'll come in and pick up you and your daughter. You don't have to fear any reprisal from Coburn. He won't hurt you. I'd stake my career on that. But you need to be brought in so I can protect you. Tell me where you are."

She held Coburn's gaze for several long moments while her common sense waged war with something deeper, something elemental that she couldn't even put a name to. It tugged at her to abandon her innate caution, to stop playing it safe, to forsake what she *knew* and to go with what she *felt*. The feeling was powerful enough to make her fear it. She feared it even more than she feared the man looking back at her with fierce blue eyes.

She went with it anyway.

"Didn't you hear what Coburn told you, Mr. Hamilton? If you send other agents in after us now, you'll never get The Bookkeeper." Before Hamilton could respond, she returned the phone to Coburn.

He took it from her and said, "Too bad, Hamilton. No sale."

"Have you brainwashed her?"

"Forty-eight hours."

"Waterboarded?"

"Forty-eight hours."

"Jesus Christ. At least give me a phone number."

"Forty-eight hours."

"All right, goddammit! I'll give you thirty-six. *Thirty-six,* and that's—"

Coburn disconnected and dropped the phone onto the bunk, then asked Honor, "Do you think this tub will float?"

Chapter 23

———❖———

When Tom got home, Janice was deep into a word game on her cell phone. She didn't even know he was there until he moved up behind her and spoke her name, then she nearly jumped out of her skin. "Tom! Don't do that!"

"Sorry I startled you. I thought you would have heard me come in."

He tried but failed to keep his bitterness from showing. She was playing word games with someone she'd never met who lived on the other side of the world. His world was crumbling. It seemed to him an unfair imbalance. After all, everything he did, he did to try and win her approval, to elevate her regard of him, to make their godawful life a little better.

Of course it wasn't her fault that he was having a bad day. She didn't deserve being the scapegoat for it. But he felt defeated and resentful, so rather than saying something that would set off a quarrel, he left his briefcase there in the den where he'd found her and went into Lanny's room.

The boy's eyes were closed. Tom wondered if they simply hadn't reopened after blinking, or if Lanny was actually sleeping. Did he dream? If so, what did he dream about? It was masochistic to ask himself these questions. He would never have answers to them.

He continued to stare down at the motionless boy and recollected something that had happened shortly after Lanny's birth, when he and Janice were still trying to come to terms with the extent of his limitations and how they would impact their future. A Catholic priest had called on them. He came to comfort and console, but his platitudes about God's will had upset and angered them. Within five minutes of his arrival, Tom had showed him to the door.

But the cleric had said one thing that had stuck with Tom. He'd said that some believed impaired individuals like Lanny had a direct line to God's mind and heart, that although they couldn't communicate with us here on earth, they communed constantly with the Almighty and his angels. Surely it was another banality that the priest had taken from a how-to-minister-to-the-flock manual. But sometimes Tom wanted desperately to believe it.

Now he bent down and kissed Lanny's forehead. "Put in a good word for me."

When he entered the kitchen, Janice, who had prepared a meal for him, served the plate at the single place setting on the table, saying apologetically, "I didn't know when you'd be home, or if you would be, so I didn't cook."

"This is fine." He sat down at the table and spread the napkin over his lap. Although the shrimp salad, buttered French bread, and sliced melon had been artfully arranged on the plate, he had no appetite.

"Would you like a glass of wine?"

He shook his head. "I've got to go back to the office for a while. I should be there if something breaks."

Janice sat down in the chair across from him. "You look done in."

"I feel done in."

"Nothing new on the kidnapping?"

"Nothing, and everyone including the dogcatcher is out looking for them. Or their bodies."

Janice crossed her arms over her middle and hugged herself. "Don't even say it."

He placed his elbow on the table and leaned his head into his hand, rubbing his eye sockets with his fingers. Janice reached across the table and covered the hand resting beside his water glass.

"I don't think he'll kill them, Tom."

"Then why did he take them?"

"Ransom?"

"No call. We're monitoring the father-in-law's home phone. He's had a lot of concern calls from acquaintances, but nothing else. Same on his cell phone." He picked up his fork and thoughtfully tapped it against the rim of his plate, but he didn't take a bite of food. "I don't think this is about ransom."

"Why do you say that?"

"Coburn doesn't fit the profile of a guy who shoots up his place of employment, or an office, or a school."

"How so?"

Realizing he wouldn't be eating, he set down his fork and tried to organize the thoughts that had been bouncing around inside his head. "Typically those guys are making a final and defiant stand against the dirty, rotten world and everybody in it who's wronged them. By golly, they're going to make a statement that will have a memorable impact, then go out in a blaze of glory.

"When they don't commit suicide at the scene, they usually go home, kill their wife and kids, their parents, their in-laws, whoever, *then* kill themselves." He lowered his hands and looked at Janice. "They may hold some hostages for a while before either killing them or releasing them. But they typically don't disappear with them."

"I understand what you're saying, but..." She gave a small shake of her head. "I'm sorry, Tom. I don't know how to respond because I don't know what you're getting at."

"What I'm getting at is that Lee Coburn isn't your textbook mass murderer."

"Is there such a thing?"

"Of course there are exceptions, but he doesn't fit the accepted profile." He hesitated, then added, "Even Hamilton picked up on it."

"Clint Hamilton? I thought he was in Washington now."

"He is. But he called me today, wanted to know what the hell is going on down here and what I'm doing about it."

Janice made a small sound of dismay. "He was checking up on you?"

"Essentially."

"He's got his nerve." She pushed back her chair and indicated his untouched plate. "Are you going to eat that?"

"Sorry, no. It looks good, but..." He ended on a helpless shrug.

She carried his plate to the counter, cursing his predecessor under her breath. "If he didn't think you were up to handling the job, why did he appoint you to the position?"

What Tom believed to be the answer to that was too humiliating to speak aloud, especially to Janice. She abhorred defeatism. She particularly abhorred it in her husband.

He said, "I don't know where Hamilton got his information, probably from other agents in the office, but he must have noticed the same discrepancies in Coburn's M.O. that I did. He even asked me if Coburn was an agent from my office working undercover at the trucking company."

She sputtered a laugh, then sobered so quickly it was comical. "Was he?"

Tom gave her a crooked smile. "No. At least I didn't place him there." His smile slipped. "Someone in New Orleans who outranked me could have, I suppose. Or someone from another agency."

"Without informing you?"

He merely shrugged, again not wanting to admit that he was inconsequential. Or at least was regarded so by coworkers.

She rejoined him at the table. "Hamilton has no right to interfere. Of course the man has an outrageous ego."

"You've never even met him."

"Based on everything you've told me about him, I doubt he could get his head through that door. It makes me mad as hell that he's monitoring you."

He decided against telling her that he wasn't the only one in his office who had heard from Hamilton today. Many agents had disapproved of his appointment and had made no secret of it. But there were some who, either by word or general attitude, had demonstrated their support.

One of those agents, a data analyst, had confided in him today that others in the office had received calls from Hamilton. "For some reason," she'd told Tom behind closed doors, "this case has showed up on Hamilton's radar. He's following it closely and asking questions about you."

"What kind of questions?"

She had held up her hands, palms out. "I won't get

involved in office politics, Tom. I need this job. But I thought you should know that you're being scrutinized."

Tom had thanked her. For the rest of the day, he sensed whispering behind his back. Which may only have been his paranoia, but he didn't think so. He resented Hamilton's intrusion. Whatever the reason for it, it was insulting and worrisome.

He pushed back his chair and stood up. "I'd better get back."

He left the kitchen before the troubling conversation could continue. He washed up in the powder room and retrieved his briefcase from the den. Janice met him at the back door with a sack lunch. "Emergency relief in case you need it. Peanut butter crackers and an apple."

"Thanks."

She didn't kiss him this time, and he didn't kiss her. But before he could turn away, she placed her hand on his arm. "You're doing a good job, Tom. Don't let Hamilton or any-one else browbeat you into thinking otherwise."

He gave her a weak smile. "I won't. The hell of it is, Hamilton's right."

"In what way?"

"Any fool following this case would realize that it's no ordinary kidnapping. In all likelihood, Mrs. Gillette wit-nessed Coburn shooting Fred Hawkins. Murderers don't leave eyewitnesses. Coburn has a reason for keeping her alive."

Chapter 24

Doral paid a dutiful visit to his mama.

As expected, she was prostrate with grief. Female relatives hovered around her, pressing her hands and applying damp cloths to her forehead. Rosary beads clacked as they prayed for Fred's soul and petitioned for comfort for the loved ones he'd left behind.

There was no more room in the kitchen for all the food that had been brought by friends, family, and neighbors. The air-conditioning fought a losing battle against an approaching storm, which had lowered the barometric pressure and raised the humidity.

The male faction, to escape the drama inside the house, carried their overloaded plates out into the yard. They sat in lawn chairs, stroking the rifles and shotguns that lay across their laps, which was as second nature to them as scratching the ears of their hunting dogs. They passed around bottles of cheap whiskey and, in low voices, plotted revenge against Fred's killer.

"He'd better hope the law catches up to him before I do," said one uncle, a mean son of a bitch who'd lost an eye in Vietnam but could still outshoot most anybody, except possibly Doral.

"By this time tomorrow, I'll have this Coburn's balls in a Mason jar. See if I don't," vowed one cousin who was below the legal drinking age but was so drunk he was nearly falling off the tree stump on which he sat.

One of Doral's younger brothers yelled at his rowdy kids, who were chasing each other in the yard. "Show some fucking respect!" he shouted, then pledged not to rest until Coburn was dead. "I don't take kindly to people messin' with our fam'ly."

As soon as they'd eaten their fill and drunk the bottles dry, they piled into pickup trucks and set out to assigned territories to resume the search for their kinsman's killer.

Doral said goodbye to his weeping mother, pulled himself free of her clammy, clutching hands, and left along with the rest, except that he went alone. Despite being half drunk, he easily navigated the winding back roads at a high rate of speed. He'd traveled these roads all his life and knew them intimately. He'd driven them a lot drunker than he was tonight. He and Fred. He and Eddie.

Thoughts of Eddie called to mind that fishing trip that had been captured in the framed photo that Crawford had bagged as evidence. Doral remembered that excursion as one of the best times the four of them had had together.

From thoughts of that day, his mind drifted to his fishing boat and his pre-Bookkeeper years. He and Fred had been born poor, and it had been an uphill struggle all their lives to make ends meet. Fred had sought financial stability by signing on with the police department. But wearing a uniform, working a shift, wasn't for Doral. He enjoyed flexibility.

He'd bought his boat on credit extended to him by a banker so tight-assed he squeaked when he walked. The rate of interest had been usurious, but Doral had never even been late on a payment.

Then for years he had run charters into the Gulf, putting up with groups of rich, drunken sons of bitches—doctors, lawyers, stockbrokers, and such—who thought of themselves as far above a fishing guide with callused hands and a Cajun accent. He had endured their verbal abuse, and their vomiting up their expensive booze, and their griping about the heat and the sun, rough seas, and uncooperative fish. He'd tolerated their crap because his livelihood had depended on it.

In a way, he'd been grateful to Katrina for destroying his boat and putting an end to it. No more kissing up to abusive assholes for Doral Hawkins, thank you very much.

That's when The Bookkeeper had approached him and Fred with a moneymaking idea. The work was going to be a lot more exciting and lucrative than any enterprise they could have dreamed up on their own. Even in a state where taking graft was as commonplace as crawfish, the scheme was a way to get filthy rich.

Doral hadn't shied away from the danger involved. The payoff was worth the risks. He liked walking a tightrope and enjoyed the inside joke of being a public official by day and something else entirely by night.

His job description was to intimidate, maim, or kill if necessary. He had a natural propensity for stalking and hunting, and now he could make a living at it. The only difference was that the prey was human.

So here he was speeding along back roads, his prey Lee Coburn. And his best friend's widow and child.

When his cell phone rang, he slowed down only marginally in order to answer the call, but after hearing the urgent message the caller imparted, he floorboarded his brake pedal and skidded to a stop, sending up a cloud of dust that enveloped his car. "Are you shitting me?"

There was a lot of background noise, but the whispering caller made himself heard above it. Not that Doral wanted to hear anything of what he had to report.

"I thought you should know so you could pass it along to The Bookkeeper."

"Thanks for nothing," Doral muttered. He disconnected and pulled his car off the road, letting it idle on the edge of a ditch as he first lit a much-needed cigarette, then called The Bookkeeper.

He was stone cold sober now.

He skipped traditional greetings. "It's rumored that Coburn is a federal agent."

The Bookkeeper said nothing, just breathed slowly and deeply. Malevolently.

Doral, envisioning a seething volcano about to erupt, swiped at a bead of sweat rolling down his temple and into the outside corner of his eye.

"When did you hear this?"

"Ten seconds before I called you."

"Who told you?"

"One of our plants in the P.D. He heard it from a feeb who's working with them and the sheriff's office on the kidnapping. The buzz is that Coburn is an agent who's been working undercover."

A long silence ensued. Then, "Well, as you so astutely pointed out this morning, he does seem unusually smart for a dock worker. I only wish you had realized that before you let him escape the warehouse."

Doral's gut clenched as tight as a fist, but he didn't say anything.

"What about Honor's friend? Anything from her since you paid her a call this morning?"

"Tori hasn't left her house. I honestly don't think she's heard from Honor or she wouldn't be sitting tight. One thing I did find out, she's got a new boyfriend. Bigwig banker in New Orleans name of Bonnell Wallace."

"I know him. We've got money in that bank."

"No shit? Well, I caught up with the health club's bimbo receptionist at Subway when she went out for lunch. Made it look like a chance meeting. Schmoozed her, and it didn't take much. She was only too happy to unload about Tori, who she referred to as a royal *B* with a capital letter, and that's a quote."

Doral was now breathing a little easier. He was pleased to have something positive to report following the rumor about Coburn. He hadn't been idle today. He'd been proactive and was making progress. It was important that The Bookkeeper know that.

"The bimbo—her name's Amber—her guess is that Wallace doesn't want any of his banking customers or highfalutin friends to know he requires a personal trainer, so that's why he started coming down here for his workouts. He's got a fat belly, but a fatter purse. Tori was all over him in a New York minute. Sank her claws into him, and now he's ga-ga. Tori is under the misconception that their affair is a secret, but all the employees know that it's not just iron Mr. Bonnell Wallace is pumping whenever he comes to Tambour."

After a lengthy silence, The Bookkeeper said, "Good

information to hold in reserve in case we need it. Unfortunately, it hasn't moved you any closer to locating Coburn, has it?"

"No."

"You and Fred left us with a mess, Doral. At a time when we least need a mess. No matter what Coburn is, he should have been killed along with the others. I haven't forgotten who let him get away. Find him. Kill him. Don't disappoint me again."

The cheap whiskey surged into the back of Doral's throat, scalding and rancid. He gargled it down. "How were Fred and I to know—"

"It's your business to know." The Bookkeeper's tone of voice sliced to the bone, silencing any excuses Doral might have made. And just in case the message hadn't quite sunk in, The Bookkeeper added, "You've heard me speak highly of Diego and his razor."

Goosebumps broke out on Doral's sweat-dampened arms.

"The only problem with using Diego is that it's over too quickly for the person who failed me. He doesn't suffer long enough."

Doral barely made it out of his car before throwing up in the roadway.

Chapter 25

Honor was stunned to realize that Coburn seriously planned to move her father's shrimp trawler.

Her protests fell on deaf ears.

Within minutes of hanging up on Hamilton, Coburn was in the wheelhouse, flinging back the tarp that had been placed over the control panel. "Do you know how to start the engine?" he asked impatiently, motioning to the controls.

"Yes, but we'd have to get it into the water first, and we can't do that."

"We've got to. We gotta relocate."

Several times over the next hour she tried to convince him that it was an impossible project, but Coburn wouldn't be deterred. He found a rusty machete in a toolbox on deck and was using it to whack at the fibrous vegetation that clung to the hull. It was backbreaking work. Once again she tried to dissuade him.

"Hamilton gave you his word. You don't trust him to keep it?"

"No."

"But he's your boss. Overseer, supervisor? Whatever you call it in the FBI."

"He's all of that. And the only thing I trust him to do is to cover his own ass first. Remember, Lee Coburn no longer exists."

"He gave us thirty-six hours."

"He'll renege."

"What makes you think so?"

"I know how he thinks."

"Doesn't he know how you think, too?"

"Yeah, which is why we need to hurry. As we speak, he's probably already trying to get a location on my cell number."

"You didn't give it to him. You said disposables were untraceable. You said—"

"Yeah, I said. But I don't know everything," he muttered.

Anxiously, she looked into the sky, where clouds were scuttling in off the Gulf. "Would he send a helicopter?"

"Unlikely. Hamilton would opt for something more covert, something that wouldn't give us warning. Besides, there's a storm coming. He won't come by air."

"Then why are you in such a hurry?"

He paused to wipe his sweating forehead with the back of his hand. "Because I could be wrong."

But the harder they worked, the more hopeless it seemed. Honor suggested that they take their chances in the recently stolen pickup. "No one's looking for that truck. You said so yourself."

"Okay, and go where?"

"To my friend."

"Friend."

"A lifelong friend who'd give us a hiding place, no questions asked."

"No. No friends. They'll be watching your friends."

"We could spend the night in the truck."

"*I* could," he said. "*We* couldn't."

Eventually she stopped wasting energy on trying to change his mind. She lacked his stamina and skills, but she applied herself to helping and did whatever he asked of her.

Emily awakened from her nap. She was chatty and excited by the activity. She got in the way, but Coburn worked around her with surprising patience. She stood on deck and called down encouragement to them as, together, they put their backs to the prow and pushed the unfettered craft off the bank into the water.

Coburn checked for leakage and, finding none, joined Honor at the controls. Her dad had taught her how to start the engine and to steer. But it had been years. Miraculously, she remembered the steps, and when the engine belched to life, she didn't know who was the more astonished, her or Coburn.

He asked about fuel. She checked the gauge. "We're okay. Dad was preparing for a hurricane. But the other gauges..." She looked at them dubiously. "I don't know what all of them are for."

He spread a yellowed nautical map over the control panel. "Do you know where we are?"

She pointed out their location. "Somewhere along here. If we head south toward the coast, we'll become more exposed. On the other hand, one shrimp boat in a marina lined with them won't be as obvious. Further inland, the bayous are narrower. There's more tree coverage. Waters are also shallower."

"Since we'll probably have to bail out, I vote for shallow water. Just get us as far as you can."

He traced their progress on the map. They chugged for about five miles through the winding waterways before the engine began to cough. The waters became thick with vegetation. Several times, Honor narrowly missed running over cypress knees that poked up through the opaque surface.

Coburn nudged her elbow. "Over there. It's as good a place as any."

Honor steered the boat closer to the marshy shore, where a dense cypress grove would provide partial concealment. Coburn dropped anchor. She cut the engine and looked at him for further instruction.

"Make yourselves comfortable."

"What?" she exclaimed.

He folded the map and stuffed it into the pocket of his jeans, then checked his pistol and set it on the control panel, well out of Emily's reach. "I'll take Hawkins's .357. You keep this one. It's ready to fire. All you have to do is point and pull the trigger."

"What are you doing?"

Before she'd even finished asking, he was out of the wheelhouse. When she reached the deck, he was lowering himself over the side of the boat into the knee-deep water. "Coburn!"

"Can't leave the truck back there." He hesitated, then, swearing under his breath, pulled her cell phone and its battery from his pocket. "I guess I should leave you a phone. Just in case something happens to me. But I'm trusting you not to use it. If you have to call someone, call 911 and only 911." He passed her the two components.

"How do you..."

"Lucky for us, yours is an older phone. It's easier to do than with the newer models." He removed the back of her phone and demonstrated how to replace the battery. "Line up the gold bars, snap it into place. Emily could do it." His eyes met hers. "But—"

"I promise I won't unless you don't come back."

He bobbed his head once, then turned away from the boat.

He slogged his way to solid ground, then disappeared into the undergrowth.

Diego was shopping in a Mexican supermarket when his cell phone vibrated again. He stepped outside the store to answer. "You ready for me?"

"Yes," The Bookkeeper said. "I want you to watch someone for the next couple of days."

"What? Watch someone?"

"Isn't that what I said?"

"What about Coburn?"

"Just do as I tell you, Diego. The man's name is Bonnell Wallace."

Who cared what the hell his name was? It wasn't Coburn. Before he could voice his objections, he was given two addresses, one for a bank on Canal Street, the other a residence in the Garden District. It wasn't explained to him why this man needed watching, and actually, Diego didn't give a flip. It was a bullshit job.

With exaggerated boredom, he asked, "Do you want him to know he's being watched?"

"Not yet. I'll let you know when another move is called for. *If* one is called for."

"Okay." His cavalier tone didn't escape The Bookkeeper.

"Am I keeping you from something, Diego?"

Yeah, he thought. *You're keeping me from a high-paying hit.* Instead he put The Bookkeeper on the defensive. "I haven't been paid for the massage parlor girl."

"I don't have proof that she's dead."

"What, you want me to send you her head in a box like those vultures in Mexico do?"

"No need to go that far. But I haven't seen anything on the news about a body being found."

"It won't be. I saw to that."

"But you didn't give me any details."

"Like what?"

"When you tracked her down, was anyone with her?"

"No. She was soliciting conventioneers there where the riverboats dock."

"The Moonwalk."

"Whatever."

"She was alone? No pimp? Somebody helped her get away. She wouldn't have had the courage to leave on her own."

"All I know is that she was alone when I found her. No pimp, or she would have been doing more business," he said, putting a chuckle behind it. "She was easy pickings. I negotiated a ten-dollar blowjob, then when I got her under some pilings, I slit her throat. For good measure, I opened up her belly, filled it with rocks, and sank her in the river. If her body ever pops up, it won't look like her no more."

Referring to Isobel in these terms made him wince, but he had to keep up appearances. The laugh, the cockiness was fake, but he must make himself believed.

The Bookkeeper kept him waiting an interminably long time before speaking. "All right. You can pick up your money tomorrow. Where do you want it left?"

Paydays came in the form of an envelope of cash, left for him in a designated spot that changed each time. He gave The Bookkeeper the location of a dry cleaning establishment that had been abandoned since Katrina.

"There's an old cash register on the counter. Have it left in the drawer."

"It will be there. In the meantime, keep me posted on Bonnell Wallace. I want to know anything he does that's not part of his daily routine."

"Oh, like that's a big fucking deal." Before The Bookkeeper could respond to that, Diego clicked off and returned to the store. He got another cart and started over. He never left anything unattended, fearing a transponder or something worse being planted on it.

And, as nice as an envelope containing five hundred dollars would be, he wouldn't pick it up for several days. First, he would watch the dry cleaner's building to make certain that a trap wasn't being laid for him. The Bookkeeper might not trust him entirely. But he trusted The Bookkeeper not at all.

It was raining by the time he left the store with his purchases and one shoplifted canned ham. Regardless of the weather, he took a long, rambling route home, checking over his shoulder frequently and approaching blind corners with his razor in hand.

Isobel greeted him with a sweet smile and a dry towel. Her shyness toward him lessened a little each day. She was coming to trust him, starting to believe that he wasn't going to harm her or sell her services.

He had stopped touching her. He no longer trusted himself even to stroke her cheek, not when the sight of her melted his heart but made his cock swell with desire.

At night she clutched her silver crucifix in her tiny fist

and cried herself to sleep. She would awaken screaming from nightmares. When bad memories caught up with her, she would weep for long periods of time, covering her face and moaning, overcome with shame for having been sexually coupled with hundreds of men.

But to Diego, she was pure and good and innocent. It was he who was evil, he who was stained with a vileness that could never be washed way. His touch would have tainted her and left a scar on her soul. So he refrained, and loved her only with his eyes and brimming heart.

He emptied the sacks of groceries. They shared a carton of ice cream. He turned on his iPod, and he would swear the music sounded better because she was there to share it. She laughed like a child when her goldfish blew her kisses through the glass bowl.

He thought of her as an angel who had filled his underground room with an essence as bright and clean as sunlight. He basked in her light and was reluctant to leave it.

The Bookkeeper's stupid assignment could keep for an hour or two.

Honor was sitting on the bunk beside her sleeping daughter, listening to the rain and her own anxious heartbeat, when she heard a bump and actually felt the vibration of it. She slid the pistol from beneath the mattress and held it in front of her as she crept up the steps and peered through the opening.

"It's me," Coburn said.

With profound relief, she dropped her gun hand to her side. "I'd almost given up on you."

"It was a long way back to the truck, especially going overland. By the time I got there, it was getting dark and raining hard. Then I had to find a road. Only waterways were on the map. I finally found a gravel road that runs out about a quarter mile from here."

It was a miracle to Honor that he'd found his way back at all.

"Everything okay?" he asked.

"Emily wanted to wait up until you got back, but we ate, then played with Elmo a while. I started telling her a story, and she fell asleep."

"Probably better."

"Yes. She would've been afraid of the dark, and I didn't want to turn on the lantern. Although I considered putting it on the deck to guide you back. I was afraid you would miss us in the dark. You left me few instructions before you left."

If he noticed the implied rebuke, he ignored it. "You did right."

Her eyes had adjusted to the darkness, and she could make him out. His clothes were soaked, his hair was plastered to his head. "I'll be right back," she told him.

She descended the steps and replaced the pistol beneath the mattress, then gathered up some items and returned to the wheelhouse. She passed him a bottle of water first. He thanked her, uncapped it, and drained it.

"I found these." She handed him the folded pair of khakis and a T-shirt. "They were in one of the storage compartments. The pants will be too short, and they smell moldy."

"Doesn't matter. They're dry." He peeled off Eddie's LSU T-shirt and replaced it with one that had belonged to her father, then began unbuttoning the jeans.

She turned her back. "Are you hungry?"

"Yeah."

She went back down the steps and flicked on the lantern only long enough to locate the food she'd set aside for him. By the time she returned to the wheelhouse, he had swapped out the pants. She set the foodstuffs on the console. "You forgot to get a can opener."

"I got cans with pull tabs."

"Not the pineapple. And of course, that's what Emily wanted."

"Sorry."

"I found a can opener in a drawer under the stove. It's rusty, so we may get lead poisoning, but she had her pineapple."

Using his fingers, he ate his meal of canned breast meat chicken, pineapple slices, and saltine crackers. He washed it down with another bottle of water that Honor fetched from below. She'd also brought up a package of cookies to appease his noticeable sweet tooth.

He was sitting on the floor, his back propped against the console. She sat in her dad's captain's chair, which had suffered the ravages of the elements like everything on the boat.

The silence was broken only by the pelting rain and the crunch of cookies.

"It's raining harder than ever," she remarked.

"Um-huh."

"At least the rain keeps the mosquitoes away."

He scratched at a place on his forearm. "Not all of them." He took another cookie from the package and bit off half.

"Will they find us?"

"Yes." Noticing that his blunt answer had startled her, he said, "It's only a matter of time, depending largely on when Hamilton kicks things into full gear. He probably has already."

"If they find us—"

"When."

"*When* they find us, will you..." She searched for the word.

"Go peacefully?"

She nodded.

"No, I won't."

"Why?"

"Like I told Hamilton, I'm not quitting until I get this son of a bitch."

"The Bookkeeper."

"It's not just an assignment any longer. It's one-on-one, him against me."

"How did it work, exactly? The business between him and Marset?"

"Well, let's see. Here's a for-instance. Each time a truck passes from one state into another, it has to stop at a weigh station. Have you seen these arms that extend over the interstate near state lines?"

She shook her head. "I don't routinely cross state lines, but in any case, no, I've never noticed."

"Most people don't. They look like streetlights. But they're actually X-ray machines that scan trucks and cargo, and they're constantly being monitored. Agents see a truck that looks suspicious, or that hasn't stopped at the weigh station, it's pulled over and searched."

"Unless the person monitoring it is on the take and lets it pass."

"Bingo. The Bookkeeper created a market out of doing just that. His business strategy was to corrupt the people enforcing the laws, effectively making the laws a joke. A human trafficker would pay for the protection and consider it a cost of doing business."

"Sam Marset was a...?"

"Client. I believe one of the first, if not *the* first."

"How did it come about?"

"Along with his honest business, Marset was doing a brisk trade in illegal goods. Since he was legit, no one suspected. Then Marset's trucks started getting stopped often, his drivers hassled. The increased vigilance was enough to scare him. Above all, the elder of St. Boniface didn't want to get caught. Enter The Bookkeeper with a solution to his problem." Coburn grinned. "Thing was, The Bookkeeper had created the problem."

"By orchestrating the searches."

"And probably Marset knew it. But if The Bookkeeper could put a cog in his wheels, he could see to it that the cogs were removed. It was either pay The Bookkeeper for protection, or risk getting caught with a shipment of drugs. Life as he'd known it would be history."

"Others would be forced to do the same."

"And did. The Bookkeeper now has an expanded client base. Some are large commercial operations like Marset's. Others are small-time independents. Men out of work due to the oil spill who have a pickup truck and kids to feed. They drive over to south Texas, pick up a couple hundred pounds of marijuana, drive it to New Orleans, their kids eat for another week.

"They're breaking the law, but the bigger criminal is the individual who's making it profitable for them to become felons. The smugglers run a much greater risk of being caught, and when they are, they can't rat out the facilitator because they rarely know who it is. They only know their contact person, and that individual is low on the totem pole."

"If Marset was such a good customer, why was he killed? You mentioned something to Hamilton about his whining."

"Things rocked along okay for a time. Simpatico. Then The Bookkeeper started getting greedy, started increasing his commission for the services provided. Marset didn't need a crystal ball to tell him that without a ceiling, the cost would keep going up, and soon a large slice of his overhead was going to be The Bookkeeper's fee. But if he refused to pay it—"

"He'd get caught, exposed, and sent to prison."

"Right. And The Bookkeeper could make it happen, because his tentacles reach into the entire justice system. So Marset, ever the diplomat, and a little naive as it turns out, proposed that they meet last Sunday night and settle on terms that both could live with."

"You smelled a rat."

"The Bookkeeper is the freaking Wizard of Oz. I couldn't see him strolling into that warehouse, shaking hands, and negotiating."

"Did Marset know his identity?"

"If he did, he died without telling. I've been through his files, read every scrap of paper I could get my hands on, including the one with your husband's name on it."

"Surely you don't suspect Eddie of being The Book-keeper."

"No, The Bookkeeper is alive and well."

"How do you think Eddie fit in?"

"You said he had moonlighted for Marset. Maybe he was in on the illegal side of his business. Or maybe he was a dirty cop on The Bookkeeper's payroll. Maybe he was playing both ends against the middle, or holding out for a larger take. Maybe blackmail was his angle. I don't know."

She stared him down until, with a trace of reluctance, he added, "Or he was a cop trying to make a case against one or both. But crooked or straight, he would have tried to protect himself by collecting hard evidence that he could use for whatever his purpose was."

Honor was steadfast in her confidence of Eddie's integrity, but for the time being she let the matter drop. "Royale Trucking. Are all the employees crooked?"

"Not at all. Those six who died with Marset, yes. He had a separate set of books that only he and one other guy ever saw. People in the corporate office, even members of his own family, didn't know about his sideline."

"How could they not?"

He shrugged. "Maybe they didn't look too deep. They didn't want to. All they knew was that the business continued to do extremely well in a weak economy."

"So they'll be okay? Mrs. Marset?"

"In terms of prosecution, yes. Won't be easy for her when the truth about her husband is exposed."

Honor pulled her feet up to the edge of the seat, looped her arms around her legs, and propped her chin on her knees. Quietly she said, "They'll kill you."

He bit into another cookie, saying nothing.

"Doral or one of the Hawkins clan. Even the honest policemen, who only see you as Sam Marset's killer, would rather bring you in dead than alive."

"Hamilton's told everybody I'm already dead. Wonder how he'll wiggle out of that one."

"How can you joke about it? It doesn't bother you that you could be killed?"

"Not particularly."

"You don't think about dying?"

"I'm only surprised that it hasn't happened yet."

Honor picked at a cuticle that had been torn loose while they were working on the boat. "You know how to do things." She glanced at him. He was looking up at her curi-ously. "Survival things. Lots of things."

"I don't know how to bake cupcakes."

For the first time since she'd found him lying facedown in her yard, he was teasing her, but she wouldn't let it divert her. "Did you learn all those skills in the Marine Corps?"

"Most of them."

She waited, but he didn't elaborate. "You were a differ-ent kind of Marine than my father-in-law."

"He's a recruiting poster?"

"Exactly."

"Then, yeah, I was different. No marching in formation for the kind of Marine I was. I had a uniform, but didn't wear it but a few times. I didn't salute officers, and nobody saluted me."

"What *did* you do?"

"Killed people."

She had suspected that. She'd even deluded herself into thinking she could hear him admit it without flinch-ing. But the words felt like tiny blows to her chest, and she feared she would only feel them stronger if she heard more, so she carried the subject no further.

He finished his last cookie and dusted crumbs off his hands. "We need to get to work."

"Work?" She was so exhausted her whole body ached. She thought that if she closed her eyes she would fall asleep where she sat. Stained mattress or not, she looked for-ward to lying down on it beside Emily and sleeping. "What work?"

"We're going through it again."

"Through what again?"

"Eddie's life."

Chapter 26

—◦—

Diego approached the property under cover of darkness, rain, and dense, sculpted shrubbery. Bonnell Wallace's home was one of the stately mansions on St. Charles Avenue.

From an intruder's standpoint, it was a fucking fortress.

Landscape lighting had been well placed for flattering accent. The risk it posed was negligible. Diego saw a hundred ways that the artificial moonlight could be avoided.

Problematic, however, were the spotlights projecting from ground level up onto the exterior walls and bathing them with thousands of watts of illumination. A shadow cast by that light would be thirty feet tall and would look like an ink-print on the gleaming white brick.

He assessed the perfectly maintained lawn and the eighty-thousand-dollar car parked in the circular driveway, and determined that the security system's quality would also be the best that money could buy. State-of-the-art contacts would be on every door and window, with motion and

glass breakage detectors in every room, and, in all likelihood, an invisible beam around the perimeter of the property. If it was broken, a silent alarm would be activated,
so that by the time an intruder reached the house, police
would already be surrounding it.

None of these obstacles made breaching it impossible,
but they presented difficulties that Diego would rather
avoid.

Through the front windows, he could see into a room
that looked like a study. A heavyset, middle-aged man was
seated in a large chair, his feet up on an ottoman, talking
on the telephone and frequently sipping from a glass he
kept close at hand. He looked relaxed, uncaring that the
lighted room was on display and that he could be seen
from the street.

That was a statement in itself. Mr. Wallace felt safe.

In this neighborhood, someone who looked like Diego
would immediately arouse suspicion. He was confident of
his ability to be invisible when he needed to be, but even
so, he kept a wary eye out for patrol cars and nosy neighbors out walking their dogs. Rain trickled beneath his collar and down his back. He disregarded it. He hunkered
there, nothing except his eyes moving as they periodically
scanned his surroundings.

He watched and waited for something to happen. Nothing did, except that Mr. Wallace traded his telephone for a
magazine that held his attention for almost an hour. Then
he tossed back the remainder of his drink and left the
room, switching out the light as he went. A light on the second story came on, remained on for less than ten minutes,
then went out.

Diego stayed where he was, but after another hour,
when it became apparent to him that Wallace had gone to

bed, he decided that his time was better spent somewhere else. He would resume his surveillance in the morning. The Bookkeeper would never be the wiser.

He slithered from his hiding place and walked a few blocks to a commercial area where several bars and restaurants were still open. He spotted a car in a dark and unattended lot and used it to drive himself to within a mile of his home, where he walked away from it, knowing that within minutes urban predators would have it stripped down to the wheels.

He went the rest of the way on foot and let himself into his building without turning on a light. He didn't make a sound as he entered his underground living quarters. For once, Isobel was sleeping free of bad dreams. Her face was peaceful.

Diego wasn't at peace and he didn't sleep.

He sat gazing at Isobel's serene face and puzzling over why The Bookkeeper had assigned a talent like him to such a Mickey Mouse job as "keeping an eye on" Bonnell Wallace.

"I don't know."

Honor's voice had grown hoarse from repeating those three words. For two hours, Coburn, who was seemingly inexhaustible, had been hammering her with questions about Eddie's life, going back as far as his early teenage years.

"I didn't even know him then," she argued wearily.

"You grew up here. He grew up here."

"He was three classes ahead of me. We didn't notice each other until he was a senior, I was a freshman."

He wanted to know about every aspect of Eddie's life. "When did his mother die? How did she die? Does she have family he was close to?"

"Nineteen ninety-eight. She was on chemotherapy for breast cancer. Her system was weakened by the treatments, and she died of pneumonia. She had one surviving sister. Eddie's aunt."

"Where does she live?"

"She doesn't. She died in 2002, I think it was. What does she, or any of this, have to do with what you're looking for?"

"He left something with someone. He put something somewhere. A file. Record book. Diary. Key."

"Coburn, we've been through this. If such a thing exists, I don't know what it is, much less where to look for it. I'm tired. Please, can't we wait until morning and pick this up again then?"

"We may be dead in the morning."

"Right, I may die of exhaustion. In which case, what's the point?"

He dragged his hand over the lower half of his face. He stared at her long and hard through the darkness, and she thought he was about to relent, when he said, "You or his dad. One of you has to have it."

"Why not another cop? Fred or Doral? Besides Stan and me, Eddie was closest to the twins."

"Because whatever it is, it surely implicates them. If they had it, they would have destroyed it. They wouldn't have been hovering around you for two years."

"Waiting for me to produce it?"

"Or just to make certain that you never did." While he thought, he repeatedly socked his fist into his opposite palm. "Who ruled Eddie's car wreck an accident?"

"The investigating officer."

He stopped the hand motions. "Let me guess. Fred Hawkins."

"No. Another cop. He happened upon the wreckage. Eddie was already dead when he arrived."

"What's this officer's name?"

"Why?"

"I'd like to know how he happened upon the wreckage."

Honor stood up quickly and went out onto the deck but stayed near the exterior wall of the wheelhouse so the slender overhang of the roof would protect her from the rain.

Coburn followed her. "What?"

"Nothing. I needed some air."

"My ass. What?"

She slumped against the wall, too tired to argue with him. "The officer who investigated Eddie's car crash was found floating in a bayou a few weeks later. He'd been stabbed."

"Suspects?"

"No."

"Unsolved homicide."

"I suppose. I never heard any more about it."

"Thorough sons of bitches, aren't they?" He stood shoulder to shoulder with her, staring out at the rain. "What did Eddie like to do? Bowl? Golf? What?"

"All that. He was a good athlete. He liked to hunt and fish. I've told you that."

"Where's his fishing and hunting gear?"

"At Stan's."

"Golf bag?"

"At Stan's. And so are his bowling ball and the bow-and-arrow set he got for his twelfth birthday." She said it with asperity, but he nodded thoughtfully.

"Sooner or later, I'm gonna have to pay Stan a visit." Before she could address that, he asked her to describe Eddie.

"You've seen his picture."

"I mean personality-wise. Was he serious and studious? Lighthearted? Moody? Funny?"

"Even-tempered. Conscientious. Serious when called for, but he liked to have a good time. Loved telling jokes. Liked to dance."

"Liked making love."

She figured he was trying to get a rise out of her, but she wouldn't give him the satisfaction. Looking him straight in the eye, she said, "Very much."

"Was he faithful?"

"Yes."

"You're sure?"

"Positive."

"You can't be positive."

"He was faithful."

"Were you?"

She glared at him.

He shrugged. "Okay, so you were faithful."

"We had a good marriage. I didn't keep secrets, and neither did Eddie."

"He kept one." He paused in order to give the statement significance, then lowered his voice to a whisper. "Everybody keeps secrets, Honor."

"Oh really? Tell me one of yours."

A corner of his mouth tilted up. "Everybody but me. I don't have any secrets."

"Absurd thing to say. You're wrapped up in secrets."

He folded his arms over his chest. "Ask away."

"Where did you grow up?"

"Idaho. Near the state line with Wyoming. In the shadow of the Tetons."

That surprised her. She didn't know what she had

expected, but not that. He didn't look like her image of a mountain man. Of course, he could very well be lying, inventing an unlikely past to protect his cover. But she went along. "What did your father do?"

"Drank. Mostly. When he worked, it was as a mechanic at a car dealership. He drove a snowplow in the winter."

"He's deceased?"

"For years now."

She looked at him inquisitively. He didn't respond to the silent question for so long that she didn't think he would.

Finally he said, "He had this old horse that he kept in a corral behind our house. I named it, but I never heard him call it anything. He rarely rode it. Rarely *fed* it. But one day he saddled it and rode off. The horse came back. He didn't. They never found his body. Of course they didn't look very hard."

Honor wondered if the bitterness lacing his voice was aimed at his alcoholic father or at the searchers who had given up on finding his remains.

"Dad had ridden that horse near to death, so I shot it." His folded arms dropped back to his sides. He stared out into the rain. "No great loss. It wasn't much of a horse."

Honor let a full minute pass before she asked about his mother.

"She was French Canadian. Tempestuous by nature. When riled, she would launch into French, which she never bothered to teach me, so half the time I didn't understand what she was screaming at me. Nothing good, I'm sure.

"Anyhow, she and I parted ways after I graduated high school. I attended two years of college, decided it wasn't for me, joined the Marines. My first tour of duty, I got word that she'd died. I flew to Idaho. Buried her. End of story."

"Brothers or sisters?"

"No."

His facial expression was as devoid of feeling as his life had been devoid of love from any source.

"No cousins, aunts, uncles, nobody," he said. "When I die, 'Taps' won't be played. There'll be no twenty-one-gun salute, and there won't be anyone there to get a folded flag. I'll just be history, and nobody will give a shit. Especially me."

"How can you say something like that?"

He turned his head toward her, registering surprise. "Why does that make you angry?"

Now that he'd asked, she realized she was angry. "I genuinely want to know how someone, anyone, could be so indifferent when speaking about his own death. Don't you value your life at all?"

"Not really."

"Why not?"

"Why do you care?"

"You're a fellow human being."

"Oh. You care about mankind in general, is that it?"

"Of course."

"Yeah?" He turned the rest of his body toward her, until only his right shoulder was propped against the wall of the wheelhouse. "Why didn't you beg him to come get you?"

She didn't follow the shift in topic. "What?"

"Hamilton. Why didn't you tell him where you were so he could send someone to pick you up?"

She took a shaky breath. "Because after what I've seen and heard over the past day and a half, I don't know who to trust. I guess you could say I chose the devil I know." She meant it in jest, but he didn't crack a smile.

He inclined an inch toward her. "Why else?"

"If I have something that will convict The Bookkeeper, then I should help you find it."

"Ah. Patriotic duty."

"You could put it that way."

"Hmm."

He moved closer still, his nearness making her aware of her heartbeats, which had become stronger and faster. "And...and because...of what I've already told you."

He stepped around until he was facing her, seemingly unmindful of the rain falling on him. "Tell me again."

Her throat was tight, and not only because she had to tilt her head back in order to look up into his face. "Because of Eddie."

"To preserve his reputation."

"That's right."

"That's why you're here with me?"

"Yes."

"I don't think so."

And then he pressed into her. First his thighs, then his middle, his chest, and finally his mouth. She made a whimpering sound, but its definition was unclear even to her, until she realized that her arms had gone around him instinctually, and that she was clutching his back, his shoulders, her hands restless and greedy for the feel of him.

He kissed her openmouthed, using his tongue, and when she kissed back, she felt the hum that vibrated deep inside his chest. It was the kind of hungry sound she hadn't heard in a long time. Masculine and carnal, it thrilled and aroused her.

He cupped the back of her head in his large hand. He pushed his thigh up between hers, high, and rubbed it against her, and continued kissing her as if to suck the very breath from her. She reveled in every shocking sensation.

He broke the kiss only to plant his hot mouth at the base of her throat. Boldly and possessively his hand covered her breast, squeezed it, reshaped it to fit his palm, felt her hard nipple, and hissed his pleasure.

And that brought Honor to her senses.

"What am I doing?" she gasped. "I can't do this." She shoved him away. He stood, impervious to the torrent beating at his head and shoulders, his chest rapidly rising and falling as he stared at her through the gloom.

"I'm sorry," she said, meaning it to the bottom of her soul. But was she sorry for him, or sorry for herself? Sorry about letting it happen, or sorry she'd stopped it?

She didn't know, and she didn't allow herself to debate it. She rushed through the door of the wheelhouse, down the steps, and into the cabin.

Emily came awake, sat up, and looked around.

It was still kind of dark, but she could see, so she wasn't scared. Mommy was there, lying beside her on the smelly bed. Coburn was in the other one. They were both asleep.

Mommy was lying on her side, her hands under her cheek. Her knees were pulled up until they were touching her tummy. If her eyes had been open, she would have been looking at Coburn. He was lying on his back. One of his hands was resting on his stomach. The other one was hanging off the edge of the bed. His fingers were almost touching Mommy's knee.

She hugged Elmo against her and dragged her bankie along as she scooted to the end of the bed and climbed down. She wasn't supposed to walk barefoot on the floor because it was so nasty. Mommy had said. But she didn't want to sit down on it to put her sandals on, so she went on tiptoe up the steps and looked into the room with all the funny stuff in it.

Her mommy had sat her in the crooked chair and told her that it used to be her grandpa's seat, and that he had let her sit in his lap while he steered the boat. But she'd been a baby, so she didn't remember. She wished she did, though. Driving a boat would be fun.

Her mommy had got to drive it yesterday, but when she asked Coburn if she could drive it too, he said no because they were in a hurry, and he had better things to do than to entertain her. But then he'd said maybe later, we'll see.

Coburn had told her not to get too close to the broken windows because the glass could cut her. She had asked him why glass cut people, and he said he didn't know, it just could, and for her to keep away from the windows.

It wasn't raining anymore, but the sky looked wet, and so did the trees that she could see.

Her mommy probably wouldn't like it if she went any farther, so she tiptoed back down the steps. Mommy hadn't moved and neither had Coburn, except that his stomach went in and out when he breathed. She pressed her hand to her stomach. Hers went in and out too.

Then she spied the forbidden phone and the battery lying at the foot of Coburn's bed.

Yesterday, while her mommy and Coburn were cutting bushes off the boat, she'd asked if she could play her Thomas the Tank Engine games on Mommy's phone. Both of them had said "No!" at the same time, except that Coburn had said it a little louder than Mommy. She hadn't understood why they said no, because sometimes when Mommy wasn't using the phone she would let her play games on it.

Mommy wasn't using her phone now, so she probably wouldn't mind if she played a game.

She had watched when Coburn showed Mommy how to put the battery in. She could do it. Coburn had said so.

He didn't move when she picked up the phone. She lined up the gold bars on the battery and snapped it into place, just like Coburn, then turned on the phone. When all the pretty pictures came on the screen, she tapped on the picture of Thomas the Tank Engine. Of all the games, she liked the puzzle best.

Concentrating hard, she started with the wheels, then added the engine and the smokestack, and all the other parts, until there was a whole Thomas.

Each time she worked the puzzle, Mommy told her how smart she was. Mommy knew she was smart, but Coburn didn't. She wanted him to know that she was smart.

She crept toward the head of his bunk and lowered her face close to his. "Coburn?" she whispered.

His eyes popped open. He looked at her funny, then looked over to where Mommy was sleeping before looking back at her. "What?"

"I worked the puzzle."

"What?"

"The Thomas puzzle. On Mommy's phone. I worked it."

She held it up for him to see, but she didn't think he really looked at it, because he jumped off the bed so fast he banged his head on the ceiling.

Then he said a really bad word.

Chapter 27

Deputy Sheriff Crawford was surprised to discover that their destination was a derelict shrimp boat that seemed not to be floating so much as squatting in the water.

As hiding places went, it was a sorry choice. First, it was an untrustworthy-looking vessel. Bad enough. But then it was also situated between miles of hostile terrain and a labyrinth of bayous in which one could easily become hopelessly lost before reaching the Gulf of Mexico, if that was indeed the planned escape route.

Maybe Coburn wasn't as smart as he'd given him credit for. Maybe he was becoming desperate.

Using only hand signals to communicate to the men with him, they approached the craft on foot with stealth and extreme caution.

The team, working out of the temporary command center in the Tambour Police Department, consisted of himself, two other sheriff's deputies, three Tambour policemen, two FBI agents, and one state trooper who'd just happened to be in the room chewing the fat with the others when a techie came in and announced that he was getting a signal from Honor Gillette's cell phone.

His attempt to locate it using triangulation was successful.

It then took an agonizing hour of discussion to determine how best to get to the isolated location. By air, land, or water? Once it was decided that land was the best option in terms of a surprise, Crawford had yielded the floor to the closest thing that either the Tambour P.D. or the sheriff's department had to a S.W.A.T officer, who had taken a few classes in his spare time and at his own expense.

He shared his limited knowledge and summarized by saying, "Don't screw up and shoot the woman or kid," which Crawford could have told the group himself in five seconds rather than thirty-five minutes.

They piled into three official SUVs, then drove through fog and mist for what seemed like hours, but was actually only forty minutes, until they could go no farther, not even in vehicles with four-wheel drive.

Besides, Crawford didn't want their approach announced by engine noise. They'd proceeded on foot, and now were hunkered down among the trees, watching for signs of life aboard the boat, from which the phone's cell signal was emanating. Crawford thought it a miracle that there was a cell tower anywhere near this place, but he wasn't going to question either the benevolence of the gods or the foresight of the cell provider.

The sun was rising, but the eastern horizon was so heavily banked by clouds that daybreak did little to relieve the dim and gloomy atmosphere. The water in the bayou, which looked swollen after last night's torrential rains, was absolutely still, as was the Spanish moss that hung from tree branches in saturated clumps. It was too early even for birds. The silence was as thick as cotton.

Crawford motioned the men forward. They had no choice but to risk exposure as they covered the distance between the tree line and the creek bank. When Crawford reached the boat, he crouched down against its hull, checked his weapon again, then climbed over and stepped lightly onto the deck. Others followed, but Crawford was the first inside the wheelhouse, the first to hear a vicious curse and movement coming from below, the first to aim at the man coming up the steps.

Stan Gillette stepped out of the passageway into the wheelhouse with his hands raised. In one of them, he was holding a cell phone. "Deputy Crawford. You're late."

He'd made the kid cry.

When he'd wrenched the cell phone from her hand, she'd let out a howl that could've raised the dead. It got her mother up off the bunk, all right.

He'd scooped up the bawling kid and practically slung her over his shoulder, freeing his other hand to get Elmo and bankie. He'd shoved them into her chubby arms, then grabbed Honor's hand and dragged her—protesting—up the steps, through the wheelhouse, and onto the deck.

Alone, it would have taken him only minutes to abandon the boat, wade through the bayou, then sprint the half mile through sucking mire to where he'd left the pickup. Even in the semi-light of predawn, he'd have been away from there in a fraction of the time it had taken him just to get them off the boat. Honor had balked at stepping into the water, but he'd pushed her, and she'd managed to splash her way out of the shallows. Twice she'd stumbled during their mad dash to the pickup.

And all that time, the kid had kept a stranglehold on his neck, wailing in his ear over and over, "I didn't mean to."

When they reached the truck, she was still blubbering. He'd handed her over to Honor, who'd scrambled into the passenger seat. He'd slammed the door, run around the hood, vaulted into the driver's seat, and crammed the key into the ignition. The tires had spun in the mud, but eventually gained traction, and the pickup had lurched forward.

They were well away from the shrimp boat now, but he didn't let his guard down. Honor's cell phone would have been as good as a damn beacon on a lighthouse, leading the police straight to them. As soon as it was discovered that they were no longer aboard the boat, the chase would resume.

He didn't know at what time the kid had turned on her mother's phone. Minutes before she woke him up? Hours? But he had to assume the worst, in which case he was surprised they'd escaped at all. At best, they couldn't have got too much of a head start.

So he blocked out the presence of the sobbing kid and her mother and concentrated on putting as much distance as possible between them and the boat, in the shortest amount of time, without getting too lost, driving into a bayou, or hitting a tree.

Honor shushed Emily, crooning to her as she hugged her close to her chest and smoothed her hand over her hair. Eventually the kid stopped crying, although every time he glanced at them he was met with four reproachful eyes.

He finally came upon a main road. Not wanting to get stopped for speeding, he let up on the accelerator and asked Honor if she had any idea where they were.

"South and east of Tambour, I think. Where did you want to go?"

Where did he want to go?

Fuck if he knew.

Presently, all he was doing was burning precious gas, so he pulled into the parking lot of a busy truck stop, where the pickup wouldn't be noticed among so many similar vehicles. By the looks of things, the combo fuel stop and convenience store was a gathering spot for day laborers who stoked themselves on coffee, cigarettes, and microwave breakfasts before going to work.

For easily thirty seconds after he cut the engine on the pickup, no one said anything. Finally he looked over at the two females who were sorely complicating his life. He intended to tell them as much in unmitigated terms, when the kid said in a trembling voice, "I'm sorry, Coburn. I didn't mean to."

He closed his mouth. He blinked several times. He looked at Honor, and when she didn't say anything, he looked back at the kid, whose damp cheek was still lying against Honor's chest. He mumbled, "Sorry I made you cry."

"That's okay."

Her mother, however, wasn't in as forgiving a mood. "You scared her half to death. You scared *me* half to death."

"Yeah, well it would have scared me half to death if I'd woken up looking into the double barrel of Doral Hawkins's shotgun."

Honor bit back a retort she obviously was itching to say. Instead she bent over Emily's head and kissed the top of it.

The comforting gesture somehow made him feel even worse about setting the kid off. "Look, I said I was sorry. I'll get her a...a...balloon or something."

"She's afraid of balloons," Honor said. "They scare her when they pop."

"Then I'll get her something else," he said irritably. "What does she like?"

Emily's head popped up as though it was spring-loaded. "I like Thomas the Tank Engine."

Coburn stared at her for several beats, then the absurdity of his situation got the better of him, and he began to laugh. He'd been eyeball to eyeball with villains whose best chance at an afterlife lay with taking off his head. He'd ducked heavy gunfire, dodged a rocket launcher, jumped from a chopper seconds before it crashed. He had cheated death too many times to count.

Wouldn't it have been funny if he'd been done in by Thomas the Tank Engine?

Honor and Emily were watching him warily, and he realized that neither had ever heard him laugh. "Inside joke," he said.

Happy once again, Emily asked, "Can we have breakfast now?"

Coburn considered, then said under his breath, "Why the hell not?"

He got out and opened a toolbox that was attached to the back of the truck's cab. He'd discovered a denim jacket in it the day before. It smelled of gasoline and was covered in grease, but he pulled it on. Standing in the open wedge of the door, he leaned in. "What do you want?"

"Would you rather I go?" Honor asked.

"I don't think so."

"You still don't trust me?"

"It's not that. In this crowd…" His gaze moved over her tousled hair and whisker-burned lips. It took in her snug T-shirt and the clearly defined shape beneath it, which he knew by feel was the real deal, not fake. "You'd attract attention."

She knew what he was thinking because her cheeks turned pink. She had ended last night's kiss, but that didn't mean she hadn't liked it. In fact, he figured it meant she'd liked it a lot. Too much. He'd stayed on the deck for half an hour after her speedy retreat, but when he did go below, he'd known she was still awake even though she'd pretended otherwise.

Even after he'd lain down on the bunk, he'd stayed restless and hot for a long time. If she'd been as worked up over that kiss as he'd been, it was no wonder that she was blushing now and having a hard time looking him in the eye.

Face averted, she said, "Anything you get will do."

He put on the cap and sunglasses he'd found in the truck, and, as he'd expected, he blended with the other customers. He waited in line to use the microwave, then took his heated breakfast sandwiches to the cash register and paid. As soon as he'd handed the sack of food over to Honor, he started the truck and drove away.

While driving, he ate his sandwich and sipped his coffee, which was chicory-enhanced and bracingly strong. But his mind wasn't on either the hot food or the coffee, because it was busy assessing his situation and deciding on his next course of action. He was in a jam, and he wasn't certain how to proceed.

Like the time in Somalia when his weapon had malfunctioned just as his target spotted him. He'd had to make a choice: Abandon the mission and save his own skin, or carry out his assignment and ante up on surviving it.

He'd had a nanosecond in which to make up his mind.

He'd dropped the weapon and used both hands to snap the guy's neck.

He didn't have much more time for decision-making now. He couldn't see his pursuers yet, but he sensed their urgency to find him.

The odds weren't in his favor, but he wasn't ready to throw in the towel, abandon his mission, and let The Bookkeeper continue conducting business.

He wasn't even ready to call Hamilton and ask for backup from Tom VanAllen, because he didn't entirely trust his own agency. The bureau probably didn't entirely trust him either.

For all the FBI really knew, he had gone postal and mowed down everybody in that warehouse on Sunday night. If it became expedient for the bureau to pass him off as a veteran suffering from P.T.S.D., then that's what they would do, and no one, probably not even the woman sharing a stolen truck—and a wanna-fuck-you-bad kiss with him—would believe otherwise.

Chances were good that he wouldn't be around to see the smoke clear on this case. He wouldn't be available to exonerate himself for the warehouse massacre. He'd wind up on a slab, growing cold in infamy. But by God, he wasn't going to take the fall for The Bookkeeper's handiwork without putting up a hell of a fight.

This morning had been a close call. As sure as he was still breathing, that engaged cell phone had brought people running to that damn tub, and in all probability Doral Hawkins had been leading the pack. If Emily hadn't awakened him when she had, they'd all have been shot in their bunks.

Risking his own life was a job requirement. Risking theirs, no way.

Mind made up, he said, "You mentioned a friend yesterday."

Honor looked over at him. "Tori."

"Aunt Tori," Emily chirped. "She's funny."

The gender of Honor's friend shouldn't have mattered to him at all. He was surprised by how glad he was to learn it was a woman. "Good friend?"

"Best friends. Emily thinks she's family."

"You trust her?"

"Implicitly."

He pulled off the road, rolled to a stop on the shoulder, and dug his cell phone from his front pants pocket. Then, turning to Honor, he laid it on the line. "I gotta dump the two of you."

"But—"

"No buts," he said emphatically. "Only thing I need to know, when you're free of me, are you going to call in the cavalry?"

"You mean Doral?"

"Him, the police, the FBI. Last night, you enumerated all the reasons you came with me. One of them was mistrusting the authorities. Does that still hold?"

She nodded.

"Say it."

"I won't call in the cavalry."

"All right. Do you think your friend would hide you for a couple of days?"

"Why a couple of days?"

"Because that's how long Hamilton gave me."

"He gave you less than that."

"Will she hide you?"

"If I ask her to."

"She wouldn't betray your trust?"

Without an instant's hesitation, she gave an emphatic shake of her head.

"That means she can't call in the cavalry either," he said.

"That would be the last thing Tori would do."

It went against his nature, as well as his training and experience, to trust anyone. But he had no choice except to give Honor the benefit of the doubt. As soon as he was out of sight, she might very well sic Doral Hawkins on him, but that was a risk he had to take.

The alternative was to keep her and Emily with him. If he did, they could very well get hurt or killed. He didn't think even he, who'd seen unimaginable atrocities, and had inflicted a few himself, could handle watching the two of them die. It was his fault they were in this. He should have left Honor blissfully ignorant.

But second-guessing was a waste of energy, and he didn't have time for regret.

"Okay. You're about to put that implicit trust in your friend to the test. What's her number?"

"It won't work if you call. I'll have to."

He shook his head. "If you do, you could be implicated."

"Implicated? In what?"

He glanced at Emily, who was singing along with Elmo. The ditty had annoyed him at first, but he was used to it by now and, most of the time, able to tune it out. Coming back to Honor, he spoke softly. "Implicated in any shit that may come down when my deadline expires." Her green eyes stayed fixed on his; he read the question in them. "If I do nothing else, I'm going to take care of Doral Hawkins."

"Take care of?"

"You know what I mean."

"You can't just kill him," she whispered.

"Yeah, I can. I will. I am."

She turned her head away and stared through the

bug-spattered windshield at the glowering sky. Visibly distressed, she said, "I'm so far out of my element here."

"I realize that. But this is my element, so you've got to trust my judgment."

"I know you're doubtful about Stan. But he would—"

"Not an option."

"He's my father-in-law, Coburn. He loves us."

He lowered his voice even more, so that Emily wouldn't be distracted from her singing. "Do you want Emily around to witness the confrontation between him and me? Because you know it will eventually come down to that. Do you think he's going to let me just walk into his house and start going through Eddie's things? No. Whether he's guilty of partnering with The Bookkeeper or Marset, or an honest citizen safeguarding his dead son's good name, he's going to resist my intrusion. With force. Not only that, he'll be good and pissed with me for dragging you and his granddaughter into this."

Her expression was a giveaway. She knew he was right. Even so, she continued to look miserably indecisive. He gave her only a few seconds before prodding her again. "What's Tori's number?"

She raised her chin stubbornly. "Sorry, Coburn. I can't."

"You don't trust her enough?"

"This is my mess. How can I drag Tori into it? I'll be placing her in danger, too."

"Tough choice, I know. But it's the only one you've got. Unless..." He tipped his head toward Emily. "You trust Doral Hawkins to spare her life. *I* wouldn't bet on it. *You* might."

She gave him a baleful look. "You always use that."

"Because it always works. What's Tori's number?"

Chapter 28

———⇒·•·⇐———

Even before Tori checked the light beyond her shutters, she knew by instinct that it was an ungodly hour for her phone to be ringing.

She groaned and buried her head deep into her pillow to escape the noise. Then, remembering the events of yesterday, she rolled toward her nightstand and grabbed her phone. "Hello?"

"Tori, did I wake you up?"

Not Honor and not Bonnell, who were the only people on earth whom she might forgive for calling her at dawn. "Who's this?"

"Amber."

Tori scowled and flopped back down onto her pillow. "What? And it had better be good."

"Well, just like you instructed me, the first thing I do each morning after turning off the alarm is to turn on the sauna and whirlpool in both locker rooms so they can be getting hot. Then when all the lights in the studio have been turned on, I unlock the front door, because some-times there are people waiting—"

"For godsake, Amber, get to it."

"That's when I check the main number's voice mail. This morning, somebody left a weird message at 5:58, just a few minutes before I opened up."

"Well, what was it?"

"'What does Barbie see in Ken?'"

Tori sat bolt upright in bed. "That's all she said?"

"Actually it was a man."

Tori thought on that for several moments, then said, "Well, isn't it obvious to you that it was a crank call? Don't bother me with crap like this again."

"Are you coming in today?"

"Don't count on it. Cover for me."

Tori ended the call and bounded out of bed. She skipped doing her hair and makeup, which she *never* skipped, and dressed rapidly in the first clothes her hands touched when she reached into her closet. Then, grabbing her keys and handbag, she left through the front door.

But halfway to her car in the driveway, she noticed a beat-up panel truck parked at the curb across the street, about a third of the distance to the corner. Anyone inside it would have an unobstructed view of her house. She couldn't tell whether or not anyone was behind the wheel, but Doral's words came back to her. *I'll be on you like white on rice.*

Maybe she'd been watching too many crime shows on TV, maybe she was being super-paranoid, but she'd never seen the truck on her street before, her best friend had been kidnapped yesterday, and she'd been threatened and manhandled by a local hoodlum.

She'd rather be paranoid than stupid.

Rather than continuing on to her car, she bent down and picked up the morning issue of the newspaper that was lying in the wet grass. Pretending to read the front page, assuming a casual saunter, she retraced her steps back into the house and soundly closed the door behind her.

Then she quickly went through her house, slipped out her back door, and, cutting a path that couldn't be seen from the street, walked across her lawn, which melded into that belonging to the house directly behind hers. There was a light on in the kitchen. She knocked on the door.

It was answered by a handsome, buff young man. He was cradling a smug-looking cat in his arms. Tori despised the cat, and the feeling was mutual. But she adored the man, because he'd once told her that in his next life he wanted to be an unapologetic diva bitch just like her.

He was a client who never missed a workout. Well-defined biceps bulged when he pushed open the screen door and motioned her in. "This is a surprise! Hon, look who's come to call. Tori."

His partner in this, the only gay marriage in Tambour, whose body was equally buff, entered the kitchen as he speared a cuff link into his sleeve. "Hell must have frozen over. I didn't know you ever got up this early. Sit down. Coffee?"

"Thanks, no. Listen, guys, can I borrow a car? I gotta go...somewhere...in sort of a hurry."

"Something wrong with your Vette?"

"It's making a funny noise. I'm afraid it'll quit on me, and I'll be stranded."

She hated telling them such a transparent lie. They'd been excellent neighbors, and over the years had become loyal friends, dispensing expensive wine and commiseration each time she got divorced. Or married, for that matter.

They looked at her, then at each other, then back at her. She knew that they knew she was lying, but if she tried to explain, they would drive her to the nearest loony bin.

Finally the one with the cat asked, "The Lexus or the Mini Cooper?"

Upon seeing Stan, Crawford exclaimed, "What the *hell*?"

Under other circumstances, Stan might have enjoyed the deputy's humiliation and bafflement, but he could feel the egg on his own face. Unused to being made a fool of, he was trying very hard to keep his dignity intact and his fury under control. It wasn't Crawford he wanted to lash out at, however. It was the man who, twenty-four hours ago, had robbed him of Honor and Emily.

"My daughter-in-law's cell phone," he said, extending it to Crawford.

He snatched it from Stan. "I know what it is and who it belongs to. How the hell did you get it, and what are you doing here with it?"

"Well, one thing I'm *not* doing with it is playing Thomas the Tank Engine games," Stan retorted.

Crawford activated the phone. From the screen, the cartoon steam engine smiled up at him.

"It's Emily's favorite game," Stan told him.

"So they have been here."

"Those are my late son's clothes," he said, motioning to the damp heap on the boat console. "There's food and water below. Empty cans and wrappers. Yes, they were definitely here, but they're gone."

To Crawford's further consternation, Doral joined them from the cabin below. The deputy holstered his gun and placed his hands on his hips. "Mrs. Gillette must have called you and told you where she was. Why didn't you notify me?"

"Honor didn't call anybody," Stan said stiffly. "I already checked her call log. It's been cleared. Even the calls she and I exchanged yesterday are no longer on there."

The deputy's eyes shifted back and forth between them, landing on Doral with an accusatorial glare. "If she didn't call you, then one of your late brother's friends in the police department must have tipped you that we'd got the signal."

He was right, of course. A police officer, who was a friend to both Fred and Doral, had called Doral with news of this latest development. Out of loyalty, Doral had in turn called Stan. While Crawford was still pulling together a team, the two of them had been speeding here.

But even with the head start, they'd arrived only minutes before Crawford, which had been long enough for Stan to determine that the ramshackle boat had recently been inhabited. The sheets on the bunks were still warm, although he'd hated making that observation, especially in front of Doral. It unnerved him to think of his late son's widow, and Emily, of course, being that cozy with Lee Coburn.

Coburn wasn't so careless as to leave the phone behind. He'd left it deliberately, using it as a decoy to attract the posse to the boat, while he was moving away from it and taking Stan's family with him.

It was galling.

He and Doral had been talking about Coburn's caginess before the arrival of Crawford and his team. "I've bribed everybody I know to bribe, Stan," Doral had said with disgust. "Nobody can, or will, say definitely."

It hadn't taken long for the rumor to circulate through

the police department, then beyond, that Lee Coburn might be a federal agent who'd been working undercover in Sam Marset's trucking firm. Which would put an entirely different spin on Sunday night's massacre.

About that, Stan's feelings were ambiguous. He hadn't quite determined what he thought of that and how, if it was true, it affected him.

But Doral had. He'd told Stan, "It doesn't matter to me one way or the other. Coburn shot my brother in cold blood. I don't care if he's a felon, a feeb, or the prince of darkness, I'm gonna kill him."

Stan understood the sentiment. Regardless of who or what Coburn was, he'd made an enemy of Stan when he'd cast suspicion on Eddie. And now Honor's reputation was being compromised. If Coburn had taken Honor and Emily as insurance for a safe getaway, why hadn't he abandoned them by now? If his reason for taking them had been ransom, why hadn't he demanded it?

And if Honor was a hostage, why hadn't she left them a trail they could follow? She was a clever girl. She must realize that dozens of law enforcement personnel and volunteers were scouring the countryside in search of her and Emily. Surely she could have figured out a way to leave subtle signposts.

If she had wanted to. That's what gnawed at Stan. What kind of sway did this man Coburn hold over her?

Doral had remarked on the close quarters of the cabin below, and then had looked at Stan, his eyebrows raised. And now Stan could tell that Crawford's thoughts were moving along that same track.

Stan bluffed. Taking an aggressive stance, he said to Crawford, "I suggest you stop wasting time and begin tracking where Coburn took my family from here."

"I'll get on that myself," Doral said and started to go.

Deputy Crawford put out a stiff arm to stop him. "Don't you have a funeral to plan?"

"Meaning what?"

"Meaning that I understand why you'd want to hunt down your brother's killer and get revenge. But this is a police matter. Nobody invited you to participate. And if I find out who's feeding you information from inside the P.D., or from inside the sheriff's office, I'm going to nail his ass to a fencepost."

Doral moved Crawford's arm aside. Smirking, he said, "I'd pay to see that," then left the boat.

Crawford ordered two of the officers to search the craft for clues, starting with the cabin. They clumped down the steps. He sent the rest out to search the surrounding area for footprints, tire tracks, anything.

When he and Stan were alone, Crawford said, "I couldn't help but notice the name of the boat, Mr. Gillette. *Honor.*"

"It belonged to her father."

"Past tense?"

"He died several years ago."

"She owns it now?"

"I suppose." Honor hadn't mentioned her father or his boat since his demise. It had never crossed Stan's mind to ask what had become of the trawler. It was hardly a coveted legacy.

Crawford said, "You might have mentioned the boat yesterday."

"I didn't think of it. In any case, I wouldn't have known where it was moored."

"You didn't keep track?" he asked, sounding surprised. Or maybe skeptical.

"No. I didn't like her father. He was an aging, dope-smoking hippie who called himself a shrimper but was actually a ne'er-do-well who never had two nickels to rub together. He wore beads and sandals, for godsake. Look around," he said, raising his arms. "He lived on this boat. The condition of it speaks to the kind of person he was."

"And yet your daughter-in-law came here to hide."

Stan actually took a threatening step toward the deputy. "I resent the implication that Honor is *hiding* from me."

Crawford wasn't intimidated. He didn't back down. "You've heard the rumor about Coburn being a fed."

He stated it as fact. Stan said nothing.

Crawford pulled a knowing frown. "Come on, Mr. Gillette. You've heard the rumor. What do you think about it?"

Stan wasn't going to confirm or deny anything to this man in whom he had little confidence. "All that concerns me is the safe return of my daughter-in-law and grandchild. I'm going to leave you now and try to find them myself."

Crawford sidestepped to block Stan's path. "Couple of things first." He paused for a beat, then said, "Mrs. Gillette obviously had access to her cell phone. So why didn't she call 911? Or you? If she wanted to be found, wouldn't she have done that instead of letting her little girl play games on her phone?"

Stan schooled his expression not to change. "You said a couple of things."

"You might want to reconsider who you ally yourself with."

"Why?"

"I received an initial ballistics report. The bullet that killed Fred Hawkins didn't match any of the ones fired during the warehouse mass murder."

Stan was quick with an explanation. "Coburn would have dumped the guns he used at the warehouse. They're probably at the bottom of a bayou. He used another to shoot Fred."

"Or," the deputy said, drawing out the qualifier, "he wasn't the warehouse shooter."

Chapter 29

Shes a babe."

It was the first time either Coburn or Honor had spoken in five minutes. Even Emily sat still and untalkative in Honor's lap, having stopped the game of her own invention with Elmo and lapsed into the same brooding silence.

Coburn looked at Honor. "Come again?"

"Tori will knock your eyes out. She's a babe."

"What Tori is," he said tightly, "is not here."

"She will be."

"We've been waiting for over an hour."

"She's a busy lady."

"At six o'clock in the morning?"

"Her fitness center opens early." Although she knew that Tori didn't personally open the club each morning, she was trying to reassure Coburn, and possibly herself, that Tori would show up. "Eventually someone will check the business line for voice mail messages. If you had called her cell phone—"

"We've been through that."

They had. He'd rejected calling Tori's personal phone for the same reason he didn't want Honor placing the call herself. "Anything that goes down will be on my head, not yours," he'd said.

"Tori and I could be accused of aiding and abetting."

"You could say I used your kid to coerce you."

"I could swear to that under oath."

"There you go."

Now, as they sat waiting for a sign from Tori, Honor said, "As soon as she gets the message, she'll come. We just need to be patient."

But he looked like a man whose patience had run out an hour ago when they had arrived at the designated place. He looked around now and, not for the first time, expelled his breath while mouthing words that Emily shouldn't overhear. "We're like sitting ducks. Right out in the open."

"Well, what did you expect of a secret meeting place?"

"I expected it to have walls," he fired back.

"It's safe. No one knows about it except Tori and me."

"Maybe she forgot that silly code."

"She didn't forget."

"What's it mean, anyway?"

"It means Ken's a dork."

He muttered another vulgarity.

Okay, so the phrase *was* silly, considering their ages now. But when she and Tori had first sworn an oath on it, they'd been giggling girls. Then they'd continued to use it into their teens to communicate whenever one needed to see the other immediately. It meant, "Drop everything, come now, this is an emergency."

Of course when they were in high school an emergency had amounted to an adolescent trauma like heartache over a boyfriend, a hateful teacher, a failing grade, and, in Tori's case, a missed menstrual period. Today's emergency was for real. "Why here?" he asked.

"Here" was an ancient live oak tree that had roots bigger around than Honor, snaking along the ground in every direction from its enormous trunk. It had withstood centuries of hurricanes, blights, land developers, and other hazards. Imposing and magnificent, it almost appeared artificial, like something a Hollywood set designer had constructed and plunked into the clearing.

"Meeting out here in the countryside added to the thrill of sneaking out, I suppose. We discovered this place on the day I got my driver's license. We were exploring because we could. We came across the tree out here in the middle of nowhere and claimed it as our own.

"From then on, we met here to talk about things that were too sacred even to share over the telephone." She could tell he wasn't quite getting it. "Teenage girls can be terribly dramatic, Coburn. It's hormonal."

He made a nonverbal sound that she couldn't interpret, and wasn't sure she wanted to. Threading her fingers through Emily's hair, she said wistfully, "I suppose one day Emily will be sneaking out to meet—"

She broke off when Coburn sat up, suddenly alert. "What kind of car does she drive?"

"A Corvette."

"Then that's not her." He reached for the pistol at his waistband.

"Wait! That's not her car, but that's Tori. And she's alone."

The small, unfamiliar red-and-white car bumped across the creaky wooden bridge and then followed the rutted path toward the tree, stopping twenty yards short of it.

Honor opened the passenger door so Tori could see her. Emily scrambled out, jumped to the ground, and broke into a run, shouting, "Aunt Tori!"

Tori alighted from the Mini Cooper and was waiting to catch Emily and swing her up into her arms. "You're getting so big! I won't be able to do this much longer."

"Guess what," Emily said, wiggling free of Tori's hug.

"What?"

"Coburn said if I would just be quiet and let him think, then he would get me an ice cream. Only not now. Later. And guess what else. We slept on a boat that used to be where my grandpa lived. Not Grandpa Stan, my other grandpa. The beds were funny and didn't smell nice, but it was okay because we're on a 'venture. I woke Coburn up, and when I did, he said a bad word. But Mommy told me that sometimes grown-ups say words like that when they're very upset. But Coburn isn't mad at me, just at the sidjee-ashun."

When Emily wound down, Tori said, "My goodness. We've got a lot to catch up on, don't we?"

Over Emily's shoulder, she was looking at Honor and telegraphing a hundred unspoken questions. She kissed Emily's cheek, then set her down. "Let me talk to your mommy for a minute."

She extended her open arms to Honor, and the two of them embraced. For several moments they just held each other tightly. Finally, Tori released her and sniffed back tears. "I could kill you for causing me such a fright. I've been worried sick."

"I knew you would be, but there was no help for it."

"The news stories led me to fear...Well, I'm just awfully glad to see that you and Emily are still in one piece. Did he...? Are you...? God, I'm so *relieved*," Tori said emotionally. "You look like something the cat drug in, but you seem fine."

"We are. Basically. I'm sorry you were so afraid for us. He wouldn't let me call you until this morning. And even then he wouldn't let me call you directly. I wasn't sure you'd get the message. But he—"

"'He' being *him*?" Tori was watching Coburn as he came toward them. When her gaze moved back to Honor, her perfectly waxed eyebrows were raised. Speaking in an undertone, she said, "Kidnapper? I should be so lucky."

Ignoring the remark, Honor made the introductions. "Tori Shirah. Lee Coburn."

Tori gave him the inviting smile that men couldn't resist. "Charmed."

He didn't acknowledge either the greeting or the smile. Instead he was looking toward the far side of the bridge that Tori had crossed in order to reach them. "Is your cell phone on?"

She was taken aback by the question and the abrupt manner in which he'd asked it, but answered immediately, "Yes."

"Get it." She looked at Honor, and when Honor nodded, she dropped her coquetry, retrieved her cell phone from her handbag in the car, and handed it to him.

Coburn asked, "Were you followed?"

"No." Then, "Hey!" when he took the battery out of her phone.

"You're sure?"

"I made sure." She told them about the panel truck she'd seen parked on her street that morning. "I didn't like the looks of it, so I went out the back way and borrowed the Mini from my neighbors. No one followed me."

"What made you suspicious of the panel truck?" he asked.

"I thought someone might be watching the house. Doral Hawkins came to see me yesterday." She went on to relate what had happened. "He's more than a little pissed that you shot his brother. At least it's said that you shot and killed Fred."

To her implied question, Coburn merely nodded.

She eyed him speculatively, but when no explanation was forthcoming, she continued. "Doral told me that if I heard from Honor, I had better notify him first, or else."

"He threatened you?" Honor asked.

Tori shrugged. "Let's just say that he made himself understood. But screw him. Stan, too."

"When did you talk to Stan?"

She recounted their conversation. "It vexes me to give him any credit at all, but I must admit that he was less obnoxious than usual. I guess fear has taken the shine off his brass."

"What's he afraid of?" Coburn asked.

Tori sputtered a laugh. "You left a trail of dead bodies, then you disappeared, taking Honor and Emily with you. Stan has a right to be more than a little concerned, don't you think?"

"Coburn didn't murder those men in the warehouse," Honor said. "And he didn't take Emily and me by force."

Tori shifted her gaze from one to the other and said drolly, "I sorta gathered that." Then, placing her hands on her hips and glancing down at her disassembled phone, she asked, "So, what gives?"

"The fact is that he's—"

"No." He put his hand on Honor's arm to stop her from revealing his identity. "The only thing she needs to know is that you and Emily must stay underground until all this shakes out."

"She deserves an explanation," Honor argued.

"You said she would help with no questions asked."

"I know that's what I said. But it's unfair to let her go on thinking that you—"

"I don't give a damn what she thinks."

"Well, I do. She thinks you're a killer."

"I am."

"Yes, but—"

"Excuse me." Tori held her raised hand palm out to stop Honor from continuing, but it was Coburn she addressed. "Keep your secrets. I've already volunteered my services." Then she said to Honor, "Emily isn't afraid of him, and kids are supposed to be good gauges of someone's character. Like dogs."

"Emily is four. She's infatuated because he's a novelty."

"Yeah, well, I trust her instincts. Possibly even more than I do yours. In any case, you summoned me, and I'm here. Tell me what you want me to do."

"Get them away from Tambour," Coburn said before Honor could speak. "Right now. Don't stop for anything, don't return home, don't tell anybody that you're going. Can you do that?"

"Of course. Where do you have in mind?"

"I don't." He looked at Honor, who shook her head.

"My dad's shrimp boat was my only ace."

Tori said, "I own a house on the far side of Lake Pontchartrain. Across the bridge. Would that do?"

"Who knows about it?" Coburn asked.

"Husband number two. I got it from him in the divorce settlement. The house in exchange for me keeping quiet about his...Never mind. It turned ugly. Anyway, the only reason I wanted the house was to spite the jerk. I don't use it on a regular basis, I don't even like it that much. It's been months since I was there."

Honor was listening to them, but she was watching Emily, who was still wearing the clothes in which Honor had hastily dressed her yesterday morning before fleeing their house. Her hair was unbrushed. There was a patch of dirt on her knee and a tear in the armhole of her top. Meals had been irregular and not very tasty. She'd slept in an uncomfortable, smelly bunk.

Yet she seemed perfectly content and carefree, heartbreakingly innocent of the seriousness of their situation. She'd found a stick and was humming happily as she used the tip of it to etch patterns in the mud.

"She'll need some things," Honor remarked.

"We'll get whatever she needs." Tori gave Honor's arm a reassuring pat. "No one is looking for me. I'll take care of everything." To Coburn, she added, "But I'll wait until we're almost there before I stop to shop."

"As of now, you can't use credit cards. Do you have plenty of cash?"

"I have some," Honor reminded him.

"Money is one thing we don't have to worry about," Tori said. "I can get what I need. All I have to do is ask."

"Ask who?" Coburn wanted to know.

"My current beau."

"No. Nobody can know where you are."

"He wouldn't tell."

"Yeah, he would. If the right people got to him, he'd tell."

He said it with such conviction that even Tori was daunted by what he implied. "We'll pool our resources and make do."

He appeared satisfied with that, but stressed that Honor and Emily must get into hiding before being spotted.

"Gotcha," Tori said. "No one would know to look for me

in this car." Then her expression clouded. "The only person I worry about is Stan. If he tries to contact me again, and I don't respond, he'll smell a rat. I would be the logical person that Honor would come to for help."

"He may figure out that she's with you, but he can't know where," Coburn said.

Tori turned to Honor. "That's okay with you? There's no love lost between him and me, but the man is beside himself with worry over you and Em."

"I know it seems cruel to keep him in the dark." Honor glanced over at Coburn, but saw no softening of his resolve. "But that's how it's got to be. For a little while longer at least."

"You have your reasons," Tori said. "But I dread the showdown when Stan finds out that I provided the wheels when you ran away from home."

"I'm not going with you."

Honor's declaration startled Tori speechless. Coburn was more outspoken. "The fuck you're not."

She had been silently debating this with herself and had come to the conclusion that she couldn't just dust her hands of this, which would be the safe and practical thing to do. It had occurred to her, not in one blinding instant of enlightenment but gradually over the past couple of days, that she was done with being safe and practical.

Since Eddie's death, she often had resented Stan's interference in her life, but she'd done nothing to discourage it. She had allowed him and others to protect her, to shepherd her through rough times, and to oversee her decisions as though she was a child who needed constant guidance.

She'd had much more independence when she was married. Eddie had regarded her as an equal, a woman who was allowed and, indeed, encouraged to form her own opinions and to act on her decisions.

Widowhood had fettered her. It had made her inse-
cure and cautious, afraid to relocate, or explore employment options, or to do anything other than remain in a rut
comfortably lined with memories of her happy past. Stan's
supervision had fostered her timidity. She didn't like this
woman she was now. She missed the more confident Honor
Gillette that she had been.

Squaring off against Coburn, she said, "I'm not going
to let you just brush me off."

"Not going to *let me*? Watch, lady."

"You're the one who dragged me into this."

"I didn't have a choice then. Now I do."

"So do I."

"That's where you're wrong. My choice is the only one
that counts, and I choose for you to go with your friend
here."

"I'm going to see this through, Coburn."

"You could get killed." He pointed toward Emily where
she was still playing with her stick. "You want to leave her
an orphan?"

"You know better than to ask that," she shot back
angrily. "But this time I won't be cowed or coerced. I want
answers to the questions about Eddie."

"I'll get them for you."

"That's just it. *I* need to get them."

"Not your job."

"But it is!"

"Yeah? How's that?"

"Because I didn't do it before."

His chin went back.

She hadn't expected to blurt out that admission of
guilt, but now that she had, she pressed on. "I should have
insisted on a more thorough investigation of Eddie's car

wreck. I didn't. I was told it was an accident, and I took the explanation at face value. I never posed a single question about it, not even after the officer who found Eddie was murdered so soon after.

"I let everyone hover around me and start taking over my decision-making." She dug her index finger into her chest. "I'm making this decision. I'm staying on until I know what really happened to my husband."

Tori placed her hand on Honor's arm. Softly, she said, "That's honorable and all, honey, but—"

"I'm not doing it just for me. He needs me." She nodded toward Coburn even though they had maintained eye contact. "You do. You said so yourself."

He muttered an expletive. "That's what I said, but I was—"

"Manipulating me, I know. But you've convinced me that I'm indispensable. You can't find what you're looking for without my help. Not in time. You're on a deadline. Without me, you won't know where to search. You don't even know your way around the area. You had to ask me for directions this morning, remember?"

He clamped his jaw shut.

Honor said, "You know I'm right."

He stewed for a few moments, but Honor knew she'd won the argument even before he returned Tori's phone to her and began reiterating his instructions.

When asked, she gave him the general location of her house on the lakeshore. "It's about a two-hour drive, depending on freeway and bridge traffic. Shall I call you when we get there?"

"Is there a landline at the house?"

She recited the number, which Honor memorized, as she knew Coburn did. He said, "Let us call you. Don't answer the phone unless it rings once, and then again two minutes later. And leave your cell phone off. No battery."

Honor protested. "What if there's an emergency at her fitness center? No one would know how to reach her."

Tori waved off that concern. "It's a building, you and Em are my family. Besides, it's insured to the hilt."

Finally, all the details that they could think of had been discussed, and it came time for Honor to part with Emily.

Struggling to keep her tears in check, Honor hugged her close, reminding herself that as heartwrenching as it was to let her go, it was the best thing she could do for her child. The risk of Emily's becoming collateral damage if she stayed with her and Coburn was simply too great.

Honor was laying her own life on the line, but it was something she had to do for Eddie's sake. And even more for her own.

Emily was too excited over the prospect of having time with her Aunt Tori to notice Honor's emotion. "Are you and Coburn coming to the lake, too?"

"Maybe later. Right now, you're going with Aunt Tori all by yourself. Just you! Like a big girl. Won't that be fun?"

"Is this part of the 'venture?"

Honor tried to keep a brave face. "It's the best part."

"Sleeping on the boat was the best part," Emily countered. "Can we sleep there again sometime? And maybe I could drive it."

"We'll see."

"That's what Coburn said, too, but I think he'll let me."

Leaning down to her, Honor said, "You need to be on your way. Give Mommy a kiss."

Emily bussed Honor's cheek enthusiastically, then held her arms up to Coburn. "Coburn. Kiss."

He'd been acting as though on sentry, obviously ill at

ease with being so exposed and impatient with the protracted farewell scene. Now his head snapped around and his gaze dropped to Emily.

"Kiss," she repeated.

After a long, expectant moment, he bent down. Emily looped her arms around his neck and kissed his cheek. "Bye, Coburn."

"Bye." He stood up, pivoted quickly, and started walking quickly back toward the truck. "Hurry up," he told Honor over his shoulder.

Emily scrambled into the backseat of the Mini Cooper. Honor wasn't happy about her riding without her child seat, but Tori promised to drive with special care until she could stop and buy one.

When it came time for the two women to say goodbye, Tori eyed her warily. "You're sure you're doing the right thing?"

"I'm not at all sure. But I've got to do it anyway."

Tori smiled ruefully. "You always were the Girl Scout." She hugged Honor tightly. "I can't even pretend to understand it all, but even I'm smart enough to realize that you're trusting me with Emily's life. I'd die before letting something bad happen to her."

"I know you would. Thanks for this."

"You don't have to thank me."

The two friends shared a long look of unspoken trust, then Tori got into the Mini. As Honor closed the car door for her, Tori said through the open window, "I don't care who or what Coburn is, I just hope you're finally getting laid."

Chapter 30

Clint Hamilton had been on the telephone for ten minutes with Tom VanAllen, who was giving him a full account of the morning's events. He sounded reluctant, hesitant, and apologetic, which didn't surprise Hamilton, because the upshot of the report was that Coburn had outfoxed and eluded the authorities again.

When VanAllen concluded, Hamilton thanked him absently, then remained silent for nearly a full minute while he absorbed and analyzed the new information. Finally he asked, "Any sign of a struggle aboard the boat?"

"I'm sending you some pictures by email. Our agent took interior and exterior shots. As you'll see, it's a shambles, but if you're asking if they found fresh blood or anything like that, then no."

"Coburn left the phone there, and it was on?"

"Deputy Crawford and I agree that he left it behind intentionally."

"To draw everyone to the boat, while he was going the opposite direction."

"Yes, sir."

Hamilton had no doubt that had been Coburn's intention. "The footprints. Did they indicate that Mrs. Gillette was being dragged from the boat? Heel skid marks, anything like that?"

"No, sir. In fact, Crawford has come right out and suggested that she's not a hostage as originally believed."

"I sense a *furthermore*."

"Well, we've been given no indication that she's attempted to escape from Coburn."

"How could she without risking her child's safety?"

"I understand, but, as Crawford pointed out, she obviously had access to her telephone, yet she didn't use it to make any distress calls."

Everything that Tom was saying lent even more credibility to what Hamilton had heard from the widow herself during their phone conversation yesterday. Forsaking law and order, trusted lifelong friends, and even her father-in-law, who by all accounts was her personal guard dog, Honor Gillette had allied herself with Lee Coburn.

"What about the tire tracks?"

"Their footprints led us right to them a couple hundred yards from the boat. The tread is clearly defined and has already been typed. The tires came as standard issue on several makes of Ford pickups, model years 2006 and 2007."

"Jesus. That narrows it down to several thousand pickups in Louisiana alone."

"It's a daunting number of vehicles, yes, sir."

"I'm sure the locals are running checks on stolen Ford pickups."

"None reported so far."

Not surprising. Coburn would have chosen his vehicle wisely.

"State agencies have ordered that every Ford truck of those model years be stopped and checked," VanAllen was saying. "Meanwhile, Mr. Gillette is very concerned about his daughter-in-law and granddaughter. He came straight here from the shrimp boat and was—"

"Explain to me what he was doing there when the authorities arrived."

VanAllen shared Deputy Crawford's suspicion that Doral Hawkins and Stan Gillette had a direct pipeline into the Tambour P.D. "Crawford thinks they've got moles inside the sheriff's office, too. Courthouse. Everywhere."

"The good ol' boy system," Hamilton remarked.

"Yes, sir." VanAllen continued by describing Stan Gillette's state of mind. "He went ballistic over Crawford's insinuation that his daughter-in-law was 'in cahoots'—his words—with Coburn. He caused quite a scene in our lobby, insisted on seeing me personally, gave me an ass-chewing for not putting this 'upstart deputy sheriff' in his place. Said I was being derelict in my duties and that if his family wound up dead, their blood would be on my hands. Which," he said around a sigh, "I know without his telling me."

Hamilton considered his decision for several seconds, then said, "Tom, Mrs. Gillette and her little girl are in danger, but not from Coburn. He's one of ours. He's an agent."

After a momentary pause, VanAllen said, "Crawford asked me point-blank if he was. I said no."

"Where did he get the notion?"

"Rumor mill, he said."

That was troubling. The rumor had to have originated in Tom VanAllen's own office, based on the fishing Hamilton had done yesterday. Apparently his inquiries hadn't been as subtle as he'd thought. Shelving that issue for the moment, he gave Tom background information on Coburn.

"I recruited him straight out of the Marines and trained him personally. He's one of the best undercover agents in the bureau. He always worked deep, but never as deep as he did at Marset's company.

"He took Mrs. Gillette and the little girl from their home for their own protection. I spoke with her on the phone yesterday. Neither she nor the child has suffered any harm from Coburn. Nor will they. On that score, you can ease your mind." He paused, then said, "What you should be concerned about is the seepage of information out of your office."

VanAllen didn't say anything for the longest time, but Hamilton could feel the man's slow burn coming through the phone. When he did speak, his voice vibrated with anger. "Why did you deliberately mislead me about Coburn?"

"Because his mission was sensitive. Before revealing who he was, I had to know how he was perceived."

"You made a fool of me."

"No, I—"

"What would you call such gross manipulation?"

"Tactics, Tom." Hamilton raised his voice to match the angry level of VanAllen's. "There's some bad shit going on down there, and everyone is susceptible to corruption."

"That's a chickenshit response."

"Ours is a chickenshit business. In order to be good at it, you can't trust anybody."

"If you didn't trust me, why did you appoint me to this job? Or *is* that why? Because you *didn't* trust me."

"I appointed you because you were, and are, the best man for that position."

VanAllen gave a bitter laugh. "Well, in light of my position, can you tell me why Coburn was planted inside Sam Marset's trucking company?"

"Is this line secure?"

"Is any?"

"Good point," Hamilton said dryly.

"The building was swept for bugs this morning. We're as safe as we ever can be. What was Coburn's mission?"

Hamilton talked him through the nuts and bolts of Coburn's secret op. "Essentially he went in to unmask all the players. Discovered more than he bargained for."

"The Bookkeeper."

"The Bookkeeper. Coburn says he was on the verge of making an ID."

"So why haven't you made arrangements for him to come in, share what he knows?"

"I tried," Hamilton said. "He's reluctant."

"Why?"

"He wants to finish what he started."

"How noble," VanAllen said snidely. "The truth is, he doesn't trust this office and his fellow FBI agents."

Hamilton said nothing. Some statements didn't need any elaboration.

"Where does Mrs. Gillette fit into this?" VanAllen asked.

"Not her per se. Possibly her late husband. Coburn thinks Gillette died with secrets to reveal about The Bookkeeper."

"That explains why Stan Gillette was yelling about false accusations against his late son."

"Chalk up another reason for him to hate Coburn.

And then there's Doral Hawkins, who's out to avenge his brother. The target on Coburn's back gets bigger every minute he's out there."

"Which makes his reluctance to come out of hiding understandable."

"It's a volatile situation, and the whole thing could blow up in our faces." Having reached the heart of the matter, Hamilton waited several beats, then said, "That's why I need you to be in top form, Tom."

"You want me to bring them in."

"I do. Bring them in along with any knowledge either has of The Bookkeeper. We need to finish this thing."

"I understand, sir."

"Understanding alone isn't good enough, Tom. I need to know that I can count on you."

Chapter 31

As soon as Coburn climbed back into the pickup truck, he placed his hands on the steering wheel and tried to ignore the damp spot on his cheek where Emily had planted a kiss.

He wanted to wipe it away, but doing so would be an acknowledgment that it was there and that he felt it. Better that he attach no significance to it whatsoever. But as he watched the Mini Cooper disappear around the bend on the other side of the bridge, he realized that he was going to miss the kid's chatter.

When Honor joined him in the pickup, he gave her a dirty look for having lagged behind, but he didn't say anything because she was trying unsuccessfully to hold back tears, and the last thing he needed was for her to have a crying jag.

He started the truck, glad to be leaving this so-called secret meeting place. As they crossed the groaning wooden bridge, Honor said, "You mentioned to Tori that the authorities would be on the lookout for this pickup by now. What makes you think so?"

He explained about the tire tracks they had left near the boat. "No way they could have missed them. If these tires were put on this truck at the factory, they'll be on the lookout for this make and model."

"Which means we risk being stopped."

"Until we get another set of wheels."

"You plan to steal another car?"

"I do."

"From?"

"The same family that supplied the truck."

They drove for almost twenty minutes along back roads on which even natives to the region could have become lost. But Coburn had a photographic memory of places he'd been and a flawless sense of direction, so he was able to relocate the house from which he'd taken the pickup.

The house was half a mile away from its nearest neighbor. It sat roughly seventy yards off the road, and was screened by a dense grove of pine trees. The mailbox at the turnoff was the only giveaway that there was a house at all. The box was still bulging with uncollected mail.

As he slowly guided the pickup up the private drive, he was relieved to note that nothing had changed since he'd been there eighteen hours earlier. The owners hadn't returned.

"How did you get here yesterday?" Honor asked. "How'd you find it?"

"I was driving around looking for a car that would be easy to steal. Noticed the mailbox. I went past, ditched the other car about two miles from here, then doubled back on foot." He pulled the truck to its original spot behind the house and cut the engine.

"Nice place," she remarked.

He shrugged. "I guess. It serves my purpose."

Honor, looking thoughtfully at the shuttered windows on the back of the house, said, "I was married to a police officer sworn to safeguarding people and property. Do you ever feel guilty about stealing cars or trespassing?"

"No."

She turned her head and looked at him with a combination of dismay and disappointment.

Both of which vexed him. "If you're nursing qualms about trespassing and stealing cars, you should have gone with your friend. But, for Eddie's sake, you wanted to see this through. If you want to see it through and stay alive, you'd better start thinking mean."

"Like you."

"Me? No. Mean like the bad guys who transport young girls from city to city to be sex slaves to degenerates. *That's* mean. And your darling Eddie might have been part of it."

He opened the door to the pickup and got out. He didn't look back to see if Honor would follow. He knew she would. That had been a cheap shot, but it was calculated to snap her out of her conscientious slump.

Besides, he'd had it up to here with Saint Eddie. And who knew? Maybe Eddie *had* specialized in trafficking girls.

The garage was about twenty yards from the house. Stairs attached to the exterior wall led to quarters above it, but Coburn was interested only in the car he'd seen inside the garage yesterday when he peered through a window in the door. There was an old-fashioned hasp and padlock securing it, but he used a crowbar from the toolbox in the pickup, and within seconds was raising the garage door.

The sedan was at least a decade old, but, despite a layer of dust, the body was in good shape, and none of the tires was flat. The keys were dangling from the ignition. He climbed in, pumped the gas pedal a couple of times, cranked the key, and held his breath. It took a couple of tries and some sweet talk, but it started. The gauge indicated more than half a tank of gas. He drove the car out of the narrow garage far enough to clear the door, then put it in park and got out.

He pulled down the garage door and fixed the broken padlock to make it appear, from a distance anyway, to still be intact. Then he looked at Honor, who was silently fuming, and hitched his chin toward the passenger-side door. "Get in."

"Has he got an alarm system?"

"Yes."

"Do you know the code?"

"Yes."

"Is the backyard fenced?"

"Yes."

"Can we get in without being seen?"

"Possibly. At the back corner of the house, there's an exterior door going into the garage. It has a keypad, but I know the code. There's access to the kitchen through the garage."

They'd already driven past Stan Gillette's house twice, but Coburn wanted to be damn certain that he wasn't walking into a carefully laid ambush. He had no choice except to take the risk. He had to get into that house.

Befitting Gillette's character, his was the neatest house on the street. Basic Acadian in style, its white paint was so fresh it hurt the eyes. Nary a blade of grass defied the perfect edging along the curb and front walkway. Old Glory hung from one of four square columns on the front porch, which provided support for the overhang of the red tin roof. It was so perfect, it could have been ordered already assembled from a catalog.

Coburn drove past it and circled the block again.

"He's not there," Honor said, emphasizing it now, since she'd already told him that several times.

"How do you know for sure?"

"Because he doesn't put his car in the garage except at night. If he were in the house, his car would be in the front driveway."

"Maybe this is a special occasion."

Two blocks away from Gillette's street was a green belt with a small playground. Two cars were parked in the lot. One must've belonged to the young mother shooting video of her daughter who was hanging upside down from a bar on the jungle gym, the other to the teenage boy who was hitting tennis balls against a backboard.

No one gave them a look as Coburn pulled the car into the lot. As long as the rural family stayed away from home, he considered the sedan a relatively safe mode of transportation. No one would be looking for it. All the same, it was less conspicuous here than parked on a neighborhood street where it could arouse curiosity.

He looked across at Honor, who he could tell was still pissed at him for the crack he'd made about her late husband. "Ready?"

Her expression said *no*, but she nodded *yes* and got out of the car. "We're in no particular hurry," he said. "Just a couple out for a leisurely stroll. Okay? Wouldn't hurt for you to smile."

"This coming from the man who doesn't own one."

They fell into step and walked along the perimeter of the green, unnoticed by those on the playground. The mom was laughing and shouting directions to her daughter, who was still hanging upside down and making funny faces at the camera. The tennis player had iPod earphones in, so he was completely oblivious to his surroundings.

Nudging Honor along with him, Coburn skirted the green belt, then walked into a yard that backed up to it. Honor looked around nervously. "What if a homeowner comes out and asks what we're doing?"

"Our dog ran off before we could get his leash on. Something like that. But no one will ask."

"Why not?"

"Because if they see us, they will in all likelihood recognize us and immediately notify the police. I'm armed and dangerous, remember?"

"Okay, so what happens if we hear sirens coming this way?"

"I run like hell."

"What do I do?"

"You collapse to the ground, and cry, and thank them for saving you from me."

But the point was moot because no one accosted them, and they reached the back corner of Stan's house without mishap. Honor raised the cover on the keypad and pecked in the code. Coburn waited to hear the metallic nick, then turned the knob and pushed open the door.

They slipped into the garage, and he pulled the door shut behind them. Daylight coming through three high windows enabled them to see their way to the kitchen door. Honor stepped inside and disarmed the alarm system. Its warning chirp fell silent.

But when she would have moved farther into the kitchen, he placed his hand on her shoulder and shook his head. He mistrusted the ease with which they'd breached the house. So he remained on the threshold, muscles tensed, ready to bolt.

Silences weren't all the same. They had qualities that he'd been trained to distinguish. For sixty long seconds he listened, until, finally, he determined that the house was truly empty. Then he removed his hand from Honor's shoulder. "I think we're okay."

Most operating rooms weren't as sterile as Stan Gillette's kitchen. Coburn figured the sterility was a reflection of the man himself. Cold, impersonal, unyielding, no areas that could become cluttered with emotional junk.

Which, he realized, was also an accurate description of himself.

Shoving that thought aside, he asked Honor where Eddie's stuff was.

"All over the house, really. Where do you want to start?"

She led him into what had been Eddie's bedroom when he was growing up. "It hasn't changed much since the first time I came here. Eddie brought me to meet Stan. I was so nervous."

Coburn didn't give a shit, and his indifference must have been apparent because she ended the stroll down memory lane and stood in the center of the room, her hands awkwardly clasped in front of her.

"What?" he asked.

"It's strange being in this house, in this room with..."

"Without Eddie?"

"I was going to say *with you.*"

Several responses sprang to mind, but all of them were either vulgar or otherwise inappropriate, and he didn't have time to deal with the bickering that a lewd comment would inevitably spark. Keeping the comebacks to himself, he pointed her toward a bureau. "Empty the drawers. I'll start on the closet."

He gave it the same thorough treatment that he had the closets in Honor's house. It seemed that Gillette hadn't disposed of anything belonging to his son. Resisting the temptation to rush, Coburn tried not to overlook anything or to dismiss an item until he'd searched it.

Thinking that Eddie's police uniforms would be a logical hiding place, Coburn examined each seam, lining, and pocket of every garment, looking for something sewn inside. He didn't find anything except lint.

When an hour had passed and he had nothing to show for it, he began to feel the pressure of time. "Is Gillette usually away from the house during the day?" he asked Honor.

"He has his various activities, but I don't keep close tabs on his schedule."

"Do you think he's out doing one of his various activities?"

"No. I think he's out looking for Emily and me."

"So do I."

Another hour went by, increasing his frustration. He was on borrowed time and it was getting away from him. He glanced over at Honor to ask her another question about her father-in-law's daily routine, but the question died before he asked it.

She was sitting on the double bed, going through a box of keepsakes, most of which were medals and ribbons Eddie had won for sporting contests throughout his schooling. She was crying silently.

"What's the matter?"

Her head came up. Tears spilled from her eyes. "What's the matter? What's the *matter*? This is the matter, Coburn. This!" She dropped the medal that she'd been rubbing between her fingers and shoved the box away from her with such force that it slid off the edge of the bed and landed bottom side up on the floor. "I feel like a grave robber."

What did she want him to say? *I'm sorry, you're right, let's leave.* Well, he wasn't going to say that, was he? So he didn't say anything. A moment passed while they just looked at one another.

Eventually she made a resigned sound and wiped the tears off her cheeks. "Never mind. I don't expect you to understand."

She was right. He didn't understand why this was so upsetting to her. Because he *had* robbed a grave once. After thoroughly searching for survivors in the decimated village, where even the pathetic livestock hadn't been spared, he'd plunged down into a pit where body was heaped upon body.

He'd plowed through the rotting corpses of dead babies and naked old ladies, strong men and pregnant women, looking for clues as to which of the warring tribes was responsible for this particular massacre. He'd been under orders to find out. Not that the answer mattered all that much, because the guilty faction soon would be subjected to retaliation that was just as horrific.

He'd failed to gather any intel. All his search had produced was a canteen of water that miraculously had escaped the hail of bullets fired into the pit from automatic weapons. His own canteen had been running low, so he'd slid the strap of the canteen off the shoulder of a dead man, a boy really, no more than twelve or thirteen by the looks of him, and had slipped the strap onto his own shoulder as he climbed out of the mass grave.

That had been a lot worse than this. But Honor didn't need to know about it.

"Where's Stan's room?"

*   *   *

Two hours later, Stan Gillette's house was in a state similar to Honor's when Coburn had finished with it. The yield
was also the same. Nothing.

He'd thought perhaps Stan's computer would contain
incriminating information, but getting into it didn't even
require a password. Coburn had searched through his
documents file and found little beyond letters to the editor,
which Stan had composed either in support of or opposition to political editorials.

His emails were mostly exchanges with former Marines,
relating to upcoming or past reunions. There was a progress report on one former comrade's prostate cancer, the
death notice of another.

Likewise the websites Gillette routinely visited were
devoted to the Corps, veterans' organizations, and world
news, certainly nothing pornographic or relating to the
trafficking of illegal substances.

The hoped-for treasure trove turned out to be a big fat
bust.

Finally, the only place that hadn't been searched was the
garage. Coburn had never lived in a place with a garage,
but he knew what they were supposed to look like, and this
one was fairly typical, except for one major difference: its
extraordinary organization.

In the extra bay, a spick-and-span bass fishing boat
sat on its trailer. Hunting and fishing gear was so nicely
arranged it looked like a store display. Along the back of a
work table, carefully labeled paint cans had been perfectly
lined up. Hand tools were neatly arrayed on a pegboard
wall. A power lawnmower and edger, along with a red gas
can, were sitting on a pallet of bricks.

"Shit," Coburn said under his breath.

"What?"

"It would take days to go through all this." He nodded toward the small loft that was mounted just under the ceiling in one corner. "What's up there?"

"Mostly Eddie's sporting gear."

A ladder constructed of two-by-fours had been built into the wall. Coburn climbed it and stepped onto the loft. "Hand me a knife." Honor got one from the work table and passed it up to him. He used it to slice through the packing tape on a large box. Inside, he found an archery target, baseball, basketball, soccer ball, and football.

"Watch out."

One by one, he tossed them down. A bowling ball was in the bottom of the box. The finger holes were empty. Coburn opened a second box to find uniforms for each of the sports, a baseball glove, a football helmet, shoulder pads. He searched them all. Found nothing.

When he came down, Honor was holding the football, turning it over in her hands. She ran her finger along the leather lacing. Smiling, she said, "Eddie was quarterback of the high school team. His senior year, they went to district. That's when we started dating. That season. He was too small to play college ball, but he still loved the game and would go out and throw passes whenever he could get somebody to catch them."

Coburn held out his hand. Honor gave him the football. He plunged the blade of the knife into it.

She cried out and reflexively reached out to take the football back, but he worked the knife to increase the size of the hole, then shook it so that anything inside it would fall out. Nothing did. He tossed the deflated ball onto the work table.

When he came back around, she slapped him. Hard.

"You're a horrible person," she said. "The coldest, most heartless, cruelest creature I can imagine." She stopped on a sob. "I hate you. I really do."

At that moment, he pretty much hated himself. He was angry and didn't know why. He was acting like a complete jerk and didn't know why. He didn't understand his compulsion to want to hurt and rile her, but he seemed incapable of stopping himself.

He took a step toward her and made it intentionally intimidating. "You don't like me?"

"I *despise* you."

"You do?"

"Yes!"

"Is that why you sucked my tongue down your throat last night?"

She seethed for a count of five, then spun away from him, but before she'd taken a single step he reached out and brought her back around. "That's what you're really pissed about, isn't it? Because we kissed." Lowering his face closer to hers, he whispered, "And you liked it."

"I hated it."

He didn't believe that. He didn't want to believe it. But he forced himself to appear indifferent to whether she had liked it or not. He released her arm and stepped away from her. "Don't beat yourself up over it. Humans are animals, and animals mate. They also sneeze and cough and fart. And that's about as much as that kiss meant. So relax. You didn't cheat on your dead husband."

She hiccupped a sound of affront, but before she could articulate a response, he took out his cell phone and turned it on. By now Hamilton would know about this morning's close call on the shrimp boat. Coburn wanted to know what the fallout of that had been.

He placed the call. Hamilton answered immediately. "Coburn?"

"Good guess."

"You pulled a fast one this morning."

"By the skin of my teeth."

"Which was enough. Where are you?"

"Try again."

"I've set it up with Tom VanAllen for you and Mrs. Gillette to come in. He's as solid as Gibraltar. It'll be safe. I give you my word."

Coburn held Honor's stare. His cheek still stung where she'd slapped him, where hours ago her daughter had left the wet imprint of a goodbye kiss. He wasn't used to dealing with people who wore their emotions on their sleeves, and these Gillette women had made it an art. No wonder he was cranky.

"Coburn?" Hamilton said, repeating his name for the third time.

"I'll call you back," he said, and clicked off the phone.

Chapter 32

———⊰•⊱———

He lied to you."

Tom VanAllen made a motion with his shoulder that could have been either a shrug of indifference or of concession. "Not outrightly."

"He deliberately misled you," Janice said. "What would you call it?"

He would call it lying. But he didn't want to use that term with Janice to describe how Hamilton had manipulated him. Essentially, he was defending Hamilton's manipulation, and he hated himself for it. But to admit how gullible he'd been would make him look even more ridiculous to his wife.

He'd come home to help her with Lanny, who'd kept them up most of the night moaning. It was a distress signal they knew well. Those pitiable sounds were his only means of communicating that something was wrong. Sore throat? Earache? Muscle cramp? Headache? He wasn't running a fever. They checked him daily for bedsores. Because they didn't know why he was suffering, they couldn't do anything to relieve it, and, as parents, that was torture.

Maybe he'd only been afraid, and their presence at his bedside had comforted him, because eventually he'd fallen asleep. But it had been a rough night. That, coupled with Tom's professional crisis, was making both of them feel particularly whipped today.

After tending to Lanny, he'd declined her offer to make lunch, and had instead chosen the den as the room in which to tell her about Hamilton's trickery. He'd noticed the computer was on, and when he remarked on it, she admitted to having spent several hours that morning investigating the websites of some of the better perpetual care homes within a reasonable distance.

Tom regarded that as a step forward. Of sorts. Paradoxically it was a forward step that led to an end. He was almost relieved to have another crisis diverting his attention from that one.

"How do you know he's telling the truth now?" Janice asked.

"You mean about Coburn being an undercover agent?"

"That man seems no more like an FBI agent than—"

"Than I do."

Her stricken expression was as good as an admission that he'd taken the words out of her mouth. She tried to recant. "What I meant was that Coburn sounds like someone who's cracked. He killed eight people, counting Fred Hawkins."

"Hamilton claims Coburn didn't shoot those men in the warehouse."

"Then who did?"

"He didn't say."

"Does he know?"

Tom shrugged.

She exhaled a gust of breath, her annoyance plain. "So he's still playing head games with you."

"He's paranoid." Hamilton had come right out and accused Tom's office of being riddled with holes through which information was flowing. Deputy Crawford had groused about the moles in the various law enforcement agencies. "Everyone is paranoid, with reason," he told Janice.

"Why didn't Coburn call you for help when all hell broke loose? Why did he run away from the massacre, ransack the Gillette house, and make himself look a criminal?"

"He wanted to maintain his cover for a while longer. Besides, Hamilton is his exclusive go-to guy. Hamilton put him there in Marset's company, and no one else knew. I wasn't even Coburn's fallback contact."

"Until now." Janice didn't even try to disguise her bitterness. "Now that Hamilton's boy wonder has his back against a wall, he dumps it on you to bring him in. You know what that means, don't you? It means that if something bad happens, you catch the blame. Not Clint Hamilton, who's safe and sound up in his carpeted office in D.C."

She was right, of course, but it irked him to hear his gnawing resentment put into words by his wife. He grumbled, "It may not even happen."

"What do you mean?"

"First, Hamilton has to contact Coburn, who's being very coy about staying in touch. Then he has to persuade him to place himself in my custody, and that's going to be a tough sell."

"Why wouldn't he want safety and protection?"

"He doesn't trust me—the bureau—to provide it. If he did, he would have called me in the first place, like you said. Frankly, he'd be crazy not to be cautious. If Marset was as dirty as alleged, God knows what kind of evidence Coburn has collected. Anyone who did illicit trade with Marset probably has a contract out on Coburn.

"And then there are the personal vendettas. I'm told Doral Hawkins is out for his blood. So is Mrs. Gillette's father-in-law. The vigilante mindset has Hamilton worried."

"He wants Coburn alive."

"He wants the evidence Coburn obtained." He glanced at his wristwatch and then reached for his suit jacket. "I need to get back. I've got to be on hand and ready for whatever happens."

As he walked past her toward the door, she reached for his hand to detain him. "What if he doesn't?"

"What if who doesn't what?"

"What if Coburn doesn't come in?"

"Status quo for me. I won't be the hero, but I won't have a chance to screw up, either."

"Don't talk about yourself that way, Tom." She stood up and clasped his shoulders. "Don't even think that way. This could be an opportunity for you to prove your mettle."

Her confidence in him was misplaced, but he appreciated her loyalty. "I'm just pissed off enough to seize that opportunity."

"Good! Show Hamilton your stuff. And Coburn. And everybody."

"I'll do my best."

Her expression softened. "Whatever you do, be careful."

"I will."

"This man may be an FBI agent, but he's dangerous."

"I'll be careful. I promise."

Before leaving, he stopped in Lanny's room. The boy's

eyes were open, but he lay still, silent, staring, and Tom almost wished for the agitation he'd exhibited last night. At least that demonstrated that he felt *something*, that he shared some level of humanness with his father. Any connection would be better than none at all.

"I would do anything for you, Lanny," he whispered. "Anything. I hope that . . . that on some level, you know that." Tom touched his son's hair, then leaned down and kissed his forehead.

He got as far as the front door before realizing that he'd left his keys in the den. He retraced his steps and was about to reenter the room when he drew up short.

Janice had returned to her seat on the sofa. She had her cell phone in hand, her thumbs furiously tapping the touch screen. In under a minute, he and his problems had been discarded and forgotten. She was totally engrossed in her own world, a world in which he had no part.

He remembered that just a few days ago—or was it yesterday?—he'd caught her similarly absorbed in her telephone.

"Janice?"

She jumped. "Jesus, Tom!" she gasped. "I thought you'd left."

"Obviously." He set his briefcase on the end table and walked toward her.

She came to her feet. "Did you forget something?" Her pitch was unnaturally high, her smile unusually bright.

He nodded down at the phone in her hand. "What are you doing?"

"Playing my word game."

"Let me see." He extended his hand.

"What? Why?"

"Let me see."

"You're interested in my word game?" She posed the question around a phony-sounding laugh. "Since when have you—"

He lunged and snatched the phone from her hand.

"Tom?" she cried in shock.

Then, "Tom!" spoken in a strident tone that matched her gesture when she stuck out her hand, palm up, demanding that he give her cell phone back.

Then, when he didn't, when he held it out of her reach and read the text message on the small screen, she said his name again, this time with a soft, plaintive, remorseful groan attached.

"I've called to put you on alert. Be ready to move at a moment's notice."

Diego gave a sarcastic huff. "What? And miss all this fun?"

He'd been at the Garden District mansion before sunrise and had followed Bonnell Wallace when he drove out of its front gate. Now, for hours, he'd been watching the banker's car where it had remained since 7:35 that morning when Wallace had parked it in its designated slot in the employees' parking lot of the bank building.

Watching as the sun faded a high-gloss paint job was boring as shit.

In addition to being bored, Diego disliked being idle for this long. He stayed on the move, like a shark, cruising invisibly below the surface, striking hard and fast before continuing on. *Fluid.* That was the word. He liked being fluid, not stationary.

Mainly, he resented that The Bookkeeper had held out the carrot of Lee Coburn, then had assigned him to do a mindless job that any moron could do. He thought of a dozen other activities that he could be enjoying more, not the least of which was spending time with Isobel at home.

Home. That's the term with which he thought of his underground bunker now.

The Bookkeeper was keeping him from that most pleasant of pastimes.

"I sense some discontent in your tone, Diego."

He stayed sulkily silent.

"I have a reason for assigning you to watch Wallace."

Well, so far that reason had escaped Diego. He didn't really care what the reason was. But The Bookkeeper was on the phone now, and the prospect of a more exciting and higher-paying job perked him up. "Today's the day I get Coburn?"

"Coburn is an undercover FBI agent."

Diego's heart bumped, not with anxiety, dread, or fear, but with excitement. Taking out a fed, that was trippy, man.

"You know what that means, Diego."

"It means he's toast."

"It means," The Bookkeeper said testily, "you'll have to move with extreme caution, but swiftly. When I give the go-ahead, you won't have much time."

"So give me time. Tell me now, when and where?"

"Details are pending. You'll know what I want you to know, when I'm ready for you to know it."

Which Diego translated to mean that The Bookkeeper didn't know the details yet either. He grinned, thinking about how aggravating that must be. But he wasn't stupid, and he wanted the contract, so he spoke with affected humility. "I'll be here whenever you're ready for me."

The Bookkeeper usually got in the last word, and this time was no exception. "The New Orleans authorities still haven't discovered that whore's body."

"I've told you. They won't."

"Which begs a question, Diego."

"What question?"

"How is it that you're so sure of that?"

Then the line went dead.

Chapter 33

Honor and Coburn made it back to the playground parking lot without incident.

The mother and child had left. The teenager had taken a break from his tennis practice and was now lying under a tree, earphones on, doing something on his cell phone. He didn't notice the couple who got into a stolen car and drove away.

Only then did Honor ask Coburn about his brief exchange with Hamilton. "What did he say?"

"He wants us to turn ourselves over to Tom VanAllen. He gave me his word that VanAllen is solid and that we'll be safe in his custody."

"Do you believe him?"

"If VanAllen is that solid, why didn't Hamilton let him in on my op? Now, all of a sudden, Hamilton trusts him. That makes me nervous. I'd have to be eyeball to eyeball with VanAllen before I could gauge his trustworthiness, and I won't have that much time before placing our lives in his hands."

"And the other part? About his ability to protect us."

"I have even less confidence in that." He looked over at her. "The hell of it is, I'm running out of options."

"I would say so. You've resorted to puncturing harmless footballs."

He ignored that, but she hadn't really expected an apology.

"The thing is, I know I'm right." He looked over at her as though daring her to contradict him.

"All right, say Eddie did have something, how long can you continue to search for it alone? What I mean is," she said, rushing to continue before he could interrupt, "with all the technology that the FBI has at its disposal, if you were working with other agents, with a network of personnel, wouldn't you stand a better chance of discovering what Eddie had stashed?"

"My experience with a network of personnel? Things usually get fubared, and I'm talking on a colossal scale. Even good agents get hamstrung by bureaucratic red tape, and the federal government has miles and miles of it, most of which is wound around the DOJ. That's why Hamilton had me working alone."

"And why it's only your life that's in jeopardy now."

He shrugged. "Goes with the job." Then he tipped his head for emphasis. "*My* job. Not yours."

"I'm here because I chose to be."

"You chose wrong."

They'd been keeping to the outskirts of town, where there were clusters of houses now and then, but no organized neighborhoods like the one they'd left. Sad-looking strip centers and lone businesses were either run-down or had been closed for good, some abandoned after Katrina and never reopened, others victims of the economic crash caused by the BP oil spill.

Coburn pulled into the parking lot of a strip center that had a Dollar General store, a barber shop, and a small market and liquor store that featured homemade boudin sausage and antitheft bars on all the windows.

He cut the motor, then propped his elbow in the open window and cupped his mouth and chin with his hand. For several minutes he sat still, as though in deep thought, but his eyes remained in constant motion, watching everyone who went into or out of one of the businesses, warily evaluating each car that drove into the parking lot.

Finally he lowered his hand and reached for his cell phone. "I'm going to make this quick, okay?"

She nodded.

"Whatever I say to Hamilton, you go along."

She nodded, but with less surety.

"You gotta trust me on this." His blue eyes bore into hers.

She gave him another nod.

"Okay then." He placed the call.

She heard Hamilton's brusque voice. "I hope you're calling to tell me you've come to your senses."

"There's an old train on an abandoned track."

He gave Hamilton the location on the outskirts of Tambour. She was acquainted with the general area, but had never noticed the railroad track or the old train parked there.

"VanAllen only," he said. "And I mean it. I feel one tingle down my spine and we're outta there. I send Mrs. Gillette to VanAllen. But I'm keeping her kid with me until I'm certain that everything's—"

"Coburn, that—"

"Is how it's going to be. Ten o'clock."

He disconnected and turned off the phone.

When Stan raised his garage door using the remote on his car's sun visor, Eddie's basketball rolled out onto the driveway.

That could only mean one thing.

He killed his car's engine and got out. As he did so, he slid his knife from the scabbard strapped to his ankle. He approached the open maw of his garage with caution, but he could see that no one was inside.

When he spotted Eddie's deflated football on the work table, he was seized by a cold fury. He hefted his knife, enjoying the familiar balance of it in his hand.

Stan moved swiftly but silently toward the door that led into his kitchen. He turned the knob, then thrust the door open. The warning beep of his alarm didn't engage. No one sprang out at him. The house was soundless, perfectly still. Honed instinct told him that there was no one inside. Nevertheless, he kept his knife at the ready as he moved from room to room, surveying the damage.

Coburn.

Then and there, Stan resolved that when he came face-to-face with the man, he would tear him apart with the same level of ruthlessness with which Coburn had disemboweled his house, particularly Eddie's room.

Standing on the threshold of the bedroom that, until today, had remained largely unchanged since Eddie's youth, Stan tried to determine whether or not anything had been taken from it. However, that was almost beside the point. The room had been desecrated, and that was more untenable than theft.

Searching the rooms this thoroughly would have taken a while. Hours, Stan estimated. A near impossible task for one man working alone.

Honor.

The thought caused Stan's heart to painfully constrict. Had his daughter-in-law actually participated? Stan tried denying that such was possible. As Eddie's widow, shouldn't she, more than anyone, want to preserve his good name, if not for her own sake, then for Emily's? But the evidence before him indicated that she had assisted the man bent on tarnishing Eddie's reputation.

Stan felt her betrayal keenly. Before she made a fatal mistake, he had to reach her, talk sense into her.

Toward that end, he'd been beating the bushes all day. He'd come close to making an ass of himself at the FBI office, railing at Tom VanAllen, in whom he had even less confidence than in Deputy Crawford or the agencies the two of them represented. If he wanted Honor and Emily found and brought home, it was up to him.

He'd gone to every place he could think of where she might be. He'd called on some of Honor's faculty members, other friends and acquaintances, but had met with no success. Even the priest of the church where she worshiped insisted that he hadn't heard from her, but he was praying for her and Emily's safe return. Stan had put the verbal thumbscrews on everyone he'd talked to, and he believed he would have known if he was being lied to.

Doral, who had a man watching Tori Shirah's house, informed him that she hadn't left it all day except to retrieve her newspaper just after dawn. Her car was still in the driveway.

Stan's gut instinct said otherwise. He remembered a place out in the countryside that Eddie had once shown him, a place that Honor mistakenly believed was her secret. Eddie had confided to Stan, with a goodly amount of chagrin, that he'd followed Honor from home one night when, following a brief telephone call, she'd abruptly left the house with a flimsy and transparently false explanation.

But her mysterious errand had amounted to nothing more than a meeting with Tori. Eddie had laughed it off, saying their clandestine meeting was probably a holdover from their high school days.

It was just possible that the tradition continued.

When Stan had talked to Tori the day before, she had seemed genuinely shaken and worried about Honor's so-called kidnapping. He wondered if she'd been playing him. Or if, since then, Honor had sent her a distress signal that she had deliberately withheld from him and the authorities.

So, acting on that hunch, he'd driven out to the remote spot. In the years since Eddie had shown him the place, the old wooden bridge had become more rickety. The live oak tree seemed to have spread even wider, its roots become even more gnarled.

Immediately Stan had noticed tire tracks that looked as if they'd been recently made. But they didn't particularly excite him. Honor and her friend couldn't be the only two people to have discovered this picturesque spot. It would be a perfect out of the way place for teenagers looking to park and make out, or smoke pot, or drink purloined booze. Movie companies were constantly scouting out the area looking for scenic spots for location filming.

He was about to leave and resume his search elsewhere when he noticed some characters that had been drawn in the mud. He was looking at them upside down, but when he squatted down to take a closer look right side up, his breath escaped his body in a slow hiss.

Etched in the mud, the letters were irregularly sized and shaped, but readable:

EmiLy.

On the way back to town, he'd called Doral. "Your man needs his ass kicked. Tori Shirah isn't inside her house. She's with Honor and Emily."

They had agreed to meet at Stan's house to discuss how they would go about tracking down the Shirah woman, believing that if they applied themselves to it, they could get Honor's whereabouts from her.

Now, hearing a car door close, Stan retraced his steps through his house and into the garage. Doral was standing there, hands on hips, his eyes on the punctured football.

He turned around as Stan approached. "That son of a bitch."

"That's the least of it. The inside of my house looks like Honor's."

Doral expelled a long breath that carried with it several choice words. "Any sign that Honor and Emily were here, too?"

Stan said a terse no, and just that. He wasn't going to share with anyone his misgivings about Honor's loyalty. "But I know where they were at some point recently, and Tori Shirah was probably with them."

Doral's cell phone rang. He held up a finger to tell Stan to hold the thought while he took the call. He listened, then said, "Soon as you know."

When he clicked off, he grinned. "We may not need Tori. That was my guy at the FBI office. Coburn is sending Honor in."

"When? How?"

"My guy's standing by for details."

Chapter 34

Hamilton had been very specific about timing. "If you're already there when Coburn arrives, he'll be suspicious. If you come late, he'll probably scotch the plan altogether, and you'll never even see him or Mrs. Gillette. So get there with only a couple minutes to spare."

Tom VanAllen had arrived at the designated place at exactly two minutes before ten o'clock. He'd turned off the motor of his car, and after the popping of the cooling engine had stopped, the silence was complete except for the sound of his own breathing and the intermittent screech of a cricket.

He wasn't cut out for this cloak-and-dagger stuff. He knew it. Hamilton knew it. But Coburn had set the terms, and they'd been given no other choice except to agree.

The rusting train was to Tom's right, a darker bulk against the surrounding darkness. It crossed his mind that Coburn might be hiding somewhere on the train, watching and waiting, assuring himself that his conditions had been met before producing Mrs. Gillette.

Praying to God he wouldn't screw up, Tom slid back his cuff and checked the lighted hands on his wristwatch. Only thirty seconds had elapsed since his arrival. He wondered if his heart could withstand the pounding for an additional minute and a half.

He watched the second hand tick off another few seconds, marking more time since he'd called home.

He made an involuntary sound of utter despair when his mind tracked back to the scene that had played out this afternoon when he'd caught his wife on her cell phone. Caught her in the act, so to speak.

He lunged and snatched the phone from her hand.

"Tom?" she cried in shock.

Then angrily, "Tom!"

And finally, "Tom," on a soft, plaintive, remorseful groan as he read what was on the screen.

Some of the words were so blatantly sexual, they seemed to jump out and strike him. But he couldn't associate them with Janice. His wife. With whom he hadn't had marital sex in... He couldn't even remember when the last time had been.

But whenever it was, the words he was reading off her cell phone screen hadn't been part of their foreplay or whispered in the heat of passion. In fact, before today he would have bet a month's wages that language like this had never crossed her lips, that she would abhor it. Beyond bawdy, it was the dirtiest vernacular of the English language.

He scrolled up to the last text that someone—who?—had sent her. It was a salacious invitation, outlining in explicit detail what the sender would like to do with her. The reply she'd been so busily composing was an equally graphic acceptance.

"Tom—"

"Who is it?" When she just looked at him, her mouth moving but no words coming out, he repeated the question, stressing each word.

"It's no one . . . I don't know . . . he's just a name. Everybody uses code names. Nobody knows—"

" 'Everybody'?"

He tapped on the word "Messages" at the upper left-hand corner of the screen in order to display the index of senders from whom she'd received text messages. He tapped on one and several exchanges appeared. Then he accessed those sent by another sender with an equally suggestive code name. The names were different, but the content of the messages was nauseatingly similar.

He tossed the phone onto the sofa and looked at her with a kind of horrified wonderment.

Her head dropped forward, but only for a moment, then she flung it back and met him eye to eye. "I refuse to be ashamed or to apologize." She didn't so much speak the words as hurl them at him. "What I have to live with day in, day out," she shouted, "God knows I need something to amuse myself. It's a pastime! Rather pathetic and lowbrow, I'll grant you. But harmless. It doesn't mean anything."

He stared at her, wondering who this person was. She wore Janice's face, her hair, her clothes. But she was a total stranger.

"It means something to me." He picked up his car keys and stalked from the room, leaving her chasing after him, calling his name.

She must have sensed something in his tone of voice, or read something in his expression that frightened her and took the starch out of her defiance. Because the last thing he heard her say was, "Don't leave me!"

He slammed the front door on his way out.

Now, hours later, the sound of the slamming door and her plea echoed inside his head.

He'd been so damned angry. First Hamilton's machinations. Then to discover his own wife was exchanging filthy text messages with God knew who. Perverts. Sex addicts. It turned his stomach to think about it.

But leave her? Leave her to cope with Lanny alone when she couldn't handle more than a few hours without assistance? He couldn't do that. He couldn't simply walk out of their situation and leave her to cope with it alone. And even if he was inclined to abandon her, he couldn't desert Lanny.

Actually he didn't know what he would do about this. Probably nothing.

Doing nothing seemed to be the way in which he and Janice handled most of their problems. They were without friends, without sex, without any happiness whatsoever simply because neither of them had done anything to stop the erosion of it. Her "sexting" would be just another aspect of their lives that they would pretend wasn't there.

They were strangers who lived in the same house, a man and a woman who'd known one another a long time ago, who had laughed and loved, and who now were forged together by a responsibility that neither could forsake.

Jesus, they were pitiful.

He scrubbed his face with his hands and ordered himself to focus on the job at hand. He checked the time. Straight up ten o'clock.

Make yourself seen, Hamilton had told him.

He opened the car door, got out, and walked forward, stopping several yards beyond the hood of the car.

He held his hands loosely at his sides, slightly away from his body, also as Hamilton had directed. The cricket continued to fill the night air with its grating racket, but above it Tom could hear his own heartbeat, his own staggered respiration.

He didn't hear the man. Not at all.

He had no forewarning that he was there until the barrel of a pistol was jammed into the base of his skull.

When Coburn had told Honor what she was to do, she'd protested. "That goes against your own plan."

"It goes against the plan I gave to Hamilton."

"You never intended to send me to meet VanAllen?"

"Hell no. Somebody in this op is working for The Bookkeeper. Whether or not it's VanAllen, somebody is dirty. Probably lots of somebodies. The Bookkeeper will be afraid of what you know, or at least suspect, and will want you taken out as bad as he does me."

"He can't just have me shot."

"Of course he can. I told you, situations like this, hostage exchanges in particular, get fucked up real easy. Sometimes on purpose. You could become an 'accidental' casualty."

It was a sobering thought that had silenced her for several moments. He had parked their stolen car in the garage of a defunct paint and body shop, where the gutted chassis of other cars had been left to the mercy of the elements. When she'd asked him how he knew about these hiding places, he'd said, "I make it my business to know."

He hadn't elaborated, but she reasoned that he had mapped out several escape routes, planning against the time when he would need one. Like tonight.

They had waited in the stifling garage for more than an hour before he began giving her instructions. "Stay here," he'd said. "Either I'll come back within a few minutes after ten o'clock, or I won't. If I don't, drive away. Collect Emily and—"

"And what?" she'd asked when he stopped talking.

"Depends on you. You either call your father-in-law or Doral. You tell them where you are, and you get welcomed back into the fold. For a while anyway."

"Or?"

"Or you keep driving and get as far away from here as this car will take you. Then you call Hamilton. You tell him you won't come in to anybody except him. He'll come pick you up."

"Why does it have to be one way or the other?"

"Because I came to your house on Monday morning. I wish now that I hadn't. But I did. So thanks to me, The Bookkeeper and everyone on his payroll will assume you know something. The good guys will assume the same. You've got to decide which team you're on."

She looked at him meaningfully. "I already have, haven't I?"

He'd held her gaze, then said, "Okay, good. Listen up." He gave her his cell phone, recited a telephone number, and told her to memorize it.

"Hamilton's? Won't it be on the phone?"

He shook his head. "I clear the log after each call. You should, too. Got the number?"

She had repeated it back to him.

Then he'd gone through it all again, stressing to her that she couldn't trust anyone, except possibly Tori. "I got a good vibe from her. I don't think she would betray you, but she might give you up unintentionally."

"How?"

"These aren't imbeciles we're dealing with. Tori pegged it this morning. They're gonna get suspicious when they discover she's split. They'll try to pick up her trail in the hope of it leading to you."

"Why do you think so?"

"Because that's what I would do."

She smiled faintly, but her mind was busy trying to assimilate everything he was telling her. "How do you think VanAllen will react when you show up in my place?"

"I have no idea. But I'll find out soon enough. Remember, if I don't come back within a reasonable period of time, that means things went to shit. Get away from here."

When he'd said all he had to say, he got out of the car, rubbed his fingers over a spot in the garage floor where dirt had collected in a pool of motor oil, and then spread the gritty residue over his face and arms.

Then he'd gotten back into the car, checked the clip of his pistol to make certain there was a bullet in the chamber, and tucked it back into his waistband. He passed her Fred's revolver. It was huge and heavy and sinister.

Coburn must have sensed her repugnance. "It sounds like a cannon and spits flames when it fires. You may not hit your target, but you'll scare him. Don't talk yourself out of pulling the trigger, or you'll be dead. Okay?"

"Okay."

"Honor."

She shifted her gaze from the pistol to him.

"You'll be dead," he repeated, emphasizing it.

She nodded.

"Don't let your guard down for a second, for a *nanosecond*. Remember me telling you this. When you feel the safest, you'll be the most vulnerable."

"I'll remember."

"Good." He took a deep breath, let it out in a gust, then said the words that Honor had dreaded to hear. "Time to go."

"It's not even nine o'clock yet."

"If there are snipers in place—"

"Snipers?"

"—I need to know where they are."

"You made it clear to Hamilton that VanAllen must come alone."

"I wish VanAllen was the only one I had to worry about."

He'd put his left foot on the garage floor and was about to step out of the car when he stopped. For several seconds he stayed like that, then he turned his head and looked over his shoulder at her.

"As kids go, yours is okay."

She opened her mouth to speak, but found she couldn't, and wound up merely nodding.

"And the football? It was a rotten thing to do. I'm sorry."

Then he was gone, his shadow moving swiftly across the littered garage floor and slipping through a narrow opening in the corrugated tin door. The wheels squeaked on the rusty track as he rolled the door shut behind himself. She'd been left alone in the darkness.

And here she had remained for more than an hour now, sitting in a stolen car in an abandoned cavern of a building, her only company the mice she occasionally heard scratching through trash, her thoughts in turmoil.

She was worried about Emily and Tori. Coburn had allowed her to call the house. After she let the phone ring once and dialed again, Tori had answered, assured her that they had safely arrived and that all was well. But that had been hours ago. Something could have happened since then and she wouldn't know about it.

She thought of Stan, and how worried for them he must be, and how bad she felt about turning his home inside out. For all his sternness, his affection for her and Emily was genuine. She didn't doubt that for an instant.

Would he ever understand that what she had done,

she'd done strictly in order to preserve Eddie's reputation? In the final analysis, wasn't that much more important than saving a box of track-and-field medals from his school days?

But she feared Stan wouldn't see it that way and would never forgive her for invading the sanctity of Eddie's room. He would look upon her actions as a betrayal not only of him, but of Eddie and their marriage. The relationship with Stan would suffer irreparably.

And her thoughts frequently returned to Coburn and the last things he'd said to her. For him, what he'd said about Emily had been very sweet. His apologies for involving her in the first place, for ruining the football, were significant because he rarely explained or excused anything he did. When he'd apologized to Emily for making her cry, he'd done so clumsily.

It was a rotten thing to do. It might not have been the most eloquent of apologies, but Honor didn't question its sincerity. His eyes, their startling qualities emphasized even more by the makeshift camouflage on his face, had conveyed his regret as well as his words. *I'm sorry.* She believed he was.

His harsh childhood had made him cynical, and the things he'd seen and done while in service to his country had hardened his heart even more. He was often cruel, possibly because he'd witnessed how effective cruelty could be toward getting results. Whatever he said or did was unfiltered and straightforward because he knew that hesitation could be fatal. He didn't worry about future regret because he didn't expect to live to a ripe old age when one typically reexamined the pivotal decisions and actions of his life.

Everything he did, he did as though his life depended on it.

The way he did everything—ate, apologized...kissed—was like it was for the last time.

That thought brought Honor's mental meandering to a complete standstill, and she experienced a jarring realization.

"Oh, God." It was a whimper, spoken in the quietness, spoken from the heart.

Suddenly flying into motion, she pushed open the car door and scrambled out. She stumbled over debris in her path as she made her way toward the door of the garage. It took all her strength to push the heavy door along its unoiled track far enough to create a space that she could squeeze through, which she did, not even considering what dangers might be lurking beyond that door.

She paused for only a second to get her bearings, then struck out in a dead run in the direction of the railroad tracks.

Why hadn't she realized it before now? Coburn's instructions to her had been a farewell. He didn't expect to return from this meeting with VanAllen, and in his own untutored and unsentimental way, he had been telling her goodbye.

He'd said all along that he didn't expect to survive, and tonight he'd gone in her place, probably sacrificing himself to save her.

But his thinking was flawed. No one was going to shoot her. If The Bookkeeper believed she had something that would incriminate him, she wouldn't be killed until he had discovered what that something was and had taken possession of it.

She was indispensable to the criminals the same way she was to Coburn, and Hamilton, and to the Department of Justice. What The Bookkeeper perceived her to know or to have was as good as a bulletproof vest.

But Coburn had no such protection.

She was his protection.

Chapter 35

———◦———

Coburn?"

Coburn pressed the pistol more firmly against Van-Allen's neck. "Pleased to meet you."

"I was expecting Mrs. Gillette."

"She couldn't make it."

"Is she all right?"

"She's fine. Just tied up at the moment."

"That's not funny."

"It wasn't supposed to be. I'm just letting you and the sharpshooters who've got me in their night vision sights know that if they kill me, Mrs. Gillette and the kid will stay perpetually lost."

VanAllen gave a small shake of his head. "You made yourself clear to Hamilton, who made himself clear to me. There aren't any sharpshooters."

"Tell me another one."

"It's the truth."

"Wireless mike? Are you talking for the benefit of every-body out there listening in?"

"No. You can search me if you don't believe me."

Coburn deftly stepped around VanAllen, but kept his pistol aimed at his head. When he came face-to-face with the man, he sized him up. Desk jockey. Unsure. Out of his league.

Threat to him, next to nil.

Dirty or clean? Coburn would guess he was honest, because he appeared not to have either the guts or the cunning to be on the take.

Which is why Coburn believed the man truly didn't know about the sniper on the water tower over Coburn's left shoulder at seven o'clock. Or the one in the caboose window at four o'clock. Or the one he'd spotted on the roof of the apartment complex three blocks away.

That shooter would have to be extremely good, and the angle was lousy, but it could be done, and after blowing Coburn's head off, the bastard would have all the time in the world to get away.

Either VanAllen was really good at playing dumb, or he truly was in the dark, which was even more alarming.

"Where are Mrs. Gillette and the child?" he asked. "They're my chief concern."

"Mine, too. Which is why I'm here and she's not." Coburn lowered the pistol to his side.

VanAllen followed the motion, looking relieved that he was no longer staring into the bore. "You didn't trust me?"

"No."

"What reason have I given you not to?"

"None. I'd just hate to leave you out."

"You mistrust everybody."

"A life-preserving policy."

VanAllen nervously wet his lips. "You can trust me, Mr. Coburn. I don't want this fouled up any more than you do. Is Mrs. Gillette all right?"

"Yes, and I want to make damn certain she stays that way."

"You believe she's in danger?"

"Yeah, I do."

"Because she has incriminating information on The Bookkeeper?"

On the outside chance that VanAllen had lied about wearing a wireless mike, Coburn wasn't about to answer that question. "Here's what's going to happen. You're going to order the local P.D. to call off the manhunt for me. Like you, I'm an agent for the Federal Bureau of Investigation in performance of my duty. I can't have a bunch of trigger-happy yokels on my ass."

"Crawford isn't going to shrug off eight murders."

"Homicide detective?"

"For the sheriff's office. He's investigating Fred Hawkins's murder. He sort of inherited the warehouse murders when Fred—"

"I get the picture," Coburn said, cutting him off. "Talk this Crawford into granting me a reprieve until I can bring Mrs. Gillette in safely. Then I'll thoroughly brief him on the warehouse shootings and Fred Hawkins."

"He won't go for it."

"Twist his arm."

"Maybe if you gave me some exculpatory information that I could pass along—"

"Thanks, but no thanks. Your office leaks like a sieve and so does his."

VanAllen sighed, looking worried. "It all relates to The Bookkeeper, right?"

"Right."

"And it's big?"

"Right again."

"Can't you tell me anything?"

"Can. Won't."

"Why not?"

"Because if you were supposed to know, Hamilton would have already told you. He would have started by telling you about me."

The man winced, as though it pained him to hear that. He also must have sensed Coburn's resolve and decided that trying to bargain was pointless. "Okay, I'll do my best with Crawford. What are you going to do?"

"Disappear. I'll bring Mrs. Gillette in, but no one will be given notice. I'll choose my time and place."

"I'm not sure that'll fly."

"With who?"

"Hamilton. He said to tell you that time is up."

"Hamilton can go fuck himself. Tell him I said so. Better yet, I'll tell him myself. I'm still on the trail of something, and I intend to finish the job that he assigned me. If you need to go back to him with something, tell him that. Now, let's get in the car."

"What for?"

"We're gonna make it look like I'm going peaceably."

"Look like?" VanAllen glanced around, and again, Coburn thought that if he was faking his ignorance, he was good at it. "Look like to who?"

"To the snipers who've got me in their crosshairs."

"Who would want to shoot you?"

Coburn frowned at him. "Come on, VanAllen. You

know who. And the only reason they haven't taken me out already is because they still wouldn't know where Honor Gillette is. You and I will get in the car and drive away."

"Then what?"

"At some point between here and your office in Lafayette, I'll get out. When you arrive, surprise! I'm no longer in the car with you. Whoever balks first is the person you arrest immediately, because that's the person who had the snipers in place. Got it?"

VanAllen nodded, but Coburn hoped he felt more certainty than his nod demonstrated.

Coburn said, "Let's go."

VanAllen turned and walked to the driver's side of the car and opened the door. The dome light came on, convincing Coburn yet again that the agent had no field experience. But he was glad of the light because it afforded him a check of the backseat. There was no one crouched between the seats.

He opened the passenger-side door and was about to get in when he sensed motion in his peripheral vision. He turned toward the train. A shadow streaked past the gap between two of the freight cars. Coburn dropped to look beneath the train and saw a pair of legs on the other side of it sprinting away. He started crawling in that direction and was almost under the train when a cell phone rang.

Coburn swiveled his head, caught VanAllen as he reached for the ringing telephone attached to his belt.

Coburn looked beneath the train and at the man fleeing from it.

Then to VanAllen, he shouted, "*No!*"

Honor was winded and her left side was cramping, but she continued to run at full tilt. She hadn't thought the train tracks were that far from the paint and body shop garage until she began covering the distance. Running in darkness over unfamiliar ground made it even more difficult.

This was an industrial area of town comprised of warehouses, machine shops, and small manufacturing plants, all of which had been deserted for the night. Twice she plunged down blind alleys and had to retrace her steps, which became slower the farther she ran.

Only once did she allow herself a few moments to try and catch her breath. She put her back to a crumbling brick wall that formed one side of an alley. She gulped air. She pressed both hands into her side to try and ease the cramp.

She didn't linger there for long, however. Rats scuttled nearby. She couldn't see the dog that snarled at her from behind a cyclone fence at the dark end of the alley, but the sound conjured up menacing images.

She continued on.

Finally she reached the tracks. They were overgrown with weeds, but the steel rails reflected some ambient light and made the going a little easier, although her heart felt on the verge of bursting. Her lungs labored. The cramp in her side was causing her to gasp with pain.

But she ran on because Coburn's life could very well depend on her reaching him. She didn't want him to die.

When she finally spotted the old train near the water tower, she would have cried out in relief, had she had enough breath to make a sound. Seeing her goal gave her additional strength, and she pumped her legs even faster.

She made out the automobile parked near the train. She saw the two figures standing in front of the hood. As she watched, they separated. Coburn went around to the passenger side. The driver got in and closed his car door.

A heartbeat later a ball of flame bloomed into the night sky, illuminating everything around it in the red glow of hell.

The concussive blast of the explosion knocked Honor to the ground.

Chapter 36

———⇒⊶⊙⊷⇐———

Doral had the dubious pleasure of informing The Book-keeper.

"My guy in the FBI office had just enough time to plant the bomb on the car and program in the cell phone number. But it worked exactly like it was supposed to. Bam! They never had a chance."

The silence on the other end was palpable.

Doral continued. "I witnessed it myself from the top of the water tower. All of us got the hell away from the area immediately. Nobody ever knew we were there."

Still silence.

Doral cleared his throat. "There is one thing, though."

The Bookkeeper waited in stony silence.

"It wasn't Honor who showed up. It was Coburn." Unsure how The Bookkeeper would receive that piece of news, he hastily added, "Which is better when you think about it. It'll be easier to track down Honor than it would have been to deal with him."

"But those weren't your instructions. That wasn't my plan for Coburn."

Doral understood The Bookkeeper's letdown. Between Coburn and Honor, the undercover agent was naturally the bigger trophy. For personal reasons, Doral would have enjoyed killing him in a manner that was painful and protracted. Instead, the son of a bitch had gotten off light. He'd gotten the instantaneous death planned for Honor and Tom VanAllen.

When given his orders a few hours earlier, Doral had diplomatically questioned the necessity of killing the FBI agent. "He really doesn't know anything."

To which the Bookkeeper had said, "He's in a perfect position to ruin things, if unintentionally. Even a blind squirrel finds a nut every now and then. And it will look good to the Mexicans that we killed a federal agent."

"We got two FBI guys tonight," Doral said now. "That should really impress that cartel."

But The Bookkeeper didn't seem all that impressed.

Jesus, what did he have to do to make up for letting Coburn escape the warehouse? Now that Coburn and VanAllen were dead, the only remaining threat was Honor. She was just a pawn, but she was a dangerous one who had to be eliminated. Doral accepted that. Just as he'd accepted having to kill Eddie.

He and Fred had tried to persuade The Bookkeeper to rethink that mandate. They'd bargained for his life to be spared. Did Eddie, their boyhood friend, really have to *die*? Maybe just a stern warning or a threat either real or implied would work.

No loose ends. No mercy. The Bookkeeper hadn't made an exception even for Eddie. He'd crossed a line. He had to go. The order had been issued in language that a one-year-old could understand, but for the sake of all concerned, he and Fred had made it as quick and painless as possible, while still making it look like an accident.

Doral hoped he could devise something that easy for Honor.

But if she died badly, she had only that friggin' Coburn to blame, first for involving her—because Doral was convinced that she didn't know Eddie's secret—and then for stealing the quick death she should have had.

Of course before Doral could do anything, he had to find her.

With the mind-reading skills that often gave Doral gooseflesh, The Bookkeeper said, "Coburn's dead, and he was the only person who knew where Honor is. How do you plan to find her?"

"Well, now that Coburn is ashes, she may come out of hiding."

"You're willing to wait on that?"

The implication being that waiting would be a bad idea. "No, of course not. I'm going to focus on Tori Shirah. Because I'm convinced that when we find her, we find Honor and Emily."

"For your sake, I sincerely hope you're right, Doral. For once."

The Bookkeeper hung up without saying more. Doral closed his phone and realized as he started his pickup truck that his hand was shaking.

He hadn't even been congratulated for getting Coburn, the asshole who was to blame for this whole fiasco. Instead, he'd received another veiled threat. He was still on The Bookkeeper's shit list, where nobody wanted to be.

He drove his pickup out of the crowded parking lot of a tavern, where, even before calling The Bookkeeper, he'd stopped to toast his success with the car bomb. He joined the stream of vehicles that were homing in on the area near the train tracks where Tom VanAllen's car had been blown to hell and back and was still smoldering. It was attracting gawkers like moths to a giant light bulb.

It did his smarting ego some good to know that he had caused all this commotion. Too bad he couldn't crow about it.

Some of the curious had felt the impact of the blast, others had heard it, a few had actually seen the fireball that had lit up that side of town. Doral had to park two blocks from the tracks and go the rest of the way on foot... for the second time that night.

The area had been cordoned off by first responders. Uniformed police officers were still needed to keep the gathering crowd back and to make way for arriving emergency vehicles. The flashing strobes gave the whole scene a surreal aspect.

New arrivals asked questions of those already there.

Doral heard a dozen different versions of what had taken place and who was responsible, none of which were right. It was al Qaeda, it was dope dealers running a meth lab out of the trunk of their car, it was two lovesick teenagers with a suicide pact. Doral was amused by all the hypotheses.

He received condolences for the loss of his twin, who had been a victim of this crime wave. A mass murder on Sunday. A kidnapping on Tuesday. Now a car bomb. Concerned citizens wanted to know, what had happened to their peaceful little town?

Playing the role of city manager, Doral somberly pledged that the city government and local law enforce-

ment were doing all they could to catch those responsible
and put a stop to the series of violent crimes.

He'd been glad-handing for about an hour when he saw
the coroner backing his van away from the burned-out car.
Doral positioned himself to be on the driver's side when
the van stopped while officers cleared a path for it through
the crowd.

Doral motioned for the coroner to lower his window.
He obliged and said, "Hey, Doral. Had some excitement
tonight, huh?"

Doral tilted his head in the direction of VanAllen's car.
"Any guess who it was?"

"The driver?" He shook his head. "No idea. Wasn't
enough to make a positive ID just by looking." Lowering his
voice, he said, "But don't quote me on that. License plates
were destroyed, too. They're trying to get the car's VIN
number, but the metal is so hot—"

"What about the other one?"

"What other one?"

"The other person. On the passenger side." He hitched
his thumb over his shoulder. "Somebody said there
were two."

"Then somebody said wrong. There was just the one."

"What?"

"There wasn't anybody on the passenger side."

Doral reached through the open window and grabbed
the man by the collar.

Stunned by the sudden move, the coroner pushed
Doral's hand aside. "Hey, what's with you?"

"Are you sure? There was only one body?"

"Like I said, only one."

The earth dropped out from under Doral.

*   *   *

Coburn had been partially beneath the train when the bomb detonated, which is what had saved him. Triggered when VanAllen answered his cell phone, the explosion had instantly vaporized most of VanAllen and demolished the car.

When Coburn crawled out from under the boxcar on the other side, burning debris showered him, scorching his skin, hair, and clothing. With no time to drop and roll, he batted out the most dangerous of the burning patches as he ran like hell the length of the train.

The man in the caboose had saved his life. Had it not been for his running away, Coburn would have been standing in the open passenger door when VanAllen answered his phone. He rounded the caboose and ran in a crouch along the weed-choked tracks, trying to keep a low profile against the fiery glow of the burning car.

He was almost on top of Honor before he saw her, and even then it took him a second to process that the huddled form on the tracks was a body, a woman, Honor.

With full-blown panic, he thought, *Oh, Jesus, she's hurt. She dead? No!*

He bent over her and dug his fingers into her neck, looking for a pulse. She reacted by slapping at his hands and screaming bloody murder. He was glad she was alive, but at the same time furious with her for endangering herself. He hooked one arm around her waist, scooped her off the ground and up against him.

"Stop screaming! It's me."

Her legs gave way and she slumped.

"Are you hurt?"

He turned her and, holding her upright by her shoulders, looked her over. She didn't have any wounds that he could see, nothing grisly like shards of glass protruding from her torso, or shattered bones poking through her skin, no deep gashes. Her eyes were open and staring at him, but unfocused.

"Honor!" He shook her slightly. "We've got to get away from here. Now come on!"

He jerked hard on her hand as he struck out running, trusting her to come along. She did, although she stumbled several times before gaining her footing. When they reached the garage, he opened the door, shoved her inside, then rolled the door shut. He didn't even wait for his eyes to adjust to the darkness, but guided her by feel to the car. He secured her in the passenger seat, then went around and got in on the driver's side.

He pulled off his T-shirt and used it to wipe off the grease camouflaging his face and arms. The shirt came away blood-smeared. He checked his reflection in the rearview mirror. He looked exactly like what he was: a man who had barely escaped becoming a human Roman candle by clambering beneath a freight train.

He reached into the backseat and retrieved the ball cap that he'd found in the pickup truck. It helped some to conceal his face. But he figured that anyone on the streets of Tambour in the next half hour would be curious about the explosion, not about a man in a ball cap driving an old sedan.

He looked over at Honor. Her teeth were chattering, and she was hugging herself tightly as though to hold herself together against the violent shudders that seized her. He didn't even attempt to snap her out of her daze. For the time being it was just as well that she had shut down.

He got out of the car and opened the garage door. Once in the car again, he placed his hand on the top of Honor's head and pushed it down below the level of the window.

"Stay out of sight." He started the engine and drove out of the garage, his destination the only place he knew to go.

This job sucked.

By now, Diego should have been washing Coburn's blood off his razor.

Instead, the whole day, wasted.

He could have spent it with Isobel. He'd even thought it was safe enough now to take her out into the open. They could have gone to a park, sat on a bench and fed ducks, shared a blanket under a tree. Something like that.

He'd seen people doing things like that, and he'd scorned such unproductive pastimes. But he realized now why people enjoyed them. It was all about being close to another person and letting nothing distract you from the joy of simply being near them.

He could have spent the day gazing into Isobel's lovely eyes, teasing small, shy smiles out of her, perhaps daring to hold her hand. He could have seen for the first time how her hair and skin looked in sunlight, how a breeze from off the river would mold her clothes to the dainty body that tantalized him.

He would have enjoyed that.

He would have enjoyed killing the fed.

Instead, he'd wasted all day babysitting the fat guy's car.

Bonnell Wallace hadn't even left the bank for lunch. He'd parked his car in the bank employee lot that morning, and there it had stayed until he left for home at ten after five. The Bookkeeper had said to follow him, so Diego had followed him through rush-hour traffic. He'd gone straight home.

Fifteen minutes after he got to the mansion, a black

woman driving an SUV and wearing a domestic's uniform had left. She drove through the property gate, and it had closed behind her automatically.

That had been hours ago, and no one else had come or gone.

Diego was bored stiff. But if The Bookkeeper wanted to pay him to watch a gate, that's what he would do. For now. But never again. After collecting his pay for this job, plus the five hundred he was being paid for Isobel's believed extermination, he'd get himself a new phone and disappear off The Bookkeeper's radar.

As though conjuring up a call, his cell phone vibrated. He pulled it off his belt and answered.

"Are you ready for some action, Diego?"

"You hafta ask?"

The Bookkeeper issued him new instructions, but they were a far cry from what he had waited all day to hear. "You're shitting me, right?"

"No."

"I thought I was on standby to do the fed. 'Be ready, Diego. At a moment's notice, Diego,'" he mimicked. "What happened to that?"

"Change of plans, but this is related."

"How?"

"It's been a busy and trying night. Just do as I tell you without giving me an argument."

Diego stared at the big white house and considered The Bookkeeper's order. He was here and he'd invested a hell of a lot of time already; he'd just as well do it. Mumbling, he asked, "What do you want me to do with him after?"

"That's a stupid question. You know the answer. Get on it. I need this information as soon as possible. Immediately."

Fuck immediately, Diego thought as he disconnected. *I've waited on you all fucking day.*

For several minutes after, he remained in his hiding place and analyzed the mansion. As before, he mentally ticked off all the reasons why breaching it would be dicey.

He didn't like it. He had a bad feeling about this job, and had from the get-go. Why not heed his gut instinct and just walk away from it, let The Bookkeeper find someone else to do this?

But then he thought of Isobel. He wanted to get her pretty things, and he couldn't always steal them. He would need money, especially if he planned to vacation for a while and spend idle days with her. The Bookkeeper's money was good. An hour, two at most, and he would be due a hefty payday. After collecting, he could leave The Bookkeeper's employ for good.

Mind made up, he came out from his hiding place. Keeping to the shadows and moving with the stealth of one, he found a place at the back of the Wallace property where the wisteria vine on the estate wall was thick and the lighting thin.

He went over the wall.

Chapter 37

———⇒•◦•⇐———

The place was still deserted. The padlock on the door of the detached garage was exactly as Coburn had left it. The black pickup hadn't been moved from where he'd parked it that morning.

He pulled the sedan to a stop beside it and together they got out. Honor, functioning in a fog, looked to him for direction.

"Let's see what's up there." He nodded toward the room above the garage.

They climbed the staircase attached to the exterior wall. The door at the top of the stairs was locked, but within ten seconds Coburn had found the key above the doorjamb. He unlocked and opened the door, then felt the inside wall for a light switch and flipped it on.

The small room obviously had been occupied by a young male. Posters and pennants for various sports teams were tacked to the walls. The bed was covered with a sta-dium blanket. Two deer heads with eight points each stared at one another from opposite walls across a floor of clean but scuffed hardwood. A nightstand, a chest of drawers, and a blue vinyl beanbag chair were the only other pieces of furniture.

Coburn crossed the room and opened a door, revealing a closet in which were stored a tackle box and rod and reel, a few articles of winter clothing zipped into garment bags, and a pair of hunting boots standing upright on the floor.

A matching door opened into a bathroom that wasn't much larger than the closet. There was no tub, just a pre-formed fiberglass shower stall that was slightly discolored.

Honor stood in the center of the room, watching Coburn as he explored without any sign of compunction. But to her, it all felt very wrong. She wished for some background noise. She wished for more space and a second bed. She wished for Coburn not to be shirtless.

Mostly she wished that the tears pressing against her eyelids would dry up.

Coburn tested the taps on the bathroom sink. After some knocking of pipes inside the wall and gurgling sounds, water gushed from both faucets. He found a drinking glass in the medicine cabinet above the sink, filled it with cold water, and passed it to Honor.

She took it gratefully and drained it. He ducked his head into the sink and drank straight from the faucet.

When he came up, he wiped his mouth with the back of his hand. "Home sweet home."

"What if the family comes back?"

"I hope they won't. At least not until I've used their shower."

She tried to smile, but thought it probably fell flat. It felt as though it had. "Who blew up the car?"

"The Bookkeeper has somebody inside the FBI office.

Somebody privy to information." His lips formed a grim line. "Somebody who's gonna die as soon as I find out who he is."

"How are you going to do that?"

"Find your late husband's treasure, and I'll bet we find that person."

"But we haven't found it."

"We haven't looked in the right place."

"Was VanAllen—"

"He was clueless."

"What did he say when you showed up instead of me?"

Speaking tersely, Coburn recounted his brief conversation with Tom VanAllen. Honor hadn't known him, but she knew that he'd married a girl from Eddie's high school class.

"Janice."

Coburn, who had continued talking while her mind wandered, looked at her strangely. "What?"

"Sorry. I was thinking about his wife. Her name is Janice, if I'm remembering correctly. She became a widow tonight." Honor could empathize.

"Her husband should have been smarter," Coburn said. "The naive bastard really thought we were all alone out there."

"Somebody set him up to die."

"Along with you."

"Except that you took my place."

He shrugged with seeming indifference.

She swallowed the emotion that was making her throat ache and focused on something else. She pointed toward his shoulder. "Does that hurt?"

He turned his head and looked at the patch of raw skin. "I think a piece of burning car upholstery fell on me.

It stings a little. Not bad." His eyes moved over her. "What about you? Are you hurt anywhere?"

"No."

"You could have been. Seriously. If you'd been closer to the car when it blew, you could have been killed."

"Then I guess I'm lucky."

"Why'd you leave the garage?"

The question took her off guard. "I don't know. I just did."

"You didn't do what I told you to. You didn't drive away."

"No."

"So why not? What did you plan to do?"

"I didn't *plan* anything. I acted on impulse."

"Were you going to throw yourself on VanAllen's mercy?"

"No!"

"Then what?"

"I don't know!" Before he could say anything further on that subject, she motioned toward his head. "Your hair's singed."

Absently he raked his hand over his hair as he moved to the chest of drawers. In one he found a T-shirt, in another a pair of jeans. The T-shirt would do, but the jeans were six inches too short and six inches too large in the waist. "I'll have to make do with your dad's khakis."

"We're both pretty much a mess." She was still wearing the clothes she'd had on when they'd fled her house yesterday morning. Since then she'd waded through a swamp, run through a marsh, and barely escaped an explosion.

"You use the shower first," he said.

"You're worse off than I am."

"Which is why you won't want to get in it after me. Go

ahead. I'll see if I can find us something to eat in the main house."

Without another word, he left. Listlessly, Honor stared at the closed door and listened as he went down the outside stairs. Then for several minutes she stayed exactly as she was, lacking the wherewithal to move. Finally she forced herself.

The bar soap in the shower was locker room variety, but she used it liberally, even washed her hair with it. She could have luxuriated in the hot water all night, but, remembering that Coburn needed it even worse than she, she got out as soon as she had thoroughly rinsed.

The towels were thin but smelled reassuringly of Tide. She finger-combed the tangles out of her hair, then dressed in her dirty clothes. But she couldn't bring herself to put her feet back into her damp sneakers. She carried them out with her.

Coburn had returned, bringing with him staples similar to what he'd brought to her father's boat. He'd set out the selection on top of the chest of drawers.

"No perishables in the fridge, so they must have planned to be gone for a while. But I found one lone orange." He had already peeled and sectioned it. "And these." He held up a pair of kitchen scissors, the kind used to cut up poultry. "For your jeans. Only the lower part of the legs is really dirty."

He had already used them on her dad's pants. They'd been hacked off at the knees.

She took the scissors from him. "Thanks."

"Dig in." He motioned toward the food, then went into the bathroom and closed the door.

She hadn't eaten since the breakfast sandwich from the

truck stop, but she wasn't hungry. She did, however, take the scissors to her jeans, leaving them with a ragged, stringy edge just above her knees. It felt worlds better to be rid of the fabric that was stiff with dried mud and swamp water.

The ceiling light was glaring, so she turned it off and switched on a small reading lamp on the nightstand. Then she moved to the window and separated the inexpensive, no-frills curtains.

It had been an overcast day, but the clouds had thinned out. Now only wisps of them drifted across a half moon. *I see the moon, and the moon sees me.* The song she and Emily sang together caused her heart to clutch with homesickness for her daughter. She would be fast asleep by now, hugging her Elmo and bankie close.

Honor wondered if she had cried for her at bedtime, when homesickness was always the strongest. Had Tori told her a story, listened to her prayers? Of course she had. Even if she hadn't thought to do so, Emily would have reminded her.

God bless Mommy and Grandpa, and God bless Daddy in heaven. Emily prayed the same prayer each night. And last night, she'd added, *God bless Coburn.*

Hearing him emerge from the bathroom, Honor hastily wiped the tears off her cheeks and turned back into the room. He had dressed in the cut-off khakis and the oversized T-shirt he'd pilfered from the chest of drawers. He was barefoot. And he must have found a razor because he had shaved.

He looked up at the extinguished ceiling light, then over at the lamp on the bedside table, before coming back to her. "Why are you crying?"

"I miss Emily."

He raised his chin in acknowledgment. He glanced at the food items. "Did you eat anything?"

She shook her head.

"How come?"

"I'm not hungry."

"Why are you crying?" he asked again.

"I'm not. Not anymore." But even as she said it, fresh tears slid down her cheeks.

"Why'd you risk your life?"

"What?"

"Why'd you leave the garage on foot? Why were you coming toward the train?"

"I told you. I just...I...I don't know." The last three words rode out on a sob.

He started walking toward her. "Why are you crying, Honor?"

"I don't know. I don't know." When he reached her, she said once again in a hoarse whisper, "I don't know."

For what seemed like the longest time, he did nothing except stare deeply into her tearful eyes. Then he raised his hands to either side of her face, slid his fingers up through her damp hair, and cupped her head. "Yeah you do."

Angling his head, he kissed her as passionately as he had the night before, but this time she didn't fight the sensations it evoked. She couldn't have even if she had wanted to. They were explosive, consuming, and she gave herself over to them.

The stroking of his tongue, the mastery of his lips, even the placement of his large hands when they moved to her hips and drew her up against him made the kiss intensely sensual and caused dark and seductive curls of arousal deep within her lower body. And when he growled against her lips, "Are you gonna stop?" she shook her head and drew him back to continue the kiss.

He lifted the hem of her T-shirt and worked it up her torso, then unhooked her bra and took her breasts in his hands. Honor whimpered with pleasure at the light tugging of his fingertips and gasped his name when he bent his head and closed his mouth around her nipple.

With one hand, he unfastened the khakis, then raised his head and held her mesmerized by the blue-hot intensity of his eyes as he took her hand, placed it on himself, and moved it up and down. He lifted his hand away, but hers remained and stroked him. He hissed a curse of surprise and delight when her thumb rubbed the tip.

Leaning into her, with his mouth against her ear, he whispered, "I think I'm gonna like the way you fuck."

They kissed recklessly and hungrily as he kicked out of his pants and whipped the T-shirt over his head. He removed her T-shirt and bra just as quickly, then dropped to his knees and undid her jeans and pulled them down her legs along with her panties. He pressed a kiss just below her navel as he drew her down onto the floor.

Moving between her thighs, he stretched out above her, then thrust into her. Once. Because, as he did everything, he acted without hesitation or apology to claim her entirely. Her eyes went wide and her breath caught. Holding her gaze, he pressed himself deeper, barely easing back before pressing deep again.

She loved his weight on her, loved the heat of his clean skin, the feel of the hair on his chest against her breasts, the pressure he applied from inside and out, the smell and rough texture of his body, his maleness. Boldly, he pushed her knee back toward her chest, changing the angle of his thrusts and heightening the friction, and the pleasure increased tenfold.

It was immense. Almost unbearable. She bit her lower lip. She covered her eyes with the back of one forearm, while with her other hand she tried to get a grip on her spinning universe by attempting to dig her fingers into the hardwood floor. But she continued slipping, slipping, slipping toward...

"Honor."

Gasping, she lowered her arm from over her eyes and looked into his face.

"Put your hands on me. Pretend this means something."

With a whimper, she wrapped her arms around him and clutched his back, then slid her hands down over his ass and drew him even deeper into her. He groaned, buried his face in the hollow of her neck, and rocked his body against hers. An orgasm burst through her at the same time he came.

She pretended nothing.

Chapter 38

For Clint Hamilton the wait was agonizing.

An hour ago, an agent in the Lafayette office had called to inform him that the scheduled meeting between Honor Gillette and Tom VanAllen had ended disastrously with a car bomb explosion.

Since receiving the staggering news, Hamilton had been alternately pacing his Washington office or sitting with his elbows propped on his desk supporting his head while he massaged his forehead. He considered taking a shot from the bottle of Jack that he kept in his bottom desk drawer. He resisted. Whatever the forthcoming update from Tambour was, he needed to receive it with a clear head.

He waited. He paced. He wasn't a patient man.

The anticipated call came shortly after 01:00 EDT.

Unhappily the update confirmed that Tom VanAllen had died in the explosion.

"My condolences, sir," the agent in Louisiana said. "I know you had a special regard for him."

"Yes, thank you," Hamilton replied absently. "And Mrs. Gillette?"

"VanAllen was the only casualty."

Hamilton nearly dropped the phone. "What? Mrs. Gillette? Coburn? The child?"

"Whereabouts unknown," the agent told him.

Mystified, Hamilton processed that, but couldn't come up with an explanation. He asked, "What is the local fire department saying about the explosion?"

He was told that an arson inspector from New Orleans had been asked to assist in the investigation. ATF agents had also been summoned. There were many unanswered questions, but of one thing the authorities were certain: Only one body was discovered in the burned-out car.

Hamilton asked if VanAllen's wife had been notified. "I want to call her myself, but not before she's been officially informed."

"Two agents have been dispatched to the VanAllen home."

"Keep me posted on that. I also want to know anything else you hear, whether it's official or scuttlebutt. Anything. Especially about Coburn and Mrs. Gillette."

He ended the call and slammed his fist onto his desk. Why the hell hadn't Coburn called to advise him of his present position and situation? Damn the man! Although, he grudgingly admitted to himself, a car bomb wouldn't exactly inspire an agent's confidence in his agency, would it?

Hamilton decided that the situation down there could no longer be handled by long distance. He needed to go himself. In hindsight, he wished he had jetted to Louisiana immediately after receiving that first SOS call from Coburn. Since then, the shit had only gotten thicker.

He placed a series of calls and secured clearance from

his superiors. He asked for a squad of agents trained for special ops. "No less than four men, no more than eight. I want them at Langley, geared up and ready to board the jet at 02:30."

Everyone with whom he spoke asked why he was flying men and equipment down there when he could use personnel from the district office in New Orleans.

His answer to all of them was the same. "Because I don't want anyone to know I'm coming."

When her doorbell rang, Janice VanAllen ran to answer it, mindful that she was wearing only her nightgown, but uncaring about her lack of modesty. She had her phone in her hand and a look of concern on her face when she pulled open the front door.

Two strangers looked back at her. One was male, the other female, but their dark suits and serious expressions were practically identical.

"Mrs. VanAllen?" The woman palmed a leather ID wallet and extended it toward Janice. Her partner did the same. "I'm Special Agent Beth Turner, this is Special Agent Ward Fitzgerald. We're from Tom's office."

Janice's chest rose and fell on several short breaths. "Where's Tom?"

"May we come in?" the woman asked kindly.

Janice shook her head. "Where is Tom?"

They remained silent, but their stoicism spoke volumes.

Janice made a keening sound and gripped the edge of the door for support. "He's dead?"

Special Agent Turner reached for her, but Janice jerked her arm back before the woman could touch her. "He's dead?" she repeated, this time on a ragged cry. And then her knees gave way and she crumpled to the floor.

The two FBI agents lifted her and supported her between them, half carrying her into the living room where they deposited her on the sofa. All the while Janice was screaming Tom's name.

Then Agents Turner and Fitzgerald began asking her questions.

Is there someone we can call to come be with you?

"No," she sobbed into her hands.

Your minister? A friend?

"No, no."

Is there a family member who should be notified?

"No! Just tell me what happened."

Can we make you some tea?

"I don't want anything! I only want Tom! I want my husband!"

Is your son . . .

Clearly they knew about Lanny, but didn't know how to phrase a question regarding him. "Lanny, Lanny," she chanted mournfully. "Oh, God." She buried her face in her hands and sobbed. Tom had loved their son. As hopeless as it was that his love would ever be returned, Tom's love for Lanny had never wavered.

Special Agent Turner sat down beside her and placed a comforting arm across her shoulders. Fitzgerald had moved away and was now standing across the room with his back to them, speaking softly into a cell phone.

Turner said, "You'll have the full support of the bureau, Mrs. VanAllen. Tom was well liked and respected."

Janice threw off her arm and wanted badly to slap her. Tom wasn't respected at all, and, to hear Tom tell it, few of his fellow agents had liked him.

"How did it happen?"

"We're still trying to determine—"

"How did it happen?" Janice repeated harshly.

"He was alone in his car."

"His car?"

"He was parked near some abandoned railroad tracks."

Janice raised trembling fingers to her lips. "Oh, God. Suicide? We...we had a quarrel this afternoon. He left the house upset. I've been trying to call him, to...to explain. Apologize. But he wouldn't answer his phone. Oh, God!" she wailed and shot to her feet.

Turner grabbed her hand and pulled her back down onto the sofa. She stroked her arm. "Tom didn't take his own life, Mrs. VanAllen. He was killed in the performance of his duty. The initial report is that a bomb was planted on his car."

Janice gaped at her. "A *bomb*?"

"An explosive device, yes. A full investigation is already under way."

"But who...who—"

"It pains me to tell you that the person suspected of involvement is another agent."

"Coburn?" Janice whispered.

"You know of him?"

"Of course. First because of the warehouse massacre. Then Tom told me he was an agent working undercover."

"Did they have contact?"

"Not to my knowledge. Although Tom told me earlier today that he might be called upon to bring Coburn in." She read the pained expression on the agent's face. "That's the duty Tom was performing?"

"Mrs. Gillette was supposed to be at the train tracks. Tom went there to get her."

"Coburn set him up?"

"We're trying to ascertain—"

"Please tell me that Coburn is in custody."

"Unfortunately no."

"Jesus Christ, why not? What have you people been doing? Coburn is obviously crazy. If he'd been apprehended before tonight, as he should have been, Tom would still be alive." Composure deserted her. She sobbed, "The whole freaking bureau is incompetent, and because of it, Tom is *dead*."

"Mrs. VanAllen?"

Janice jumped. She wasn't aware that Fitzgerald had rejoined them until he laid a hand on her shoulder and spoke her name.

He held his cell phone out to her. "For you."

She stared at him, then at the phone, and eventually took it from him and put it to her ear. "Hello?"

"Mrs. VanAllen? This is Clint Hamilton. I just heard about Tom. I wanted to call and tell you personally how profoundly—"

"Fuck you." She disconnected and handed the phone back to the agent.

Then she forcibly composed herself. She wiped her face and took several deep breaths, and when she felt more in control, she stood up and walked toward the door. She left the room, saying, "Let yourselves out. I need to check on my son."

Chapter 39

Did you?"

"Did I what?

"Like the way I..." Honor let the unfinished question hang.

Coburn turned his head and looked at her. "No. I was faking it. Couldn't you tell?"

She smiled shyly and burrowed her face into his chest.

He gathered her close. "I liked it."

"Better than a sneeze or a cough?"

"Can I think about that and get back to you?"

She laughed softly.

They had moved from the floor to the bed and were lying with their legs entwined. Lightly she blew on the chest hair tickling her nose. "What was its name?"

"What?"

"The horse you had to shoot. You'd named it. What was its name?"

He glanced down at her, then away. "I forgot."

"No you didn't," she said softly.

He lay perfectly still and said nothing for the longest time, then, "Dusty."

She propped her fist on his breastbone and rested her chin on her fist, and looked into his face. He held out for several moments, then lowered his gaze to her. "Every day when I got home from school, he'd amble over to the fence like he was glad to see me. He liked me, I think. But only because I fed him."

She reached up and ran her thumb along the line of his chin. "I doubt that was the only reason he liked you."

He made an indifferent motion with his shoulder. "He was a horse. What did he know?" Then he turned to face her and said, "Dumb thing to be talking about." He tugged on a strand of her hair, then studied it thoughtfully as he rubbed it between his fingers. "It's pretty."

"Thank you. It's seen better days."

"You're pretty."

"Thanks again."

He took in all the features of her face, but eventually his eyes rested on hers. "You hadn't been with anybody since Eddie."

"No."

"It felt good to me. But I think it might have hurt you."

"A little at first. Then it didn't."

"Sorry. I didn't think about that."

In a husky whisper, she said, "Neither did I."

It was a difficult admission to make, but it was the truth. She was glad that thoughts of Eddie hadn't intruded upon the moment, although even if they had, they wouldn't have stopped her from being with Coburn.

Two men, two entirely different experiences. Eddie had been a wonderful and ardent lover, and she would cherish forever sweet memories of him. But Coburn had a distinct advantage. He was alive, warm, virile, and inclining toward her now.

His kiss was languid and sexy. Their hands explored. She discovered scars on him that she kissed in spite of his mild protests. He called her depraved when she brushed her tongue across his nipple, but also claimed to be a big fan of depravity. Her hand glided over the hard muscles of his abdomen and followed the tapering shape of his body down to his sex.

"Do that thing with your thumb," he whispered. She did as requested, and when she picked up moisture, he groaned a litany of swear words.

His fingertips went unerringly to her most sensitive places that, when he stroked them, left her breathless. She became hot and achy in her center again and moved against him in shameless appeal. He lowered his head to her breasts, where he took his time, loving them with his mouth.

He raised her arm above her head and kissed the sensitive underside, then down her rib cage, gradually turning her until she was on her stomach. He moved her hair aside and softly bit the back of her neck, then started pecking kisses down her spine.

His breath was warm against her skin when he released a short laugh. "My oh my. Who would have guessed?"

Knowing what he had discovered, she said primly, "You didn't corner the market on tats." She had spent several minutes admiring the barbed wire encircling his biceps.

"No, but a tramp stamp? On a second-grade schoolteacher? I can remember my second-grade teacher, and I seriously doubt she had one." He leaned down and took her earlobe between his teeth. "But it makes me hot as hell to think about it. What inspired you?"

"Two Hurricanes at Pat O'Brien's. Eddie and I spent a three-day weekend in New Orleans while Stan kept Emily."

"You got drunk?"

"Tipsy. I was easily persuaded."

Coburn had kissed his way down and now his tongue was drawing tantalizing circles around her tattoo. "What is it?"

"A Chinese symbol. Maybe Japanese. I can't remember." She moaned with pleasure. "In fact, with you doing that, I can't even think."

"No? What happens when I do this?" He worked his hand between her and the mattress and began massaging her from the front, while he settled heavily upon her back. "That day in your bathroom…" he murmured, his lips brushing her ear. "When I had you up against the door."

"Um-hum."

"This is what I wanted to be doing. Touching you… here."

What he was doing caused her breathing to turn choppy, but she managed to say, "I was very afraid."

"Of me?"

"Of what you would do."

"To hurt you?"

"No, to make me feel like I do now."

He stilled. "Is that the truth?"

"Shamefully, yes."

"Turn over," he growled.

He helped her onto her back, then knelt between her legs and rubbed his lips over her belly. He planted soft kisses on her hipbone and the hollow beneath it. Then nuzzled lower.

"Coburn?"

"Shh."

His palm settled between her hipbones, and his fingertips caressed her belly while his thumb dipped down to separate and stoke. Then he deep-kissed her. The dual caress
of mouth and thumb soon had her gasping his name and
begging him with her arching body not to stop.

He didn't. But he was inside her when she climaxed,
inside her when she felt his own release, and when she
finally regained the strength to open her eyes, he was still
there, cupping her face between his hands and stroking
her cheekbones with his thumbs.

The intensity of his expression caused her to tentatively
ask, "What?"

"I've never been a big fan of the missionary position."

Not quite sure how to respond to that, she said simply, "Oh."

"I preferred making it any other way."

"Why?"

"Because it didn't have anything to do with getting off."

"What didn't?"

"Looking into the woman's face." He murmured the
statement as though puzzled by it.

Her throat grew tight. She reached up and stroked his
cheek. "You wanted to look into mine?"

He continued to stare into her eyes for several moments,
then pulled away from her so abruptly that the emotional
withdrawal was as definitive as the physical separation.

Reluctant to let that happen, she followed him, turning
onto her side toward him. He lay on his back, looking up at
the ceiling, suddenly but completely detached.

She spoke his name.

He turned only his head toward her.

Quietly she said, "When this is over, I'll never see you
again, will I?"

He waited for a beat or two, then gave an abrupt negative shake of his head.

"Right," she whispered, smiling ruefully. "I didn't think so."

He returned to his study of the ceiling, and she thought that would be the end of it. Then he said, "I guess that changes your mind about this."

"This?"

"Fucking me. But you knew what you were getting," he said as though she'd disputed him. "Or you should have known. I haven't made a secret of who I am, what I'm like. And, yeah, I've wanted you naked from the minute I saw you, and I made no secret of that either.

"But I'm not a hearts and flowers guy. I'm not even an all-night guy. I don't hold hands. I don't cuddle..." He paused, swore. "I don't do any of that stuff."

"No, all you've done is risk your life to save mine. More than once."

He turned his head and looked at her.

"You repeatedly asked me why I left the garage," she said. "Now I want to ask you something. Why were you coming back to it?"

"Huh?"

"You had told me that if you didn't return within a few minutes of ten o'clock, I was to drive away and get as far from Tambour as possible. So, for all you knew, that's what I had done. After nearly dying in that explosion, with a burn on your shoulder, and your hair singed, you could have run in any given direction in order to get away, but you didn't. When you found me on the railroad tracks, you were racing back to the garage. To me."

He didn't say anything, but his jaw tensed.

She smiled and moved closer to him, aligning her body along his. "You don't have to give me flowers, Coburn. You don't even have to hold me." She laid her head on his chest just below his chin. Her hand curved around his neck. "Let me hold you."

Chapter 40

Diego held the edge of his razor to Bonnell Wallace's Adam's apple.

Wallace was proving to be a stubborn son of a bitch.

Getting into the house had been easier than Diego had anticipated. The alarm hadn't been set, so he hadn't had to strike immediately and then run like hell to get away before the cops showed up. Instead, he'd been able to sneak in and get the layout of the house before Wallace knew he was there.

He thought he'd caught every break, until he realized that Wallace was in the study in the front of the house where he'd seen him the night before, in plain view of anyone who happened by on the street.

The soundtrack of a television show had covered his footsteps as he'd climbed the curved staircase. The second floor had bedrooms along both sides of a long hallway, but Diego soon discovered the one that belonged to the master of the house. The gray pinstripe suit that Wallace had worn to the bank that day had been slung over the back of an easy chair. His dress shoes were in the center of the floor, his necktie lying on the foot of his giant bed.

Diego had made himself at home inside the walk-in closet. A long hour and a half had elapsed before Wallace came upstairs.

From inside the closet Diego had heard the chirps of the security system as Wallace punched in the code numbers to set it for the night. Which posed a problem, of course. It meant that Diego couldn't get out of the house without tripping the alarm. But he'd decided not to worry about that until the time came. First he'd had to figure out how to overpower a man who was twice his size.

Wallace had obliged him. As soon as he'd entered the bedroom, he'd headed for the adjacent bathroom and unzipped. He'd used both hands to aim.

Diego had come up behind him, placed one hand on his forehead and jerked it back at the same time he pressed his razor to the banker's exposed throat. Wallace had cried out, not so much in fear as from shock. Reflexively he'd reached behind him with both hands and tried to twist around to ward off his attacker. Pee had sprayed the wall behind the commode.

Diego had sliced the back of his hand to show him he meant business. "You fight me, I'll slit your throat."

Wallace stopped struggling. Breathing heavily, he asked, "Who are you? What do you want? Money? Credit cards? Take them. I haven't seen you. I can't identify you. So just take what you want and get out."

"I want your bitch."

"What?"

"Your bitch. Tori. Where is she?"

Wallace had been taken aback by that. Diego could

practically feel the thoughts racing through the banker's head as he'd held it secure against his chest.

"Sh...she's not here."

"I know that, jerk face. Why do you think I've got a razor to your throat? I want to know where she is."

"Why?"

Diego's hand had moved like lightning and cut an inch-long slice into Wallace's cheek.

"Jesus!"

"Oh, I'm sorry. Did that hurt?" He'd thrust his knee into the back of Wallace's, causing it to buckle, but it didn't completely give way. The man was heavy and it was getting harder to hold him. "Get down on your knees."

"Why? I'm cooperating here. I'm not fighting you."

"Down on your knees," Diego had said, straining the words through his teeth.

Wallace had complied. Diego liked this angle better. It afforded him more flexibility and options. It was also the position of a beggar, which worked to Diego's advantage.

"Tell me where Tori is."

"I don't know. I haven't seen or heard from her today."

Diego flicked the razor and the bottom half of Wallace's earlobe dropped onto his shoulder. Again, he'd cried out.

"It's the whole ear next time. And then Tori won't want you no more, you fat turd. Or any other snatch for that matter, because you'll look like a freak. Where is Tori?"

The ear trick usually worked. Typically that was the last thing to go before they told Diego what he needed to know, and then he would end it with one deep cut across their throat. He'd had one man hold out until both ears and his nose were gone, but he'd been exceptionally ballsy.

Diego hoped the banker wouldn't take that long. He didn't like being inside this house. It occurred to him that

Wallace might have activated a silent alarm, some kind of panic button that alerted police to an intruder and duress. He didn't think so, but he hadn't lived this long by being careless.

So now, after five minutes of this song and dance, he was ready to be done with Wallace and to say adios to The Bookkeeper forever. "One more time. That's all I'm giving you, just because I'm a nice guy. Where is Tori?"

"I swear to you that I don't know," Wallace said. "I had one short text from her early this morning, saying she had to leave town on short notice."

"Going where?"

"She didn't say."

"Where's your phone?"

"I left it at the office."

"Do you think I'm an idiot!" His shout echoed off the marble walls of the bathroom. He severed off a chunk of Wallace's other ear.

Wallace sucked in air, but this time he didn't cry out. "I tossed my phone on the chair when I came in here to pee. Go look. You'll see."

"I'll see that you're jacking me around."

"No, I'm not. I swear."

"You want me to go see if your phone is in the bedroom? Fine. Only thing is, I'll have to kill you first, because I'm not letting go of you until you tell me what I want to know or until you're dead." He let that sink in. "Makes no difference to me, but you could make it easier on yourself."

"I think you're going to kill me anyway."

"Tell me where Tori's at."

"I don't know."

"Where is she?"

"If I knew I'd be with her."

"Where is she?"

"I don't know. But even if I did, I wouldn't tell you."

"Tell me, or you die in the next five seconds."

"I'm not telling you shit. I love her."

Diego moved like a striking snake, but he didn't cut the man's throat. Instead, he bashed his head against the toilet. The big man fell heavily to the marble tile floor. His forehead left an interesting pattern of blood on the white porcelain toilet bowl.

Diego used a monogrammed towel to wipe his razor clean, then folded it closed and left the bathroom. The cell phone was exactly where Wallace had said. Diego, from his vantage point inside the closet, had missed him dropping it there on his way into the john.

Rapidly he made his way downstairs, avoiding the windows on the front of the house. He'd entered the house by way of the kitchen. There was only one light on and it was the one above the range. He held Wallace's cell phone up to it and accessed his text messages. Tori. Eight forty-seven a.m. She said she was leaving town on short notice, but didn't say where. Next Diego looked at Wallace's call log. Many had been placed to Tori's number. None had come in from her. The fat man had been telling him the truth.

Diego used his phone to call The Bookkeeper. "I've got Tori Shirah's cell phone number."

"I asked for her location."

Diego recited the number and explained the text message.

"All well and good," The Bookkeeper said tightly, "but where is she?"

"Wallace doesn't know."

"You didn't get it from him?"

"He doesn't know."

"Doesn't? Present tense?"

"What good would it do to kill him?"

"What's the matter with you, Diego? A dead man can't identify you."

"Neither can Wallace. He didn't see me."

After a sustained silence The Bookkeeper asked, "Where are you now?"

"Still inside his house."

"So try again. He's got fingers, toes, a penis."

"It wouldn't do any good." Above all else, Diego trusted his instincts, and Wallace seemed the type who would die protecting his ladylove.

"He says he doesn't know where she is, and I believe him," he stressed to The Bookkeeper.

"No loose ends, Diego."

"I'm telling you, he didn't see me, and I never mentioned you."

"You've never left a victim alive. Why now? Why have you gone soft?"

"I haven't. But I haven't lost my marbles either. Killing Wallace would be risky because I can't just sneak away. Once I open a door to this place, all hell's gonna break loose. If I can't outrun the police, I don't want to be caught with a dead man."

"You're refusing to deliver what I asked for?"

"What you asked for can't be had. It would be a waste to kill a man over information he ain't got."

There was a long silence on the other end, then, "This is the second time this week that you've disappointed me, Diego." The silkiness of The Bookkeeper's tone sent a tingle down Diego's spine.

Anyone who knew anything about The Bookkeeper knew what happened to people who disappointed or failed.

Diego didn't fear being rubbed out. He was too talented to be squandered. No, The Bookkeeper would use some other means to punish him, some other—

Sudden realization came crashing down on him like a ton of bricks. *This is the second time.*

Diego's stomach lurched. He thought he might vomit. He disconnected and, without even considering the consequences, opened the kitchen door. Alarm bells went off. The noise was deafening, but it barely registered with Diego. The fear clamoring inside his head portended something far worse than arrest.

He sprinted across the stone terrace and over the lawn. By the time he reached the estate wall, he was winded, but he didn't even pause to catch his breath. He scaled the wall using the leafy vine for footholds and handholds. When he reached the top, he threw his legs over and jumped. He landed hard on the ground twelve feet below. His knees absorbed the impact, and it hurt like hell, but the pain didn't slow him.

He heard the whoop-whoop of approaching police car sirens, but he took the most direct route to his stolen car, even though it meant being out in the open as opposed to keeping to the shadows.

No one apprehended him. When he reached the car, he was wet with sweat and shaking so uncontrollably he barely managed to get it started. Heedless of it drawing notice, he pulled the car away from the curb with a squeal of tires.

He leaned into the steering wheel, gripping it with fingers that had turned bone-white with fear and fury. He'd never been taught to pray and knew no god, so he bargained with abstractions and fervently appealed to whatever unnamed supreme power was listening.

He broke his unbroken law and drove directly to his

building. The tires smoked when he brought the car to a jarring halt. He bolted out, not even bothering to cut off the engine or close the door.

A cutting torch had been used to excise the lock on the exterior door, which stood ajar. Diego plunged through it into total darkness. He raced through the dank corridors and bolted down the staircases that he knew by feel.

When he reached the lower level and saw the door to his domain standing open, he drew up short. His breath made a horrible sawing noise, and that was the only sound in the entire building. He thought he might die from the pain in his chest. He almost hoped he would, so he wouldn't have to know.

But he had to know.

He forced himself to walk to the lighted doorway and look into the room that had been his safe haven. Until tonight.

Isobel was lying on her back on the bed. She'd been stripped naked and obscenely positioned. Her face had been brutalized. Her limbs were bruised and bore scratches. There were bite marks, so deeply impressed that they'd broken through her golden skin. There was dried semen. And blood.

He'd been kept away all day so that The Bookkeeper's facilitators could take their time terrorizing, torturing, and killing Isobel and, by doing so, teach Diego a hard lesson in blind obedience.

Only her beautiful, silky black hair had escaped the assault. When Diego knelt beside the bed, it was her hair he stroked, her hair that he crooned to, that he held against his face and cried into.

His knees had grown numb by the time he finally got to his feet. He rearranged Isobel's body to restore her modesty. He gently unclasped her silver crucifix. He kissed her cut and swollen lips, their first kiss also being their last. Finally, he pulled a blanket over her.

He surveyed the room, taking account of everything in it, and deciding there was nothing there he cared to salvage, not even the expensive rug. He poured the goldfish into the toilet and flushed. It was a mercy killing. Better that than to boil to death.

He made a pile of his belongings in the center of the room, set a lighter to them, and waited to make certain that the fire would catch. When he turned his back on the room, flames were already licking at the covers on the bed, Isobel's funeral bier.

Slowly, laboriously, he made his way up through the former factory to street level. He could already smell smoke, and reasoned that it wouldn't take long for the blaze to eat the building whole.

The car was gone, of course. It didn't matter. He struck off down the sidewalk, staying close to the buildings, keeping his right hand around the razor in his pants pocket, thinking that possibly The Bookkeeper wasn't finished with him yet.

He for sure as hell wasn't finished with The Bookkeeper.

Chapter 41

When Bonnell Wallace regained consciousness, he was lying face up on the floor of his bathroom. Someone was bending over him, shining a flashlight into his eye, which he held pried open with a gloved hand.

"Mr. Wallace, can you hear me?"

"Turn off that goddamn light." It was driving splinters of pain through the top of Wallace's skull from the inside. The EMT didn't do as asked. Instead he pried open Wallace's other eye and waved the flashlight an inch from his eyeball.

Wallace swatted at the hand wearing the blue glove. Or tried. He connected with nothing but air and realized that he was seeing double and that he had aimed for the wrong image.

"Mr. Wallace, lie still, please. You've got a concussion."

"I'm all right. Did you catch him?"

"Who?"

"The bastard who did this to me."

"The back door was standing open when we got here. Your assailant got away."

Wallace was struggling to sit up while the pair of EMTs were trying to hold him down. "I need to talk to the cops."

"They're searching the property, Mr. Wallace."

"Go get them."

"You can talk with the officers later. They'll want your statement. In the meantime, we'll transport you to the ER and let them X-ray—"

"You're not transporting me anywhere." Wallace knocked aside the young man's arm, and this time his aim was perfect. "Get off me. I'm all right. I've got to warn Tori. Bring me my phone. It's on the bedroom chair."

The two EMTs consulted each other with a look. One got up and disappeared through the doorway. Seconds later, he called back, "No phone on the chair."

Wallace gave a low moan. "He took my phone. My phone has her number in it."

"Whose number?"

"Jesus! Whose do you think? Tori's."

"Sir, please lie back and let us—"

He grabbed the young man by the front of his uniform shirt. "I told you, I'm fine. But if anything happens to Tori, I'm coming after you first, and I'll make your life a living hell. So you had better get a cop in here *now!*"

Coburn had been trained to sleep as efficiently as he'd been trained to do everything else. He woke up after two hours, feeling revived if not completely rested.

Honor was still lying as though welded to him. His right arm had gone to sleep. It tingled, but he left it where it was, sandwiched between her breasts. He didn't want to wake her up until he had to. Besides, his arm felt good there.

Her right hand was on his chest, and he was shocked to realize that, in sleep, he'd covered it with his left hand, keeping it there, directly over his heart.

He had to admit: She'd got to him. This demure second-grade schoolteacher, who'd been faithful to her husband, but who had fucked him with the same fervor with which she'd fought him two days ago, had crawled under his mean ol' hide.

Her features were soft and feminine, but she was no creampuff where and when it mattered. Even those times when he'd been ready to strangle her for doing something reckless, he'd admired her courage. He believed she would have killed him, or died trying, if he'd harmed her kid.

Thinking of Emily caused him to smile. The little chatterbox. It relieved him to know that she was safe, but he wasn't as glad to be rid of her as he had thought he would be. He probably wouldn't see her again, but he would never look at one of those red bug-eyed things without thinking about her. He also knew that whenever he recalled her kissing his cheek with such unqualified trust and acceptance, it was going to ache just a little in the vicinity of his heart.

It ached now.

But he pushed those thoughts aside. Lately, he'd been thinking a lot of stupid shit, and he couldn't explain the sentimentality except that this was one crazy, mucked-up mission and had been ever since he'd fled the warehouse. No wonder he'd gone sappy. No wonder that, instead of planning what he was going to do next, he was lying here soaking up the warmth of Honor's nakedness, letting it seep into his body like a healing balm.

Damn, she'd been sweet. Tight and hot and slick for want of him. Go figure.

And when he realized that he was the first lover she'd

taken since her husband died, he'd felt like Superman. But that was also when it became confusing, when it had evolved from straight screwing into something else, when he'd wanted to feel her hands on his body, when he'd wanted her to know that it wasn't a memory or a ghost, but a flesh-and-blood man who was rocking her world, making her come. He had wanted her to know that it was him.

And that scared him.

Because never before in his life had he needed or wanted anybody needing or wanting him.

Good thing that this setup was short-term and when it was over he could walk away, no strings attached. They would return to their previous lives and never see each other again. He'd made it clear that's how it would be, and she'd accepted it.

So, okay, yeah, he had let her snuggle up next to him to sleep. If she wanted to hold him, fine. Fine. As long as they both understood that the intimacy was temporary.

But there was no denying how good it felt having her against him. Each breath she took wafted across his skin. The soft, smooth inside of her thigh was resting on top of his. Her breasts pillowed his arm. The back of his hand was nestled in the V of her thighs, and if he turned his hand and cupped her with his palm...

His cock woke up and stretched.

They could do it just once more, right? What could it hurt? He wasn't going to tell anybody. She sure as hell wasn't. If he turned his hand into her and began stroking her *there*, she would wake up smiling and drowsy and ready for him again.

They would kiss. Erotically. Her mouth would be so damn enticing, he'd dip into it again and again to gather the taste that was now familiar to him. He would touch his tongue to her nipples, and she'd rub her thumb around the tip of his cock and feel that he was about to burst, and then he'd be inside her, moving.

Or maybe not. Maybe he would do something he'd never done with a woman. Maybe he would just... *be*. Be still. No movement except their heartbeats. Not working toward something so it would be over with and he could move on to the next thing, physically sated maybe, but unaffected.

No, maybe this time, he would just savor being joined to another person as tightly as two people could be. He would savor being joined with Honor.

Maybe, while they were fitted together like that, he would kiss her. And if she kissed him the way she usually did, he would probably lose it. He'd have to move. He'd have no choice.

Afterward, he would tease her about how easy she was, and she would pretend to take exception. He would tease her about her tattoo, so wickedly positioned between twin dimples just above her shapely ass.

He'd say the tattoo artist had been one lucky son of a bitch to have had that luscious view while he plied his trade. *I'll bet he took his sweet time*, he'd say. Then he'd tell her that's what his vocation would be in his next life. He would be a tattoo artist who specialized in primary school teachers who went on Hurricane binges and got tattooed in places that weren't—

Seen by just anybody.

His lazy train of thought suddenly derailed.

He pushed her off him and leaped from the bed. "Honor, wake up!"

Startled out of her deep sleep, she came up on her elbows and shaded her eyes against the glare when he turned on the ceiling light. "What's the matter? Is someone here?"

"No. Turn over."

"What?"

"Get on your stomach." He planted his knee beside her on the bed and flipped her facedown.

"Coburn!"

"You said 'persuaded.'"

"What? Let me up."

He placed his wide hand over her bottom and held her down. "Your tattoo. You said you got tipsy and were easily persuaded. Persuaded to get tattooed?"

"Yes. I didn't take to the idea at first, but Eddie—"

"Insisted?"

"Eddie never *insisted* I do anything."

"Okay, he *persisted.*"

"Sort of. He double-dog dared me. I finally gave in."

Coburn was on his knees beside her, examining the intricate design. "And he chose the spot."

"He said it was sexy."

"It is. Sexy as all get out. But I don't think that's why he wanted it here." Coburn squinted down at the swirling pattern while tracing it with his fingertip. "What does it say?"

"It doesn't say anything." She was watching him from over her shoulder. "I told you, it's a Chinese symbol of some kind."

"It's gotta mean something or else why'd you choose it?"

"I didn't. Eddie did. In fact he—"

Coburn's head came up.

Her eyes connected with his. "He designed it."

They stared at one another for several seconds, then Coburn said, "We just found the treasure map."

*   *   *

For the umpteenth time Tori considered her empty cell phone. And for the umpteenth time she was sorely tempted to replace the battery and call Bonnell. She longed to talk to him. So what if he wasn't extraordinarily handsome and well built? He wasn't an ogre. She liked him. She knew his adoration for her was genuine and might have advanced from infatuation into—dare she think it?—full-blown love. He would be concerned over her sudden departure, wondering why she'd taken off to parts unknown without an explanation, why she wasn't answering the calls he was surely placing.

If he'd put two and two together, he would have figured out that her leaving town was connected to the friend she'd told him about, the one who'd been kidnapped. Maybe he had late-breaking news regarding Honor and the search for her and Emily.

After sending the one short text to Bonnell informing him that she was leaving town, she had heeded Coburn's instructions to the letter, even though she'd questioned the necessity of taking such precautions. A half hour after arriving at the house, she and Emily were making mud pies on a playground near the lakeshore. She'd been enjoying herself so much that it was easy to forget for short periods of time why the two of them were on this excursion.

But whenever she was reminded of the grim circumstances, she experienced a pang of longing for Bonnell's solid presence. She also felt a touch of resentment for Coburn and his strict orders. Tori had an innate aversion to rules and had spent most of her life defying them.

Her resentment had mounted with each passing hour, until now, lying alone in bed and wishing for Bonnell's raunchy company, she decided that no harm could come from one short conversation just to assure him that she was all right, as horny as ever, and desperately missing him.

She sat up and was about to reach for her phone on the nightstand. Instead she screamed.

A man wearing a ski mask was standing at the foot of her bed.

He lunged and clamped his gloved hand over her mouth, trapping her scream. She fought him like a swamp panther, shaking his hand off her face, then baring teeth and nails as she went on the offensive. Her incredibly muscled and toned body wasn't just for show. She was as strong as most men and had the reflexes to utilize that strength effectively. Her attacker narrowly escaped a heel aimed at his testicles with the impetus of a pile driver.

She tried to yank the ski mask off his face, but he got his fingers around her wrist and jerked it so hard she heard bones snap. In spite of herself, she screamed in pain.

Then he knocked her in the temple with his pistol grip. Darkness descended like a velvet blanket. Her last thought was of Emily and Honor and how miserably she had failed them.

Doral whipped off his mask and bent over Tori's sprawled form, hands on his knees, trying to catch his breath and sniff back the blood dripping from his nose. The bitch had landed at least one good punch.

He would show her the stuff he was made of. He would show her that he wasn't the kind of man who'd take crap like that from a woman. He still owed her for that time in high school when she had not only turned him down, but had done so laughing at his fumbling attempts to seduce her.

The thought of finally teaching her a lesson delighted him and got him hard. He reached for the fly of his pants.

However, even as he grappled with his zipper, he stopped and reconsidered. The Bookkeeper wouldn't like it. Not because of scruples, but because of the timing.

The Bookkeeper was impatiently waiting for his call, and this time the news had to be good.

The car bomb had failed to dispense with either Coburn or Honor. The Bookkeeper had received that bad news with even more fury than Doral had anticipated, and he'd anticipated something along the lines of Hitler getting news of the Third Reich's defeat.

"You goddamn idiot! You told me he was there."

"He was. I saw him myself."

"Then how could he have got away?"

"I don't—"

"And why didn't you check to make sure he was dead before you left?"

"The car was in flames. There was no way to—"

"I'm sick of your excuses, Doral."

It had continued that way for several minutes. But Doral preferred the ranting to the cool, distant tone of The Bookkeeper's final words. "If you can't do any better than this, I don't need you, do I?"

In that moment Doral realized that unless he delivered Coburn and Honor, he was a dead man.

Or.

It occurred to him that he did indeed have another option. He could kill The Bookkeeper.

That treasonous thought had wormed its way into his mind and coiled around his imagination. He fantasized about it and found the prospect enormously appealing. Why not?

The main *why not?* was because the end of The Bookkeeper would spell the end of his livelihood. But who was
to say that he couldn't take over the whole operation, now
that the groundwork had been so meticulously laid?

In the interest of time, Doral decided to shelve that
enticing thought for future consideration and, in the meantime, to find Honor and Coburn. He wanted that asshole
dead whether The Bookkeeper had ordered it or not.

With that goal in mind, he had called Amber, the air-
headed receptionist at Tori's fitness center. He reintro-
duced himself as the guy she'd met at the sandwich shop
the day before and had asked her out for a drink.

She'd played hard to get. It was after eleven o'clock,
she'd said peevishly. Why had he waited so late to call? She
had to open the center at six a.m.

Doral had said the first thing that popped into his
mind. "I just hate to see a good kid like you get blindsided."

"What do you mean?"

"Tori is interviewing other girls for your position."

The plausible lie had worked like a magic wand. He
was invited to come to her place for a nightcap, and all it
took was two vodka tonics for her to start enumerating all
the advantages that Tori Shirah had over her, including
a house on Lake Pontchartrain that she'd cheated an ex-
husband out of.

He left Amber with a promise for dinner at Command-
er's Palace soon and immediately reported his findings
to The Bookkeeper. Laying it on real thick, he had volunteered to personally drive to Tori's house on the lake and
check it out.

His efforts had paid off. Big-time. He hadn't located
Coburn or Honor, but he'd discovered Emily sleeping in
one of the guest bedrooms, and that was almost as good.

The sooner he reported something positive to The Book-keeper, the better the working climate, and the healthier for everybody.

Cursing his own sound judgment, which was preventing him from sampling what he'd lusted after since adolescence, he zipped up, then bent down and whispered, "Your pussy will never know what it missed."

He backed away and aimed the pistol down at Tori's head.

Hamilton's jet set down at Lafayette Aero at 03:40 Central time, gaining him an hour. The FBO was virtually shut down at that hour of the morning, so the only personnel there were the ground crew.

Hamilton was the first off the aircraft. He pleasantly greeted the man with the chocks and told him that they were an advance team sent by the State Department to set up security for the upcoming visit of a government dignitary.

"Really, who? The president?"

"I'm not allowed to say," Hamilton replied, smiling genially. "We don't know how long our errand will take. Our pilots will stay with the plane."

"Yes, sir."

Meanwhile the six men who had disembarked with Hamilton unloaded their gear and stowed it in the two black Suburbans with the darkly tinted windows that Hamilton had requested to be waiting for them on the tarmac.

If the young man wondered why an envoy from the State Department required automatic weapons and S.W.A.T. gear, he wisely contained his curiosity.

Within minutes of the jet's landing, the team was speeding away in the Suburbans. Hamilton gave his driver the

VanAllens' home address, and he programmed it into the built-in GPS. Hamilton wanted to stop there first and pay his respects to Tom's widow. He owed it to Tom. He owed it to her. After all, it was he who had sent Tom to that meeting on the abandoned railroad tracks.

It was incredibly presumptive to call at this hour of the night, but hopefully she would be up, surrounded by friends, neighbors, and kinfolk, who had rushed to her in response to the news of Tom's death.

What he feared, however, was that he would find her alone. Their son's circumstances had been extremely isolating for the couple, and in large part that isolation had been self-inflicted. Based on what Hamilton knew of Janice, it wouldn't be out of character for her to withdraw from society completely now that Tom was dead.

The agents from Tom's office who had delivered the tragic news had reported to Hamilton that they'd been asked to leave shortly after their grim duty was dispatched.

Agents sent to question her in connection to the murder of her husband had emailed him afterward that Mrs. VanAllen had been cooperative in answering all their questions but had shown them to the door as soon as they concluded the interview and had refused offers of a chaplain or grief counselor to stay with her overnight.

She had rebuffed Hamilton by cursing him and then flatly refusing to speak to him when he called a second time. He strongly suspected that all extensions of consolation had been similarly rejected.

He hoped he was wrong. He hoped he would find her house filled with people, making this meeting between them less awkward, less conspicuous, and his purpose less obvious.

Because, although his main reason for coming was to

pay his respects, he also had an ulterior motive. Call it a
fishing expedition.

There was an outside chance that Janice knew something about The Bookkeeper, even if it was tidbits of information that Tom had scattered and that, over time, she'd
picked up and put together as one does the spilled pieces
of a jigsaw puzzle. Even accidentally, pieces got linked
together to form at least a partial picture.

Hamilton needed to know what Janice VanAllen was
privy to.

Meanwhile, he didn't waste the travel time in the van.
He placed a call to the sheriff's office in Tambour and
demanded that he be connected to Deputy Crawford. He
was told that Crawford was in the temporary command
center but had gone down the hall to use the john.

"When he comes back, tell him to call me. This
number."

He disconnected and checked his phone yet again to
see if Coburn had tried to reach him. Nothing. Two minutes later the phone vibrated in his hand. He answered
curtly, "Hamilton."

"This is Deputy Crawford. You asked me to call. Who
are you?"

Hamilton identified himself. "The bureau lost a man
down there tonight. *My* man."

"Tom VanAllen. My condolences."

"Are you investigating the case?"

"I was initially. Once VanAllen was IDed, your guys took
over. Why aren't you talking to them?"

"I have been. But I think there's something you should
know since it relates to your other cases."

"I'm listening."

"Tom VanAllen went to that abandoned train track

tonight with the sole purpose of picking up Mrs. Gillette and bringing her into protective custody."

Crawford took a moment to assimilate that, then asked, "How do you know?"

"Because I brokered the deal with Lee Coburn."

"I see."

"I doubt it," Hamilton said. "No offense."

The deputy was quiet for several moments, but whether because of pique or concentration, Hamilton didn't know. Nor did he care.

Crawford said, "We've only got one body in the morgue. So what happened to Mrs. Gillette?"

"Excellent question, Deputy."

"Did Coburn set up VanAllen?"

Hamilton chuckled. "If Coburn had wanted VanAllen dead, he wouldn't have troubled himself to use a bomb."

"Then what are you telling me, Mr. Hamilton?"

"Somebody besides Coburn and me knew about that meeting, and whoever it was wanted Mrs. Gillette dead. Somebody planted that car bomb expecting to get two birds with one stone, a cop's widow and a local FBI agent. Somebody was made awfully nervous by that pairing, so they acted swiftly and lethally to prevent it."

"'Somebody.' Any idea who?"

"Whoever is listening in on this conversation."

"I don't follow."

"Like hell you don't. Your department is a freaking sieve. So is the P.D., and I sadly suspect Tom's office, too." He paused to let the deputy dispute that. It was telling that he didn't. Whether Crawford was dirty or not, he must not have seen the point in denying the allegation. "I'm not telling you how to do your job, Deputy—"

"*But?*"

"But unless you want a higher body count than you've already got, double your efforts and manpower to find Mrs. Gillette and Coburn."

"Is she with him voluntarily?"

"Yes."

"Thought so. Does Coburn work for you?"

Hamilton said nothing.

"Did Coburn, I don't know, *recruit* her for some reason? That's what it looks like to me. What are they on to that's got people wanting them dead?"

Hamilton didn't answer that one either.

The deputy sighed. Hamilton could imagine him running his fingers through his hair. If he had hair. "They've successfully stayed under the radar for three days, Mr. Hamilton. I don't know what else I can do, especially since, as you say, other forces always seem to be several steps ahead of me. But if I get lucky and manage to flush them out, what then?"

Hamilton said tersely, "I'm the first person you call."

Chapter 42

When Coburn pulled the car to a stop at the curb in front of Stan Gillette's house, Honor said, "I envisioned us sneaking in like we did this afternoon."

"I'm tired of dicking around. It's time he and I had a face-to-face."

As they moved up the front walkway, she looked at him nervously. "What are you going to do?"

"You ring the doorbell. I'll take it from there."

He could tell she was conflicted about what they had to do, but she resolutely stepped onto the porch and rang the doorbell. They heard it chiming inside the house. Coburn pressed his back to the wall adjacent to the door.

Honor saw him slip the pistol from his waistband, and that alarmed her. "What are you doing with that?"

"He may not welcome our company."

"Don't hurt him."

"Not unless he forces me to."

"He takes medication for high blood pressure."

"Then I hope he thinks twice before doing something stupid."

Hearing approaching footsteps, he sliced the air with his free hand. The door was opened, then several things happened in rapid succession.

The alarm system began chirping its warning.

Stan exclaimed his surprise upon seeing Honor, seized her arm, and drew her across the threshold.

Coburn sprang into the entryway behind her and kicked the front door shut.

He ordered Honor to disarm the security system.

Then he pushed her out of harm's way when Gillette lunged forward and swiped at his midsection with a knife.

"No!" Honor shouted.

Coburn bowed his back, making his gut concave, but the tip of the blade cut through the oversized T-shirt and found skin.

Coburn was more astonished by the ferocity of the attack than he was hurt, and immediately realized that Gillette had planned on that. He took advantage of Coburn's astonishment by kicking the pistol out of his hand.

Coburn hissed a curse and tried to grab Gillette's knife hand. He missed, and Gillette drew another vicious arc with the blade, this time catching skin on Coburn's shoulder.

"Stop it, old man," Coburn shouted as he dodged another stabbing motion. "We need to talk to you."

Gillette was having none of it. He continued to attack Coburn with a vengeance.

Honor, who'd silenced the incessant warning beep of the alarm system, was practically weeping. "Stan, please! Stop!"

Either the older man was maddened to the point of deafness, or he chose to ignore her plea. He seemed determined to kill or seriously maim Coburn, giving Coburn no choice except to be equally aggressive. He had expected resistance, harsh arguments, maybe some chest-thumping from the former Marine. But he hadn't expected a full-out assault.

Each man fought to win. They fell over furniture, toppled lamps, knocked pictures off the walls. They gouged and kicked and slugged. Coburn couldn't let up long enough to locate his pistol and aim without giving Gillette an open invitation to plunge the knife into him. So they fought hand to hand, as they'd both been trained to fight, as though it was a life-or-death contest.

And all the while Honor was begging for them to stop.

"Give it up," Coburn growled as he deflected the knife yet again.

But Gillette didn't relent. He was out for blood. Coburn's blood. When the blade of his knife connected with Coburn's forearm, cutting it clear to the bone, Coburn yelped an obscenity. He thought, to hell with the man's age, his high blood pressure, and Semper Fi. He attacked with everything he had in him and kept at it until a well-placed blow to Gillette's head caused him to lose his footing and stagger backward.

Coburn followed and seized his knife hand. Gillette didn't let go of the knife voluntarily, nor would he ever have. But Coburn twisted his wrist until Gillette cried out in agony. His fingers went lifeless around the hilt of the knife and it fell from his hand.

Coburn got him facedown on the floor, planted a knee in his back, and jerked his hands up between his shoulder blades.

Honor was openly weeping.

Coburn said to her, "There's a roll of duct tape on the work table in the garage. Bring it."

She left to do as he asked, seeming to understand that arguing would only prolong both his and Gillette's suffering. In any case, Coburn was glad he didn't have to explain it to her because he'd barely had enough breath to say that much.

Lying with his cheek against the floor, Gillette snarled, "You're a dead man."

"Not yet." But the cut on his arm was gushing blood.

Honor returned with the roll of tape. Coburn told her to tear off a strip and use it to bind her father-in-law's hands. She looked down at the man who shared her name, then back at Coburn, and shook her head in refusal.

"Look," Coburn said, panting from pain and exhaustion, "I may need him to testify, so the last thing I want to do is disable or kill him. But we can't do what we came to do if I'm having to fight him, and he's gonna keep fighting me if I don't restrain him."

He wasn't certain he could stave off Gillette if he should happen to get his second wind and resume his attack. He needed to subdue the tough old bird while he had the strength to do so and before his injured arm became completely useless. He blinked sweat from his eyes and looked up at Honor.

"Tying him up is the only way I can guarantee that one of us won't badly injure or kill the other. Don't wimp out on me now, Honor. Tear off a strip of the goddamn tape."

She hesitated but eventually pulled a strip of tape from the roll and bit it off with her teeth, then wound it around Gillette's wrists. The two of them got him secured to a straight chair that Coburn had Honor bring from the kitchen.

The man's face was a swelling, bleeding mess, but Honor got the full brunt of his animosity. "I thought I knew you."

"You do, Stan."

"How can you do this?"

"*Me*? You came at Coburn like you would kill him. You gave me—us—no choice."

"There's always a choice. You've been making very poor ones."

Meanwhile, Coburn was tightly winding duct tape around the knife wound on his arm in an attempt to stanch the bleeding.

Honor knelt in front of her father-in-law and looked imploringly into his face. "Stan, please—"

"Even if you have no regard for Eddie's memory, how dare you put my granddaughter's life at risk."

Coburn could tell that Gillette's sneering tone pissed her off, but she replied in an even voice, "Actually, Stan, I've been protecting Emily and myself."

"By teaming up with him?"

"He's a government agent."

"What kind of agent stages a kidnapping?"

"I knew that would make you frantic with worry. I wanted to call and tell you what had really happened, but I couldn't without jeopardizing our safety. Mine. Emily's. Coburn's too. He's been working undercover in a highly dangerous position, and—"

"And he's flipped," he said, giving Coburn a scornful once-over. "Wacked out. It happens all the time."

Coburn had already lost patience with the man, but Honor continued to address him in a reasonable tone. "He hasn't flipped. I've spoken with his supervisor in Washington, a man named Clint Hamilton. He has absolute trust in Coburn."

"So you thought you could, too?"

"The truth is, I had placed my trust in him even before

I spoke to Mr. Hamilton. Coburn saved our lives, Stan. He protected Emily and me from people who would've harmed us."

"Like who?"

"The Hawkins twins."

Gillette barked a laugh, but, reading her serious expression, followed it up by saying, "Surely you're joking."

"I assure you I'm not."

"That's ridiculous." He shot Coburn a furious look. "What kind of nonsense have you been feeding her?" Turning back to Honor, he said, "Those men wouldn't touch a hair on your head. Doral hasn't stopped searching for you and Emily since you disappeared. His brother lay dead, but he's been—"

"Pumping you for information about them, about where they might be, who might be sheltering them?" Coburn came to stand beside Honor so he could address Gillette directly.

Gillette's chin went up a notch. "Doral has been a loyal friend. He's gone without meals, sleep. He's been turning over every rock."

"Getting information from his moles in the police department?"

Gillette said nothing.

"Doral used that info to stay one jump ahead of the authorities, am I right? While he should be in mourning, he's been desperate to find us before any branch of law enforcement did. Why is that, I wonder?" He let Gillette chew on that for several seconds before continuing. "Doral and Fred Hawkins shot Marset and the other six."

The older man stared up at Coburn, then laughed a dry, mirthless laugh. "You say. You who stands accused of that mass murder."

"Fred would have killed Honor, and probably Emily, too, if I hadn't shot him first. Ever since last Sunday night, Doral has been trying to mop up the mess he and his brother made in that warehouse. And it was a mess. Sam Marset and the others didn't stand a chance. The twins slaughtered them."

"And only you lived to tell about it."

"That's right."

"I don't believe you. I've known those boys practically their whole lives."

"Are you sure you know them? Are you sure you know what they're capable of? For instance, did Doral tell you that he broke into Tori Shirah's house and ambushed her? Yeah," he said when he noticed a glint of surprise in the older man's eyes.

"And then when she told him she hadn't heard from Honor, he threatened her if she failed to contact him if and when she did. Did Doral mention that to you, Mr. Gillette? Never mind. I can see that he didn't."

"How do you know it's true?"

"How do you know it isn't?"

"Well, if you heard it from that slut, I'd say the source is unreliable." He switched his attention back to Honor. "Is Emily with her?"

"Emily is safe."

"Not from moral corruption."

"Let's put the character assassination of Tori on ice," Coburn said. "We haven't got time for it."

"On that I agree with you, Coburn. Your time is up."

"Really?" Coburn leaned down, putting his face within inches of Gillette's. "You say that with a lot of conviction. How do you know my time is up?"

Gillette's eyes narrowed fractionally.

Coburn continued. "The Hawkins twins are clever, but they don't strike me as bright enough to run an organization as sophisticated as The Bookkeeper's."

Gillette looked beyond Coburn to Honor. "What's he talking about?"

"Hey." Coburn nudged the man's knee, drawing his attention back to him. When Gillette's fierce eyes met his again, he continued. "Somebody with an authoritative personality and a god complex has been giving Fred and Doral their marching orders. I've got my money riding on you."

"I have no idea what you're talking about."

Coburn made a show of checking his wristwatch. "You're either staying up awfully late or getting up very early. Why aren't you groggy from having been woken up when the doorbell rang? Why aren't you dressed in pajamas or skivvies? Instead, here you are, Mr. Gillette, fully dressed. Even wearing shoes. How come? Why are you all spit-and-polished at this time of morning?"

Gillette only glared.

"You know what it looks like to me?" Coburn continued. "Like you're on standby for something. For what? For a showdown with me, the federal agent who's put a real crimp in your crime chain?"

Hostility radiated from Gillette, but he remained silent.

Coburn straightened up slowly but continued to hold the man's stare. "The only reason I might second-guess myself is because I really can't see you ordering the murder of your own flesh and blood. Not because you might have some moral hang-up about it, but because your overblown ego wouldn't let you destroy your own DNA."

Gillette had had enough. He began struggling against the tape binding him, gnashing his teeth in frustration and rage. "You have maligned my character. You've insulted me as a man and as a patriot. And furthermore, you're a luna-tic." His gaze shifted to Honor. "For godsake, why are you just standing there, saying nothing? Has he brainwashed you into believing this bullshit?"

"He's convinced me that Eddie's car wreck wasn't an accident."

Gillette stopped struggling as suddenly as he'd begun. His eyes darted between her and Coburn, landing on him. Coburn nodded. "Eddie died because he had incriminat-ing evidence on a lot of people. Not just low-life types, but prominent, outstanding-citizen types like Sam Marset and law enforcement personnel who streamline the trafficking of drugs, weapons, even human beings."

Honor said, "They had Eddie killed before he could expose them."

"Or," Coburn countered, "before he could blackmail them."

"Drug dealing? Blackmail? My son was a decorated police officer."

"Yeah, well, I'm an agent of the federal government, but five minutes ago you accused me of wacking out. It hap-pens all the time, you said."

"Not to my son!" Gillette shouted with such force he sprayed spittle. "Eddie wasn't a crook."

"Then prove it," Coburn challenged. "If you're so damn sure of Saint Eddie's honor, if *you're* innocent of criminal activity, you should be eager to help us find whatever it was that Eddie stashed before he was killed."

Honor took a step closer to her father-in-law. "I believe Eddie died a hero, not the victim of an accident. My actions this week might appear out of character, bizarre even. But, Stan, everything I did, I did with one purpose in mind, and that was to dispel even a hint that Eddie was corrupt."

"This man," Gillette said, hitching his chin toward Coburn, "who you claim to *trust*, is the one who has brought Eddie's reputation into question. Doesn't that strike you as a paradox?"

"Coburn questions everything and everyone. That's his job. But no matter what Coburn says or suspects, I haven't lost faith in Eddie." She paused, then asked softly, "Have you?"

"Certainly not!"

"Then help me prove just how valorous he was. Help us find what we're looking for."

He released a gust of breath. He looked from her to Coburn, patent dislike in his burning gaze.

Coburn felt the old man needed some goading. "How come you hate me so much?"

"You have to ask?"

"We've explained why I took Honor and Emily away, why I kept them separated from you. Now that you know I'm not a kidnapper, now that you know they're safe, I'd think a little gratitude for saving their lives would be in order.

"Instead, you attack me, nearly cut off my arm. You wouldn't even have talked to me if I hadn't secured you to that chair. You despise me on principle, Gillette. Why?" He waited a beat, then said, "Is it because you think my suspicions of Eddie are so very wrong? Or because you're afraid they're *right*?"

Gillette's glare turned even more malevolent, but finally he ground out the question, "What the hell *is* it that you're looking for?"

"We don't know, but we have a clue." Coburn motioned to her. "Show him."

She turned her back to Gillette, raised her shirt, and tipped down her waistband to expose the small of her back.

She explained when and how she'd gotten the tattoo. "That long weekend was only two weeks before Eddie was killed. He drew the design for the tattoo artist. He didn't want to place me in danger by giving me the item outright, so he left me with the clue of where to find it."

"You still don't know what this item is?" Stan asked.

"No, but Coburn figured out that the tattoo says 'Hawks8.'"

It had taken a while to decipher the figures concealed within the intricate swirls and curlicues of the seemingly random pattern. The significance of the time and intimacy required to unravel the puzzle wasn't lost on Gillette.

"You went to bed with this guy."

Although the old man bristled with censure as he snarled the words, Honor didn't flinch. "Yes, I did."

"For the purpose of vouchsafing your husband's integrity. Is that what you expect me to believe?"

She glanced at Coburn, then looked her father-in-law straight in the eye. "Frankly, Stan, I don't care what you believe. The only reason I slept with Coburn was because I wanted to. It had nothing to do with Eddie. Judge me to your heart's content, but I'll tell you right now that your opinion on this matter makes no difference to me whatsoever. I didn't need your permission to sleep with Coburn. I don't have to justify it. I don't regret it. I won't apologize for it, now or ever." She squared her shoulders. "Now, what does 'Hawks8' mean?"

Coburn knew the instant that Gillette realized he was defeated. Diminished pride transformed him physically. His chin lowered to a less belligerent angle. His shoulders relaxed, fractionally but noticeably. The ferocity in his eyes faded several degrees, and there was weariness in his voice when he spoke. "The Hawks was a soccer team up in Baton

Rouge. Eddie played one season with them. He was number eight."

Coburn asked, "Does he have a framed picture of the team? A roster? Trophy? Uniform?"

"Nothing like that. It was a ragtag league and soon disbanded. What they mostly did was get together on Saturday afternoons and drink beer after the games. They played in shorts and T-shirts. Nothing fancy. No team photos."

"Keep an eye on him," Coburn said to Honor, then left them and went into Eddie's bedroom, where he remembered finding a pair of soccer cleats in the closet. He had examined each shoe, but perhaps he'd missed something.

He took the cleats from the closet, dug his fingers into the right shoe, then ripped out the innersole. Nothing. He turned the shoe over, studied the sole, and realized he'd need a tool in order to pry it off. He searched the left shoe in a similar manner, but when he ripped out the innersole, a minuscule piece of paper dropped into his lap.

It had been folded once so that it would lie flat inside the innersole without causing a wrinkle. He unfolded the note and read the single printed word: BALL.

On his dash from the room, he rounded the corner of the door so fast, he grazed his shoulder, which jarred his injured arm and sent a bolt of pain straight to his brain. It hurt so bad it made his eyes water, but he kept running.

"What is it?" Honor asked as he raced through the living room.

On his way past her, he slapped the small note into her hand. "His soccer ball."

"I put it back in the box in the loft," Gillette called after him.

Coburn made it through the kitchen and into the garage within seconds. He flipped on the light, then rounded Gillette's car and hastily climbed the ladder to the loft. He ripped open the box and upended it, catching the soccer ball before it bounced off the loft and down to the garage floor. He shook it, but heard nothing moving inside.

Cradling the ball in his elbow, he retraced his path back into the living room. With Honor and Gillette watching expectantly, he pressed the ball as one would test a melon's ripeness. Noticing that one of the seams was crudely sewn, not at all like the factory stitching on the rest of the ball, he picked up Gillette's knife from off the floor and used it to rip the seam. He pulled back the leather flap he'd created.

A USB key fell into his palm.

He locked eyes with Honor. The contents of the key would either exonerate or indict her late husband, but Coburn couldn't let himself consider what impact this find might have on her. He'd spent a year of his life working Marset's freight dock waiting for this payoff, and now he had it.

Gillette was demanding an explanation for the key and its significance. Coburn ignored him and walked quickly to the master bedroom, activated the computer, which was in sleep mode, and inserted the key into the port. Eddie hadn't bothered with a password. There was only one file on the key, and when Coburn clicked on it, it opened immediately.

He scanned the contents, and when Honor joined him, he couldn't contain his excitement. "He's got the names of key people and companies all along the I-10 corridor between here and Phoenix where most of the stuff from Mexico is dispersed. But better than that, he's also got the names of corrupt officials.

"And I know the information is solid because I recognize some of the names. Marset had dealings with them."

He pointed to one of the names on the list. "He's a weigh station guy who's on the take. Here's a used car dealer in Houston, who supplies vans. Two cops in Biloxi. Jesus, look at all this."

"It must've taken Eddie a long time to compile the information. How did he get access to it?"

"I don't know. And I don't know if his motive was noble or criminal, but he's left us with the goods. Some are nicknames—Pudge, Rickshaw, Shamu. Diego has an asterisk beside his name. He must be real important to the organization."

"Does it identify The Bookkeeper?"

"Not that I see, but it's a hell of a start. Hamilton's gonna piss his pants." He pulled his cell phone from his pocket and tried to turn it on but immediately saw that the battery was dead. "Shit!" Quickly he took Fred's phone from his pocket and snapped in the battery. When it came on and he saw the readout, he frowned.

"What?" Honor asked.

"Doral has called three times. And all in the last hour."

"Doesn't make sense. Why would he be calling Fred?"

"He wouldn't," Coburn said thoughtfully. "He's calling me." Suddenly overcome by a foreboding that squelched the elation he'd felt only moments earlier, he depressed the call icon.

Doral answered on the first ring. In a jolly voice, he said, "Hello, Coburn. Good of you to finally call me back."

Coburn said nothing.

"Someone here wants to say hi to you."

Coburn waited, his heart in his throat.

Elmo's song came through loud and clear.

Chapter 43

When Honor heard the song, she clapped both hands over her mouth, but started screaming behind them.

Coburn didn't silently scream, but he felt like it. Fear, a foreign emotion to him, struck him to his core, and the mightiness of it stunned him. Suddenly it was clear to him why fear was such an effective motivator, why it reduced hardened men to mewling children, why, in the face of fear, individuals were willing to barter their god, country, *anything* for the threat to be removed.

His mind became a slide show of horrific images that he'd seen in war zones, the bodies of children burned, beaten, hacked at, until they no longer retained human form. Their youth and innocence hadn't protected them from a violent, unconscionable egomaniac demanding absolute surrender. Such as The Bookkeeper.

And The Bookkeeper had Emily.

"Okay, Doral, you've got my attention."

"I thought I might."

His smug chuckle rankled. "Or are you bluffing?" Coburn asked.

"You wish."

"Singing Elmos are easy to come by. How do I know it's Emily's?"

"Nice place Tori has got there on the lake."

Coburn's hand formed a fist. Through gnashed teeth, he said, "You hurt that little girl and—"

"Her fate is up to you, not me."

Honor still had her fingers clamped over her lips. Above them, her eyes were watery, wide, and stark with anguish. Entering into a pissing contest with Doral wouldn't get Emily returned to her unharmed. Although it galled him, he dispensed with the threats and asked what the terms were for getting Emily back.

"Simple, Coburn. You disappear. She lives."

"By disappear, you mean die."

"You're nothing if not smart."

"Smart enough to survive the car bomb."

Doral didn't address that. "Those are the terms."

"Your terms suck."

"Nonnegotiable."

Mindful of the time he'd been on a phone that might possibly be traced, Coburn asked, "Where and when?"

Doral told him where to go, what time to be there, and what to do when he arrived. "You follow these instructions, Honor drives away with Emily. Then it's you and me, pal."

"I can hardly wait," Coburn said. "But one last thing."

"What?"

"Since you've botched everything so bad, why are you still breathing? The Bookkeeper must have a reason for keeping you alive. Think about it."

*   *   *

Doral disconnected, muttering a stream of vile language.

Coburn was playing him. He was well aware of that. But Coburn was good at it.

Because he had tapped into Doral's worst fear: He was nothing more than a flunky, and after everything that had gone wrong over the past seventy-two hours, an expendable one.

He looked over his shoulder into the backseat where Emily was sleeping, dosed with the Benadryl that he had given her so she wouldn't be afraid or put up a fuss when it became clear to her that Uncle Doral had fibbed about why he'd taken her in the middle of the night from Tori's lake house.

Just as he'd pulled the trigger to end Tori's life, a piping voice came from behind him. "Hi, Uncle Doral."

He spun around and there had stood Emily in the doorway of Tori's bedroom, wearing a nightie, holding her Elmo and bankie, and, most disconcerting of all, happy to see him.

"Aunt Tori and I made mud pies. And guess what? Tomorrow she's going to let me play in her makeup. How come you've got gloves on? It's not cold outside. Why's Aunt Tori on the floor?"

It had taken him several seconds to process her unexpected appearance. She started coming farther into the room, and with only seconds to spare, he had a burst of inspiration.

"She's hiding her eyes and counting because we're going to play hide-and-seek."

With complete trust, Emily had played along. *Sneaking* downstairs with him, and out to the car that he'd borrowed from his cousin for the night, and into his backseat, Emily had stifled her conspiratorial giggles. They were several miles from the house before those gave way to wariness.

"I don't think Aunt Tori can find us if we hide this far away." And then, "Are you taking me to Mommy? Where's Coburn? He's gonna buy me an ice cream. I want to see them."

The questions had become numerous and unnerving, and he was glad that one of his sisters had once remarked on the effectiveness of the liquid antihistamine for sedating kids. He'd stopped at a 7-Eleven, bought a cherry Slurpee and a bottle of the medication, and soon after drinking the laced slush, Emily was sleeping soundly.

That's when he'd called The Bookkeeper to report his success. He wasn't praised for a job well done, but he actually thought he heard a sigh of relief. "See if you can get Coburn to answer your brother's phone. Set it up."

Now things were in place and all he had to do was wait for the appointed time. He faced forward, unable to look into Emily's angelic face and acknowledge what a creep he was for exploiting her affection for him. This was Emily, for crissake. Eddie's kid. He'd killed her father. He would have to kill her mother, too. Sourly he thought that making an orphan of a sweet little girl like Emily was some fucking career, wasn't it?

He wondered how he'd come to sink this low without his noticing. He was in so deep he couldn't even see the surface anymore.

He'd chosen this path and there was no going back. Initially he'd thought that closing all his escape hatches was a good thing. He'd thrown off his old life the way a snake shed its skin. Having had his fill of kowtowing to his fishing charter clientele, and his usurious creditor, he had turned his back on that business and had exchanged customer service for adventure and violence. He'd relished being licensed to bully and intimidate and, if necessary, kill.

Looking back now, however, he remembered those days on his charter boat as being much less complicated than his days were now. The work had been backbreaking and the income dependent on factors beyond his control, yet he remembered that time with a nostalgia that bordered on yearning.

But when he'd signed on with The Bookkeeper he'd made a covenant with the devil, and it was a commitment for life. There was no do-over. He couldn't throw his life into reverse.

As for his grandiose idea of eliminating The Bookkeeper and assuming control of the operation, who was he kidding? It would never happen. Even if he had the courage to attempt it, he would blunder and wind up dead anyway.

No, he would stick to the path he'd chosen until he came to a dead end.

But before he cashed out, whether it was twenty years or twenty minutes from now, he was going to kill Lee Coburn for killing Fred.

Immediately after Coburn disconnected from Doral, he punched in the number of Tori's lake house and got an automated voice mail message.

"What's Tori's cell number?" he asked Honor, hoping that Tori had defied him and restored her phone's battery.

She lowered her hands from her mouth. Her lips were white from the pressure her fingers had applied to them. They barely moved as she dully recited the number.

That call also went straight to voice mail. "Dammit!"

Tremulously she asked, "Coburn? Is Emily alive?"

"If they had killed her, they wouldn't have anything to bargain with."

He could tell she wanted to believe it. *He* wanted to believe it.

She hiccupped a sound. "Is he holding her hostage at the lake house?"

"Sounded like he was in his car."

"Do you think Tori is—" She couldn't bring herself to finish the question and ended on a whimper.

Coburn punched in 911, and when the operator answered he gave her the address of Tori's lake house. "A woman at that address has been assaulted. Send police and an ambulance. Got it?" He made the operator repeat the address, but when she started asking questions, he disconnected.

Honor was trembling. "Will they kill my baby?"

As bad as the bald truth was, he refused to lie to her. "I don't know."

She made a sound of such abject despair that he put his good arm around her and pulled her hard against him, laying his cheek on the top of her head.

"We've got to call the police, Coburn."

When he didn't say anything, she raised her head and looked up at him. "We can," he said quietly.

"But you don't think we should."

"She's your kid, Honor. You've got to make the decision. Whatever you decide, I'll go along. But I think if you bring the cops into it, The Bookkeeper will know in a matter of minutes."

"And Emily will be killed."

He nodded bleakly. "Probably. The Bookkeeper wouldn't back down. He'd have to follow through on the threat or he'd look weak. He won't let that happen. I know that's not what you want to hear, but I won't bullshit you."

She gnawed her lower lip. "The FBI office?"

"Is no better. Case in point, VanAllen."

"So it's up to us?"

"I'll do whatever it takes to save her life."

"Whatever it takes." Both of them knew what that implied. "That's the deal, isn't it? You for Emily."

"That's the deal." But he didn't say it with his customary shrug. He wasn't as indifferent to his mortality as he had been only a few days ago. Death was no longer a possible outcome he regarded with nonchalance.

"I don't want you to die," she said huskily.

"Maybe I won't. I've got another good bargaining chip."

He released her, sat down at the computer desk, and accessed the contents on the USB key.

"We don't have time for this." Honor stood at his shoulder, wringing her hands. "Where do they have Emily? Did you hear her crying?"

"No."

She made a mournful sound. "Is that good or bad? She has to be afraid. Why wasn't she crying? Do you think that means...What do you think that means?"

"I'm trying *not* to think about it."

Her near hysteria was justified, but he tried to tune her out long enough to concentrate on what he needed to do hurriedly but without making any mistakes. He opened Gillette's web browser, went into a web-based email service, and used his password to access his account. He sent the file on the USB key as an attachment to an email, then reversed the process by rapidly logging out and closing the browser, but not before remembering to clear the browser history, so that no one could tell, not in a timely fashion anyway, that he'd visited an email service.

The email address to which he'd sent the file was assigned to only one computer, and it could be opened with a password known to him and Hamilton exclusively. The location of the computer was also known only to the two of them.

The job done, he pulled the key from the port, stood up, and placed his hands on Honor's shoulders. "If it wasn't for me, you could have died of old age without ever knowing the significance of that tattoo. None of this would have happened."

"You're apologizing?"

"Sort of."

"Coburn," she said, shaking her head frantically. "I don't care about an apology now."

"Not for what I've done. For what I'm about to ask you to do. If you want Emily back alive—"

"You always use her as leverage."

"Because it always works."

"Tell me what to do."

Following his conversation with Hamilton, Crawford had stepped outside the building, whose walls had ears, and used his cell phone to call police officers and sheriff's deputies he trusted implicitly. He'd asked for their immediate assistance. It was imperative that he beef up his search for Mrs. Gillette, her daughter, and Lee Coburn.

He had a brief and secret meeting with those whom he enlisted and emphasized discretion. Some he asked to patrol areas they'd already patrolled. "Go back to the boat, Coburn's apartment, Mrs. Gillette's house. We might have missed something."

He dispatched others to follow up on various leads, everything from the crazy lady on Cypress Street who called in at least once a day reporting sightings of Mussolini, Maria Callas, and Jesus—who's to say she hadn't mistaken Coburn for one of them?—to a rural couple who'd returned home from a two-week Mediterranean cruise to discover that during their absence a car had been stolen from their locked garage, their kitchen had been rummaged through, and the apartment above the garage had been inhabited by what appeared to be at least two people. The occupation looked recent. The towels in the bathroom were still damp.

Probably these would be dead ends, but at least he was being proactive, not reactive, and he hadn't liked having his hand spanked by Hamilton of the big, bad FBI. He decided to interview Mrs. Gillette's father-in-law himself.

Stan Gillette, who popped up anywhere the action was, had what seemed to be a direct line into local law enforcement. His association should have ended when his son died. It hadn't. And that bothered Crawford. A lot. Just how much did Gillette know about Honor's so-called abduction? What was he withholding?

He didn't want to wait until daylight to pose these questions to Gillette. He would wake him up and go at him hard. People dragged from bed were groggy and disoriented and more likely to make mistakes, like giving up information they wouldn't ordinarily disclose.

But when he arrived at Gillette's house and saw that it was lit up inside like a Christmas tree, Crawford felt a tingle of apprehension. A veteran Marine might be in the habit of rising early, but *this* early?

Crawford got out of his car and went up the walkway. The front door was standing ajar. He pulled his service weapon from its holster. "Mr. Gillette?"

Getting no answer, he tapped on the front door with the barrel of his pistol and, when that received no response, pushed the door open and stepped into a living room that looked like a cyclone had gone through it. Drops and smears of blood showed up bright red on the beige carpeting.

In the center of the room, securely taped to a straight chair, was Stan Gillette. His head was bowed low over his chest. He appeared to be unconscious. Or dead. Moving quickly but carefully around the bloodstains, Crawford made his way toward him, calling his name.

The man let out a moan and raised his head just as Crawford reached him. "Is anyone else in the house?" the deputy whispered.

Gillette shook his head and replied hoarsely, "They left."

"They?"

"Coburn and Honor."

Crawford reached for his cell phone.

"What are you doing?" Gillette asked.

"Calling this in."

"Forget it. Hang up. I won't have my daughter-in-law arrested like a common criminal."

"You need an ambulance."

"I said forget it. I'm okay."

"Coburn beat you?"

"He looks worse."

"Mrs. Gillette was complicit?"

His lips hardened into a firm, straight line. "She had her reasons."

"Honest ones?"

"She thinks so."

"What do you think?"

"Are you going to get me out of this chair or not?"

Crawford replaced his pistol in the holster. As he sawed through the tape with the sharp point of his pocketknife, Gillette filled him in on what had taken place. By the time he'd finished with his story, he was free from the chair, stamping to restore feeling to his feet, flexing and extending his fingers to increase circulation.

"They took the USB key with them?" Crawford asked.

"As well as the soccer ball."

"What was on that key?"

"They refused to tell me."

"Well, it had to be something significant or your late son wouldn't have gone to such great lengths to hide it."

Gillette said nothing to that.

"Did they tell you where they were going?"

"What do you think?"

"Give you any hint? Did you pick up on anything?"

"They were in an awful rush when they left. As they raced through here, I demanded to know what was going on. Coburn stopped and leaned down, putting us eye to eye.

"He reminded me that when a Marine has a duty to perform, he doesn't let any obstacle stand in the way of performing that duty. I told him yes, of course, what of it? Then he said, 'Well, I'm a former Marine, and I've got a duty to perform. Intentionally or not, you could be an obstacle. So you should understand why I gotta do this.' Then the son of a bitch slugged me, knocked me out. Next thing I know, you're here."

"Your jaw is bruised. Is it okay?"

"Have you ever been kicked by a mule?"

"I don't suppose you saw what kind of car—"

"No."

"Where's your computer?"

Gillette led him down a hallway and into the master bedroom. "It's probably in sleep mode."

Crawford sat down at the functional desk and activated the computer. He checked the email server, the home page on the web browser, and even Gillette's documents file. He didn't find anything, nor had he expected to.

"Coburn wouldn't have left us a trail that was that easy to follow," he said. "I'd like to take your computer with me, though. Give it to the department techies, see if they can find what was on that key. I guess all we can do now—"

He drew up short when he stood up and turned around. Stan Gillette was holding a deer rifle in one hand and pointing a six-shot revolver at him with the other.

Chapter 44

———⟫•◦⟪———

I t's Coburn."

Hamilton yelled at him through the phone. "About time. Damn you, Coburn! Are you still alive? Mrs. Gillette? The child? What happened with VanAllen?"

"Honor is with me. She's okay. But they've got her daughter. I just talked to Doral Hawkins. The Bookkeeper wants to trade. Me for Emily."

Hamilton exhaled noisily. "Well, that sums it up."

"It does."

After a beat, Hamilton asked, "VanAllen?"

"Honor didn't meet him, I did. I suspected a trap, but I thought it would be him springing it. As it turned out…"

"Tom was clean."

"Maybe."

"Maybe? I understand he was practically vaporized."

"Bad guys get double-crossed, too. Anyway, he answered his phone before I could warn him not to."

"Where are you now?"

"Later. Listen, I found what I've been after. Turned out to be a USB key loaded with incriminating information."

"On who?"

"Lots of people. Locals. Some not. A shitload of stuff."

"You've actually seen it?"

"I'm holding it in my hand."

"To swap for Emily."

"If it comes to that. I don't think it will."

"What's that supposed to mean?"

"It means that I don't think it will come to that."

"No more fucking riddles, Coburn. Tell me where you are, I'll get—"

"I emailed you the file a few minutes ago."

"Nothing's come in from you on my phone."

"I didn't send it to your regular email address. You know where to look."

"So it's good stuff?"

"Yes."

"But it doesn't ID The Bookkeeper."

"How'd you know?"

"If it had, you'd have told me that first."

"You're right. We weren't that lucky. But this will make him traceable. I'm almost positive."

"Good work, Coburn. Now tell me—"

"No time. I've got to go."

"Wait! You can't do this without backup. You could be walking into another trap."

"That's a chance I gotta take."

"No way. And I'm not going to argue with you over this. I spoke with Deputy Crawford. I think I can safely vouch for him. Call him and—"

"Not until Emily is back with Honor. Then she'll notify the authorities."

"You can't confront these people alone."

"That's the condition of the swap."

"That's the condition of every swap!" Hamilton shouted. "Nobody sticks to the conditions."

"I do. This time I do."

"You could get that little girl killed!"

"Maybe. But it's a sure thing she'll die if cops and feds swarm the scene."

"Doesn't have to be that way. We can—"

Coburn disconnected, then turned off the phone. "Bet he had some choice words for me," he said to Honor as he tossed the phone onto the backseat.

"He thinks you should call in reinforcements."

"Just like in the movies. Give him his head, he'd have S.W.A.T. guys, choppers, every badge within fifty miles converging on the scene, an army of Stallones who'd only fuck it up."

After a moment, she said quietly, "I was very angry at you."

He glanced over at her with silent inquiry.

"When you ruined Eddie's football."

"Yeah, I know. My cheek still stings where you slapped it."

"I thought you were being unreasonably cruel. But actually your intuition was right. You just picked the wrong sport."

It hadn't been intuition that had caused him to plunge the knife into that football. It had been jealousy. Raw, fierce, animalistic jealousy over her facial expression as she'd stroked the football's lacing and lovingly reminisced about her late husband. But they'd both be better off if he didn't correct her misconception. Let her think he was an intuitive jerk rather than a jealous wannabe lover.

She was rubbing her upper arms, a sign of her anxiety.

"Honor." When she turned her head toward him, he said, "I can call Hamilton back. Have him send in the cavalry."

"Two days ago, you wouldn't have given me an option," she said, her tone throaty and intimate. "Coburn, I—"

"Don't. Whatever else you were about to say, don't." Her misty expression alarmed him more than if she'd launched an RPG at him. "Don't look at me all calf-eyed. Don't nurse any romantic notions about me just because I told you that you're pretty or related a sob story about some old horse.

"The sex? Mind-blowing. I wanted you, and you wanted me back, and I think even before we kissed on the boat we both knew it was a sure thing, only a matter of time. And it felt terrific. But don't delude yourself into thinking that I'm a different person than I was when I crawled up into your yard. I'm still mean. Still me."

He made himself sound harsh, because it was important that she understand this. In an hour, possibly less, one way or another, he would exit her life as swiftly as he'd entered it. He wanted to make that exit painless for her, even if it meant wounding her now. "I haven't changed, Honor."

She gave him a wan smile. "I have."

Tori's eyes refused to open, but she received intermittent impressions of motion and light and noise, all of which were magnified to an excruciating level, followed then by a darkness so absolute it swallowed every stimulus until she was jarred into awareness again.

"Ms. Shirah, stay with us. You've been seriously injured, but you're on your way to the trauma center. Can you hear me? Squeeze my hand?"

What a stupid request. But she obliged and was congratulated by a voice that then said, "She's responding, Doctor. We're two minutes out."

She tried to lick her lips, but her tongue felt thick and uncooperative. "Emily."

"Emily? She's asking for Emily. Anybody know who Emily is?"

"There was nobody else in the house."

The blackness descended again, causing the disconnected voices to waft in and out.

"No, Ms. Shirah, don't try to move. We've had to secure you to the gurney. You sustained a gunshot wound to your head."

Gunshot wound? Doral wearing a stupid ski mask. A fight with him over—

Emily! She had to get to Emily.

She tried to sit up but couldn't. She tried to remain conscious but couldn't. *Oh, Jesus, here comes that blackness again.*

When next she emerged from it, the lights were bright against her closed eyelids and there was a lot of racket and activity surrounding her. Oddly, she had the sensation of floating above it all, watching from a distance.

And was that Bonnell? Why was he wearing that silly bandage on his forehead? And were his ears bloody?

He was clutching her hand. "Sweetheart, whoever hurt you..."

Was he crying? Bonnell Wallace? The Bonnell Wallace she knew was *crying*?

"Everything will be all right. I swear to you, I'll make it all right. You'll get through this. You have to. I can't lose you."

"Mr. Wallace, we have to get her to the OR."

She felt Bonnell's lips brush hers. "I love you, honey. I love you."

"Mr. Wallace, please step aside."

"Will she survive?"

"We'll do our best."

She was being pulled away from him, but he kept hold of her hand until he was forced to let go. "I love you, Tori."

She tried to outrun the encroaching oblivion, but as it enveloped her, her mind cried out, *I love you, too.*

Since Coburn was bent on staging a one-man show, Hamilton had to find a way to stop him before he had a total disaster on his hands. Tom VanAllen's death hadn't convinced Coburn of the agent's innocence, so it was more vital than ever that Hamilton talk to his recent widow to gauge what she knew, if anything.

But when he and his team arrived at the VanAllen home, as Hamilton had predicted, there were no other vehicles there. The widow was passing the night alone. But she wasn't sleeping. Lights were on inside the house.

Hamilton alighted from the Suburban, strode up the walk, rang the doorbell, and waited. When she didn't respond, he wondered if maybe she was asleep after all. Perhaps, because the son needed around-the-clock care, the lights in the VanAllen household never went out.

He rang the bell again, then knocked. "Mrs. VanAllen? It's Clint Hamilton," he called through the wood door. "I know this is an extremely difficult time for you, but it's important that I speak to you right away."

Still getting no response, he tried the latch. It was locked. He reached for his cell phone, scrolled through his contacts, and found the house phone number. He called it and heard the phone ringing deep inside the house.

After the fifth ring, he hung up and shouted back to the vehicles parked at the curb. "Bring the ram."

The S.W.A.T. team joined him on the porch. "This isn't

an assault. Mrs. VanAllen is in a delicate state of mind.
There's also a disabled boy. Take care."

Within seconds they had busted through the front
door. Hamilton barged in, the others fanned out through
the rooms behind him.

Hamilton found Lanny's room at the end of the wide
central hall. The room had the sweetly cloying odor unique
to the bedridden. But except for the hospital bed and other
medical paraphernalia, everything was perfectly normal.
The television was on. Lamps provided a soothing ambient
light. There were pictures on the walls, a colorful rug in the
center of the floor.

However, the tableau of the motionless boy lying on the
customized bed was almost gothic. His eyes were open but
his stare was blank. Hamilton walked to the side of the bed
to assure himself that he was breathing.

"Sir?"

Hamilton turned to the officer who had addressed him
from the open doorway. He didn't say anything, but his
aspect conveyed, SITUATION, as he jerked his helmeted
head toward another part of the house.

Doral saw the car headlights approaching from the side
street. Showtime.

Seated in his borrowed car, he took one last drag on
his cigarette, then flicked it through the open window. The
cigarette sketched a fiery arc in the darkness before falling
to the pavement and burning out.

He activated his phone and called The Bookkeeper.
"He's right on schedule."

"I'll be there soon."

Doral's heart hitched. "What?"

"You heard me. I can't afford for you to screw up again."
Then the phone went dead.

It was a slap in the face. But, he supposed, the collaboration with the Mexican cartel hung in the balance, so
The Bookkeeper was taking no chances of something else
going wrong.

And this wasn't strictly business anymore. Not like Marset, who'd been gumming up the works. Not like the state
trooper who'd balked at carrying out an order. Not like all
the others. This was different. The Bookkeeper had a personal score to settle with Lee Coburn.

Coburn had stopped the car about forty yards away, its
idling motor an uneven growl in the stillness beneath the
football stadium bleachers, where Doral had chosen to do
this. This time of year, the place was deserted. It was on the
outskirts of town. Ideal location.

Coburn had the headlights on high beam. The car
itself looked like little more than a rattletrap, but somehow
it seemed menacing, reminding Doral of a Stephen King
story about a car that went psycho and killed people. Doral
pushed the ridiculous thought aside. Coburn was screwing
with his head again.

But the fed also wasn't going to come any closer until he
saw that Doral did indeed have Emily.

Doral had made sure the interior lights wouldn't come
on when he got out of his car. Crouching lower than the
roof, he opened the rear door, slid his hands under Emily's
arms, and lifted her out. Her body was limp, her breathing deep, her sleep peaceful as he placed her on his left
shoulder.

*What kind of man would use thirty-five pounds of sweet little
girl to save his own skin?*

He would. He was.

Coburn had mind-fucked him into feeling lower than whale shit, into being nervous and unsure of himself. But he couldn't allow himself to buy into that or he was as good as dead. All he wanted was one crack at Coburn. If he had to use Emily in order to take out Coburn, well, that was just life, and nobody had ever said that life was fair.

He placed his right hand, his gun hand, in the center of Emily's back so that it could be seen. Then he stood up and walked around the hood of the car, forcing himself to appear in charge, in control, and perfectly relaxed, although in reality his palms were slick with sweat and his heart was knocking.

Coburn's car began to roll forward at a snail's pace. Doral's gut tightened. He squinted against the headlights. The car came to within fifteen feet of him and stopped. He called out, "Turn off the headlights."

The driver got out, but despite the glare, he made out Honor's form.

"What the *hell*? Where's Coburn?"

"He sent me instead. He said you wouldn't shoot me."

"He said wrong." *Shit!* Doral hadn't counted on having to kill Honor while face-to-face. "Move away from the car and raise your hands where I can see them. What kind of trick is Coburn trying to pull?"

"He doesn't need tricks, Doral. He doesn't even need me any longer. He's nailed you, thanks to Eddie."

"What's Eddie got to do with this?"

"Everything. Coburn found the evidence he had collected."

Doral's mouth went dry. "I don't know what you're talking about."

"Of course you do. That's why you killed him."

"Are you wearing a wire?"

"No! Coburn has already got what he came for. He doesn't care what happens to me or Emily now. But I care. I want my daughter."

Doral gripped his pistol tighter. "I told you to get away from the car."

She stepped from behind the cover of the open door, hands raised. "I won't do anything, Doral. I'm leaving you to the legal system. Or to Coburn. I don't care. All I care about is Emily." Her voice cracked on her daughter's name. "She loves you. How could you do this to her?"

"You'd be surprised what a person can do."

"Is she...?"

"She's fine."

"She's not moving."

"You've got only your friend Coburn to blame for this. All this."

"Why is Emily so still?"

"*Where is Coburn?*"

"Is she *dead*?" Honor screamed hysterically.

"Where's—"

"You've already killed her, haven't you?"

Her screeching roused Emily. She stirred, then lifted her head and murmured, "Mommy?"

"Emily!" she shouted and extended her arms.

Doral began backing away toward his car. "Sorry, Honor. Coburn screwed the pooch."

"*Emily!*"

Hearing her mother, Emily started squirming against him.

"Emily, be still," he hissed. "It's Uncle Doral."

"I want my mommy!" she wailed and began thumping him with her small fists and kicking at his thighs.

Honor continued shouting her name. Emily screamed in his ear.

He released her. She slid to the pavement, then ran toward the car, directly into the bright headlights.

Doral aimed his pistol at Honor's chest.

Before he could get off a shot, something smacked him in the back of his head hard enough to make his ears ring.

Simultaneously the car's headlights went out, their twin beams replaced by two bright purple circles on a field of black.

He blinked wildly, trying to restore his vision, even as he realized what Coburn's strategy had been. Blind him, rattle him, deafen him, and then attack from behind. He spun around in time to catch the full brunt of Coburn's impetus as he launched himself over the hood of Doral's car, landing on him like a sack of cement and forcing him down onto the pavement on his back.

"Federal agent!" he shouted.

Coburn's impact had knocked the wind out of Doral, but he'd been fighting all his life. Instinct kicked in along with a surge of adrenaline. He whipped his gun hand up.

A gunshot rang out.

Coburn backed off Doral.

There wasn't much blood, actually, because Coburn had fired point-blank into the man's chest. In death, he didn't look all that sinister, only bewildered, as though wondering how someone as clever as he could have been done in by a soccer ball. Doral had stalked prey. His target was always in front of him. He hadn't thought to check his back.

"You should have learned from your brother. I don't negotiate," Coburn whispered.

He patted down the body and found Doral's cell phone. He feared it would conveniently disappear when the police investigated, so he slipped it into his pocket before standing up and walking quickly to the car where Honor was sitting in the driver's seat, clutching Emily to her, rocking back and forth, crooning to her.

"Is she okay?"

"Limp as a dishrag and already asleep again. He must've given her something. Is he..."

"In hell."

"He refused to surrender?"

"Something like that." He paused, then said, "You did good."

She smiled shakily. "I was scared."

"So was I."

"I don't believe that. You aren't afraid of anything."

"First time for everything." His words telegraphed a much more meaningful message than he would allow himself to say. But Honor seemed to understand both the message and why he wouldn't say anything more. They shared a long look, then he said briskly, "You get Emily to a doctor and have her checked out."

He lifted Emily from her and gently placed her in the backseat.

"What are you going to do?" Honor asked.

"Call this in to Hamilton. He'll want the skinny. He'll want me to wait here till agents arrive. Then—"

"Lee Coburn?"

The quiet voice, coming from behind him, surprised them both. Honor looked beyond him and registered puzzlement. Coburn turned.

The woman was completely expressionless when she pulled the trigger.

Chapter 45

Coburn grabbed his middle and sank to the pavement.

Honor screamed.

Coburn heard Emily react to the commotion, asking groggily where Elmo was.

But the sounds seemed to come to him from the pinpoint of light at the end of a very long tunnel. He struggled to remain conscious, but it was a hell of a fight.

He'd been shot twice before. Once in the shoulder and once in the calf. This was different. This was bad. He'd seen allies and foes alike get gut-shot, and most of them died. A small-caliber bullet could make you just as dead as a big one.

He worked his way into a half sitting position but kept his palm clamped over the pumping hole in his belly. He braced his back against the side of the car and tried to bring into focus the ordinary-looking woman who had shot him.

She was ordering Honor at gunpoint to stay put inside the car. Already she had disarmed him. He could see his pistol lying on the pavement a short distance away, but it might just as well have been a mile. Fred's .357 was under the driver's seat of the car, but Honor couldn't get to it without getting shot, too.

She was sobbing, asking the woman, "Why, why?"

"Because of Tom," she replied.

So. Tom VanAllen's wife. *Widow.* At least he wouldn't die without knowing why. But for a woman who'd just committed a crime of vengeance, she seemed remarkably cold-blooded. She didn't even appear angry, and Coburn wondered why not.

"If Tom hadn't gone to those train tracks to meet Coburn," she said, "he would still be alive."

She blamed him for her husband's death tonight. *Last night,* Coburn corrected himself. The eastern sky had taken on the blush of predawn. He wondered if he would live to see the sun break the horizon. Watching one more sunrise would be nice.

He just hated that he would bleed out with Honor watching. And what if Emily woke up and saw blood gushing out of him? She would be afraid, when up to this point he'd done everything within his power to protect her and guard her against fear.

He'd dragged Honor and her through enough shit already. Strangely enough, he thought both of them liked him. A little bit, anyway. And now he was going to put them through one more trauma, and he wouldn't even be around to apologize for it.

He'd always thought that when his number came up, it would be way overdue, and that he would be okay with it. But, Jesus, this sucked.

Lousy timing. He'd just learned what it was like to make love to a woman. Not just satisfy a hard-on, but really soak up the person that belonged to the body. Fat lot of good it would do him to know the difference, now that he had gone and got shot.

Yeah, this sucked really, really bad.

These were silly thoughts to be entertaining when he should be trying to figure out something. Something just beyond his grasp. Dammit, what was it? Something important, but teasingly elusive. Something winking at him like that last holdout star that he could see in the lightening sky just beyond Janice VanAllen's head. Something he should've caught before now. Something—

"How'd you know?" Not until he gasped the question did he realize what that something was.

Janice VanAllen looked down at him. "What?"

His breath soughed through his lips. He blinked against the collecting darkness of unconsciousness. Or death. "How'd you know I was at the tracks?"

"Tom told me."

That was a lie. If Tom had told her anything before leaving for that meeting, he'd have told her that he was to meet Honor, because that's who Tom had expected to be there. Tom hadn't been around later to tell her differently.

She'd learned it from somebody else. Who? Not the agents who would have been sent to notify her of her husband's death. They wouldn't have known. Even Hamilton hadn't known until about a half hour ago when Coburn himself had told him what had transpired at the railroad tracks.

The only people who could have told her were the ones he'd spotted near the tracks, the ones who'd planted the bomb and who'd been there to make sure it did what it was supposed to—obliterate Tom VanAllen and Honor.

Honor was begging her to call for help. "He's going to die," she sobbed.

"That's the point," Janice VanAllen said coldly.

"I don't understand how you can blame Coburn. He's a federal agent like your husband was. Tom was only doing his job, and so was Coburn. Think of your son. If Coburn dies, you'll go to prison. What will happen to your boy then?"

Suddenly Coburn sagged forward and groaned through clenched teeth.

"Please, let me help him," Honor implored.

"He's beyond help. He's dying."

"And then what? Are you going to shoot me, too? Emily?"

"I won't harm the child. What kind of person do you think I am?"

"No better than me." Saying that, Coburn cut a vicious swath with Stan Gillette's knife, which he'd slid from his cowboy boot while hunched over. It connected with Janice VanAllen's ankle and, he thought, probably had sliced through her Achilles' tendon. She screamed. Her leg buckled, and when it did, he found enough strength to topple her with a push from both his feet.

"Honor!" He tried to shout, but it came out barely a rasp.

She practically fell out of the car, seized the pistol that Janice had dropped while falling, and aimed it down at her, ordering her not to move.

"Coburn?" she asked breathlessly.

"Keep the gun on her. Cavalry's here."

Honor realized that squad cars were speeding toward them from a dozen different directions. The first to reach them bore the sheriff's office insignia. Stopping the vehicle, the driver laid rubber on the pavement. He and his passenger, Stan, were out of the car in a flash. The uniformed man had his pistol drawn. Stan was carrying a deer rifle.

"Honor, thank God you're all right," Stan said as he ran up to her.

"Mrs. Gillette, I'm Deputy Crawford. What happened?"

"She shot Coburn."

Crawford and two fellow deputies took over guarding Janice, who was writhing on the pavement, clutching her ankle and alternately groaning in pain and cursing Coburn. Others who were now out of their cars ran over to Doral's corpse.

Stan reached for Honor and hugged her. "I forced Crawford at gunpoint into bringing me along."

"I'm glad you're here, Stan. See to Emily, please. She's in the backseat." Honor pushed herself free of his hold and shouted for the EMTs scrambling out of the ambulance to hurry, then dropped to her knees beside Coburn.

She touched his hair, touched his face. "Don't die. Don't you dare die."

"Hamilton," he said.

"What?"

He nodded and she turned. Two black Suburbans were disgorging officers wearing assault gear, along with a man who looked even more intimidating than they, although he was dressed in a suit and tie.

He made a beeline for her and Coburn, although his eyes darted about, taking in the various elements of the grisly scene. "Mrs. Gillette?" he said as he approached her.

She nodded up at him. "Coburn is badly wounded."

Hamilton nodded grimly.

"Why aren't you in Washington?" Coburn growled up at him.

"Because I've got a pain-in-the-ass agent working for me who won't follow orders."

"I have it under control."

"I beg to differ." His tone was querulous, but Honor could tell that the seriousness of Coburn's wound was obvious to him. "I'm sorry I couldn't get here in time to stop this. We were at her house," he said, nodding toward Janice, who was being attended by other paramedics.

"We found evidence that she was going to skip out. Even leave the country. We found notes, texts on various cell phones, indicating that she had a vendetta against Coburn over what had happened to Tom. I contacted Crawford, who had just received word of gunshots in this area. I left one man behind to stay with her son and got here as quickly as I could."

"Let go," Coburn snarled up at the paramedic who was trying to get an IV into his arm. He wrestled with the EMT and won, managing to slip his hand inside his pants pocket—the khakis that had formerly belonged to Honor's father, now soaked with blood.

He took out a cell phone and held it up where Hamilton could see. "Doral's. Moments before he got out of his car, he made a call."

While speaking in starts and stops, his voice growing increasingly weak, Coburn had used his bloodstained thumb to work the phone. He depressed a highlighted number and said, "He called The Bookkeeper."

Seconds later, all heads turned toward the sound of a ringing cell phone coming from the pocket of Janice Van-Allen's windbreaker.

For Honor the next hour and a half passed in a blur. After making the startling revelation that Janice VanAllen was The Bookkeeper, Coburn lost consciousness, which made it far easier for the EMTs to see to his immediate needs and get him into the CareFlight helicopter that had been summoned.

Honor considered it a miracle that Emily had slept

through the entire traumatic event. On the other hand, a sleep that deep was worrisome. She was transported to the ER via ambulance.

Honor was allowed to ride to the hospital with her, but once there, her insistence on remaining with Emily was overruled.

While she was being examined by a pediatric team, Honor and Stan waited anxiously with cups of tepid coffee he bought from a vending machine. There was an awkwardness between them that had never been present before.

Finally he said, "Honor, I owe you an apology."

"Hardly. After what I did to your house? After leaving you bound to a chair? After letting Coburn take your 'magic knife'?"

He gave her a quick grin, but apparently he had something he wanted to say. "You tried to explain your motivations. I didn't listen. I dismissed them out of hand."

"It was a lot to take in."

"Yes, but my apology goes beyond what's happened over the last couple of days. Ever since Eddie died," he said uneasily, "I've held you in strict control. No, don't try to deny it when we both know it's true. I've been afraid that you would meet a man, fall in love, marry, and I'd be ousted from your lives. Yours and Emily's."

"That would never have happened, Stan," she said gently. "You're our family. Emily loves you. So do I."

"Thanks for that," he said huskily.

"I'm not just saying it. Honestly I don't know what I would have done without your support these past two years. You've been there, and I'll never be able to thank you enough for everything you've done for us."

"I tend to come on a little heavy-handed."

She smiled and said softly, "Sometimes."

"I made some ugly remarks earlier about your personal life. I'm sorry."

"I know it offended you to think of Coburn and me together."

"As you said, it's none of my—"

"No, let me finish. It's occurred to me that Eddie knew my tattoo would be discovered only by a lover. Who else would have seen it? He trusted me to choose wisely who that man would be. Eddie knew he would have to be a man of integrity or I wouldn't be intimate with him."

She paused before continuing. "I loved Eddie. You know that, Stan. He'll be enshrined in my heart until I draw my last breath. But..." She reached for his hand and squeezed it as she added, "But he can't be enshrined in my life. I've got to let go and move on. So do you."

He nodded, but possibly didn't trust himself to speak. His eyes were suspiciously moist. Honor was grateful for his stalwart presence. She was still clasping his hand when Deputy Crawford joined them.

"Your friend, Ms. Shirah? N.O.P.D. responded to your 911. They arrived to find her alone in the house. She had a gunshot wound to the head."

"What! Oh my God!"

He patted the air. "She underwent surgery to have the bullet removed. I spoke with a friend of hers, a man named Bonnell Wallace, who's there with her. She's in fair but stable condition. The surgeon told Mr. Wallace that it appeared the bullet hadn't done any permanent damage. He was guarded, naturally, but predicted she'll make a full recovery."

Weak with relief, Honor leaned her head against Stan's shoulder. "Thank God."

"Mr. Wallace gave me his cell phone number. Said for

you to call him when you're up to it. There's a lot he has to tell you and a lot he wants to hear. But he wanted you to know that Ms. Shirah has recognized him and that they've exchanged a few words. Her first concern was for you and Emily. He told her that you'd been rescued and were safe."

"I'll call him soon. Have you heard anything about Mrs. VanAllen?"

"She's receiving treatment under close guard."

"And Coburn?" she asked huskily. "Do you know any-thing?"

"I'm afraid not," Crawford replied. "I'm sure Hamilton will be in touch when there's something to report."

The waiting seemed interminable, but not long after that, the pediatrician who'd examined Emily arrived with good news. He confirmed that she'd ingested an excessive amount of antihistamine. "I'll put her in a room and let her sleep it off. She'll be closely monitored. But she shouldn't have any lasting effects." He touched Honor's arm reassuringly. "I saw nothing to indicate that she was harmed in any other way."

She and Stan were allowed to go along as the staff trans-ferred Emily to a private room. She looked small and help-less lying in the hospital bed, but measured against what could have been, Honor was grateful to have her there.

She was bending over her, stroking her hair, loving the feel of her, when Stan quietly spoke her name. She rose up and turned.

Hamilton was standing just inside the door of the room. Holding her gaze, he walked slowly toward her. "I thought I should tell you in person."

"No," she whimpered. "No. *No.*"

"I'm sorry," he said. "Coburn didn't make it."

Epilogue

———◦———

Six weeks later

"You sound surprised, Mr. Hamilton. Didn't Tom ever mention to you that I'm brilliant? No? Well, I am. Most people don't know that before Lanny was born and I became a virtual prisoner in my own house, I had a bright future as a business consultant and financial planner. All my career plans had to be abandoned. Then, a few years ago, when I'd had my fill of living a shadow life, I decided to apply my know-how to another, uh, field of endeavor.

"And I was in a perfect position to do so. Who would suspect poor Janice VanAllen, mother of a severely disabled child and wife to a man totally lacking in self-confidence and ambition, to initiate and orchestrate an organization as successful as mine?"

Here she laughed.

"Ironically, it was Tom who actually planted the idea. He talked a lot about illegal trafficking, the unlimited profits to be made, the government's futile attempts to stop the ongoing tide. Mostly he talked about the 'middleman,' whose risk of capture is limited *because usually he's hidden behind a screen of respectability. That sounded very smart and attractive to me.*

"Tom was an unchecked and guileless source of information. I asked questions, he gave me answers. He explained to me how criminals got caught. All I had to do was get to the men who caught them and, through men like Doral and Fred Hawkins, offer them a handsome bonus for slacking.

"The smugglers paid me for providing the protection. And those who didn't lived to regret it. Most are serving time. They couldn't rat me out as part of a plea bargain or deal for leniency because none knew who I was. There were always human buffers between us.

"Suffice to say, Mr. Hamilton, my little cottage industry expanded and became extremely lucrative. I had virtually no over-head except for my cell phones. Doral or Fred would deliver dispos-ables every other week or so when Tom was at work.

"I paid my employees well, but even so, profits surpassed my expectations. That was important. You see, I had to save up for the day when Lanny would no longer be an impediment. After he died, I wasn't about to stick around. I'd had it with that house, with Tom, with my life. I'd earned an easy and luxurious retirement. I never resented Lanny, but I resented the diapers I had to change, the meals I had to pump into his stomach, the catheters...

"Well, you don't need to hear all that. You want to know about The Bookkeeper. Clever name, don't you think? Anyway, millions of dollars were waiting for me in banks all over the world. It's amaz-ing what you can do over the Internet.

"But then Lee Coburn came along, and I had to accelerate my plan to skip the country. Lanny..." Here her voice turned thick. "Lanny would never have known the difference. It's not like he would have missed me, is it? In exchange for a guilty plea, you swear to me that he'll be placed in the very best facility in the country?"

"You have my personal word on it."

"And he'll get Tom's pension?"

"Every cent will go toward his son's care."

"Tom would want that. He was devoted to Lanny. Often I envied his capacity to love Lanny in ways I couldn't. I tried, but..."

After a short pause, she said, "That sexting... that isn't me. I want you to know that I think that's disgusting. It was simply a means of coded communication. I wouldn't have sent Doral or Fred Hawkins a dirty text. God. Please. No, that was just a way to explain all the telephone activity in case Tom became suspicious. You understand?"

"I understand," Hamilton replied blandly. "Didn't you have any misgivings about killing Tom?"

"Of course! It was the hardest thing I had to do as The Book-keeper. Doral tried to talk me out of it, but there simply was no other way. Besides, I did Tom a favor. He was miserable. Possibly even more so than I. He was in bondage at work just as I was at home. He wasn't good at his job. You of all people should know that, Mr. Hamilton. You contributed to his misery. He knew he could never live up to your expectations."

"I thought Tom had potential and only lacked the confidence to realize it. I thought that with my guidance and encouragement—"

"Those are really moot points, aren't they, Mr. Hamilton?"

"I suppose so."

"It pains me to talk about him. I grieved him. Honestly, I did. But this way, Tom died with honor. Even with a bit of heroism. I think he would have preferred that to dying in obscurity."

After another pause, she said, "I guess that's everything. Do you want me to sign something?"

Hamilton reached across his desk and punched the button to stop the playback.

Honor and Stan, who'd been invited to the district office in New Orleans to listen to Janice VanAllen's recorded confession, had sat motionless for the duration of it, astonished by the casualness with which she had confessed her crimes to Hamilton several days earlier.

"She had Eddie killed," Honor said quietly.

"As well as a lot of other people," Hamilton said. "Based on the information on that USB key, we're making definite progress. But," he said around a sigh, "as she said, it's almost futile. The criminals are multiplying at a rate much faster than we can catch them. But we stay at it."

"There's nothing in that file that implicates Eddie," Stan averred. "And no one was more taken in than I was by the Hawkins twins. Yes, I used Doral to get information, knowing that he had ears in the police department, but I never had an inkling of what they were doing. I stand by my record. You can check it."

"I did," Hamilton said, giving him a congenial smile. "You're as clean as a whistle, Mr. Gillette. And nothing in that file implicates your son of any wrongdoing. According to the superintendent of the Tambour P.D., an honest man I think, Eddie offered to do some covert investigative work. Possibly he'd picked up vibes when he was moonlighting at Marset's company.

"In any case, the superintendent sanctioned it, but when Eddie was killed, he didn't connect the car wreck to Eddie's secret investigation, which to his knowledge had never produced any evidence. Eddie had given it to you," he said directly to Honor.

She looked across at her father-in-law, laid her hand on his forearm, and pressed it. Then she motioned toward the recorder. "How long after recording that was Mrs. VanAllen..."

"Killed?" Hamilton asked.

Honor nodded.

"Minutes. Her lawyer had insisted that her statement be taken in a private office at the rehab center where she was getting therapy for the ankle injury. There were two federal marshals posted at the door. She was in a wheelchair. I and another agent were flanking her. Her attorney was pushing her chair.

"As we emerged from the office to take her back to her room, the young man seemed to come out of nowhere. He lashed at the marshal with a straight razor and sliced open his cheek. The other FBI agent was trying to draw his weapon when the young man slashed his throat. That agent died a few minutes later.

"Mrs. VanAllen was cut swiftly, but viciously. The razor went through her neck, almost to her spinal column, and from ear to ear. It was a gruesome death. She had time to realize she was dying. The young man, however, died instantly from a fatal gunshot wound."

It had been reported on the news that Hamilton had shot him twice in the chest, once in the head.

"It was a suicide mission," Hamilton said. "He had to know there was no possible means of escape. He gave me no choice."

"And he hasn't been identified?"

"No. No ID, no information on him at all. No one has come forward to claim his body. We don't know his connection to The Bookkeeper. All we have is his straight razor and a silver crucifix on a chain."

After a silent moment, Hamilton stood up, signaling that the meeting was adjourned. He shook hands with Stan. Then he clasped Honor's hand between both of his. "How's your daughter?"

"Doing well. She doesn't remember anything of that night, thank God. She talks about Coburn constantly and wants to know where he went." After an awkward silence, she continued. "And Tori has been released from the hospital. We've been to see her twice. She's being cared for by private nurses in Mr. Wallace's home."

"How's she doing?"

"She's giving them hell," Stan said dryly.

"She is," Honor said, laughing. "She's going to be fine, which is a miracle. For once in his life, Doral didn't hit his target with precision."

"I'm glad to know that both have recovered," Hamilton said. "And I commend you for the numerous times you showed incredible courage and fortitude, Mrs. Gillette."

"Thank you."

"Take care of yourself and your little girl."

"I will."

"Thank you for coming today."

"We appreciate the invitation," Stan said. He turned and started for the door.

Honor hung back, her eyes holding Hamilton's. "I'll be right there, Stan. Give us a minute please."

He left the office and when she heard the door close behind him, she said, "Where is he?"

"I'm sorry?"

"Don't play dumb, Mr. Hamilton. Where is Coburn?"

"I'm not sure I know what you mean."

"Like hell you don't."

"Do you want to know where he's buried? He isn't. His body was cremated."

"You're lying. He didn't die."

He sighed. "Mrs. Gillette, I know how distressing—"

"Don't talk to me like I'm no older than Emily. Even she

would see through your crap. Where is he?" she repeated, stressing each word.

He vacillated for several moments, then motioned her back into her chair and sat down behind his desk. "He told me that if you should ever ask—"

"He *knew* I would ask."

"He ordered me not to tell you that he'd survived. In fact, he threatened me with bodily harm if I didn't tell you that he was dead. But he also made me swear that if you ever questioned it, I was to give you this."

Opening his lap drawer, he withdrew a plain white envelope. He hesitated for what seemed to Honor like an eternity before sliding it across the desk toward her. Her heart was beating so hard and fast she could barely breathe. Her hands had turned icy and damp, so she had butterfingers as she worked her thumb beneath the flap and opened the envelope. Inside was a single folded sheet of paper with one line handwritten on it in a bold scrawl.

It meant something.

A puff of air escaped her lips. She closed her eyes tightly and pressed the sheet of paper against her chest. When she opened her eyes, they were damp with tears. "Where is he?"

"Mrs. Gillette, heed this warning, and understand that I extend it out of genuine concern for you and your daughter. Coburn—"

"Tell me where he is."

"You went through a terrible ordeal together. It's only natural that you formed an emotional attachment to him, but you and he could never work."

"Where is he?"

"You'll only be letting yourself in for heartbreak."

She stood up, planted her palms flat on his desk, and leaned to within inches of him. "Where. Is. He?"

*   *   *

He'd been coming to the airport every day for the past two weeks, ever since he'd been able to leave his bed for more than a few minutes at a time. The third time he'd been noticed loitering in the baggage claim area, a TSA agent had cornered him and asked him what he was up to.

He'd shown the guy his badge. Although he didn't look much like the photograph anymore—he was shades paler, almost twenty pounds lighter, and his hair was longer and shaggier—the guy could tell it was him. He'd made up some bullshit story about working a case undercover, and said that if the guy didn't get away from him and leave him alone, his cover was going to be blown, and then the guy would catch the flak for screwing up the op.

From then on, they'd left him alone.

He still had to use a cane, but he figured that, with luck, he could toss the damn thing in another week or so. He'd made it all the way from his bedroom to the kitchen without it this morning. But he didn't trust himself to navigate the busy baggage claim area where people were notorious for grabbing suitcases and making a dash for the rental car counters, boisterously hugging arriving relatives, or simply not watching where they were going. After all he'd been through, he didn't want to be mowed down by a civilian.

Even with the cane, he was sweating by the time he reached the bench on which he customarily sat to await the arrival of the inbound plane from Dallas, because if you were traveling from New Orleans to Jackson Hole, in all likelihood, you took the route through DFW.

The bench afforded him a view of every passenger exiting the concourse. He cursed himself for being a fool. She probably had bought Hamilton's lie; the man could be convincing. Lee Coburn was dead to her. End of story.

One day far into the future, she would bounce her grandkids on her knee and tell them about the adventure she'd had one time with an FBI agent. Emily might have a vague memory of it, but that was doubtful. How much did a four-year-old retain? She'd probably already forgotten about him.

While telling the tale to her grandchildren, Honor would probably leave out the part about the lovemaking. She might or might not show them her tattoo...if she hadn't had it removed by then.

And even if she had questioned his demise and received his note, maybe she hadn't caught on to the message. Maybe she didn't even remember that during their lovemaking, he'd said, "Put your hands on me. Let's pretend this means something."

If he ever had it to do over, he would say more. He would make it clearer to her that it had meant something or he wouldn't have cared whether or not her hands were on him. If given another opportunity, he would tell her...

Hell, he wouldn't have to tell her anything. She would just *know*. She would look at him in that certain way, and he would know that she knew how he felt. Just like she had when he'd told her about having to shoot Dusty.

What was its name?

I forgot.

No you didn't.

Without him having to put it into words, she'd known that the day he'd had to put that horse down was the worst in his memory. All the killing that came after hadn't affected him like that had. And Honor knew it.

Thinking about her, her eyes, her mouth, her body, caused him to ache. It was a pain that went much deeper even than the one in his belly, where he'd been stitched up well enough to keep him from bleeding out, but warned against doing anything strenuous for at least six months or risk springing a leak in his gut.

He took strong medications at night so he could get past the pain long enough to fall asleep, but there was nothing he could do to get past the ache of desiring Honor, of wanting to touch her, taste her, feel her against him, sleep with her hand over his heart.

And even if she had understood what he was trying to tell her in that cryptic note, would she want to be with him? Would she want Emily around him twenty-four/seven? Would she want her little girl influenced by a man like him, who knew guerrilla tactics, knew how to kill with his bare hands, but didn't even know who Elmo and Thomas the Tank Engine were?

In order to overlook all that, she would have to see something in him that maybe even he didn't know was there. She would really have to want him. She would have to love him.

The PA system speakers crackled, jerking him out of his reverie. The arrival of the daily 757 from Dallas was announced. His gut was stitched up good and tight, but that didn't prevent it from flopping. He wiped his damp palms on the legs of his jeans and stood up shakily, leaning heavily on his cane.

He called himself a masochist for putting himself through this torture day after day.

He braced himself for the disappointment of having to go home alone.

He braced himself for happiness like he'd never known in his entire life.

He watched the door they would come through.

Acknowledgments

Cell phones have made it almost impossible for people to disappear. That's a good thing if someone is lost in the wilderness and needs to be rescued. It's bad if you're a fiction writer trying to keep your protagonists from being found.

That's why I want to thank John Casbon, who provided me with information that proved invaluable. As I'm writing this, the technology in this novel reflects the state of the art. That's not to say that it won't be obsolete tomorrow. Advances in this industry are made daily. So, if by the time you're reading this book, the technology is laughably out of date, please cut me some slack. I did the best I could, going so far as to buy my own "burner" just to test what I could and couldn't do with it.

I also wish to thank my friend Finley Merry, who, on more than one occasion, has pointed me to someone to go to for help and information. Had it not been for him, I wouldn't have met Mr. Casbon, who came to be known as "my phone guy."

Thank you both.

Sandra Brown